CP/4

Together Under the Stars

By Beryl Matthews

Hold on to Your Dreams
The Forgotten Family
Battles Lost and Won
Diamonds in the Dust
A Flight of Golden Wings
The Uncertain Years
The Day Will Come
When the Music Stopped
When Midnight Comes
Friends and Enemies
From This Day Forward
Together Under the Stars

a&b

Together Under the Stars

BERYL MATTHEWS

Allison & Busby Limited
11 Wardour Mews
London W1F 8AN
allisonandbusby.com

First published in Great Britain by Allison & Busby in 2021.

A CIP catalogue record for this book is available
from the British Library.

First Edition

ISBN 978-0-7490-2761-2

Typeset by BookType

The paper used for this Allison & Busby publication
has been produced from trees that have been legally sourced
from well-managed and credibly certified forests.

Printed and bound by
CPI Group (UK) Ltd, Croydon, CR0 4YY

FSC
www.fsc.org
MIX
Paper from
responsible sources
FSC® C020471

Per Ardua Ad Astra

– Through Adversity to the Stars

Royal Air Force motto

Chapter One

Scampton, Lincolnshire, October 1943

The lorry swung through the gates and pulled up outside a building. The men surged off, and Steven Allard gazed around, hardly able to believe he was here at last. His bright blue eyes came to rest on a sight that made the excitement rush through him, and without thinking began striding across the grass to take a closer look. Studying the beautiful object up close he knew he was in love. This was what all the training had been for.

'Sir?'

Forcing himself to turn his head towards the person who had come to stand beside him, Steve found he was looking into a pair of golden-brown eyes. She was around nineteen, he assessed, and several inches below his six foot one. He smiled and nodded towards the Lancaster. 'Isn't she beautiful?'

'And deadly, sir.' She didn't return the smile.

It was only then he noticed the dark circles under her eyes, and a deep sadness showing in them. His instinct was to reach out and put his arm around her to offer some comfort for whatever she was suffering. That was crazy, of course – they didn't even know one another.

'They are waiting for you, sir.'

'Yes, of course. I just had to have a closer look.' They walked together towards the building. 'Why is that plane down here and not with the others I can see on the airfield?'

'It's a replacement, and has only just been delivered, sir.'

'Ah, I see.' He didn't need to say anything else. The word 'replacement' said it all.

Once inside they walked along a passage and stopped by a door, which she opened, and with a smile of thanks he went through.

Nancy Dalton closed the door quietly behind him and paused for a moment, head bowed as she tried to control her emotions. These young men had left the safety of their homes in Canada to become bomber crew. Did they know their chances of surviving thirty missions were slim? Yes, of course they did, she had seen it in the eyes of that pilot when she'd told him the Lancaster was a replacement. They all knew and still they went out, night after night, knowing each mission could be their last. Just like her darling brother, Dan. He'd adored flying and had such enthusiasm for life, but sadly at twenty-one his life had been cut short. He was due to land two nights ago and hadn't returned.

She straightened up. It promised to be a clear night. Once again the planes would roar into the air, and once again they would scan the skies and count how many return. Those that didn't make it back would be briefly mourned, then everyone would carry on with what had to be done. This dreadful loss of life was happening on land, sea and air, and many kept the grief to themselves, just like Nancy. Even when she was off duty, she counted the planes as they arrived back. Many times she had considered putting in for a transfer away from the airfields, but she would still know the raids were going on. No, this was where she had to be, and here she would stay. Dan hadn't shirked his duties knowing his chances of survival were not good, and distressing as it was, neither would she.

'What are they like?' Jean, her friend, fell into step beside her. 'I saw you with one of the new arrivals.'

'He's the only one I've met. He was studying the new Lancaster and Group Captain Jackman asked me to bring him in here.'

'Well, what was he like?'

'Tall, nice soft voice . . .' she shrugged. 'I was only with him for a few minutes.'

'I saw you walking with him and you looked good together.'

Nancy stopped and glared at her. 'I am not looking for a boyfriend, and certainly not one from a bomber crew. The pain of losing my brother is unbearable and I will not lay myself open to that kind of grief again.'

'I know this is a terrible time for you, but Dan would want you to get on with your life. You will change your mind eventually.'

'Never!'

'There you are!' Luke Canning made his way across the room towards his old friend. 'Where the blazes have you been, Steve?'

'There's a new Lancaster on the field and I went to have a look at it. Didn't you see it?'

'I saw it, but we were told to come straight in here.'

'I couldn't resist, and don't look so worried, a WAAF came and tore me away from it.'

His friend's hazel eyes lit up with interest. 'Was she beautiful?'

'Exquisite.'

'Did you find out her name?'

'Name?' Steve frowned. 'She didn't have a name. It had only just arrived.'

Luke gave an exasperated sigh. 'I'm talking about the girl, not the plane. What was the WAAF's name?'

Steve shrugged. 'I didn't ask.'

'Of course you didn't.' Luke shook his head in mock despair. 'Put you in front of a plane and you don't see anything else. My friend, you have a problem. You must have noticed something about her. Was she dark, fair, tall or short?'

'Hmm.' Steve made a show of needing to think for a moment. 'She was attractive with lovely brown eyes, but she looked tired.'

'That's hardly surprising. This country has been at war since September 1939, and for most of that time it has been fighting on its own.'

'Well, it's hitting back, and now we are here to help.'

Luke laughed and, nearly as tall as him, rested his hand on Steve's shoulder. 'In the grand scheme of things, how much difference do you think our small group are going to make? I'm only twenty and so is Ricky Gregson, you're twenty-one and Sandy Jenson is the oldest at twenty-two.'

'I know we're a bunch of inexperienced boys, but we will be able to do the job we are trained for. Most of those flying are no older than us, but we are here because they badly need aircrews.'

'Gentlemen!'

They turned their attention to the officer who had just come into the room, and all chatter ceased.

'Please be seated.' He waited until they were settled, then introduced himself. 'I am James Harlow, the commander of this base. Welcome to RAF Scampton.' His gaze lingered on each of the four men in turn. Steve, Luke, Ricky and Sandy waited expectantly to hear what he had to say. 'I know you came over in a larger group and I was hoping for more, but we have only been allocated four of you. Nevertheless, we are grateful to have you join us, and you are more than welcome.' He gave a wry smile. 'There is a saying in the military I don't think any of you will have heard. Anyone know what it is?'

All heads shook in denial.

'Never volunteer for anything.'

Laughter filled the room.

'You are all volunteers so you might like to remember that, in case you need it sometime. Now, we were expecting you at the beginning of the month and not towards the end, but I know your convoy was delayed. You have had a long journey, and are no doubt curious about the country you have come to fight for, so you have three days' leave to do some exploring and adjust to your new surroundings.' He waited for the murmur of approval to die down, and then continued. 'Don't expect the kind of conditions you have come from. Many things will be different – especially the food. Being an island, our vital supplies have to come in by sea at great cost to the lives of merchant seamen, so when you are out don't criticise the food. Rationing is strict and you will often see long queues of people waiting patiently outside shops.'

'Sir, if everyone gets the same, why do they have to queue up for it?' Ricky asked.

'They do that when a shop gets something extra. News

spreads and people rush to get there before everything is sold out. Also, when someone sees a queue they will join it without knowing what the shop is selling. However, gentlemen, you will be relieved to hear that we do our best to see our aircrews are well fed, but if you are used to having large steaks, then that is a thing of the past, I'm afraid. When you are flying you will get bacon and an egg for breakfast,' he told them.

'I like three eggs, sir,' Luke called out.

'You'll get one and be grateful for that.' The commander chuckled. 'You will now be shown to your quarters, so settle in and the evening meal will be served at seven. Tomorrow you start your leave, and after that the hard work begins. Don't get into any trouble, because we need each and every one of you. Oh, and one more important thing. When you are out and about, you are not to talk about the base or what you are doing here, not to someone you know nor amongst yourselves. Remember, careless talk costs lives. You will see that notice everywhere, so be careful. You never know who is listening.'

They stood as the officer walked out, and then followed the escort to another building. The next couple of hours were spent exploring what was going to be their home for the foreseeable future. Eventually they settled in the mess.

One of the cooks approached them. 'Would you like a pot of tea, sirs?'

Luke frowned.

'Yes, please,' Steve said, before Luke could say anything.

'I was going to ask for coffee,' his friend protested.

'If coffee was available, he would have offered tea or coffee. Remember what we've been told about shortages and everyone here drinks tea, so we'll get used to it.'

'Ah, yes, I forgot for a moment.'

There were doubtful looks as the pots of tea were placed on the table near them. Back home most of them only drank coffee, but Steve's family did have tea, especially when the weather was hot, because they found it more refreshing.

'That's freshly made so let it draw for a while,' the orderly told them.

'Draw?' Ricky asked.

A slight smile touched the man's face and he patiently explained that it would be too weak if not allowed to stand. 'Would you like me to show you how to pour a good cup of tea, gentlemen?'

'Yes, please.'

'First you put a little cold milk in the cup, and then when the tea is the right colour, you fill the cups.'

They watched as he did this and then handed the cups around.

'Now, you must taste it because some of you might like sugar. Personally, I prefer my tea without, but it is a matter of taste.'

Steve was the first to sip his, and after a moment said, 'That's lovely and I don't take sugar.'

'Do you drink tea in Canada?' the cook wanted to know.

'Oh, yes, but coffee is generally the preferred drink,' Steve explained, draining the cup and holding it out for a refill. 'That was most welcome. Can I have another, please?'

The man refilled Steve's cup and gave him a smile of approval. 'There's a knack to making a good cup of tea. Call if you need anything, sirs.'

'Where are the aircrews?' Ricky asked.

'They will be sleeping, sir. The weather is good so they will be going out tonight.'

By the time they had drained the pots, the men agreed that tea wasn't so bad after all.

'We haven't tried the food here yet,' Sandy said.

'I don't care what it's like,' Luke declared. 'I'm so hungry I'll eat anything.'

They laughed, feeling relaxed and happy to have reached their destination after months of intensive training.

It had been quiet on the base since they had arrived, but suddenly there was the sound of vehicles running and voices calling out orders. Without a word the Canadians got up and went out to the airfield. It was a hive of activity, with a flood of vehicles heading towards the Lancaster planes.

'They are loading bombs for the raid tonight,' Luke murmured. 'I wonder where they are going.'

'They won't know until the briefing.' A sergeant came and stood beside them. 'No one is told the destination until the last minute.'

'When do they take off?' Steve wanted to know.

'In two hours. I have been told to inform you that dinner is about to be served. Do you know where to go?'

Luke nodded. 'We've explored and got our bearings.'

'Off you go then, sirs.'

The mess was buzzing with talk and laughter when they took their seats.

'Late again, Steve,' Ricky, the navigator, remarked. 'Couldn't you find your way?'

'Trust you to beat us to the food,' Steve remarked dryly. 'Did you run all the way?'

The joking and friendly insults continued while they devoured the food, and not one of them complained about the simple offering. It was plentiful, and that was all the group of young, healthy men needed. It had been a long day, and after a tense sea journey the relief of reaching the base was immense.

They were all sitting around talking and enjoying a cigarette when the sudden roar of engines had them on their feet and running outside to watch the majestic planes taxi for take-off. The reaction to the sight was different for each one of them. Someone drew in a deep breath, another clenched their hands in excitement and one murmured a prayer. Apart from that, every one of them was quiet, well aware they would soon be the crews embarking on a raid.

Steve watched each of the huge Lancasters heave itself into the air with its heavy burden of bombs, and could almost feel his hands on the controls. His expression was impassive, giving nothing away.

Ricky came to stand beside him and asked quietly, 'Do you think they will let us choose our own crews?'

'I don't know. Why?'

'I'd like to fly with you, if possible.'

Steve tipped his head to one side and his mouth twitched in amusement. 'Do you think I'll get lost without a good navigator?'

'There is that, of course,' Ricky chuckled, 'but you've got the reputation of being a damned good pilot, and unflappable. I'd feel easy knowing you were with me. Try and fix it, Steve. I'm the best navigator you could have. I was top of the class.'

'I know, I'll see what I can do.'

Ricky smiled in relief. 'Thanks.'

Sandy had overheard the conversation and joined them. 'I don't know how true it is, but I've been told they put all those up for active duty in a room together and the pilots can choose who they want for a crew.'

'That would be great,' Luke exclaimed, grinning at his friend. 'If that's true, Ricky and I won't leave your side. You've already got two of your crew, a navigator and a flight engineer.'

'We'll have to wait and see if Sandy is right.'

'I hope I am because it is going to be damned important to be up there with people you like and trust.' Sandy stifled a yawn, running a hand through his dark blond hair. 'I need some sleep.'

'Good idea.' The men turned and made their way towards their quarters.

Steve was already clothed and on his feet when the others began to scramble out of bed.

'They're coming back!' someone shouted, but Steve was out of the door with Ricky and Luke right behind him.

There were people and vehicles everywhere, the fire appliances and ambulances lined up, ready to move in if needed. Two planes had landed and more were coming into view. They watched in silence and scanned the horizon, just as everyone else was doing. Plane after plane landed, then all went quiet – the sky was empty.

'Is that all of them?' Luke wondered.

'Still five more.' A man with wings on his chest came and stood with them. He held out his hand to Steve. 'Wing Commander Robert Jackman,' he said, shaking each of their hands in turn.

After introducing themselves, Steve asked, 'Have you flown on these raids?'

The wing commander nodded. 'Finished my second tour of duty last week, but most of my crew is still up there, and I'd rather be with them instead of waiting down here, but my request was refused.'

'I can hear another one, look.' Rick was pointing.

Suddenly the vehicles near them burst into life, and when the plane was nearly down they raced after it.

'Oh hell – fire!' Luke swore.

The next half-hour was a nightmare. The ground crews were pulling men out of the plane when another one came into view missing an undercarriage and badly damaged.

They breathed a sigh of relief when it stopped just before hitting the burning plane. After that the sky was empty. Three planes still unaccounted for. As the Canadians watched the drama unfold before their eyes, they were in no doubt as to the dangers they would face. The men were so absorbed in the action, not one of them noticed the young girl standing by the control tower.

Chapter Two

'You've got to stop doing this, Nancy. You are putting yourself through unnecessary anguish.'

'Unnecessary? Is that what you think this is? Night after night these young men are going out never knowing if they will survive.' Nancy shot Jean an angry look. 'Do you think they are giving their lives for nothing?'

Jean sighed. 'That isn't what I mean at all. Of course it's necessary if we are going to win this blasted war. What I meant was you are adding to your grief by scanning the sky each time and counting them as they return. It's as if you are waiting for Dan's plane to arrive.'

'I know that isn't going to happen, and don't you dare insult me by suggesting I'm stupid. My concern is for those flying now. We know them all and have even had drinks with them at the pub. Don't you care what happens to them?'

'Now you are insulting me. Of course I care.' She gestured toward the frenzy of activity going on to save the crew of the crashed plane, and there was a catch of distress in her voice when she spoke. 'I am here now because I am on duty, but you are not. You should be in bed asleep, not watching this.'

Nancy turned her head and saw a tear trickling down Jean's face and grasped her hand. 'I'm sorry for snapping at you. I know you care – we all do, but it's so bloody hard, isn't it?'

Jean nodded. 'I try not to watch them coming in, but can't avoid it when I'm on duty. I don't think you have ever missed waiting for them, though. I could understand it when Dan was flying, but why continue to put yourself through this, especially now when you are reeling from the shock of losing him?'

Nancy shrugged. 'I feel someone should be waiting and sending up a prayer for them.'

'I didn't know you were religious.'

'I've never been much of a church-goer, but I do it because I hope it will be of some help. What else can we do?'

'Who knows, but one can't help feeling powerless. Are there any more to come?'

'Three are now overdue.'

They gazed up at the empty sky and Jean murmured, 'Perhaps they've landed somewhere else.'

'Maybe, but we won't know for a while.'

'This must be torture for you, Nancy, why don't you ask for a transfer, preferably away from an airfield? We can still keep in touch and meet up from time to time.'

'I've thought about it, but Dan and all these boys have never shirked their duty, and neither will I. Don't worry about me.'

Jean placed an arm around her shoulder. 'I can't help it. I can only imagine what you are going through. You were so close to your brother.'

'He was only two years older than me, but he'd always been there for me. He was very caring, and I'm not alone in my grief.' She watched an ambulance drive away, leaving the firemen tackling the blazing plane and said softly, 'There are many like me, and after tonight there will be more.'

'There's two more!' Jean pointed to the incoming planes. 'One is in trouble, though, and it looks as if the other has been guiding it home.'

The damaged plane came in to land first while the other gained height to come round again for landing. Both girls gasped when the damaged machine's undercarriage collapsed and it began to swerve across the field. Emergency vehicles rushed towards the stricken plane and they held their breath until it came to a stop.

'No fire, thank heavens, but look at that gaping hole in the fuselage, Jean. That pilot must have fought hard to get his crew back. Here comes the one who had stayed with it. That leaves one missing.'

'One too many,' Jean murmured, turning to her friend. 'I know you're not on duty, but will you join me for breakfast?'

'Yes, of course.'

'Dalton!'

'Sir?' She spun to face the commander.

'Come with me.' He turned on his heel and headed for his office.

'I'll see you later,' she told Jean, and ran to catch up with him.

'Close the door,' he said as soon as they were inside.

She did so and stood to attention in front of his desk.

'You are on compassionate leave from this moment.'

'I am not due leave at the moment, sir, and I don't want any.'

'This isn't open for discussion, Dalton, it's an order.' When she opened her mouth to protest, he rose to his feet and stopped her. 'Go home to your family and grieve with them. Your brother was an excellent pilot and a fine young man. He is greatly missed by everyone who knew him. Your parents need your support at this time.'

She lowered her eyes as the pain shot through her.

'Go home,' he told her gently, handing her the authorisation. 'You are needed there. And when you return, I don't want to see you standing out there at dawn counting the planes. Is that understood?'

'Yes, sir.'

'Make sure you obey my orders, because if you don't, I will have you transferred to a desk job away from any airfield. Now get some breakfast and go home.'

'Sir.' She saluted and left the office, heading for the dining room.

He was right, of course, her parents did need her. She should have gone to them the moment Dan was lost, but she was hurting so much and didn't want to leave the base. She felt close to her brother here, and that had been selfish.

'What did he want?' Jean asked the moment Nancy joined her.

'I've been ordered to go home.'

'It's the right thing to do.'

'I know, but in an odd way staying on duty has helped me. Take a look at the men who have just returned. They are sitting there with empty seats around them. They've lost friends during the night. They feel the loss, I know, but they won't let grief get in the way of what they have to do.

Tonight they will go again, and tomorrow it might be their chairs that are empty.'

'Where does such courage come from?'

Nancy took a gulp of tea. 'Who knows, but their example has helped me handle the loss of my brother. Though I fear that control will crumble the moment I arrive home.'

'No, it won't,' her friend assured her. 'Your parents will need you to be strong, and you will be. You are as brave as Dan was. You have the same smile he had, and I'm sure it will comfort them to see it.'

That remark made her feel better, and for the first time in two days she smiled at Jean, though it didn't quite reach her eyes. She glanced to where the new arrivals were sitting, looking relaxed and enjoying a cigarette. 'They've been given three days' leave to help them settle in before they go on active duty. I wonder what they will do with that time.'

'Go exploring, I expect, and probably get into mischief by the look of them. Why don't we go and ask if they need any help?'

'Oh, no.' Nancy raised her hands in protest. 'They seem quite capable of looking after themselves. I must pack my kit and catch the first train to London.'

Ricky stubbed out his cigarette and sat back. 'So, what are we going to do with this leave?'

There were several suggestions about visiting places they had heard about, but only Sandy had a clear idea of what he wanted to see. 'I've always wanted to go to York,' he told them. 'What about you, Steve?'

'I'm going to London. My parents know someone there and have asked me to look him up if I have a chance.'

'Really?' Luke was surprised. 'You never told me about that.'

'Hey, I'd like to have a look at London.' Ricky leant forward. 'Let's all go. Sandy, you can visit York another time.'

'I suppose so, and London ought to be the first place we see. Where does this man live, Steve?'

'A place called Woolwich. I looked it up before we left home, and I think I can find it.'

'Right, pay attention everyone.' Luke called order. 'Who's for London?'

Four hands shot up.

'That's settled, then. All we have to do now is find out how to get there. Let's ask those two girls.'

Steve smiled wryly as the entire group got up and sauntered over to the WAAFs, and watched the girls quickly stand up as they noticed the men approach.

'How can we help you, sirs?' one of them asked.

'Ow, you don't have to call us sirs.' Luke grinned at her. 'What's your name?'

'Jean, and this is Nancy.'

After they had all introduced themselves, Luke said, 'We've got three days' leave and need advice on how to get to London.'

'Steve's got to look up a family friend,' Ricky told them, glancing round and beckoning to Steve, who was standing at the back of the group. 'Come and tell the girls where you want to go.'

He walked forward, moving with his usual fluid grace. He was tall, strongly built and there was already a look of maturity and latent power about him that made all eyes turn in his direction.

23

Luke pushed him towards the girls. 'Tell them where this person you want to see lives.'

'Where do you need to go, sir?' Nancy asked politely.

'Woolwich.' He pulled a small notebook out of his pocket and opened it at the first page. 'This is his address.'

'I can certainly tell you how to get there, but can't help you with the road. When you get there, it would be best to ask a policeman. He will be able to direct you to the house.'

'Why a policeman?'

'Well, sir, most of the road signs were removed at the beginning of the war in order to confuse the enemy if they invaded.'

'I see, but there isn't any danger of that now, is there?'

'No, sir, thanks to our air force,' she stated proudly.

'You're going to London today, why don't you take the gentlemen to the station and see they catch the right train?' Jean suggested.

Nancy gave her a withering look but nodded, turning her attention back to the pilot standing in front of her. 'Have you got all your travel documents in order?'

'We've got to collect them before we leave the base,' Luke told her.

'Do that now, because I will be leaving in the next half-hour. Oh, and you'll need English money. Have you got any?'

'Yes, we have.' Ricky glanced at the clock and frowned. 'Will the trains be running this early in the morning?'

'They will, and I want to get to London as early as possible.'

'We'll see you by the gate, shall we? Do we need transport to get to the station?' Sandy asked.

'If we don't see a bus then we can walk.'

'Right, get a move on,' Steve told the men. 'We mustn't keep Nancy waiting.'

There was a stampede to get their documents, eager to be on their way.

'Thanks,' Nancy said to her friend. 'You have just lumbered me with four Canadians.'

Jean laughed. 'It should be fun. They seem a lively crowd, and that Steve is gorgeous. Did you see those eyes? They look like the ocean on a sunny day.'

'Now, Jean, don't go all poetic about a pilot, or any of them. They will be going out on raids soon, and you know how painful it can be if you get too fond of them,' she warned.

'I know, and I do try, but I must admit I am not very good at that.'

'It's a bugger, isn't it, but the war won't last forever, and then we won't have to keep our feelings in check. Now, I had better get going and shepherd that lot to the station. With a bit of luck, I might be able to lose them on the journey.'

'Good luck with that. Try to relax a bit during your leave, and I'll see you when you get back.'

After collecting her kit, Nancy walked towards the gate and groaned inwardly when she saw her travelling companions waiting. They were lounging against anything available, smoking and laughing, but the moment they saw her they all straightened up with huge grins on their faces, except for the tall one. He crushed his cigarette end with the toe of his shoe, and just nodded when she reached them. Nancy had been intrigued by this one from the moment they met, but that was dangerous territory, and she was determined to keep a detached military attitude. She saluted smartly. 'Let's start walking and catch a bus if we see one, but it might be a little early yet.'

Sandy stepped forward. 'Allow me to carry your kit, Nancy.'

'That is kind of you, sir, but I can't let an officer do that for me.'

He smiled and bowed his head. 'I understand, but we are all on leave now, so there is no need to be so formal and salute when you see us.'

'When I am in uniform, I must treat you in the proper manner, sir. I can be reprimanded if I don't.'

'Even if we are not on the base?' Luke asked.

'It doesn't make any difference. If I see an officer in the RAF anywhere then I must salute him.'

'There will be many things we find unusual,' Steve pointed out when he noticed that Ricky was not going to let the subject drop. 'We might not adhere to their strict military rules, but we must respect them. Discipline and obeying orders without question are just two of the qualities that have been essential for this country to survive.'

They were all nodding, serious now.

'We apologise if we seem too forward, but it is just our way, and we mean no harm,' Luke told her.

'There is no need to apologise. You have only just arrived in this country and it must all seem strange to you.' She smiled at each one, her gaze resting on Steve. Jean was right. This one was different. He was a natural leader, although she doubted he was aware of it, but it was clear the others looked up to him.

As they walked along the road the laughter and chatter continued, all obviously excited about their trip to London. They had to move to the side to allow a lorry full of British soldiers to pass.

As it came up beside them, Ricky called out, 'Hey, pals, what about a lift to the station?'

The men leant out and called to Nancy. 'What you got

there, darling? They sound like Yanks. Do you want any help with them?'

'No thanks, I can manage,' she replied. 'Are you going by the station?'

The lorry came to a halt. 'Hop on, we'll take you there.'

'Hey, we're not Americans, we are Canadians!' Ricky told them as they helped Nancy climb on.

It was a bit of a squeeze, but they all managed to fit in the back of the lorry.

'Where are you off to?' one of the soldiers asked.

'London,' they all said together.

'You will have your hands full if you are going to show this bunch around London, sweetheart.'

'I'm on my way home, and I am just seeing them safely on the right train.'

Ricky nudged her. 'Hey, are they allowed to be so familiar with you?'

'That was just harmless teasing. When you get to London you will find it full of military personnel from many countries, including Americans, so be prepared for remarks like that.' She gave him an amused look. 'We may appear reserved and not to show our feelings, but you will get used to that and our sense of humour after a while.'

'I suspect that keeping your emotions in check has been necessary after all this country has been through.' There was a lot of noisy chatter going on, so Steve was able to talk to Nancy, but he kept his voice low.

'It has been a necessary requirement, sir.' She looked him straight in the eyes. 'And still is, as you will have witnessed early this morning.'

He nodded. 'I understand the hesitation of getting too close to anyone who might be in danger.'

27

'Exactly, sir, it is hard enough dealing with our own family losses. It isn't easy, though. That's the station ahead, would you ask your men to stay behind me while I see about the train?'

He raised his eyebrows. 'They are not my men. We only met when we were sent to the same training camp. I am not in charge, but I'll try and keep them in order for you.'

'That would be helpful, sir. Thank you.'

The lorry came to a stop and they all jumped off, called out their thanks, and followed Nancy into the station. Fortunately, there was a train due almost immediately and she ushered them on with a sigh of relief. It was crowded and they had to spread along the corridor. She found herself a space away from the boisterous group and closed her eyes, trying to relax. All her strength was needed if she was to be any help to her parents in their grief.

Chapter Three

The train was hot and stuffy with so many people crowded into it, so Steve pulled a window down and watched the scenery pass by. After the sea crossing, one thing had struck him as they had been driven to Lincolnshire, and that was the colour green. He liked what he'd seen so far, and couldn't wait to explore further when he had time. This small country was lovely, and he could understand why they had fought so hard to keep the powerful enemy from invading. He had watched the news as Germany walked into France and felt dismayed, then awed by the rescue of the army from Dunkirk. A victory had been snatched from defeat, but after that the general opinion was that Britain was finished. How wrong that had been. Against all the odds they had defeated the might of the enemy air force and endured the bombing of cities. And they still hadn't given up. He had trained and watched, longing for the day he could come here, anxious in case he was too late to get involved. He couldn't be happier to have arrived in time. His parents had tried hard to talk him out of flying bombers, but he wouldn't be swayed by their arguments against it. This was where he was needed, this was where he wanted to be, even if it cost him his life. Like everyone else, though, he was sure that wouldn't happen to him. It was far better to think that way than to keep worrying about being killed.

He glanced along the corridor and saw Nancy. Her brow was creased as if struggling with some strong emotion. She had lost someone close to her, he was sure of that. He had sensed it the first time they met.

'Hey, Steve,' Luke and Ricky wormed their way to him through the press of bodies. 'Can we come with you when you go to see your parents' friend?'

'Sure, if you want to.'

'Thanks.' Luke leant on the window and studied the countryside. 'What do you think London is like after all the raids?'

'I've no idea. All we know is what the news has reported, so we will have to wait and see.'

Rick nodded and glanced along the corridor at Nancy, who was sitting on her kitbag, head resting back and eyes closed. 'I don't think that girl likes us.'

'I think she just wants to be alone.'

'Why? Do you think we embarrass her?' Luke frowned.

'I'm sure it isn't that. Take a good look at her and tell me what you see,' Steve suggested.

'Well, she's a pretty girl, but sitting there as if she's unhappy.'

'Unhappy is not quite the right word. She appears to be stand-offish because she's hurting and doesn't want anyone to see her pain. I would hazard a guess that someone she loves has just been killed.'

'I've noticed you have the ability to sum people up quickly, so I believe you.' Luke sighed. 'Do you think it was one of the aircrew?'

'Maybe, but it's only speculation. However, watch what you say and do around her.'

'You could be wrong and she just doesn't want anything to do with loud-mouthed Canadians.'

Ricky pulled a face at Luke. 'That's more than likely. Pity, though, because she seems a nice girl.'

'Where is Sandy?' Steve asked, changing the subject.

'Talking to some soldiers further along the corridor. I don't know if he wants to come with us or go straight to the West End.'

'Why don't you two go and ask him?'

Luke nodded agreement. 'I expect he'll want to stick with us, and we could all visit there tomorrow.'

Before they had time to move Sandy appeared next to them.

'Ah, just the person we want. We're going with Steve to Woolwich first. Do you want to come with us?'

'Sure. We've got time.'

'We're stopping!' Ricky had his head out of the window to see what was going on. 'There are women handing out refreshments. Hey, ma'am, what does WVS stand for?'

A woman came up to the window. 'Women's Voluntary Service, young man. You're going to be stuck here for a while, so would you like tea?'

'Yes, please, ma'am. There are four of us here. We've got some English money, so how much?'

'Nothing for those in the services, son. I'll be back in a minute.'

Ricky popped his head back and grinned. 'What do you think of that? They are giving all military personnel free refreshments if they want it.'

When the woman returned, they opened the door and took the tea from her.

'Do you want something to eat, as well?' she asked. 'We do have some spam sandwiches.'

'No thank you, ma'am,' Steve replied. 'We have food with us. Do you know why we have stopped?'

'They are doing repairs further down the line. We've been told the delay should be about an hour.'

He thanked the woman and closed the door, and when his friends started talking to a couple of sailors, Steve edged his way to where Nancy was sitting. She hadn't moved. He stooped down and touched her arm gently, and when her eyes opened he handed her the tea. 'I thought you might like this.'

'Oh, thanks.' She took it from him and sipped the hot brew appreciatively. 'That's good.'

'We are going to be stuck here for about an hour for repairs on the line ahead.'

She just nodded and finished the drink.

'Would you like another one?'

'No thanks, that was just what I needed.' She dredged up a smile. 'We'll need to change trains at King's Cross. I'll let you know when we get there, and then I'll show you where to get the train to Woolwich.'

'That would be helpful.' He removed the empty mug from her hands and asked, 'Is there anything else I can do for you?'

She shook her head. 'That is thoughtful of you, but there isn't anything you can do to help me through a painful home-coming.'

'Do you want to talk about it?' When she didn't answer he began to rise. 'I know it's none of my business.'

'It was my brother,' she blurted out when he was almost

standing. Steve sat back down. 'He was a Lancaster pilot, like you, and three days ago he didn't return. He was seen to go down with no chance of anyone getting out. One of the Lancasters circled looking for parachutes, but there weren't any.'

'Where was he based?'

'Same as we are.'

His heart ached for her, and he could imagine the anguish she had suffered waiting for a plane that never arrived. 'What was his name?'

'Dan. He was so young.' She glanced up at him, her eyes brimming with tears. 'You all are.'

'Will you be asking for a transfer after your leave?'

'No, I won't run away. We won't survive by running at the first sign of loss and tragedy. We must win this war or all the sacrifices will have been for nothing.' She sat up straight, determination written on her face. 'I'll do what I have to do.'

'Yes, we all will.' He gave a slight smile, which she answered in the same way. 'The enemy has already lost the battle, although they won't admit it. This war is coming to an end, Nancy.'

'Let us pray it is. Thank you for talking to me like this. It has helped. Now, why don't you go and get yourself some tea. I'll find you when we are nearly there.'

He unwound himself from the floor, smiled at her, and went back to where his friends were standing.

'You had quite a chat,' Luke remarked the moment he reached them. 'What did she say?'

'She'll come and let us know when we reach our destination,' was all he said, leaning out of the window to catch the attention of a WVS woman. 'Any chance of another tea, ma'am?'

'I'll get you one, young man. You Americans ask so nicely by calling us ma'am.'

Ricky squeezed his head out of the same window. 'We're Canadian, ma'am.'

'Oh, I do beg your pardon. I can only see your head and your accent fooled me. Step out for a moment so I can see you properly. I don't want to make the same mistake again.'

Luke opened the carriage door and stepped onto the platform, followed by his friends, and then pointed to the name on his shoulder.

She studied all of them with care and when her eyes rested on the badges on their jackets she nodded. 'Now I can see the difference. I hope you will forgive me.'

'Of course, it is just this is the second time today we have been mistaken for Americans and I couldn't help mentioning it.'

'I understand.' She smiled at Steve and Ricky. 'I'll get tea for all of you, shall I?'

They didn't get the tea because at that moment a guard blew a whistle and waved a flag, urging them all back to the train. As it began to move again, they waved to the women and called their thanks, then settled down for the rest of the journey.

Steve found enough space to sit on the floor, leant his head back and closed his eyes.

Steve woke to someone tugging at his arm, and opened his eyes to see Nancy and his friends trying to pull him up. 'What?'

'For goodness' sake wake up, Steve. Nancy said we've got to get off here and catch another train.'

'Oh, right.' He stood up and slung his bag over his shoulder.

'You were sound asleep,' Nancy remarked. 'How can you do that on a crowded, moving train?'

'He could sleep on a clothes line,' Ricky told her, shaking his head and laughing. 'On the way over we hit a nasty storm. The ship was rolling all over the place and Steve was fast asleep. Nothing seems to bother him.'

'And that's the reason we want to fly with him,' Luke pointed out. 'Even if half the plane was missing, he'd still calmly find a way to fly it.'

'So, are you getting the same train as us?' Steve asked, quickly changing the subject when he saw Nancy wince at the mention of damaged planes.

'No, I catch a different one. Come with me and I'll show you the platform you need.'

They followed her, and after she had found out when the next train to Woolwich was due, she forced a smile. 'Enjoy your leave. When you get there a policeman should be able to direct you to the address you want.' She hesitated. 'Have your parents heard from their friend recently?'

'Not for some time. That's why they've asked me to come and see him.'

'You do realise this part of London has been badly hit, don't you? He might not be there now. What line of work is he in?'

'He works at the docks. I know,' he said when he saw her expression change. 'But we are hoping it might just be the unpredictable mail service. We want to know if he is all right.'

She smiled up at him. 'Good luck. I hope you find him.'

He nodded, returning the smile. 'We'll see you back at base?'

'Yes. Enjoy yourselves.'

'Oh, we will.' Ricky told her, a huge grin on his face.

They waved to Nancy as she walked away.

The train arrived on time and at Woolwich they hurried out of the station, eager to see some of London. 'Come on, let's find this place.'

Ricky glanced around. 'I can't see a policeman, but we should be able to find someone who lives around here. What about those people waiting at the bus stop?'

'Worth a try.' Steve strode across the road. 'Can you help us? We are looking for Fenton Street.'

The Canadians were studied with interest, and one man asked, 'What number do you want?'

'Fifty-four.'

'Hmm.' He turned to the man beside him. 'What do you think, Fred?'

'Dunno. Why are you looking for that house, son?'

'I've been asked to visit someone who lives there.'

'Ah, well, we can tell you where it is, and you might be lucky.'

'Sorry?' Steve was puzzled.

'Some of that street ain't there any more. The house you want might still be there, though, if it's far enough down.' The man turned to his friend again. 'Have you been down there, Fred?'

'No, but my missus said it had taken a right bashing.' He shrugged and turned to Steve. 'All you can do is take a look. Go down this road until you come to the second street on the right, then take the first right and that'll bring you to what's left of Fenton Street.'

'Thank you, sir.'

'Hope you find it still standing,' the man said.

They began walking and Luke was concerned. 'That didn't sound too good.'

'No, it didn't, but it seems all right here, so perhaps they are wrong.' Steve said nothing, continuing to follow the directions they had been given.

When they turned into the street they all stopped suddenly. 'They weren't wrong,' Luke said softly. 'Dear Lord, just look at that.'

Steve's expression was unreadable, but his friends were horrified as they took in the scene of destruction. Some houses had been completely destroyed, others were half-standing and roped off with danger signs on them, and some were still intact, but with windows boarded up and clearly uninhabited.

They continued walking until they reached some undamaged houses towards the end of the street.

'There's number 48,' Ricky declared, running ahead and looking at the houses. He stopped then, turned and grinned at his friend. 'Here it is, and undamaged by the look of it.'

Relief washed over Steve. For a while there he had been thinking he might have to send his parents bad news. He knocked on the door and waited. No one answered.

'Who are you looking for, lads?'

They turned to see a woman who had come out of the house next door.

'Harry Green. My parents have asked me to visit him,' Steve explained.

She came closer so she could see the name on their uniform, and then smiled. 'Ah, yes, Harry told me he has relatives in Canada. He's on the early shift, so should be home in about an hour. You'd better come in and wait.'

'Thank you, ma'am. That is kind of you.'

'Come along then, and I'll make you a nice cup of tea while you wait.'

Ricky chuckled softly as they followed her. 'More tea. I think this country runs on the stuff. And you never told us you were related to this chap, Steve.'

'My dad married his cousin.'

'Your mum's English!' Luke gasped. 'You never said – now I see why you were so set on coming here.'

Ricky punched him in the arm. 'So that's why you like tea.'

Steve chuckled as they followed the woman into the house.

'Sit yourselves down. Seeing how Harry's wife died several years ago and now his daughter is away, he comes here for his meals.'

'She's joined one of the services, hasn't she?' Steve asked.

'That's right, she's in the ATS. That's the women's army, in case you don't know. My name's Gladys, by the way.'

The boys introduced themselves and chatted while Gladys made the tea.

She brought out her best china for them, and as he sipped from the delicate cup, Steve's thoughts turned to Nancy, wondering how she was coping. He had been lucky. Harry and his daughter were alive. He sent out a silent thought to her, somehow knowing she would be strong and a comfort to her family.

Chapter Four

Nancy turned the key in the door, and the moment she stepped inside her mother, Sally, was hugging her tightly.

'I'm so glad you are home,' she said, her voice husky with emotion. She held Nancy at arm's length. 'Are you all right?'

Nancy nodded. 'Where's Dad?'

'At work, but he'll be home in a couple of hours.' Her eyes filled with tears. 'He'll want to know exactly what happened. Will you be able to tell us? All we had was a telegram saying Dan was missing, presumed dead. Is there a chance he survived?'

'No, Mum,' she told her firmly. 'I'll tell you what I know when Dad is here, but I'm gasping for a cup of tea,' she said, hastily changing the subject. It was going to be painful enough giving them the details and she didn't want to have to go through it twice.

'Of course you are. Leave your bag here and you can take it to your room later.'

She was helping her mother prepare the meal, talking

about anything but the war. Her mother was obviously holding on to the hope that somehow Dan had survived, and Nancy trembled at the task ahead of her.

The door swung open and her father, Tom, strode in, embracing her in a fierce hug. 'I saw your bag in the hall. Ah, it's so good to see you, sweetheart.'

She looked up at him with affection, seeing a strong man, but one struggling with grief.

'How long have you got?' he asked.

'Fourteen days.'

'It will be wonderful to have you home for two weeks, darling.' He kissed the top of her head, and then asked softly, 'Do you know what happened? They didn't give us any details.'

'I can tell you what another crew reported when they arrived back.'

He nodded and turned to his wife. 'Can the meal wait for a while?'

'It will keep.' Her mother pulled out chairs for them to sit at the table. 'I've made a fresh pot of tea.'

Nancy noticed her mother's hands were shaking as she poured the tea.

'Is there any chance Dan has survived?' her father asked hopefully.

'From what I've been told everyone on his plane died. The crew who witnessed it are certain no one got out.'

'How could this other crew know it was Dan's plane?'

She was hoping her father wouldn't ask that question. 'His was the only plane from our base that didn't return that night. They still had bombs on board and the plane blew up in the air. I'm sorry,' she said quickly, when she heard her mother's gasp of anguish.

Tom put his arm around his wife. 'It's best we know for sure, my dear. I want Nancy to tell us everything she knows about the raid. Are you up to hearing that, or would you rather I talk to her in the other room?'

'No.' She straightened up, wiped the tears from her face and looked at her daughter with compassion. 'Were you waiting for him to return?'

Nancy nodded and told them everything she knew. They listened in silence, and when she had finished her father asked questions until he was satisfied he had every detail.

Sally wiped the tears flowing down her face and took a deep breath before speaking. 'Thank you, darling. We know that wasn't easy for you, but we needed to know. I'll see the vicar tomorrow and arrange a memorial service for Dan. Now, we must have something to eat.'

Nancy watched her mother serve the meal, and saw in her the pain they were all feeling. It was a loss they were going to have to live with for the rest of their lives.

Her father squeezed her shoulder and said quietly, 'Thank you. I know that was hard for you, but it will help your mother to come to terms with the loss.'

'I hope it has helped you as well.'

'It has.' He gave a tired smile. 'Dan told us you were always there on the airfield waiting for them to return and I can only imagine what you went through as you watched in vain for his plane. Thank you for keeping that vigil. Will you be transferred now?'

She shook her head. 'I want to stay there, Dad. It's hard to explain, but somehow I feel that's where I need to be.'

'I know. You've got to be in the thick of things, just as Dan had to be. You are so like him, do you realise that?'

'We always got on well and thought alike.'

41

'Tell us one more thing . . .' He paused while Sally put the plates in front of them. 'Was Dan happy flying those monsters?'

'He loved it, and like all the crews he knew his chance of surviving was not good, but that never dimmed his enthusiasm for what he had to do. He always had a smile on his face, and I don't believe he would have changed a thing.'

'That's good to know,' he said. 'Now, we had better eat before it gets cold or we will be in trouble with your mother.'

'Ah, he knows me so well,' Sally remarked, forcing a faint smile.

Nancy relaxed and even managed a little laugh, knowing her mother's insistence they eat on time. She gave a silent sigh of relief as a weight lifted from her shoulders. It had been silly to dread telling them because they were strong people and would deal with the loss of their son with courage and dignity. She must do the same, and support them in any way she could.

When Harry saw the boys, his gaze rested immediately on Steve, and a huge smile lit up his face. 'Ah, lad, there's no mistaking you are Rose and Bill's son. My word, but it's good to see you.'

'And you, sir.' Steve stepped forward and shook the hand of the man he had heard so much about but never met. 'My folks asked me to look you up. They are worried because they haven't heard from you for a while.'

'I have written, and I sent one only last week, but you know how unpredictable the post can be, so I expect they'll get them all at once.' Harry looked at the other boys, who were standing by respectfully. 'Introduce me to your friends, lad.'

Steve did so, and they were then bombarded with questions

about how everyone was in Canada, and they in turn wanted to know everything about the air raids.

During a lull in the conversation Gladys stood up. 'I can offer you boys a sandwich, but I haven't enough to cook you all a meal, as much as I would like to.'

Luke was immediately on his feet. 'We don't expect you to feed us, ma'am. Is there somewhere we could get something to eat?'

'Will the British Restaurant still be open, Harry? They know you and I'm sure they would be happy to serve these boys.'

'I'll take them down there and have something to eat with them, if you don't mind, Glad?'

'Not at all.'

'That's settled, then. Come on, lads, when we've had something to eat, I'll show you around, and this evening we'll go to the pub and have a right celebration.' He slapped Steve on the back, grinning. 'It's terrific to have met you at last.'

'As soon as they knew I was coming over here they insisted I look you up.'

'It's great you've been able to, and it's lovely to hear all the news. We can't say much in letters, you know.'

Steve nodded. 'Yes, security is very strict, and that's understandable.'

Harry ushered them out of the door. 'You can all stay with me tonight. How long have you got, by the way? I didn't ask.'

'Only tomorrow and then we have to return to base,' Rick explained. 'We thought we'd spend tomorrow having a look round the West End. That's the place to go, we've been told.'

They thanked Gladys for her kindness, and as they walked up the road, Ricky asked what a British Restaurant was.

'They've been set up right across the country to provide meals for anyone who needs it. It's difficult to make the rations last, and they are a godsend for the workers. The one by the docks is always busy, so we'll have to queue.' Harry gave the Canadians an amused glance. 'That's something you'll have to get used to over here. We queue for everything.'

'So we've been told.' Steve chuckled. 'But will they serve us, Harry?'

'Of course. Those wings on your jacket will get you in anywhere. We've good reason to be grateful to the air force.'

'I listened to the news, and it was that battle that made me decide to join the air force,' Luke told him. 'I hope I get the chance to examine a Spitfire one day.'

'Well, you might, you never know.' He glanced at Steve. 'I know I shouldn't ask questions, but where have you come from today?'

'Lincolnshire.'

'Ah.' He nodded, that location telling him all he wanted to know. 'How was the journey?'

'Crowded, but interesting.'

'I expect it was – quick, run! There's the bus we need.'

They sprinted and just beat the bus to the stop. They went upstairs and Steve insisted on paying for all of them.

It was only a couple of stops and when Harry took them into the building they gawped in amazement. It was a long room with trestle tables filling every space, and an orderly queue of people collecting their meals.

A woman sitting at a table by the door greeted Harry. 'Brought some friends with you this time, have you?'

He pulled Steve forward. 'This is my cousin Rose's lad and three of his friends. They've just arrived from Canada. I know it's a bit late, Val, but they need feeding.'

She looked the youngsters over and laughed. 'I don't doubt that. They'll need a main meal, pudding and a cup of tea, then. That will be ten pence each.' She laid out different coloured tokens.

The boys looked at them, confused.

'You hand the tokens over at the counter,' she explained. 'The blue one is for the main meal, this one for the pudding and the last colour is for a cup of tea.'

Luke dug in his pocket and pulled out a handful of coins. 'I'll pay for us all. Is this enough money?'

'Far too much.' She carefully took the correct money out of his hand. 'Off you go, now, and join the queue.'

Luke studied the money left in his hand and frowned. 'Have you taken enough?'

'Yes, dear. As I said, it's only ten pence each.' She smiled at him.

Harry laughed quietly at Luke's astonishment and urged them to the end of the line.

Once served, the hungry boys devoured the food without comment, and lit cigarettes to enjoy with their cups of tea.

'I don't need to ask what you thought of the meal,' Harry remarked as he looked at the clean plates.

When they had all said politely that they had enjoyed it, Sandy leant forward and asked quietly, 'What was it?'

'Don't ask, lad.' Harry grinned and they all burst out laughing.

They spent an interesting afternoon being shown around the dock area, and although they could not go in, Harry found them a spot where they could see some of the ships.

'A convoy has just arrived,' he explained. 'That's the lifeblood of this country, lads.'

Steve nodded. 'We came over with a large convoy escorted

by battleships. Sailing time was delayed because of the late arrival of two ships, and our journey was uneventful, but we heard stories of what it had been like when the Wolf Packs had been operating.'

'Thankfully, the navy and air force got the better of them and they began losing too many subs, but it's still bloody dangerous out there.'

'After Dunkirk, nobody believed this small island could survive,' Luke remarked.

Harry snorted and laughed. 'The thing was, nobody told us that!'

'When anyone said that in front of Mum, she would tell them they didn't know what they were talking about. She pointed out that Hitler would have to cross the Channel, and there was no way he was going to be allowed to do that.'

'Ah, that sounds like my cousin. Living on an island is good in that respect, Steve, and when he couldn't defeat our air force he had to change his mind.' Harry studied the boys, knowing what they were here to do, and prayed silently that they would all survive.

They made their way back to the house where Harry produced scrambled egg on toast, and although it was made with powdered egg it was still eaten with gratitude. They were very concerned, though, that they were eating precious rations and were careful not to take second helpings.

After clearing the dishes, Harry glanced at the clock. 'Right, lads, the pub is open so let's go and have a bit of a celebration.'

The place was packed when they arrived, and the boys created a lot of interest as Harry introduced them to his friends from the docks, showing off Steve with pride.

'I'll get the drinks.' Steve began to worm his way through

the crowd towards the bar when hands caught hold of his arm.

'No, lad, you go and sit down,' Harry told him. 'You don't pay for anything tonight.'

'That's right,' another man said. 'You are our guests.'

Steve protested, but Harry and his friends insisted. Deciding he would try later, Steve eased his way back to his friends and sat down. 'They won't let us buy drinks, but we'll see if we can get a chance later.'

They soon had a large crowd round them, and when a soldier got on the piano the place erupted into song.

The boys were wide-eyed with amazement. This was not what they had expected of war-torn London. They were soon singing along.

At one point in the evening, Steve and Sandy were able to push their way up to the bar and get a round of drinks for everyone. By that time they were all too merry to notice where the drinks were coming from.

Steve sat and watched the antics of the locals as the pianist began to play some of the cockney songs, and was soon roaring with laughter when Ricky got up and joined in with 'Knees up Mother Brown'.

After closing time, they made their way back to Harry's, still laughing about the evening, a little unsteady on their feet.

'That was quite a night,' Ricky declared, doing a little dance.

Steve reached out to steady his friend when he nearly walked into a lamp post. 'Watch where you're going.'

'Ooops! Why is it so dark?'

'There's a blackout,' Luke told him. 'You know how the smallest lights can be seen from the air.'

'Course I do. Just forgot where I was for a moment.'

'Good heavens, and he's our navigator,' Steve declared jokingly. 'Do you think we had better find someone else, Luke?'

'Might be an idea.'

'Hey, I'm the best you can get.' Ricky draped his arm across their shoulders. 'You are going to need me, my friends.'

The mention of what was in front of them was like being drenched in a bucket of cold water, and they sobered up. They all started when they heard a rumbling sound behind them and gaped in astonishment as several of Harry's friends came past them, rolling a barrel of beer.

'Come on, lads, we ain't finished yet,' one of the men called.

They all piled into the house, including some of the neighbours, who were not going to miss a party. It turned out to be a night the boys would never forget.

Chapter Five

It was five o'clock in the morning when someone shook Steve awake and he saw Harry bending over him.

'I'm off to work now, lad,' he whispered.

Steve dragged himself out of bed and went to the kitchen so he could talk without waking his friends. It was only a small two-bedroom house so they had all shared the same room.

'Thanks for coming, Steve. It's been good to see you. I'm sorry Sybil wasn't here, but we'll all get together at some time. Come again when you can, and bring those bright lads with you as well.'

'I don't think they are going to be too bright this morning, after the night we've just had.'

Harry chuckled and gave Steve a bear hug, then stepped back, serious. 'You take care, and keep in touch.'

'I'll come again as soon as possible, and will certainly bring my friends with me. They won't let me come without them,' he joked.

'I must be off. Enjoy the rest of your leave. Oh, and Gladys will be in later to give you some breakfast.'

'Thanks, Harry, it's been great to meet you at last.'

'Same here, lad. I'm only sad it's at a time like this. You be careful, now, and next time you come I'll take you for another knees-up at the Jolly Sailor.'

'We'll look forward to that.'

'Write regularly. I'll need to know you are all right.'

'We will be.'

'Of course you will. You are in a strange country, so if you need anything at all you are to contact me at once. Will you do that, lad?'

'I promise.'

'Does that include us?' Luke appeared with the other two behind him. 'After last night we have decided to adopt you into our family.'

'My word, I am honoured.' Harry laughed. 'In that case I shall expect all of you to turn to me if you need any help at all.'

'Thanks, Uncle.' They all hugged him.

'Right, I will tell you what I told Steve – you boys take care.'

'Oh, we're quite safe,' Rick told him. 'We've got two of the best pilots you could ever hope for.'

'Yeah, they're unflappable, Harry.' Luke draped his arm around both pilots. 'Why do you think we are staying so close to them? We're hoping they will let us choose our own crews.'

Harry nodded and then glanced at the clock. 'I must dash. Have fun, lads.'

'We will,' they called as Harry sped out of the door, determined not to be late for his shift.

Gladys appeared immediately, and she studied them carefully while serving them toast and tea. 'I must admit you look a lot better than I expected after last night. I thought you'd all be asleep until the afternoon.'

The boys looked puzzled and she laughed. 'You were all drunk last night.'

'We were not!' they protested.

'We were happy, that's all,' Sandy informed her. 'That beer was like water.'

'You must have liked it, though, because you drank enough of it.'

'After two pints we got used to it,' Luke smirked. 'Anyway, we are fine and want to make the most of today. Can you tell us how to get to the West End?'

Armed with instructions they were soon on their way, eager to see more of London.

They got off the train at Piccadilly Circus and began walking along Shaftesbury Avenue, turning down one street after another, not knowing where they were going, but enjoying every minute.

'Just look at this!' Luke exclaimed in astonishment. 'It's crowded and nearly everyone is in uniform.'

'There are Americans everywhere,' Rick pointed out as another group passed them, grinning and calling out 'Hiya boys.'

'This country is filling up with military as they prepare for an invasion,' Steve said quietly.

'Do you really think it is imminent?' Rick wanted to know.

He nodded. 'Harry believes it will be next year. He said ships are arriving all the time filled with military personnel and equipment.'

Ricky's eyes shone with excitement. 'If that is so, then we will be a part of it.'

'That's what we are here for.'

Luke nodded. 'Then I suggest we enjoy our leave while we can. I'm starving. Where can we eat?'

'That's easy, just follow the Yanks,' Sandy suggested. 'They've obviously sussed the city out.'

They asked a group of American soldiers where they could get something to eat and were taken to a small hotel that was able to serve them a fairly decent meal. The next couple of hours were hilarious as the Americans insisted on showing them some of their favourite places.

By evening they had gathered quite a crowd, and they all agreed that the place to spend the evening was in an English pub. The Americans loved these as much as they did. Their companions knew just the place, of course, and took them down a side street to The Rose and Crown. During that evening they met men and women of all the services, ranks and different nationalities. After spending time in the pub, they went to one of the larger hotels holding a dance and were lucky enough to book the last room they had for the night.

The next morning Luke sat on the edge of the bed, head in hands, and groaned, 'I need a strong cup of coffee.'

'I need a whole potful,' Ricky muttered. 'Where did those Yanks get all that whisky from?'

The others looked around the room to see where the voice was coming from and found Ricky on the floor beside the bed.

'What on earth are you doing down there?' Steve asked, helping his friend to his feet. 'Are you all right?'

'Not sure, but I think so.'

'Why were you on the floor?'

'There wasn't enough room for all of us in those two small beds.' He gave Steve a bleary look. 'You take up a hell of a lot of room, so I was more comfortable on the floor.'

'Sorry about that. I can't help having long legs, and this was the only room they had available.'

'Hey, it's not a problem. Once we start flying missions, we will all be crammed together in that plane and living in each other's pockets.'

'True. Smarten yourselves up and let's see if we can get breakfast.'

'And coffee,' Luke sighed.

There was no sign of their companions of the night before, so after eating they made their way to the station to catch a train back to base.

They were glad they'd made an early start because the journey back was slow, with two delays and a change of trains. It was the middle of the afternoon when they arrived at base, and they went to the rest room to talk about their trip to London.

After listening for a while, Steve got up and wandered out to the airfield, gazing at the majestic planes lined up and being worked on by the ground crews.

'Did you enjoy your leave?' a voice piped up from beside him.

He turned his head and looked down at Jean.

'Very much. Are they going out tonight?'

She nodded. 'The weather forecast is good. Was Nancy all right on the train?'

'Quiet, but that was only to be expected. She told me about her brother.'

'Did she?' Jean was clearly surprised and smiled up at

him. 'I'm so pleased to hear that. She's been bottling the grief up, and that is not good.'

'She'll be all right now she is with her family. What was he like – her brother?'

'A man everyone liked and respected. Brother and sister were very much alike and very close. They were always laughing and joking together, but they were both conscious that one day he might not return from a mission. Although she fought to control her emotions, I know his death tore her apart. She scanned the skies for hours hoping he would return, and never gave up until she heard the reports from the other crews.'

He nodded in understanding. 'Will they transfer her, do you think?'

'If they try, she will kick up a fuss. She believes this is where she is meant to be and intends to stay. Of course, orders have to be obeyed and she might not have any choice.' Jean looked up at the tall young man beside her. 'Steve – I may call you that?'

'Please do.'

'Nancy may appear unfriendly, but that is not her way at all. She is hurting after the loss of her brother and will try not to get close to another member of the aircrews. She believes it is unwise to make friendships. We have seen too many young men go out and never return, and being too close to any of them would be painful. She won't risk it.'

'Do you agree that distancing yourself from relationships you will be able to avoid such distress?'

'I believe it is impossible to be detached from what is happening here. We feel the loss of every one of them, whether we are close to them or not.' Jean shrugged. 'Nancy is saying that now, but I do believe she will change her mind.

Anyway, I am pleased to hear she has already broken her rule.'

'Has she?'

Jean gave him a knowing smile. 'She warmed to you enough to talk about her brother.'

'She needed to talk and I'm a good listener, and neither of you have to worry about us because we will come through whatever we have to face.'

'That's what they all say, and I pray you are right.'

'Hello, Jean.'

She spun round and beamed a smile at Luke, Sandy and Ricky. 'Hello, did you enjoy your trip to London?'

They launched into a full description of their leave, and then Luke asked, 'We thought we'd go to the pub this evening. Would you care to come with us?'

'Thanks. I'm off duty at eight so I'll meet you there.'

'Great!' Ricky was clearly delighted about this. 'We'll have the drinks lined up. Might as well make the most of the last few hours of our leave.'

Early the next morning it was time to start preparing for raids. After several days of intensive instruction, they were told to meet in the officers' bar that evening.

It was crowded and Steve scanned the room, seeing many faces he didn't know.

'Ah,' Luke said, 'I thought I heard lorries arriving earlier today with new arrivals – and all British by the look of them.'

'Gentlemen,' the commander called order. 'Circulate and get to know each other. Everyone here is trained in the various skills needed for a Lancaster crew. Oh, and the drink being handed round is the only one you will get because you will be flying on a training run tomorrow.'

A murmur of approval rippled across the room.

'Looks like we might have a say in who we have as crew, Steve.' Sandy joined his friends who were standing together. 'I've already been approached by several men, and they seem a nice crowd.' He glanced at Luke and Ricky. 'Are you two hoping to fly with Steve?'

'Yes, if it's possible,' they both replied.

'Well, you've got two, Steve, now you need a wireless operator, bomb aimer, and a mid and rear gunner.'

'There's plenty to choose from.' Ricky handed both pilots a drink from the tray being held by an orderly.

'I've already made a note of some,' Sandy informed them. 'Now I'll wander round and chat to the others.'

Everyone began to move around the room, introducing themselves and forming large clusters of men of various disciplines. After about an hour, Steve had names for a wireless operator and two gunners. That only left a bomb aimer to complete his crew – assuming he was going to have a say in the matter, of course.

The noise from the chatter and laughter was deafening, but it was important they got to know each other; they needed to be a close-knit group who gelled together in friendship and trust. He looked around at everyone, and his attention was caught by one man standing against the wall by himself. His badges indicated he was a bomb aimer. Steve wandered over and introduced himself.

'I'm Andy Bamber,' the man said, giving Steve an appraising look.

'Good to meet you, Andy. Don't stand here by yourself. Come over and meet our crowd.'

'Thanks.' Andy stubbed out his cigarette and gave a wry smile. 'You and your colleagues caught my attention as soon as you walked in, so I started asking questions, and I liked what I heard. I've already been on a couple of missions when a crew lost their bomb aimer, so I know what it's like and how important it is to have a crew that works together as a team and hold their nerve.'

'How do you know we will do that? None of us have been in combat yet.'

'I know that remains to be seen, but as I said, I've been watching you. Your guys have been sticking to you like glue and the men you've collected appear delighted to join you. Your other pilot is getting the same kind of response, as well. I can see it in their faces, but you're the one I want to fly with – if you'll have me.'

Steve nodded. 'I'll put you on the list and hope I have a say in the choice.'

'I believe you might have. From what I've managed to find out, quite a few are coming to the end of their missions and they need crews to replace them. A lot of us only arrived today, so they need to get us together as quickly as possible.'

And replace the losses, they both thought, but neither said, as they walked over to the others.

After introductions were made, Steve told them Andy had flown on two missions, which caused huge interest.

'Tell us what it's really like,' Ricky asked.

'Words couldn't describe it,' Andy admitted. 'But I don't think it will be long before we are on active duty and you'll find out for yourselves.'

That was the feeling Steve had as he looked around the room at the men, then back to his own crowd. He regarded them carefully and was satisfied. They would be a good crew – he was sure of it.

Chapter Six

Early the next morning the pilots were called to the command-er's office and told about the urgency to get working crews together quickly. The names they had collected were consid-ered, agreed, and notices prepared to put up for everyone to see. Once they were informed who they were flying with, they were all issued with flight gear and taken out to the waiting Lancasters. Those in charge certainly weren't wasting any time!

Steve examined the plane they had been given, and then walked up to the ground crew. These men were going to be of the greatest importance as they had to keep the machines in working order.

They saluted when he approached and introduced himself. 'She looks in fine condition,' he said.

'Yes, sir,' the sergeant replied. 'She's only four months old and hasn't been damaged.'

'I'll try and keep her that way.'

'We are sure you will, sir, and we will keep her flying for you.'

'You didn't tell me your name, Sergeant.'

'Just call me Sarge, sir, everyone does.'

'Good to meet you, Sarge.' Steve smiled and then went to join the rest of the crew.

The excitement was palpable as they all took their positions, and as Steve eased himself into the pilot's seat he gave a sigh of pleasure. At last, he was where he loved to be.

Once in the air on a dummy bombing run, he was pleased with the response and efficiency of his crew. They had all worked well together.

The ground crew were waiting when they jumped to the ground. 'How was she, sir?'

'Perfect to fly, Sarge.'

'That's good. We'll check her over again now.'

Steve watched as the men examined the plane, clearly eager to get their hands on their charge again.

'We'd better treat that machine well or those men will have a few words to say about it.'

'Without a doubt, Luke. We might think the Lancaster is ours, but I suspect they are just lending her to us,' Ricky remarked as he slapped Steve on the back. 'Nice flying, skipper.' When Steve raised his eyebrows, his friend grinned. 'Just getting into the swing of things.'

'Come on, we must check in and see what they thought of our practice run.' Steve ushered the exhilarated bunch of men to the main building.

The routine for the next few days was the same, and after debriefing, all the crews gathered together to relax.

They stood when the commander entered the room.

He gazed around, and then said, 'Well, gentlemen, play-time is over. I am sorry to throw you into the mix of things so soon, but a big raid is planned and every plane that can fly will be in the air. You will be going on your first mission tomorrow night, so I suggest you get some sleep during the day. Briefing will be at eighteen hundred hours.'

'Did you sleep?' Andy asked Steve as they climbed into their flying gear the following day.

'Managed a few hours. What about you?'

'Hard to relax, but forced myself, knowing we needed to be alert for the mission.' He gave a tight smile. 'At least I know what is waiting for us, but you still have to find out.'

'I don't know what could be worse; you knowing or us trying to imagine.' Ricky was serious for a change. 'I expect we will get used to sleeping during the day.'

They all went outside and jumped on the transport waiting to take them to the aircraft.

When they reached the planes, Steve's heart rate quickened. This was the culmination of all their training, and ahead of them was something no amount of imagination could prepare them for.

'Good luck, sir,' one of the ground crew said softly.

'Thank you.' Steve smiled at him and then climbed into the plane. Settling down and strapping himself in he was totally focussed on what had to be done. This was going to be a big raid and they would be joining up with flights from other bases. Once all the checks had been carried out, the order for take-off came through.

He taxied into position, and when his turn came they climbed to the required height and assumed their position with the others.

'Wow, what a sight!' Jack, the rear gunner, exclaimed. 'The sky is full of planes.'

'When you test your guns over the sea, don't shoot any of them down,' Steve ordered. A collective chuckle could be heard, easing the tension.

During the flight to Berlin, they were constantly on the watch for night fighters. Steve glanced up and saw the stars shining brightly. It was a beautiful night, but the clear weather also made them very visible from the ground.

'Flak ahead,' Luke announced as they approached their target. 'Hell, look at those searchlights. If we get caught in one of them we'll be lit up like a Christmas tree.'

'Target ten minutes.' Ricky's voice came through, clear and calm.

'Keep her steady, skipper,' Andy said, as the anti-aircraft guns began to blaze away in earnest.

Steve listened for Andy's voice repeating – 'Steady.' A shell burst close by and rocked the plane, but he kept her on course. The tension in the plane was palpable and everyone was holding their breath.

'Steady . . . steady . . . Bombs gone! Get us out of here, skipper.'

Making sure the airspace around them was clear of other aircraft, Steve climbed and turned towards home. He soon caught up with the other Lancasters. It was then that the night fighters appeared, and he began to weave in an effort to make them a difficult target. Although the battle with them was short, one plane went down and another had been hit and was now flying with one engine not working. The fighters also suffered casualties.

'Is everyone all right?' Steve asked as they reached the sea.

One by one they reported in and all had come through unscathed.

He landed and taxied to their parking place. When

everything was shut down, he thumped his head back against his seat and closed his eyes.

Ricky swore. 'Anyone want to bet how many of these we will survive?'

'We were lucky this time, so let's hope the lady stays on our side. Let's get out of here and check in,' Steve replied. He was the last one to climb out and the ground crew were waiting, scouring the plane for damage. 'I don't think anything hit us,' he told the sergeant.

'We'll give her a thorough going over, sir.'

'Thanks.' He nodded to the crew. 'Let's get the debriefing done and then we can eat. I'm starving.'

After debriefing they went straight to the mess hall. They knew there had been casualties, but the number of empty seats shocked them. No one mentioned it, though, and they ate in silence, all the while searching the faces for Sandy. He raised his hand and called to them. Their friend had also come through their first mission unscathed.

When the meal was over Steve stood up. 'I'm going for a walk to stretch my legs.'

'Want company?' Luke asked.

He shook his head. 'I won't be long. I need to move after sitting in one position for so long. The forecast is that the weather is holding fair for several days, so I expect we'll be going out again tonight. Get some sleep.'

Ricky frowned. 'You need sleep as well. We can't have you dozing off while we're in the air.'

'Not a chance,' he assured them. He made his way out of the mess into the fresh air. It was cold but a lovely morning and he drew in deep breaths. There was still a slight smudge of pink in the sky, and it looked as if it was almost touching the trees at the end of the airfield. He strode towards them. He'd always appreciated nature, and after the mayhem of last night everything was in sharp focus. He walked for a while, head up and a smile on his face. It was good to be alive.

'Steve.'

He stopped, surprised he had almost walked back to the control tower.

Jean came up to him, looking concerned. 'I've been watching you for a while. Are you all right?'

'I'm fine, thank you. I like to walk after sitting in one position for some time. I can walk for miles in a day when I'm at home.'

'Really? What do you do?'

'We are farmers.'

'Ah, then you are used to being out in the open in all weather.' She smiled up at him then, thinking he didn't look like a farmer's son. 'How did the rest of your crew deal with their first mission?'

'Perfectly. They all remained calm and got on with what they had to do.' He gave a slight smile. 'There were a few rude remarks from Ricky, of course, but that just helped to ease the tension.'

'He's a lively character, there's no doubt about that. That was a rough night from what I've heard,' she said sadly. 'I was relieved to see you return safely.'

'Not as much as we were, I'll bet. I have just been thinking how beautiful everything looks.'

'I have time before I go on duty, so do you fancy a cup of tea?'

'No, thanks, Jean.' He yawned. 'I think it's time I got my head down.'

'Good idea.' She hesitated. 'Er . . . most of the crews carry a mascot or something they consider good luck. Do you have one?'

'Never thought about it,' he admitted.

She reached into her top pocket and held something out to him. 'Would you like this? You don't have to accept it,' she added hastily.

He took it from her, held it in the palm of his hand and then smiled, his long fingers closing over it. 'A silver star, just like the ones we fly under. Thank you, Jean; I will keep it with me all the time. Are you sure you want to part with it?'

'Oh, yes, I would love you to have it. It isn't valuable, if that is worrying you. I have an uncle who is a metalworker and he makes things out of scraps from the factory floor.'

'He's very talented.'

She nodded. 'He's an artist with his hands. When he gave it to me, I knew at once it was meant for a bomber crew, so I . . . er . . . took it to the RAF minister and he blessed it for me. It will keep you and your crew safe, Steve.' She gave a hesitant smile. 'I know that sounds silly, but I have to believe it.'

'I don't think it's silly.' He glanced around. 'Is it permitted to kiss you on the cheek?'

'You'd better not,' she laughed, her eyes glinting with amusement and pleasure that he had accepted the gift. 'We'll both be reprimanded if you do such a thing here.'

'Ah, shame. In that case, my thanks will have to do.'

They were both laughing as he strode away to get some much needed sleep.

He entered the room quietly so as not to disturb Luke, but he need not have worried because his friend was still awake.

'You've been a long time. I was about to come out and find you. Did you enjoy your walk?'

'Very much.' Steve began to empty his pockets before undressing, and put the contents on a unit by the bed.

Luke reached out and picked up the star. 'I haven't seen this before. Where did you get it?'

'Jean gave it to me. She said it will help to keep us safe. I don't believe in such things myself, but it was a thoughtful gesture, so I accepted it.'

'Well, if that's what she believes, then you had better bring it with you when we go out. Don't tell Ricky where you got it, though, because I think he's got his eyes on her, and might not like the thought of her giving you that token.'

'He needn't be concerned. Jean is a nice girl, and they would probably suit each other. The star was a gift for all the crew.' With a sigh of relief, Steve settled in the bed and closed his eyes.

'Aren't you interested in Nancy?'

But Steve never replied. He was already fast asleep.

Chapter Seven

Nancy's parents managed to arrange the memorial service for Dan the day before she was due to return to base. The small church was crowded with family, friends and neighbours, all wanting to pay their respects to the young man they had loved.

Nancy stood with her parents in her best dress uniform, dry-eyed, having shed all of her tears in private, knowing her brother would want her to keep her composure for their parents' sake. It was all so very painful, though, and she struggled to keep the picture of his smiling face as he greeted her after every mission. She closed her eyes and could almost see him walking across the airfield towards her, a big grin on his face. But she hadn't been fooled; the bright look couldn't hide the strain in his eyes. Putting their lives on the line night after night took its toll, but he never complained – none of them did.

This service was really so her family could say goodbye to their son, even though there wasn't a body to bury. They had insisted that it be upbeat, and for that she was grateful.

Once the service had finished, a few came back to the house, and it was good to see her parents a little more relaxed. They would always mourn the loss of their son, of course, but at least they could now move on with their lives, as she had to herself.

Nancy walked into the garden for a moment, ignoring the slight drizzle, wanting to get away from the chatter in the house. Tomorrow she would return to the airfield, and couldn't help but wonder how many of the familiar faces would no longer be there. Her heart seized slightly as Steve's face flashed through her mind.

The next day she spent as much time as possible with her mother and father, leaving it as late as she could to catch the train. Her homecoming had been sombre and she wanted to leave seeing a smile on their faces, so she told them about the Canadians Jean had saddled her with. It made her mother smile and shake her head and even made her father laugh when she told them about the lift they were given to the station, how insistent they were in making it clear they were Canadians and not Americans.

'When you come on leave again bring some of them home with you,' her mother suggested. 'Those poor boys are a long way from home and family.'

'That's a good idea,' her father said before she could protest. 'We've got plenty of room for three or four, and it would be good to have the house full of young men again. Do bring them, Nancy.'

'It would mean them being on leave the same time as me, but I'll see what I can do.' The thought of having them here filled her with apprehension, but her parents were obviously enthusiastic about the idea. Would it help them? On reflection she thought it might.

'Try, darling.' Her mother squeezed her hand. 'This place is so empty without you and Dan, and we could give them a touch of home for a few days.'

'I'll do my best, but you don't know what you will be letting yourself in for,' she teased. 'Oh, my, look at the time. I really must be going!'

'We'll come with you to the station.' Her father smiled at her. 'We want to hold on to you for as long as possible.'

There was a train just arriving when they got there, so there wasn't time for lingering goodbyes.

The journey was slow and tedious, and it was dark by the time she walked through the gates. Suddenly, the familiar roar of engines ripped through the air as the Lancasters began to soar into the sky. Nancy hurried to check in and then went to the control tower where she could see Jean standing outside.

They watched in silence until the last plane was in the air, and then Jean asked, 'How did it go at home?'

'Quite well. Have you finished for the day? I'm going for a cup of tea.'

'Yes, I'm not on duty again until eight tomorrow. Let's go to the mess and you can tell me all about it.'

They settled at a table and Nancy looked around. 'Are the Canadians at the pub?'

Jean shook her head. 'No, they've just taken off.'

'What? They are flying missions already? How many raids have they been on?'

'This is their second. More crews were needed urgently so they are on missions much sooner than anyone expected.

A batch of British airmen arrived, and they are all flying.'

Nancy was dismayed, and her expression showed it. She hadn't expected them to be thrust into active service this quickly. It must mean losses had been high while she had been away, but she didn't ask.

Jean studied her friend's face. 'Are you sure you want to stay here?'

'Definitely.' Nancy straightened up. 'That news took me by surprise, that's all.'

'Hmm, well don't stand on the airfield counting them back or the commander will transfer you.'

'I promise.'

'Good. Now tell me how your parents are doing, and then go to bed. You look worn out.'

'It was a tiring and emotional couple of weeks, but do you know, I feel more at peace now.'

Jean listened intently to Nancy's recount of her leave and her eyes opened wide when she heard about the request to bring the Canadians home with her next time. Jean grinned. 'That should be interesting. Can I come too?'

'I'd be glad to have you there.' Nancy shook her head and grimaced. 'I would really need some support with that lot running around the house.'

'I can just imagine. Are you going to tell them?'

'Not likely! Anyway, there isn't much chance of that happening now they are flying.'

'True. Shame, though, because they could be just the tonic your parents need. Don't dismiss the idea, as they will probably get a few days off now and again, and a change of scene would be good for them.'

'I'll keep it in mind.' Nancy yawned and stood up. 'I must turn in now. I'm on duty early in the morning.'

'Can we meet for breakfast around eight? And don't you dare go out to the airfield at dawn.' Jean gave her a stern look. 'I mean it.'

'I know.' Nancy raised her hands. 'I'm not going to do anything to risk being transferred, so no watching planes return, I promise.'

'Night.'

Right on time the next morning, Nancy and Jean had breakfast together. She knew the planes had returned from their mission but didn't ask about casualties; she'd rather not know, and Jean did not offer any information.

When they'd finished eating there was still a short time left of their break, so they stood by the control tower and watched the men on the airfield.

'The ground crews are busy caring for their babies, I see,' she remarked, noting the activity around the planes.

'Babies!' Jean laughed. 'I'd hardly call those monsters babies.'

'They are to the ground crews.'

A lone figure walking by trees on one side of the airfield caught her attention.

Jean noticed and said, 'That's Steve. He likes to walk after a raid. Everyone copes in their own way, as you know: some sleep at once, others read or listen to the wireless. Steve likes to walk, and I suspect be on his own for a while.'

Nancy had a small pair of binoculars her father had given her for her nineteenth birthday and she always carried them with her. She put them up to her eyes and studied the figure in the distance. 'I expect he likes the feel of fresh air after being in the plane for hours.'

'Probably. I spoke to him after his walk yesterday.'

'Oh, how was he?'

'Relaxed, and a little cheeky.'

'Really? In what way?'

Jean then told her about his offer to kiss her cheek after accepting her gift of the star. 'He didn't have a lucky mascot, and to be honest I don't believe he thinks such a thing is necessary, but he accepted it with good grace.'

'Why did you give him that? You're not falling for him, are you?'

'No, he's a man I like and respect, but I'm more attracted to Ricky.' Jean gave a quiet laugh. 'I met them at the pub when they came back from London, and he had me crying with laughter about the things they'd got up to. I think he likes me, too.'

'Oh, Jean, we said we wouldn't get too close to any of the crews. It could all end in heartbreak.'

'I know, but I can't help liking them.' She shrugged. 'Still, there won't be many more chances to get to know them while they are flying missions. They will fly, eat and sleep all the time the weather holds.'

Nancy glanced at her watch. 'I'll have to hope Mum and Dad forget that idea of them coming home with me. Now, I must go.'

When she walked back into the stores, two airmen who had just arrived on duty sighed with relief. She grinned at them. 'Have you had a busy time?'

'You could say that,' Denny told her. 'What with a batch of new recruits who needed kitting out, and ground crew shouting at us for parts that didn't come the day before they were even ordered,' he exaggerated. 'We've been rushed off our feet and asked for help while you were on leave, but we never got it.'

'How was everything at home?' Colin asked, sympathy showing in his eyes.

'It was a tough time, but my parents were pleased to have me there. We held a memorial service for Dan and that helped all of us. So, where do you want me to start?'

'Paperwork,' they answered in unison, pointing to a desk in the corner piled high.

'Right. What deliveries are you expecting today?'

'We've been promised a new Lancaster and, hopefully, two new engines.' Colin grinned. 'If they don't arrive, we'll let you deal with the irate ground crews.'

'Cowards,' she teased. When they laughed and went back to their work, she realised how much calmer she felt. The ache at the loss of her darling brother was still there, and always would be, but she felt more able to cope with it. Her thoughts went to those on active duty – the Canadians in particular. There wasn't anything she could do for those who didn't return, but the living needed friends who cared for them. So, regardless of the pain she was liable to experience, she would try to help these boys who were far from their homes.

The rest of the day was so busy there wasn't time to think about anything but the work at hand. The Air Transport Auxiliary delivered two new planes instead of the one expected, which everyone was delighted about. The engines arrived as well, along with two lorry loads of other necessary spares. Keeping the planes flying was the top priority, as many of them came back damaged in one way or another.

Nancy was working her way through a mound of delivery notes when someone tapped her on the shoulder.

'The next shift has arrived,' Colin told her. 'Let's go eat.'

'My goodness! Where has the day gone?'

Denny joined them and they headed for the mess.

When they'd finished their meal and the men had left, she wandered outside and gazed up at the sky. It was November now and the daylight hours shorter. The evening was clear, but not too cold, so she sat on a seat outside the building and relaxed. Across the airfield the planes were being loaded and the ground crew were making sure they were in good order. She took the binoculars out of her pocket and held them up to her eyes, focussing on the men jumping out of the transport and walking towards their planes. The tall figure of Steve was easy to pick out, and she watched until the last one had taken off, then closed her eyes in a silent prayer for the safety of the entire flight.

It was too early to go back to her quarters, and she doubted she would sleep much tonight anyway, so she went in search of Jean. She needed some company and a beer or two.

Chapter Eight

The Lancasters were soon over the sea and the bright moon was dancing on the water. It was a lovely sight, but also a reminder that they would soon cross the coast and be in danger.

Ricky came through. 'Don't ever dump us in that, Steve. I can't swim.'

There were chuckles and Andy remarked, 'Don't worry, you would soon learn.'

'I'll try to see we are on dry land, but I can't make any promises,' Steve replied, pleased to hear the teasing banter. This was a rare moment to relax a little because soon they would need to be alert for trouble. He had fallen in love with this plane the moment he had seen her, and adored it all the more as he flew. Even the prospect of danger couldn't dampen the pleasure of being at the controls and soaring upwards.

This was a big raid planned and they were heading for the industrial heartland of Germany. It would be well protected, and they knew what was waiting for them.

With their destination close, the sky lit up with searchlights, and flak began bursting around them. There was a loud crash and the plane shuddered. Andy's calm voice came through, 'Steady . . . steady . . .'

Steve knew everyone was concerned about possible damage as they flew through the barrage. They were being buffeted from constant attack from the ground. Something had hit them but he still had control, so it didn't appear to have damaged anything vital.

'Bombs away!'

It was only after he had turned for home and away from the searchlights and guns, he asked, 'Is everyone all right?'

They all came through except Ricky. 'Navigator!' Luke demanded. 'Respond.'

'He's all right,' the wireless operator told them. 'He's just indicated to me that his headset isn't working. It's a bit draughty where he's sitting, though.'

'How bad is the damage?' Steve wanted to know.

'Nothing the boys on the ground can't fix.'

'Good.' Knowing his crew were unhurt and the plane didn't appear to be in trouble, Steve concentrated on getting them home safely.

After landing, they all went to look at the damage. There was a small hole the size of a tennis ball close to Ricky's position.

The next few minutes were hilarious as Ricky told everyone just what he thought about those who had been shooting at them. Even the ground crew were grinning, and so were the many who had gathered to see what was going on. Steve and Luke had to take him by the arms and lead him to debriefing, still complaining.

At breakfast there were no new empty seats, and everyone breathed a sigh of relief.

It had just started to drizzle when Steve went for his walk, but that didn't bother him. He looked up at the leaden sky and smiled. They had eventually managed to quieten Ricky down and Steve laughed out loud. Ricky was a lively character and anything he did was with great energy and dedication, but he also had guts to fool around after such a close shave.

Later that morning, Nancy was taking some needed goods to one of the hangars when she saw the small hole in the Lancaster being towed inside. Wing Commander Jackman was watching so she went up to him. 'Whose plane is that, sir?'

'Allard's.'

Her heart skipped a beat. 'Was anyone hurt?'

'No, but the shrapnel must have parted the navigator's hair when it came through.' He began to laugh softly.

Nancy was surprised to see him so amused and frowned. 'Is that funny, sir?'

'No, but the reaction of the navigator was. While inspecting the damage he began to tell everyone, in very colourful terms, just what he thought about the enemy.'

'Oh, what did he say?'

Jackman burst into laughter. 'It isn't fit for the ears of a young lady. When he'd run out of expletives, he began begging the ground crews forgiveness for bringing their baby back with a hole in it. It was the funniest thing I've seen in a long time.'

'From what I've seen and heard about him, he's the comedian of the group.'

'I can believe that, but he's also wise. From reports it was rough up there and knowing they had taken a hit, albeit a small one, would have made the journey back tense. His little performance had them all laughing.'

'Er . . . what about the pilot, sir, was he all right?'

'He just watched the scene with an amused smile on his face and looking as if they had just returned from a pleasure jaunt.'

She nodded, relieved, and after glancing at her watch she saluted the wing commander and hurried to deliver the parts she was holding.

It was the middle of the afternoon when Jean arrived at the stores. 'Nancy!' she called. 'I need a typewriter ribbon and paper and envelopes.'

'Coming right up.' Nancy collected the items and took them with the form for Jean to sign. 'Are they going out again tonight?'

When Jean didn't reply, she said, 'Come on, you work for the officers so you must know.'

'The weather is holding, so yes.'

'What about those who returned with damage?'

Jean gave her a stern look. 'You've been asking questions, haven't you? I thought you weren't going to take an interest in anyone on missions.'

'I'm only keeping myself up on what is happening on the base.'

'Liar.' Jean grinned. 'Did you hear what happened when Ricky got out and examined the hole on their plane?'

Nancy nodded and couldn't help smiling. 'Wing Commander Jackman told me. And you haven't answered my question.'

'The damage wasn't bad and has already been repaired, so they will be going again tonight. Want to go to the pictures later?'

'Might as well. What's on?'

'No idea. Does it matter?'

'Not at all. I'll meet you at seven.'

'Good, see you then.'

The rest of her shift flew by, and after getting something to eat she met her friend at the gate, only it wasn't just Jean. She had gathered four airmen to join them as well.

They just had time after the film to go to the pub for a drink. It was crowded with military personnel as usual and very lively.

The evening had given her little time to dwell on those flying somewhere over Germany, but once in bed the thoughts rushed in. She sighed. All the good intentions not to worry about any of them had evaporated, and to be truthful, being so close to the action it was impossible to keep detached. Even if she moved to another posting away from all this, it wouldn't be any better. No amount of distance would ever be able to erase the pilots from her mind.

Over the next couple of weeks, Nancy resisted the urge to get up when she heard the planes returning, but she did always check to see if Steve was out for his usual walk. He did it no matter the weather, and always did it alone. She didn't know what his home in Canada was like, but she had the feeling he was used to having open space around him and he missed that.

'One day I'm going to ask him why he does that.'

'He'll only smile and say he likes walking, but he told me he is a farmer, so I expect he's used to being out in any weather,' Jean said.

Nancy nodded and looked up at the heavy sky. 'Winter is closing in now and that means, hopefully, there will be times when they can't fly.'

Jean nodded. 'They must need a break soon, but they'd be the last to admit it.'

'I know, but it takes its toll on every one of them as they face constant danger, no matter what service they are in. They are experts at hiding that fact. Dan laughed and joked, as he had always done, and you would think he was untouched by what he was doing until you looked into his eyes. I can see the same happening with the Canadians. They arrived as boys, laughing and excited, but they will leave as men. Providing they survive,' she added softly.

Jean sighed. 'They've crawled into our hearts, haven't they?'

'And that makes us a couple of bloody stupid females, doesn't it?'

'Language,' Jean reprimanded, linking her arm through Nancy's. 'Let's stop all this worrying and get some breakfast. The weather is foul, so they might not go out tonight. If so, we'll met them in the NAAFI and beat them at a game of darts.'

'Good idea.' Both girls were grinning at the prospect as they headed for the mess.

The weather deteriorated even more during the afternoon and the rain was thundering down. The NAAFI was packed with airmen unwilling to get soaked going to the village.

The moment the girls walked in Ricky's face lit up, and he beckoned them over. Steve's crew were all together, which was the way they lived while flying missions. They had become a close-knit bunch who relied on each other.

The men stood up and offered seats and Luke went to get them a drink.

'We heard you have the night off, so we thought we'd challenge you to a game of darts,' Jean explained.

'You're on.' Luke placed a beer in front of each of them. 'Choose your opponents.'

'We'll play all of you, two at a time, and when we've beaten all of you, our prize will be a dinner and dance at a nice place.'

'Such confidence,' Ricky teased. 'What will be our prize if we win?'

'You won't.'

There were howls of protest, and others nearby who had heard the challenge joined in, urging the group to take them on. Nancy sipped her beer and tried to contain her amusement. Her friend was incorrigible, but this could be a fun evening, and that was a good thing for everyone.

'Have you got steady hands, Ricky?' Sandy called out.

He held them up. 'Not a tremor.'

'That's pretty good, considering someone shot at you,' Jean remarked casually.

Ricky was about to open his mouth to reply when the rest of the crew chorused, 'Don't get him started on that again. His language isn't suitable for young ladies.'

'We are quite used to bad language,' Nancy told them.

'Perhaps so, but we would rather not have to listen to his tirade again.' Steve was shaking his head in mock dismay.

Luke slapped Ricky on the back. 'You were quite safe, anyway, Steve had the lucky star with him.'

'What star? This is the first I've heard about it.'

'I gave it to him to keep you all safe,' Jean said.

'Show me,' Ricky demanded.

Steve took it out of his top pocket and handed it over.

'That's nice.' Ricky pouted slightly. 'Why did you give it to him and not me?'

'Because he's the pilot. He's the one who has to get you there and back, so he should have the star close to him.'

'Ah, yes, you're quite right.' He handed it back to Steve. 'Make sure you always have that with you.'

'I will.'

Ricky turned and reached out to Jean to give her a hug. 'Thank you for thinking about us in that way. It helps, you know?'

'I know.'

'So, who do you want to play first?' Steve asked, changing the subject.

'You and Ricky.'

When they began to play, everyone gathered round. The men were calling encouragement to the Allard crew, and the women present were cheering Nancy and Jean on.

It was close. The boys were better than the girls had expected and they needed a bullseye to win the first game.

'You can do it,' Jean whispered to Nancy as she handed her the darts. 'No one could beat you and your brother.'

That remark brought to mind happy memories of the fun they'd had, and she took a deep breath. The dart hit the target with a thud, and the room erupted.

Jean grinned at their opponents. 'One game to us.'

As the crew had an odd number, they elected Sandy to play with Andy. They turned out to be the two best players in their group and won that game, but that was the only game the girls lost.

By the end of the evening, everyone was laughing and thoroughly enjoying themselves.

'That was brilliant,' Nancy laughed as they walked back to their billet. 'Good job we won, though, or else we would have had to take all of them out somewhere for a treat.'

Her friend chuckled. 'They are gentlemen, and I'm sure they wouldn't have allowed us to pay for a night out.'

'You're right.' Nancy punched Jean on the arm. 'We wouldn't have lost whichever way the games went.'

'I was banking on it. I think I'll sleep well tonight.'

'I know I will.'

Chapter Nine

Luke gazed out of the window and sighed. 'The rain is still coming down in sheets. Wonder what the weather is like over Germany?'

'Let's go and find out.' Steve shrugged into his flying jacket. 'There might be a window of better weather tonight.'

'Hope so. I hate this hanging around,' Ricky said. 'Be a bit dicey taking off in torrential rain, though, Steve.'

The three of them ran to the operations building and found it full of airmen waiting to know what the situation was.

The commander walked in. 'Stand down, gentlemen. We are not needed tonight, but be ready tomorrow. An extra-large strike is being planned, so go easy on the booze.'

When the officer left, the men gathered together and Sandy wandered over.

'What say we take the girls out to a dance? We might as well pay our forfeit while we have a chance.'

'Good idea. I'll go and find them.' Ricky was gone before anyone could answer.

Luke laughed. 'Think he's really fallen for Jean.'

They continued talking, and in about fifteen minutes Ricky arrived back, a huge grin on his face. 'They'll be ready at seven, so it's smart uniforms tonight, boys. We mustn't let the girls down.'

'Does that mean I've got to polish my shoes?' Luke teased.

'Of course. Buttons, too! Andy and the others have found themselves dates for tonight, so it will just be the four of us.'

Steve looked out at the rain. 'I'll go and see if I can cadge some transport, or else we are going to get soaked.'

'It will have to be big enough for the six of us,' Sandy called to his retreating figure.

Steve lifted his hand in acknowledgement, and was only a few steps outside the room when he met two of his ground crew.

'Got an unexpected night off, sir.'

'Yes, Sarge. A few of us are going into town, so do you know where I can get the loan of some transport?'

'How many of you?'

'Six.'

The sergeant looked at his companion who nodded. 'You leave that to us, sir. We'll get you something.'

'Thanks. I'll be in the briefing room.'

'Right you are.'

He watched the men hurry away and went back to his friends.

Sandy raised an eyebrow. 'That was quick.'

'Two of our ground crew are finding us something.'

'Those men are guardian angels,' Luke remarked. 'They are even looking after us when we are not flying.'

'They take a personal interest in their crews.' Sandy shook

his head. 'I've seen how upset they are when their boys don't come back.'

'True, and we certainly couldn't keep flying without their expertise and care.' Steve wandered over to the window and looked up at the sky. There wouldn't be any stars visible tonight.

The men were soon back and the sergeant handed Steve a key and winked. 'You should be able to squeeze six of you in that, sir. It's just outside the door.'

'Thanks. We lost a darts match against two of the girls, so we have to treat them to a night out. We thought we'd take them dancing, so do you know a good place to go?'

Both men smirked, and the sergeant asked, 'Who did you play against, sir?'

'Jean and Nancy.'

That brought huge grins to their faces. 'Oh dear me, you don't want to play darts with those two. They are experts.'

'So we found out,' Steve replied. 'Nevertheless, we have to pay our debts, so where can we take them?'

'There are two places, but one of them is very expensive.'

'That one will do. Give me instructions how to get there.'

The sergeant wrote in his notebook, tore out the page and handed it to Steve, and they all went outside to have a look at the car.

Steve's mouth twitched in amusement. 'How did you manage to get an officer's car?'

'Best not ask, sir. Just get it back here by midnight and we will return it. It is for officer use and you are technically an officer, so enjoy yourselves.'

'We will, and thanks.'

Steve got in the driver's seat and the others all piled in,

then he drove them back to their quarters where they set about smartening themselves up for the evening ahead.

The girls were waiting for them as arranged, and Jean gave a whoop of delight when the car pulled up beside them, full of men with huge grins on their faces.

'Wow!' Nancy said as she squeezed in the back. 'Where did you get this, Steve?'

'A couple of our ground crew got it for us, but I was told not to ask where it came from.' He turned his head and smiled at her. 'They also told me we must return it by midnight.'

There wasn't any more room in the back, so Jean got in the front and was sitting on Ricky, amid much laughter and shoving. 'Midnight. Did you bring your glass slipper with you, Nancy?'

'Darn it, I forgot.'

The Canadians laughed, and Sandy said, 'Aren't we lucky. We've got two Cinderellas to take to the dance.'

'Lovely, I do enjoy a dance.' Jean pushed Ricky's leg out of the way. 'Shift over, I can't close the door.'

After much wriggling the car door clicked shut. 'All right, pilot, you can take off now,' Ricky ordered. 'I can't navigate, though, because I can't see a blasted thing.'

'I know where there is a dance, so I can direct you.'

'Thanks, Jean, but I've been told of a good place.' The directions were clear enough, and in about twenty minutes he pulled up outside a large hotel. 'This looks like it. Everybody out,' he ordered.

Nancy leant forward and tapped him on the shoulder. 'You can't take us here. It's too expensive.'

'So I've been told, but it looks perfect.' There was much

pushing and shoving going on in the seat beside him. 'Will you two get out – somebody help Jean and Rick to untangle themselves so we can go and enjoy our evening.'

It took a while, but eventually they were all out of the car and straightening their uniforms.

'Glad we put our best uniforms on,' Jean whispered to her friend. 'I've always wanted to come here, but could never afford it.'

'Neither could I, and the thing that's worrying me is, can they?'

'Well, they are better paid than our boys, and if we only drink beer that will keep the cost down.'

Steve had parked the car round the side out of the way and strode back to the group. He offered Nancy his arm and led everyone inside.

They were greeted at the door, escorted to the ballroom and given a table by the dance floor.

'Wow, this is fabulous.' Ricky gazed around the crowded room, a smile of pleasure on his face. 'It's so quaint.'

'Pilots get the first round.' Luke urged Steve and Sandy towards the bar.

There were British, Americans and more Canadians who gravitated over to them, as well as many of the local girls. They danced all the time, changing partners many times, especially in the 'excuse me' dances.

Towards the end of the evening, Steve managed to have a slow foxtrot with Nancy, and she said teasingly, 'You dance very well for a farmer's boy.'

'Why, thank you,' he replied, clearly amused.

'So, why did you decide to become a pilot?'

'I was put through for the training programme as soon as I joined up because I already had a private pilot's licence.'

She stopped dancing in surprise. 'How long had you been flying before you joined up?'

'Three years as a qualified pilot. My father took me up when I was about six, and began teaching me when I reached the age of fourteen.'

'Your father is a pilot? Was he in the air force?'

'No, but he is a very good pilot, and I'm sure could easily fly a Lancaster.'

'What do your parents think about what you're doing?'

'They understand, and to be honest, I think Dad is quite jealous.' He gave a quiet laugh. 'I have to give details of what it's like to be at the controls of such a fine plane every time I write.'

At that moment there was a tap on his shoulder and an American claimed his partner. As he walked away, she watched him with a look of utter confusion on her face.

'Lost your partner?' Luke asked, coming to stand beside him.

He laughed and nodded. 'Just as well.'

'Why do you say that?'

'She was asking a lot of questions. I told her my dad taught me to fly at a young age, and she's wondering what a farmer's boy is doing flying planes.'

Luke tipped his head back and roared with laughter.

'I'm only telling her the truth. I am a farmer's boy and Dad did teach me to fly,' he protested.

His friend couldn't stop laughing. 'Ricky told Jean he works in a department store.'

'And what have you said you do?'

'I said I'm a toolmaker in an engineering firm.'

They grinned at each other. 'Well, they are all true – to a point. At least they will never be able to accuse us of bragging, or boasting about our occupations at home.'

'Wonder what Sandy has told them he does?'

'He's told them he's a history teacher,' Steve replied. 'Which again is basically the truth.'

'Yeah, he's in the right place because there will be plenty in this country to interest him. I'll go and get the girls another drink before the bar closes and perhaps that'll take their minds off trying to find out too much about us.' Luke walked away, still chuckling quietly to himself.

The dance finished at eleven, giving them plenty of time to get the car back before midnight.

The sergeant appeared the moment they drove in, and once everyone had extracted themselves from the car, he took the key from Steve.

'Had a good night, sir?'

'Wonderful.' He pulled a half-bottle of whisky out of his pocket and slipped it to the sergeant.

The bottle disappeared immediately into his coat and he winked at Steve. 'Thank you kindly, sir. If you need anything in the future, you just come to me.'

'Thanks, I certainly will.'

It had been such a fun evening that the girls couldn't stop smiling. Jean put her head to one side and asked, 'That was terrific, so when can we play you again? Same rules apply.'

'We are not falling for that,' Steve teased. 'Since then, we've heard about your prowess with darts. We've been told you are practically unbeatable.'

'I don't know where you heard such tales, sir.' Nancy feigned a shocked expression. 'Our game is very average.'

'Oh, yeah!' Ricky exclaimed. 'You needed a bullseye to win and it flies straight to the target. I'd say that was way above average.'

'Tell you what. Give us time to practise, and in about three months we'll beat you.'

'Sandy!' Luke exclaimed, 'We'd need longer than that.'

'Let's say around May, then.'

The men all nodded.

'All right, we'll keep you to that promise.' Jean took hold of Nancy's arm and blew kisses at them all. 'Night, boys, and thanks for a really lovely dance.'

'Those two are really something, aren't they?' Ricky sighed as he watched the girls disappear.

Nancy sat on the edge of the bed, too awake to sleep. 'Did you know Steve could fly a plane before he joined up?'

'No, but that must have helped his application to train as an air force pilot. He loves flying and is earning the respect of all of his crew. Ricky says he has a wonderful temperament at the controls. They feel safe with him.'

'I'm sure he is, but I'm puzzled why he and his father are pilots. They're farmers.'

Jean stopped brushing her hair. 'His father is a pilot as well?'

Nancy nodded. 'He taught Steve.'

'Now that *is* interesting. His dad must be highly qualified to be able to teach someone.' Jean sat beside her friend. 'They say very little about their lives at home. Although we are coming to know them quite well, we haven't much idea about their background.'

'Perhaps they're homesick and it's too painful to talk about.'

Jean shrugged. 'I expect that's why, but I can tell you they're not ordinary boys. They're educated, have lovely manners, and the opulence of that hotel tonight didn't faze them at all. It was as if they are quite used to going to places like that.'

'Oh, that doesn't mean much, Jean. They go out on raids never knowing if they'll survive the night, that'd make anyone enjoy the free time they have. After what they experience up there under the stars, nothing down here will disturb them. In their situation, why hold on to any money they have?'

'Of course, you're right. You know me; I can let my imagination run away with me. They are ordinary boys doing a dangerous job. It's just that they come from a country we know nothing about.'

Instead of answering, Nancy bowed her head and silent tears streamed down her face.

'Hey, what's the matter?' Jean put an arm around her shoulder. 'Why are you crying?'

'I wish Dan was here. He would have liked those boys. I miss him so much.' She was sobbing now.

'Of course you do, and it's time you let all that grief come out.'

Nancy sat up straight and wiped her face, then took a deep breath. 'I'm sorry. It's silly of me after we've had such a lovely time.'

'No, it isn't. This evening probably reminded you of the fun you always had with your brother.'

Nancy nodded. 'You know that star you gave to Steve; well, I was wondering if your uncle would make something I could give them.'

'Good idea. I'll ask him to make a star for all of them. What would you like your one to be – the moon?'

'I was thinking of another star with their names engraved on the back. Could your uncle make that?'

'I'm sure he could. How about making it slightly different from the one I'm giving them, and very highly polished.'

'That sounds lovely.'

Jean squeezed Nancy's arm. 'I know we've become too fond of them, but that's something we have to deal with. We can let them know they're not alone here. That's what they need.'

'Yes, it's something we can do for them.'

'And we will.' Jean smiled. 'Feel better now?'

'Yes, I do.'

'Good. Now we had better get some sleep.'

Chapter Ten

The roar of planes taking off had Nancy and Jean running outside. It was always a sight to see and they watched as wave after wave of Lancasters filled the sky.

'Dear Lord,' Nancy gasped, 'every plane in Lincolnshire must be up there tonight.'

'No wonder they didn't drink much last night. I thought it was because of the cost, but they knew what was going to happen.'

They stood in silence until the sky was clear. Nancy sighed. 'I need a strong cup of tea.'

'So do I. I don't think we're going to sleep much tonight.'

When they walked into the mess all the ground crews were in getting a late supper. Serge waved them over. 'Come and join us.'

Grateful for the company, they sat with the Allard ground crew, who already had several pots of tea and a pile of sandwiches on the table.

'You're settling in for a long night,' Jean remarked as she

poured tea for all of them. 'I don't know if it's harder for those waiting on the ground or those in the air.'

'Tough on everyone, but honestly, I'd rather be down here than facing the mayhem. We've got the greatest respect for those lads, and it's agony waiting for them to return.' The sergeant gave Nancy a sympathetic glance. 'But you know all about that.'

She nodded. 'I vowed never to get too friendly with anyone flying missions again, but it's impossible, isn't it? Do you have any idea why they're sending out such a large force?'

'I think it's obvious an invasion is being planned, and they need to hit hard to disrupt Hitler's manufacturing ability. The boys are going to be busy over the next few weeks.'

They stayed talking to the men for some time and then went back to their quarters. Much to her surprise, Nancy managed to sleep for a good while, but was suddenly awake when the roar of returning planes could be heard. She sat up, head on one side listening. With the experience of many such mornings she could detect Lancasters flying normally, and those labouring with damage. She was half out of bed when Jean put the light on.

'Don't go out there,' she warned.

Nancy swung her legs back on the bed. 'Sorry, it's an automatic reaction.'

'The commander has only got to see you out there once.'

Nancy thumped her pillows in frustration, but knew Jean was right. She was being watched, and didn't want to risk being posted somewhere else. 'I get the feeling the commander is looking for any reason to move me away from here.'

'He is, but it's only because he's worried about you after losing Dan. You shouldn't have been sent here in the first place; he knows that and so do you. He believes you should be away from a fighting squadron, but you're good at what you do and are well liked, so he's holding off.'

'I know he never thought I should be here, and I'm aware he has made an exception for me.' She gave a stifled laugh. 'I daren't let him know that I can hear Dan reprimanding me and saying – don't you dare run away.'

That made Jean smile. 'He'd have you out of here so quickly your feet wouldn't touch the ground.'

'I'll be careful.' Nancy rested her head back and listened to the sound of the planes still coming in. She would be very upset to be sent away. There were only a few WAAFs stationed here, mostly to deal with the office work, or in the stores, like herself. Two were drivers for the officers and they all got on well together. Most important, though, was her friendship with Jean, and Jean's solid support had helped her through those first couple of agonising days. She hadn't drowned her with gushing sympathy, which was the last thing Nancy had needed, but she was there, quietly and steadfastly reaching out to give her support and courage to cope with the loss. In her grief she had snapped at her and everyone around her, but Jean had ignored the outbursts. She owed her a lot, and it was their friendship that was one of the many reasons she felt the need to stay here.

They were both wide awake now, so they washed, dressed and went to get something to eat. Without mentioning it, but by mutual consent, they went to the NAAFI instead of the airmen's mess.

It was only after they had emptied two pots of tea that they walked outside and over to the control tower. Dawn was coming up and they could see the airfield clearly now. Planes were everywhere. One was on its side, another had skimmed a tree on approach and bits were hanging off it, another had lost its undercarriage and had skidded right up to the boundary. Lorries and ground crew were swarming everywhere to get the airfield back into working order as quickly as possible.

'That must have been a rough one,' was all Jean said.

Nancy nodded and anxiously scanned the airfield. When she saw the tall figure of Steve walking well away from all the activity she heaved a ragged sigh of relief. They had survived another mission, and she hoped the rest of the crew were unhurt – especially Ricky, because although Jean never said much, it was clear that she had fallen hard for the lively Canadian. She sent up a prayer for all the other crews hoping the casualty list wasn't too big or too serious.

Steve still had his flying jacket on and turned the collar up. The weather was getting colder now – nothing like it was at home, of course, but the wind was blowing across the field and was biting. He turned and strode briskly to their quarters.

Luke was sitting in a chair reading a newspaper and glanced up when Steve came into the room. 'That was quicker than usual.'

He tossed his hat on the bed and ran a hand through his thick dark hair. 'I could eat a nice big juicy steak.'

At that moment Ricky looked in the door. 'So could I. We've had breakfast and I'm still famished.'

'So am I.' Andy arrived with the rest of their crew.

'Why are we all so hungry?' Luke complained. 'We should be asleep after a night like that.'

The mid gunner, Eddie, leant against the door. 'I swear I can still see those shells bursting all around us. That's one hell of a view I've got.'

Retrieving his hat from the bed, Steve put it on and said,

'We're obviously not going to sleep, so let's go and see if we can get something else to eat.'

'Do you think they've got any steaks?' Ricky asked hopefully.

'Not a chance, but we might be able to get some spam sandwiches.' Luke ushered everyone from the room and they headed for the mess.

When they walked in, most of the flight crews were there and Sandy came over to them grinning. 'I guess you're still hungry as well.'

'Hey, what's wrong with everyone this morning?' Ricky wanted to know.

'Will you men stop milling around and sit down,' one of the staff ordered. 'We know you want more food.'

Luke gave her a wistful look. 'A nice, big, rare steak would be good.'

Her smile said she understood. 'Not possible, I'm afraid, but we'll find you something.'

'We're always hungry when we get back,' Sandy remarked, 'but we're extra hungry today and it's damned difficult to sleep when your stomach is rumbling.'

'Don't worry about it. You're all young, healthy lads and, like the planes, need constant refuelling.'

When she went back to the kitchens, they pulled tables together and all sat down. The cigarettes were passed round and they talked, trying to unwind after what had been a truly nerve-jangling night.

When the plates of spam fritters and fried potatoes came round, they tucked in. It wasn't the steaks they longed for, but the ravenous men didn't stop to worry about that. After clearing their plates and drinking several cups of tea they sat back, feeling much more relaxed. Cigarettes were handed round again and they settled down to chat about anything but the war.

'That's better,' Luke sighed. 'Now we might be able to sleep.'

'Anyone know what the weather forecast is?' Ricky asked.

'Light cloud at the moment, but expected to clear by nightfall.' The wing commander pulled up a chair and sat at their table, then turned his attention to Steve. 'I'm coming with you tonight as an observer.'

'Right, sir. Glad to have you along.'

Jackman took a cigarette out of the packet on the table, lit it with a gold lighter, then called out, 'Dottie.'

The woman who had served them came over.

Indicating the empty plates littering the table, he said, 'I'm hungry. How about the same you've been feeding these men, Dottie?'

'You know we have to keep those flying on missions well fed. You can get a snack at the NAAFI if you're that desperate.'

He drew on his cigarette and blew smoke up to the ceiling and grinned at her. 'I'm flying tonight.'

She took a deep breath and let it out on a sigh. 'You can't keep out of it, can you, Robert? Your poor mother's nerves were in shreds when you were on missions and now she thinks you're safe.'

'I am safe. I'm flying with Allard and his crew as observer, so how about that food, Aunt Dottie?'

'All right.' She gave him an affectionate pat on the shoulder. 'I'll see what I can do.'

When she hurried away, Sandy asked, 'Aunt Dottie?'

'She's a friend of my mother's and I've known her for as long as I can remember. I've always called her aunt. When the war started, she was determined to do her bit by joining one of the services but was considered too old. She wouldn't give up, though, and eventually managed to get into the Catering Corps, and has been at this base for a couple of years. She enjoys keeping the airmen watered and fed.'

'Sounds as if she's a determined woman,' Luke remarked.

'Oh, she is, believe me. She's gone through two husbands and is on the third.'

The food soon arrived and once his plate was cleared, Robert stood up and slapped Steve on the back. 'See you at briefing.' They watched him walk away, a spring of anticipation in his stride.

Ricky waited until the door closed behind him and shook his head. 'What do you think he's going to observe; how thick the flak is? He can't wait to get back in the air. Do you think we'll be like that at the end of our missions?'

'Probably,' Sandy admitted. 'Dicing with danger can become addictive to some. Still, that remains to be seen, and what we need now is sleep.'

They stubbed out their cigarettes and after waving thanks to Dottie made their way out of the mess.

At the briefing later that day they were told about the invasion being planned and the vital role they would play in the run up to it. Bomber Command's job was to destroy the enemy's infrastructure as much as they could, and Robert was coming to assess the effectiveness of the raids.

When they were dismissed, Robert gathered Steve and his crew and outlined what he needed from them. They were to go in with the first wave, drop their bombs and circle back after everyone else to take a look at the target.

'Oh, great,' Ricky muttered under his breath.

Steve narrowed his eyes, seeing the danger in the operation. It would mean being over the target longer than usual. 'If I notice at any time we are too low on fuel, I will turn for home immediately, Wing Commander.'

'Understood. You are responsible for the lives of all on board and I would expect you to put safety first.'

'Why did he pick us to fly with?' Eddie murmured, as Jackman left the room.

'Because we're a good crew,' Luke replied. 'Anyway, there's nothing to worry about because Steve won't take any unnecessary chances. Now, let's get ready for what could turn out to be an interesting flight.'

'That's not what I would bloody call it,' Andy swore. 'I think we're going to be busy tonight, mates.'

While they waited for the hour to take-off they lounged around, relaxing in any way they could, and when the time came, they flew ahead of the main force.

Upon reaching the target, Steve followed orders and flew in, dropped their load, then took up position to fly behind the last of the bombers. He watched the fuel carefully, assessing how much was needed to get them home safely. Luke didn't take his eyes off the dials at this point.

'Can you go round again?' Jackman asked. 'I would like a few more pictures.'

'No, sir,' was Steve's firm reply as he turned for home.

There was a huge sigh. 'I would've liked another look, but you're quite right.'

The flight back was uneventful and when they landed at Scampton there were smiles of relief on all their faces.

At debriefing, the wing commander was able to report on what he had been able to see, praising Steve and his crew.

As they walked to the mess to have a well-earned breakfast,

Andy said, 'Steve, if he comes up with another scheme like that, then tell him someone else should have the honour of his company. By the way, how much petrol did we have left?'

'Enough, I made sure of that.'

After breakfast Steve went for his usual walk, but this time left the base and strolled along a country lane. His thoughts turned to home and he knew that once he was back there, he would never want to leave again.

Chapter Eleven

The weeks slipped by. Sometimes they flew several nights in a row, and others when they were just hanging around waiting for the next raid. By the time Christmas came they were a seasoned and efficient crew, and had been told they might not be flying again until early January.

'Any chance of leave?' Steve asked the commander, hoping he could get along to see Harry again.

'I'm afraid not. We need you on base in case orders change.'

Ricky was clearly disappointed. 'Is that likely, sir?'

'You can never tell. I've been ordered to keep the base in readiness. But, tonight is the Christmas Eve party in the officers' mess and you're all expected to attend.'

'Is that an order, sir?' Andy asked dryly.

'Take it any way you like.' He laughed quietly. 'We shall see you all tonight, then.'

Ricky loved a party.

On their way to the NAAFI to practise their darts, Luke wondered aloud if the girls would be there.

'I've no idea,' Steve replied.

'I'll go and see if I can find them.' Ricky sped off.

Eddie laughed. 'That boy is definitely in love, and from what I've seen he's picked the right girl in Jean. What about you, Steve? Nancy's a nice girl and you seem to get on well together.'

'We do,' was his only reply.

Ricky was soon back, all smiles. 'I found Nancy and they've also been invited to the party.'

Steve handed him the darts. 'Good, now see if you can hit the board.'

They enjoyed their game and complimented each other on their improvement.

'In another six months we might be good enough to beat the girls,' Steve joked.

'Six months!' Luke exclaimed. 'We had better make it sooner than that because the war might be over by then.'

'Oh, I doubt that,' Andy said, shaking his head. 'If the invasion takes place in early summer it'll be a hard fight to reach Germany. My guess is that we could see the end next year or sometime the year after.'

'That's providing the invasion is a success,' Luke pointed out.

'It will be – it has to be,' Andy replied. 'There won't be any turning back this time. It'll be a case of go in and stay in, no matter how tough that turns out to be. There won't be a repeat of Dunkirk, you can be sure of that.'

Andy spoke with passion and Steve could understand how he felt. 'It'll be a success, and you're not alone this time.'

'No, we aren't, and they don't stand a chance against our combined forces.'

'We'll toast that with the officers' beer tonight.'

Andy grinned at Steve. 'I hope it's something stronger than beer.'

Back in their quarters again, they found that a large quantity of mail had been delivered, and having time to spare they sat down to read, eager for news from their families.

The first two letters Steve opened were from his parents, and the pang of homesickness he felt as he read was firmly pushed aside. Christmas at home had always been a happy time with the house full of people and laughter. He hoped it would still be that way even with him away. The next letter was from Harry and had him laughing quietly to himself. He didn't recognise the writing of the last one, and he sat straight up in surprise when he started reading. It was from Nancy's parents, wishing him and his fellow Canadians a happy Christmas. 'Well, I'll be damned,' he said out loud.

'What's up?' Luke glanced up from his own letters.

'I've had a letter from Nancy's folks with Christmas wishes to all of us, saying we'll be welcome to stay with them anytime we're on leave.' He handed the letter over for Luke to see.

'My word, that's kind of them. Nancy must have told them about us.'

Steve nodded. 'I'll send a reply thanking them.'

'Hey,' Ricky exclaimed, 'I've got a letter from Uncle Harry, and he says that everyone at the Jolly Sailor is sorry we can't be there for Christmas.'

'Yes, that's a shame,' Steve admitted. 'I was hoping we could get to see him again.'

Luke glanced at the clock. 'We'd better start getting ready.'

All spruced up in their best dress uniforms, they inspected each other to make sure everything was perfect.

Ricky stepped in front of Steve and looked him up and down, then sighed. 'Do we have to take him with us?'

'Of course,' Luke replied. 'We don't go anywhere without our pilot. Why?'

'Just look at him. He's over six feet and oozing charm without even trying. Is it any wonder the girls can't take their eyes off him? What chance do we stand?'

Steve reached out and felt his friend's brow. 'Are you feeling all right?'

'Fine. You're a handsome bugger, but at least you're a good pilot.'

'Thanks,' he remarked dryly. 'I'm pleased to hear I have an attribute you approve of.'

Sandy looked in the door. 'Come on you guys. We're all here and ready to party.'

They made their way to the officers' bar, laughing and looking forward to a good evening.

The first person Steve saw was Nancy and he went straight up to her. 'I've just received a letter from your parents saying we would be welcome to stay with them any time. I'll write thanking them, and we'd love to do that when we have the spare time. Will you also thank them for us?'

'I will.' She gave a tight smile. 'They did mention it when I was home, but they've obviously got fed up with waiting for me to offer.'

'Why didn't you tell us?'

'Because I knew there wasn't much chance of that happening while you are flying missions. I was waiting until you finished your tour of duty.'

'And by then you were perhaps hoping the whole idea would have been forgotten?' he asked, eyes glinting with amusement.

'I was going to tell you, honestly. When they first mentioned it, I didn't think it was a good idea in the circumstances, then I saw how eager they were and knew it would make them happy to have you there.' She gazed up at him.

'The guys and I would love that. How many of us can come at the same time?'

'We have quite a large house and can easily put the four of you up at the same time.'

'That's excellent. I'll let them know we'll come at the first opportunity.'

'They'll be so pleased. I wasn't sure you'd want to stay with people you don't know.'

'Nancy, spending time in a real family home would be wonderful.'

'There you are!' Luke came up to them with a tray of drinks, quickly followed by Ricky carrying a plate piled high with food.

'Hello, Nancy. Where's Jean?' Ricky asked.

'Right behind you.'

He snapped his head round, nearly dropping the plate, grinning with pleasure at seeing Jean. 'Where have you been hiding? I searched the room for you.'

'I've only just arrived.' She helped herself to a drink and a sandwich. 'Good of the officers to put this on for us.'

Luke nodded and eyed the piano standing in the corner. 'A bit of music would make it seem more festive.'

'We could sing,' Ricky suggested.

'Don't you dare,' Jean scolded. 'I've heard you trying, and you are tone deaf.'

'So I've been told. They kicked me out of the choir at college. Can't understand why, because it sounds all right to me.'

They were laughing when the commander came over to them. 'Good to see you all enjoying yourselves. Care to share the joke?'

'Ricky was offering to sing for us.'

'Ah, that bad, is it?'

'Excruciating,' Jean said.

The commander winked at Ricky. 'Wait until the end of the evening and no one will notice by then.'

'I'll do that, sir.'

'Where did all the food come from?'

Steve indicated the long table piled high. 'There's actually chicken in some of the sandwiches.'

'The local farmers have been very generous. They've done this for us ever since the war started, and insist it's their way of showing their gratitude for what we are doing. Now, I must mingle.'

'That's something we should all do.' Steve picked up his glass and began to move around the room.

Nancy watched him, completely at ease whatever their rank.

'Why are you frowning?' Luke asked.

'I was just trying to figure Steve out. He said he was a farmer, but that just doesn't seem to fit somehow. There's an air of authority about him – he's a gentleman and clearly well educated.' She looked at Luke. 'Tell me the truth; what does he really do in Canada?'

'He is a farmer's son.' Luke stared across the room so he didn't have to look at her.

She shook her head and sighed. 'None of you ever talk about your homes. Why?'

He did turn to her then. 'Because we damn well miss it and talking about it hurts. Every time we go on a mission we wonder if we will ever see it again.'

'Oh, I'm so sorry; I didn't mean to upset you. Please forgive me.'

'Nothing to forgive,' he told her with a smile, but his eyes hardened. 'When the war is over, we'll tell you all about ourselves – until then, just let it go.'

'I will.' Her eyes filled with tears, knowing her curiosity had made her make a terrible blunder. In view of the loss her family had endured she really should have known better, and was thoroughly ashamed of herself.

'Hey.' He placed an arm around her shoulder. 'Don't be upset. It's only natural you should be curious.'

'That is kind of you, but I'm quite embarrassed.'

'You like him, don't you? I can tell you he's one of a kind – special – and we're happy to trust him with our lives. What we all did before coming over here is unimportant.'

She nodded. Dan had the same attitude. The past was gone, and the future would never be the same for these young men.

There was a burst of laughter and Luke took hold of her arm. 'Ricky's entertaining the wing commander, let's go and join them.'

Nancy's sombre mood lifted at once and for the rest of the evening they ate, drank, talked and laughed.

The next morning, the men all piled in Steve and Luke's room, surrounded by the contents of parcels each had received from home.

'Do you think Jean will like this?' Ricky held up a brightly coloured scarf. 'I asked Mum to get me something pretty for her.'

'I'm sure she will,' Luke told him.

He nodded and began to wrap the gift in the paper he had also been sent.

'So, you've told your folks about Jean, then?'

'Of course, Steve. I'm going to marry her when this bloody war is over.'

They all looked at him in astonishment.

'Does she know that?' Sandy wanted to know.

'Not yet, but she will agree,' he stated confidently. 'Have you a gift for Nancy, Steve?

'As a matter of fact, I've got something for both girls.'

'I've got something for both, as well,' Luke said. 'Those girls have been good to us.'

'Too right. They don't get many treats, so I've bought them chocolates.' Sandy held up two boxes. 'Aren't you giving Nancy anything, Ricky?'

'Of course I am. Mum sent scented soaps and that's for Nancy. What are you giving them, Steve?'

He held up six packets and fanned them out. 'Silk stockings, so can I have some of your wrapping paper?'

Ricky handed it over, grinning. 'Wait till the girls see those, they won't be able to believe their eyes. They've been without pretty things for such a long time, haven't they? You didn't say what you've got them, Luke.'

'Well, it had to be something that's almost impossible to get over here, so I asked my sister and she sent lipsticks and perfume.'

'Let's have a look.' Ricky sat on the bed next to his friend and examined the items. 'Nice colours; they'll love those.'

With the presents wrapped as best they could manage, they set off for the mess and their Christmas Day lunch.

They reserved two seats for the girls and piled the gifts on the table.

The moment Nancy and Jean walked in the door, Ricky rushed over and led them to their seats. They sat down and blinked at the parcels, saying nothing.

'Well, open them,' Ricky urged.

'You shouldn't be giving us presents.' Nancy looked concerned. 'We haven't got anything for you.'

'All we want is your company,' Steve told them. 'This is our way of saying thanks for your kindness to a bunch of fellas a long way from home.' He watched Nancy as she opened the parcels, exclaiming in pleasure at each gift, and he remembered their first meeting. She had looked so tired and sad then, but now she was smiling, happy, and quite beautiful.

'Such luxuries,' Jean said huskily. 'We haven't seen things like this for a very long time. Thank you so much.'

Nancy swiped a hand quickly across her eyes. 'This is very kind and thoughtful of you all, and a mere thank you seems very inadequate.'

'We're glad you like them, and seeing your pleasure is thanks enough.' Steve sat back and said teasingly, 'Of course, you could always let us win the next darts match.'

'Not a chance, Mister Pilot,' Jean told him. 'We have our reputation as the best darts players on base to defend.'

'It was worth a try,' he laughed.

The meal was served, and although there was only a small piece of chicken on the plates, there were plenty of vegetables, and a pudding to follow – not quite a traditional Christmas pudding, but the best the cooks could do with limited ingredients.

In the evening there was a concert, and Sandy lifted his

glass. 'Here's to the hope that by next Christmas there will be peace.'

Everyone drank to that, and although there were doubts, it was good to think the end might be in sight.

Chapter Twelve

During January there was little time to see the boys as they were either flying or sleeping. Jean's uncle had made the small metal items they had asked for, but it had taken him a while to finish them. They had arrived two days ago and were beautiful. He also sent two extra stars for Jean and Nancy. They had put them in their bags, happy to have keepsakes for themselves.

Late one afternoon Jean rushed into the stores. 'It's snowing hard and the weather over Germany is impossible, so they aren't flying tonight. I've just seen Ricky and he said they'll meet us in the NAAFI tonight. We can give them the good luck charms then.'

'I hope they like them. They were so good to us at Christmas and I felt awful not having anything to give.'

'So did I, and this is a small way to say thanks. See you for dinner and then we'll go to meet the boys.'

When they arrived it was packed, as usual, and the Allard crew were all together. Sandy was at the table next to them with his crew. Drinks were already on the table waiting for them.

'Hey, Steve,' Robert Jackman called across the room, 'are you taking them on at darts again?'

'Not until we've improved our game. We intend to beat them next time.'

'Good luck with that.' Robert grinned.

Everyone was smiling as the girls took their seats, and as soon as they were settled Jean took out a small packet and put it on the table in front of her, then beckoned Sandy over.

'We're glad everyone's here tonight because we've got something for you. A while ago I gave Steve a star as a good luck charm, and now I have one for each of you.' She handed them round to all the crew.

'Gee, they're great.' Sandy bent over and kissed Jean's cheek. 'Steve's one has kept his crew safe, so I'll make sure this is always with me.'

'Hey, watch it,' Ricky growled. 'Who told you it was all right to kiss Jean?'

Jean laughed and pushed another packet over to Nancy. 'Your turn.'

'I wanted you to have double protection, so this star has your name on the back, and Jean's uncle has even sketched a Lancaster on the front.' She handed them round and watched as they examined them with obvious pleasure.

'Thank you so much, they're beautiful.' While everyone else was showing their appreciation of the gift, Steve studied it carefully. 'Did your uncle make this as well, Jean?'

She nodded. 'He's a wizard with metal.'

'More than that! I'd say he's an artist.'

'It's even got my gun turret on it,' Eddie said, beaming with delight. 'Thanks so much.'

113

'We'll treasure both tokens.' Andy tucked them into his top pocket, and they all did the same.

'We know you're a long way from your families and we wanted you to know that when you're up there under the stars and in danger, you aren't alone. We're praying for you,' Nancy told them. The men all gave the girls big bear hugs.

'That means a lot to us,' Steve told them, and the rest were nodding in agreement. 'To know there's someone here waiting for our return is the greatest gift you can give us. Now, how about giving us some tips on how to throw darts so they hit the target?'

That lifted the mood and everyone laughed.

'We don't usually give free lessons,' Nancy teased, 'but we might relax our rules this once. What do you think, Jean?'

Jean took a box of darts out of her bag and stood up. 'Come on then, boys; let's see if you can hit the target.'

The rest of the evening was light-hearted.

Back in their quarters, the four Canadians lounged in Steve and Luke's room drinking beer.

Ricky took the tokens out of his pocket with a smile on his face. 'The girls are cute, aren't they? Pity there isn't another two like them and then we could have one each.'

'Don't include me,' Sandy told them. 'You know I have a girl waiting for me at home. We intend to marry as soon as the war is over.'

'Let's have another look at her picture?'

'Sure.' He took a small photo out of his wallet and handed it to Luke.

They all gathered round to study the picture of the young woman smiling back at them.

'She's very pretty,' Steve said.

'That really doesn't do her justice. You ought to see her with the sun shining on her golden hair. She's so beautiful.'

'It must've been tough leaving her.' Luke handed back the photo.

Sandy nodded. 'It was, but I've always wanted to be a pilot, and this was my chance. She understood.'

'You're a lucky man.'

'I know I am, Ricky.' Sandy yawned and stood up. 'Time for some rest. We might be flying again tomorrow night.'

'Good idea.' Steve ushered everyone out of the room.

After breakfast the next morning they went to find out if there was a raid planned for that night. There was, so they slipped into the usual routine of spending the morning writing, reading or playing cards. In the afternoon they slept.

There was still half an hour before briefing, so Steve wandered over to his Lancaster and chatted to the ground crew.

'She's really loaded this time, sir.' The sergeant was looking at the plane and frowning.

'Don't worry, she's a tough bird and can take it.'

'No doubt, but we've checked her over extra carefully and she's in good nick.'

'Thanks.' Steve checked his watch. 'Time to see what's in store for us tonight.'

The briefing was thorough, as usual, and fully armed with all the necessary information they climbed on board. Steve strapped himself in and after the usual checks the engines roared into life. He tapped his top pocket with the good luck tokens in it. The fact that one was a gift from Nancy meant a lot to him. He wanted to be more than friends with her, but was holding back from taking that step – for her sake, not his. He knew she didn't want to get emotionally involved with anyone, especially not someone on active service. He took every opportunity to be with her and let her know he thought a lot of her.

Instructions came through and everyone took their place, ready for take-off. Take-off went smoothly, and although the Lancaster was fully-loaded, it seemed eager to be on its way.

Very experienced by now, everyone knew the routine, working together smoothly and efficiently. The target was reached and bombs released without any difficulty, but as they turned for home something hit the plane, and almost immediately after that they were hit again.

'Fire in engine three,' Luke informed him. 'Shutting down. How does she feel, skipper?'

'I've still got enough control to coax her home. Keep an eye on the engines.'

'Fire looks as if it's out.'

'Good, is everyone all right? Report.' They all came through and much to his relief no one was injured. He then focussed on keeping the Lancaster steady, but he knew they were badly damaged. The rest of the crew were also aware of their perilous situation and no one spoke.

Luke tapped a dial in front of him and said, 'We're losing fuel. At this rate we won't get back to base.'

'Ricky, give me a heading for the shortest route to land,' Steve ordered. 'Away from populated areas. I want to get as close to home as possible.'

It didn't take Ricky long to send it through. By the time they were over the sea, another engine had packed up and they were losing height. Steve knew they weren't going to be able to stay in the air for much longer as he struggled to keep some control. He didn't want to ditch in the sea, but it looked unavoidable. He could see the coast in the distance and tried to gain some height, but there was no response from the plane. She was going down and he couldn't do a damned thing about it. He had to give his friends a chance.

'We're not going to make it much further,' he told them. 'We're losing height rapidly and by the time we reach land we'll be too low for you to bail out, so this is your only chance. Jump now!'

Luke shook his head. 'I'm staying; you're going to need help to get this bird down.'

One by one the men came through and said they would take their chance on him being able to land somewhere.

They were dangerously low when they crossed the coast, and as Steve turned the plane towards Lincolnshire, he was scanning the ground for somewhere with enough space to put down. Not that he was going to have a lot to do with it. The plane was leaking fuel and had been too badly damaged to go much further. It was a miracle they had managed to get this far. 'Report on fuel.'

'Nearly empty! There's a field ahead,' Luke told him.

'Seen it. Everyone, brace yourselves, this is going to be rough.'

They skimmed over a farmhouse and hit the field with such force the undercarriage collapsed, tearing part of the wing off as they hurtled across the land. They finally stopped just short of hitting some trees, and although at a crazy angle, the plane was still upright.

'Everyone out!' he shouted, fearing fire. The sweat was pouring off him and he hurt all over but didn't think anything was broken.

Luke moved swiftly, released his harness for him and hauled him out of the seat. 'Are you all right?'

'I'm okay, but that was damned hard work.'

They jumped out and joined the others a safe distance from the stricken plane. There were people running towards them from all directions. 'Any casualties?' one man asked, gasping when he reached them.

'Just shaken up, sir,' Steve replied.

'So are we, young man. You damned near took the chimney off our house.'

'My apologies, sir, I couldn't keep in the air any longer.' Steve surveyed the devastation they had caused. There was a great gouge through the field, with cabbages scattered everywhere. 'We've ruined your harvest, I'm dreadfully sorry about that.'

The man smiled and shook Steve's hand, then greeted the rest of the crew. 'I'm the farmer here and my name is Collins. Don't you worry about the damage, son. The important thing is you're all safe. Here comes the local police and the firemen. They'll take care of everything. Now, come with me, and my wife will give you a good breakfast while you wait for someone to collect you.'

Luke saw the crowd that was gathering, frowned and went over to one of the firemen. 'Could you see that no one goes near the wreckage, especially the children? It could be dangerous.'

'We'll contact the army to stand guard over it.' He studied the plane for a moment, and then turned back to Luke. 'No bombs still there, we hope?'

'No, but you'll need to be very careful.'

'We will be, son, don't you worry.' He shook his head. 'How on earth did you all get out of that alive?'

'We've got a good pilot,' Luke told him, looking over at Steve.

The sound of army vehicles arriving at speed made the crowd of onlookers move further back. 'You can go and get some breakfast. These chaps will take control of the site now.'

The farmhouse kitchen was warm and full of the sounds and smells of sizzling bacon, making them all realise that in spite of being bruised and shaken they were very hungry.

'Do any of you need medical care?' Mrs Collins asked after the introductions were completed.

'All we have are a few bruises, ma'am,' Ricky told her.

'That's good to hear. Now, sit yourselves down. I expect you could do with something to eat, and it's almost ready.'

'We can't take your rations,' Steve said. 'They'll feed us when we get back to base.'

'That could be some time and I'm sure you need food now. We have our own chickens and pigs, and the military would want us to look after you.'

They watched in amazement as plates were put in front of them, overflowing with eggs, bacon, sausages, fried bread, and after that feast there was toast, home-made jam and a pot of tea. Not another word was said as they tucked in and cleared everything, thanking her profusely.

'Do you mind if we smoke, Mrs Collins?' Andy asked.

'Of course not. Please go ahead.'

Steve lit up and drew in deeply, scarcely believing they were not only all alive, but uninjured as well. At that moment, his love and gratitude for that plane was enormous. It was nothing short of a miracle he had been able to keep them in the air as long as he did. With that amount of damage, she should have dropped out of the sky long before they had reached land. He stubbed out his cigarette and noticed a young girl of about three standing by her mother and staring at him. He smiled. 'Hello, what's your name?'

'Beth.' She clutched a rag doll tightly.

'That's a pretty name. What's your dolly's name?'

'Mary.' She came over to him then and held out the dolly. 'Mary was frightened when the house shook. She thought a bomb was coming down.'

'I'm sorry we frightened you, Mary.'

She was resting the dolly on his knees now. 'Daddy said it was a big plane. Were you the driver?'

He nodded. 'My plane wouldn't fly any more and I had to come down in your daddy's field.'

'Can I see it?'

At that moment a young boy of around eight tore into the kitchen and came to a skidding halt, gazing in awe at the strange men filling his kitchen.

'Did you find out if the constable had contacted the RAF, Johnny?'

'Yes, Dad. He said they would be coming, and I told him they weren't German. There are men out there and they won't let me in the field to have a proper look at the plane.'

'So that's where you've been.'

Johnny nodded. 'I tried to sneak in, but they've got it surrounded.'

Steve stood up and hoisted Beth into his arms, making her giggle, then he held out his free hand to the boy. 'Come on, they'll let me in, but we can't go too close because it's dangerous.'

'I'll come with you,' Luke said.

'Do we have your permission to show your children the Lancaster?' Steve asked the parents. 'They'll be safe with us.'

'Of course you can.' Mrs Collins gave the youngsters a stern look. 'You do as they say, now.'

'We will, Mum,' they both declared.

'I want to have another look.' Andy stood up. 'In fact, we all do.'

After some discussion they were allowed through the guard and stood staring at the crumpled plane. The sight wrenched at their hearts as they had all become very attached to their Lancaster.

'Wow!' Johnny couldn't believe his eyes. 'It's huge.'

Beth stared open-mouthed, then slipped her arm around Steve's neck and whispered, 'It's broken. Will you get into trouble?'

'I hope not, sweetheart.'

'Can we go closer?' Johnny was tugging at Steve's hand.

'Just a little.' Keeping a firm grip on the excited youngster they moved a few paces forward.

Eddie came and stood beside him. 'You saved our lives, mate.'

'We were lucky this field appeared just at the right time. If we'd crashed into trees, or God forbid, houses, we'd have been standing at the pearly gates now.'

'What would you have done if we had all bailed out?'

'Dumped her in the sea before we reached land to avoid any civilian casualties.'

Eddie nodded. 'We didn't give you a choice, did we?'

He smiled at Eddie. 'I'm glad it turned out this way. At least all we've done is ruin a field of vegetables.'

'That field must have looked like a postage stamp. You're one hell of a pilot to have got us safely down.'

As Eddie moved away to have a look at the plane from a different angle, Beth claimed his attention again. 'Will it fly again?'

'No, it won't.'

'What will you do without a plane to drive now?'

'They'll give me a new one.'

She leant back to look into his face. 'Will they?'

'Yep.' He touched the dolly she was still holding. 'Is Mary all right now?'

'Oh, yes, she knows you didn't mean to frighten her.'

'Good.' The others joined him, and after thanking the military guard they went back to the farmhouse to wait for someone to pick them up.

Chapter Thirteen

The mess wasn't very busy by the time Nancy arrived for breakfast, but Jean was still there.

'Sorry I'm late. I overslept, which isn't like me. I even missed seeing Steve going for his usual walk around the field.' When Jean didn't answer she studied her more closely and saw her staring at the half-empty cup in front of her. It was unusual for her to be silent. 'What's the matter, Jean?'

The anguish on her face when she looked up was clear to see. 'You wouldn't have seen him because they haven't returned.'

Nancy began to feel the room sway around her, and she wanted to cry out in despair, but she didn't. Emotions had to be kept tightly in check. 'They could have landed somewhere else. How many others are missing, and did the other crews see anyone go down?'

'I haven't been able to find out yet. The crews are still in debriefing, and no one else knows anything.'

She reached out and took hold of Jean's hand. 'Let's not

assume the worst yet. They must be out of debriefing by now, so let's go and find out if there's any news.'

All thoughts of eating were forgotten as they hurried out, and the first person they saw as they left the mess was Wing Commander Jackman. Nancy walked straight up to him and saluted. 'Sir, can you tell us how many planes are missing from last night's raid?'

'Two from here.'

'Do you have details of what might have happened to them?' She knew she shouldn't be questioning an officer like this, but Jackman was a reasonable man and what the hell. She couldn't care less if she was reprimanded.

'Not much. One was seen to go down and the other so badly damaged it was highly unlikely they could make it back. It was the opinion of the crew who saw it that they might have gone down in the sea. I don't have any definite details at present.'

'Understood. Thank you, sir.'

As he walked away, the two girls looked at each other in despair. What they had just heard was the worst possible news, and there was little chance they would ever see their lovely Canadians again.

'Oh, Sandy!' Jean sobbed and held her arms out to the man running towards them. 'Did you see them?'

'Not sure. I saw one go down over Germany, but couldn't identify it. Steve and his crew could have been in either of the two who haven't returned.'

Jean scrunched her eyes, trying to keep the tears at bay. 'I prayed so hard that all of you would come through this.'

'Don't give up hope yet. They might have bailed out, and all we can do is wait for news.' Sandy's colouring was always pale, but now he was white with worry for his friends.

'You'll let us know if you hear anything?' Nancy asked him.

He nodded and walked away.

Nancy took a steadying breath and held Jean's arm, keeping calm for her friend's sake. With such sketchy information there was hope. There had to be! 'Come on, we must report for duty.'

'I know.'

They parted, each going to their duties, and when Nancy walked into the stores, Colin came up to her. 'We've heard that Steve Allard and his crew are among the missing. You were close and I'm so sorry.'

'Thank you. We don't know what's happened yet, so all we can do is wait and hope.'

As she settled down to work, it was hard to keep this out of her mind, and every time fear crept in she fought it back. They had been daft to become close to them, but strange as it seemed, she didn't regret that for one minute. Like her brother Dan, they would always have a place in her heart – never to be forgotten.

She joined Jean for lunch, and they were just finishing when Sandy burst into the mess and hurtled towards them. He dragged the girls out of their seats. 'You've got to see this!'

Running outside they were just in time to see a lorry outside the main building and aircrew, still in their flying gear, jump down.

'Damn me, he landed that bloody stricken Lancaster.' Sandy took off at speed to get to his friends.

The girls watched with relief and joy. The predictions had been that there was little chance of them surviving and, unbelievably, here they were alive, all seven of them, and unhurt, from what they could see. The ground crew were talking to them, and the commander and Jackman were urging them inside, so it was not possible to go over to them.

However, before entering the building they all turned and waved, and the girls waved back with huge smiles on their faces.

Sandy came over. 'They're fine, but we'll have to wait for a while before hearing the details.'

The girls weren't off duty until the evening, and the moment they were free they rushed over to the NAAFI.

'They won't be flying tonight, so if they're not here we'll need to track them down. I must know what happened,' Jean declared, almost running.

The girls stepped inside and saw them immediately. They stood up and smiled, but Nancy knew the signs of shock. From the outside, no one would guess they had just had a close brush with death – not until you looked into their eyes. She had learnt to spot this when her brother had been flying.

'You gave us such a fright,' Jean growled, sitting next to Ricky.

Andy laughed. 'I bet it was nothing like the fright we had. Steve dropped our plane into a field no bigger than a back garden, and ruined the farmer's winter vegetable crop.'

They were all laughing now, and Nancy glanced at Steve, who was sitting there with a slight smile on his face. 'Tell us what happened.'

Luke launched into the story with input from the others from time to time. They were treating it as a huge joke now, but it was clear to the girls that the situation must have been desperate.

'Why didn't you bail out?' Jean wanted to know.

Ricky threw his hands up in horror. 'Steve told us to, but

we were over the sea, and there was no way I was going down there.'

John, the wireless operator, was nodding. 'We wouldn't have lasted long in the freezing water, and we knew Steve would get us down safely, if it was at all possible.'

'Boy, and were we glad we stuck with him.' Ricky slapped his friend on the back. 'You should have seen the breakfast the farmer's wife gave us.'

They continued giving more details about the mayhem they had caused by crashing the huge Lancaster in the field.

'Of course, Steve got reprimanded by the little girl of the family for frightening her dolly by nearly taking the chimney off the farmhouse.'

This caused them all to roar with laughter, and grinning, Steve got up to get the girls a drink.

As he walked away, Luke became serious, watching his friend move smoothly across the room. 'How he ever got that plane back here was nothing short of a miracle, and to get it down without any of us being killed was unbelievable.'

'Yeah, we all thought our time had come.' Ricky shook his head. 'That journey back is something I will never forget.'

'I don't suppose you will.' Jean smiled at him. 'But you're here to tell the tale, and that's what matters.'

Steve returned with the drinks and sat down again.

'What's going to happen now?' Nancy asked him.

'We have to wait for a replacement Lancaster, so we've been given some leave. There will be one waiting for us when we get back.'

'How long have they given you?' Jean looked pointedly at her friend.

'Five days.'

'What are you going to do?'

He shrugged. 'We haven't decided yet.'

'Well, you could take up my parents' offer and stay with them. There would be room for up to four of you.'

Steve glanced round at his friends. 'I'd like to do that, so who else wants to come?'

The English members of the crew all said they were going home, and that left Luke and Ricky who eagerly accepted.

'Will you be able to come with us?' Steve asked Nancy.

'I'll go and see if I can wangle some time off.' She stood up and left at once.

'It would be nice to spend time in a proper home for a while.' Ricky rolled his shoulders, trying to ease the lingering tension from the crash landing.

Half an hour passed before Nancy came back. 'That took a bit of doing, but when I said I wanted to take you to stay with my parents, they finally agreed. We can leave in the morning.'

'That's great, but how will you let your folks know we're coming?' Steve asked.

'It'll be a surprise for them.'

'Nancy, we can't descend upon your family without prior warning,' Luke told her.

'Yes, you can. Every time they write they ask me when I'm going to bring you home.'

'Well, if you're sure it's all right.'

'Positive, Steve, they'll be delighted. I assure you.'

'In that case, lads, let's go and see what food we can scrounge. We can't go empty-handed.'

The three Canadians left on their quest and Jean smiled at Nancy. 'A few days of normal home life is what they need.'

'Yes, but it's a shame you can't come as well, Sandy.'

'It is, but I'm still flying. I might be able to come some other time, though.'

'Hope so.'

They managed to get quite a few tins of food, some tea and even a couple of packets of biscuits.

'Better take cigarettes,' Ricky said as they put the items in a kitbag. 'I expect Nancy's parents smoke.'

Steve looked in the bag and frowned. 'We've got to take more than this. How is Mrs Dalton going to feed us for several days?'

'What we need is some fresh stuff as well, but where can we find that?' Luke wondered.

'A farm. There's one not far from here, so if we go early in the morning it shouldn't take us too long.'

'We'll need transport, Steve.'

'I'll see what I can do, while you ask Nancy if we can catch an afternoon train.' He strode off to try and find Sarge, and tracked him down in one of the hangars.

'Hello, sir.'

Steve explained what they wanted and why. 'Can you help us again?'

'Of course I can. Meet me at the gate at seven in the morning and I'll take you to the farm. I know the farmer and he will be happy to help you.'

'That's terrific. We'll see you then, and thanks.'

'No trouble at all, sir.'

Well pleased with the arrangement he went back to their quarters, found his friends already there, and told them about their trip early in the morning.

'I need some sleep.' Ricky yawned.

'We all do.' Luke flopped on the bed.

Although they did get some sleep, it was often disturbed, and in the morning they still felt tired and drained.

Steve was the first awake and he shook Luke, who groaned and reluctantly opened his eyes. 'Did you sleep much?'

'On and off. I kept dreaming of that field as we dropped towards it.'

Steve shrugged. 'I expect we all had nightmares about that. We've got half an hour to get to the gate, so get up while I drag Ricky out of bed.'

He found his friend sitting on the edge of the bed, head bowed and taking deep breaths. 'Are you all right?'

He nodded. 'I just had a dream that the farmer's field turned into the sea when we hit it and I was drowning.'

'You'd have a job drowning in cabbages,' Steve joked.

Ricky looked up and laughed. 'Hey, I like cabbage. We should have brought some back as souvenirs.'

Running a hand through his thick hair to bring it into some kind of order, Steve grinned, relieved to see the colour come back to his friend's face. 'Well, let's go and see if we can get some for Mrs Dalton, shall we? The sergeant will be waiting for us.'

They were soon hurrying to the gate, where Steve exclaimed, 'A lorry! Are we intending to fill that up?'

Sarge gave an amused chuckle. 'You never know, sir. Hop in; the farm is only five miles away.'

When they arrived, the farmer and his wife came out to greet them, and listened while the sergeant told them what was needed. 'I thought you might be able to help these lads.'

The farmer studied the three boys and then focussed on Steve. 'I heard some Canadian pilot dumped a Lancaster in a field and made a right mess of it. Was that you?'

130

'Yes, sir. I managed to miss the farmhouse, though,' he added dryly.

The farmer grinned. 'Not by much, from what I've heard. News of your exploits has travelled far and fast.'

'There was at least a couple of foot to spare,' Luke said, keeping a perfectly straight face.

'Well, the important thing is you all got out safely.' The farmer's wife smiled at them. 'Are you boys hungry?'

'Always,' Ricky told her immediately.

'In that case, come in and I'll cook you a good breakfast. My husband will find you plenty of fresh vegetables to take with you.'

'Thank you, ma'am,' they all responded as they followed her into the house. They had come out without anything to eat and were ravenous, as usual.

When they arrived back at base, they had so many vegetables they had to go round and borrow extra kitbags to put them all in.

They met Nancy as arranged, loaded with as much as they could carry, and she studied them in amazement. 'You've brought a lot of luggage with you.'

'We've managed to get a few things for your mum,' Steve told her.

'A few?'

Broad grins appeared on their faces as they left the base.

Chapter Fourteen

It was dark by the time they reached Nancy's house, and with the blackout hiding every crack of light it was hard to know if anyone was in.

Steve hesitated. Nancy had assured them that her parents wouldn't mind them coming unannounced, but he was still uneasy about it. 'Are you absolutely sure your folks won't mind us descending upon them without notice?'

'I'm positive.' She opened the door with her key. and pulling the blackout curtain aside. she ushered them quickly inside. 'Drop your bags in the hall and come and meet my parents.'

At that moment, the door of the front room opened, sending a shaft of light into the dark hall, and Sally Dalton gave a cry of delight when she saw her daughter. 'What a lovely surprise . . .' It was then she noticed the boys standing in the shadows.

Nancy laughed when she saw her mother's expression. 'You said you wanted to meet them, so I've finally managed to bring them with me. We all have a few days' leave.'

Sally quickly recovered. 'That is just wonderful. Come into the other room where I can see you properly.'

When Nancy introduced them, she saw her mother's eyes lingering on the wings on Steve's jacket, and knew she was picturing her son standing there with the same badge.

'I'm delighted to meet you all,' she told them. 'Tom will be as well. We've been asking Nancy to bring you home, and it's lovely you have been able to come at last. I thought there were four of you, though?'

'Sandy couldn't make it, Mrs Dalton. He's still flying,' Luke explained.

'Ah, that's a shame, but it's a pleasure to have the three of you stay with us.'

They heard the front door open, a thud, and someone swearing. 'Sally, what's all this stuff in the hall?' Tom called out. 'I nearly tripped over it.'

Nancy went out and switched the light on, and the boys were right behind her, grabbing the bags out of the way.

'Our apologies, sir.' Steve hoisted two bags onto his shoulders.

Tom stopped rubbing his shin and a huge smile lit his face, as he reached out and hugged his daughter. 'Oh, this is marvellous, and you've brought friends with you. Put those bags down, lads, and tell me who you are.'

They went back to the front room and the introductions were made. Her parents were clearly excited to have the men in their home, and Nancy admitted to herself that Jean had been right. This would be good for them.

'You must be hungry. I'll get you something to eat.' Sally left the room, smiling.

The boys were immediately on their feet, and followed

her out. 'We can't eat your rations, ma'am,' Steve told her. 'We've brought some food with us.'

'You don't need to call me ma'am, although it sounds charming. My name is Sally and my husband is Tom.'

'We'll do that, Sally.' Ricky swung a heavy kitbag up. 'Would you show us where we can unpack this, please?'

'Come into the kitchen.' Tom went to pick up one of the bags and grimaced. 'What on earth have you got in there?'

Luke grinned. 'Food, sir . . . Er, Tom.'

'No wonder it hurt when I walked into it.'

Nancy led the way to the kitchen with an amused look on her face. If the amount of luggage and its weight was any indication of what they had, then this could be interesting.

One by one the kitbags were opened, and by the time they had finished the kitchen table was covered with tins, packets and vegetables.

Sally gasped, eagerly reaching for a box and removing the lid. 'Look, Tom, eggs, bacon, sausages and a whole chicken! Where did you get all this?'

'A friendly farmer helped us out,' Steve told her.

'Not the one—'

'Oh, no, Nancy.' Ricky stopped her finishing the question. 'I'm not sure he will ever speak to us again.'

All three of the boys smirked.

'What have they been up to?'

'Don't ask, Dad.'

'Ah, like that, is it?' When she nodded, he grinned at the Canadians, standing with innocent expressions on their faces. 'Come into the front room and let the girls get on with the cooking. We'll have a pot of tea while we're waiting. Sorry I haven't got anything stronger to offer you.'

'Never mind that.' Luke dived once more into one of the bags and produced a bottle of whisky, handing it over to Tom.

Then Ricky and Steve produced boxes of cigarettes. 'Present for you,' Steve said.

Tom was gazing at the whisky and cigarettes in astonishment. 'Good heavens, lads, this is unheard of. How did you get hold of these?'

'We went on the scrounge.' Ricky winked at Nancy's father. 'We can be very persuasive.'

'I don't doubt that, and thanks very much. Let's have a drink to toast a happy and relaxing few days for you.'

Tom soon found four tumblers, poured a generous slug of whisky in each one and handed them round. He raised his glass. 'Thanks for coming. We are delighted you have made it. While you're here you are to treat this as your own home and come and go as you please. Rest and relax.'

'Thank you, Tom.' Steve sipped his drink. 'It will be a real treat for us to spend time in a proper home.'

'I expect you miss your families.'

'We do,' Luke told him, 'but we've come here to help win the war, and that's all that matters at the moment.'

They talked for some time, discussing the prospects of an invasion when the weather was better. No one knew for sure, of course, but the country was filling up with troops and equipment, indicating that something big was being planned.

Steve had taken to Tom on sight, and although he must have still been grieving the loss of his son, Tom had welcomed them into his home with obvious pleasure. There were laughing photos of Dan and Nancy everywhere, making Steve wonder how his own parents would have coped if the crash-landing had turned out differently.

The reverie was halted when Sally opened the door and announced that dinner was ready. She had roasted the chicken and used some of the vegetables they had given her. There was also an apple tart and custard for dessert. The plates were soon wiped clean of every scrap of food, and they thanked Sally and Nancy for a lovely meal.

Tom glanced at the clock. 'Anyone want to go to the pub?'

Ricky's face lit up at the mention of a pub, and the other two nodded.

'You girls coming?' Tom asked his wife and daughter.

'No, Dad, you go and have a boys' night out.'

He laughed at being called a boy and kissed her on the cheek. 'All right, but if you change your minds we'll be in The Horse and Hounds.'

The pub was crowded, and as it was his local, Tom was well known. He introduced the Canadians and, as they had found everywhere, they were welcomed with warmth.

They had a lovely evening with a lot of laughter and singing, and it was just what they needed to really unwind after their crash-landing. Steve drew deeply on his cigarette and smiled at his friends, who each gave a slight nod. The danger they faced had drawn them so close together they could almost read each other's minds.

They had expected Nancy and Sally to be in bed when they arrived back, but they were still up and waiting with sandwiches and a pot of strong tea.

When they had finished eating, Sally took them upstairs. 'You can have a room each, and are to sleep for as long as you like. As we said before, please treat this as your own home.'

After thanking her they went to their allotted rooms. Steve

took one look at the large bed, undressed quickly and dived in, sighing with pleasure and relief.

The next morning Nancy found her mother in the kitchen looking out at the back garden. 'Has Dad gone to work?'

Her mother nodded. 'He's trying to get his accountant's work up to date so he can spend more time at home while the boys are here.'

'Are our guests up yet?'

'Two are still asleep, but Steve is out there. He shouldn't be doing that, it's very cold.'

'Doing what?' Nancy went over to the window. Steve had taken a spade out of the shed and was digging over her father's vegetable plot.

'That ground must be like iron, and your dad was leaving that job until it softened up a bit.'

'Well, that doesn't seem to bother Steve because he's done over half of it. How long has he been out there?'

'I don't know. He was there when I came down.'

'Every time he returns from a mission he goes for a walk on his own, no matter what the weather. He told me that back in Canada they are farmers, so perhaps he's missing that.'

'Maybe, but he's here to rest, not work. Go and talk to him, darling, and try to make him come in.'

'I don't think he'll listen to me. I believe he's the kind of person who, when he wants to do something, won't be easily swayed.'

Sally watched him intently and then sighed. 'He's such a strong boy, and different from the other two. I like him – I like all of them.'

'I do as well. Jean and I have become rather too fond of them.'

Sally gave her a knowing glance. 'I've noticed him watching you with those gorgeous eyes.'

'We're friends, Mum,' she said firmly. 'That's all.'

'If you say so.' Her tone indicated that she didn't believe that for one minute. 'There are so many young men in danger, it doesn't bear thinking about, does it? I can only guess at the heartrending things you have seen. I don't know how you do it, darling.'

'Someone has to,' was all she said, and changed the subject. 'Start getting breakfast, and I'll drag him in. Food should make him stop what he's doing.'

Sally tipped her head to one side, listening. 'Ah, Ricky and Luke are moving around.'

'Right, I'll get Steve. They'll be hungry – they always are.'

'Of course they are.'

Nancy put on her coat and went out to the garden. 'Breakfast will be ready soon. Why are you digging over Dad's vegetable plot?'

He stuck the spade upright in the ground and smiled. 'It needed doing.'

'I didn't bring you here to work,' she scolded. 'You should be relaxing and enjoying yourself.'

He studied the beautifully prepared ground. 'I am relaxing and enjoying myself.'

'Does doing something like that remind you of your farm at home?'

His eyes glinted with amusement. 'Not really.'

Getting information out of him was a struggle, so she sensibly gave up. 'Well, come in now. Luke and Ricky are showing signs of getting up.'

'Right.' He returned the spade to the shed, and then

slipped his arm around her shoulder as they walked back into the house.

The others were already sitting at the kitchen table reading the newspapers. Steve washed his hands and joined them while Nancy helped her mother with breakfast.

'What do you want to do today?' Steve asked.

'Nothing,' was the instant reply.

'We're just going to lounge around, read, or write letters,' Luke told him. 'What about you?'

'Sounds good to me.' He turned in his chair. 'Is that all right with you, Sally? We won't get in your way.'

'Absolutely.'

'Thank you.' He turned back to his friends. 'While I'm in London, I'm going to visit Harry. Do you want to come?'

'Of course.' They both nodded agreement, and Ricky asked, 'When shall we go?'

'I thought tomorrow.'

'Perfect.' Luke grinned. 'Uncle Harry will be pleased to see us again, but if we go back to the Jolly Sailor, he'll want us to stay overnight.'

Sally had been listening to the conversation, and as she placed the plates of cooked food in front of them, asked, 'Who is Uncle Harry?'

Steve explained and she smiled broadly. 'In that case you have to visit him. We mustn't be selfish and keep you all to ourselves, as much as we would like to.'

'We'll only stay one night,' Steve told her, picking up his knife and fork to tuck in to breakfast.

Nancy watched them laughing and joking as they cleared their plates. It was lovely to see them like this, and she was glad her parents had suggested it.

Chapter Fifteen

They were about to leave for Harry's when Sally handed Steve a package. 'Give that to your uncle. I made a couple of pies out of the vegetables you brought with you. It'll make a meal for you all.'

'That's very kind of you.' He put the package carefully in his kitbag and they were on their way, looking forward to seeing Harry again.

They were in luck because he had a rare day off, and seeing them coming along the road, rushed out to meet them. There was a broad grin of delight on his face as he greeted them. 'Where's Sandy?'

'Still on duty,' Luke told him.

'Oh, shame he couldn't come as well, but it's a lovely surprise to see you again. Come in out of the cold.' When they reached the door, he leant across the fence and thumped on the next door. 'Glad, the boys are here.'

She was out in an instant and beamed at them. 'Put the kettle on, Harry, and I'll be right in. I've just made a carrot cake and it should be just about done now. I'll bring it with me in a minute.'

They were soon settled in front of a fire enjoying tea and a slice of hot cake, fresh out of the oven. It wasn't the kind of cake they were used to, but with limited ingredients it was tasty.

Harry studied them carefully. They had all changed since he'd seen them last. That was hardly surprising, though, considering what they were doing. 'How long have you got?'

'They gave us five days,' Ricky told him, and then explained about Nancy's parents inviting them to stay with them. 'We said we'd be back sometime tomorrow.'

'Great, we'll go to the Jolly Sailor, and then you can bunk down here for the night.'

Steve took the package out of his bag and handed it to Gladys. 'Sally asked me to give you this.'

She exclaimed with pleasure when she saw the pies. 'Go to the British Restaurant for your lunch and I'll make you a nice dinner with these.'

'Thanks, Glad.' Harry glanced at the clock. 'Give it another half-hour and we can go for lunch. So, why have you been given leave and Sandy hasn't?'

'We're waiting for a replacement Lancaster,' Steve told him.

'Why do you need a new one?'

'Ah, well, we broke the other one.' Ricky smirked.

Harry raised his eyebrows. 'And how did that happen?'

'Steve dumped it in a farmer's field,' Luke told him. 'Ruined his crops and nearly took the chimney off the farmhouse.'

'I wouldn't have had to do that if you'd all bailed out when I told you to,' Steve protested, managing to keep a straight face.

'And if we'd done that, we would all have ended up in the sea.' Ricky shuddered in horror. 'I nearly drowned once when I was a young kid, and there is no way I'd risk that again. Anyway, the farmer's wife took pity on us and gave us a huge breakfast.'

Luke took up the story by telling them about the little girl who had taken a liking to Steve, and they all ended up roaring with laughter.

Except Gladys, who was looking at them in amazement. 'How can you laugh? You could have been killed.'

'But we weren't, and that's why we can laugh about it,' Luke explained. 'It's the only way to deal with such mishaps, and what happened after was really funny.'

Ricky was chuckling. 'The locals were protecting the Lancaster from people who wanted to have a closer look at it. They didn't even want to let Steve through.'

That set the boys off again.

'So, what happens now?' Harry wanted to know.

'There'll be a nice new Lancaster waiting for us when we get back, and then we're in business again.'

'How many missions have you flown, Steve?' Harry asked.

He shrugged. 'I haven't been keeping a tally.'

'We still have a few more,' Luke said, 'but that doesn't mean the end of our flying. It's possible we will be asked to do more, but it depends on how things go. However, knowing Steve, he won't be happy unless he's at the controls of a plane.'

'Yes, and hopefully we can stick together.'

'Is that right, Steve?' Gladys asked.

'I love to fly and will take any opportunity offered me. What time does the pub open, Harry?' he asked, changing the subject.

'Around six.' He stood up. 'I don't know about you but I'm hungry, so let's go and get some lunch.'

When they reached the British Restaurant, the same woman was on the door and smiled when they walked in. 'Hello, lads, good to see you again.'

They paid and collected the tokens while making polite conversation with her. Then they joined the queue, and after collecting their food several of Harry's friends made room for them at their table. They had met them on their previous visit at the pub, and it proved to be an entertaining lunch.

Back at the house they walked into the kitchen to make a pot of tea, and stopped in surprise. There was a girl in ATS uniform sitting at the table.

'Sybil!' Harry exclaimed, his face lighting up with surprise and delight as she stood up and hugged him. 'I didn't know you were coming. How long have you got?'

'Only forty-eight hours, Dad.' She turned her attention to the three airmen crowding the kitchen, her eyes settling on Steve.

He grinned. 'My, how you have grown. The last picture I saw you were still in school uniform.'

She stepped up and took hold of both of his hands. 'How wonderful I get to meet you at last. Dad told me you were here, and I was so sorry to have missed you the last time. What a stroke of luck I came home today.'

'Let me introduce you to my friends, Luke and Ricky.'

'Lovely to meet you.' She shook hands with them, and then turned back to Steve. 'Are you staying for the night?'

'Yes, but we will be leaving in the morning.'

'You've certainly picked the right day. We must have a party this evening, Dad.'

'Already arranged. They're expecting us at the Jolly Sailor.'

'That'll be terrific. You go and sit in the front room while I make us some tea, then we can catch up on all the news.'

Harry walked in the pub with a huge smile on his face, and when everyone saw Sybil flanked by the three boys the place erupted with shouts of greeting and a stampede to get drinks for all of them.

Luke studied Sybil as she went round laughing with everyone, and turned to Steve. 'What a stunner.'

He nodded. 'She's turned into a beauty, and even the khaki uniform can't dim that.'

The piano pounded away and it was a wonder the roof stayed on as everyone sang at the top of their voices. Harry and Sybil made them join in the 'Lambeth Walk' and various other London songs, and had them dissolving into helpless laughter.

At closing time they went back to Harry's and the party continued, just like last time.

Sybil went next door for the night so the boys could have the only other bedroom. It was the early hours before they finally got to bed, and were instantly asleep.

The next morning, after saying their goodbyes, Steve and Ricky were out of the gate before realising Luke wasn't with them. He was still busy talking to Sybil, and when they saw them exchanging pieces of paper and hugging each other, Ricky raised an eyebrow.

'He isn't wasting any time, is he?'

Luke caught them up, tucking the paper safely in his pocket. 'Sorry to keep you waiting. We are going to write to each other, and I hope you don't mind, Steve.'

'Why would I mind?' He smiled and slapped his friend on the back. 'I could see you liked each other.'

'I think she's lovely. She told me she's a mechanic in the ATS. Fancy a young gal doing something like that.'

'It isn't unusual,' Steve pointed out. 'The women of this country have taken over many of the jobs the men do. They've had to, and she's always been interested in how things work.'

'Now we've all got a girlfriend,' Ricky declared, obviously pleased by Luke's attraction to Sybil. 'Of course, Steve's the only one who won't admit it.'

'Have you thought about what'll happen when the war is over and we return home? Are you going to just say cheerio to the girls and walk away?'

'Jean will come with me.' Ricky sounded certain.

'Will she? What if she doesn't want to leave her home and family, will you stay in this country?'

Ricky frowned. 'You know I can't do that. I have commitments at home.'

'So do we all. What I'm saying is that if we become too attached to the girls it could be complicated.'

'You're right, of course,' Luke admitted. 'It would be a lot to ask them to leave their own family and come to live in another country. Is that why you're keeping your relationship with Nancy on a friendly basis? It's obvious you care about her.'

Steve nodded. 'One of the reasons. We're all going to have to make hard decisions when the time comes to return home, but in the meantime let's enjoy their company.'

'Yeah, we'll sort it all out when the time comes.' Ricky held the station door open for them. 'Let's get back to Tom and Sally's.'

Tom was home when they arrived back and greeted them warmly. 'Did you have a good time?'

'We certainly did.' Luke laughed. 'Those dockers are a lively crowd.'

'I expect you're hungry.' Sally came out of the kitchen.

'As always,' Ricky admitted.

After dinner they sat round a log fire and talked on any subject but the war.

Steve gazed into the dancing flames and could almost imagine he was back home with his family. His thoughts dwelt on each of them and he said silently to himself – *I will see you all again and that time might not be too far away.*

Nancy's laughter brought him back to the present and he sighed as he studied her. He knew how he felt about her, the attraction was strong and undeniable, but she was now everything to her parents. He couldn't just step in and try to take their daughter away from them – he couldn't. If he lived in England then there wouldn't be a problem, but he didn't. Canada was a long way away and his commitments there were too great to leave. It was a conundrum, and one he didn't know the answer to, yet. But he sincerely hoped there was one.

'Steve.' He looked up sharply at the sound of his name.

'Tom has asked if you'd like to go to the cinema this evening, or have a lazy evening at home?'

He gave a quick smile. 'Sorry, I was miles away, Sally. For myself, I would be happy to just stay here and relax. What does everyone else think?'

They all agreed to stay in.

'He's the thoughtful kind,' Ricky teased, referring to his friend's lack of attention. 'Steve never does anything without considering it from all angles. He's the quiet one.'

'I don't know about that,' Nancy said. 'I've heard him making as much noise as the rest of you during a certain darts match.'

That set them all laughing, and it had to be explained to Sally and Tom in great detail.

Being in a real home was just what they needed, and by the end of their leave they all felt rested and relaxed.

Nancy still had one more day, so they thanked her parents for putting up with them, promising to come again when they could, then left the house and headed for the station.

The Daltons watched them striding up the road, and Sally murmured softly, 'Be safe, boys.'

Chapter Sixteen

Two days back at base and they were flying again, aware that they were getting close to completing their thirtieth mission. It wasn't mentioned, though, not wanting to tempt fate. They had seen far too many of their comrades go down or return injured.

With a reasonable spell of weather, they were going out night after night, and when their last mission arrived the ground crew were there to help them, as usual. It was clear by their faces that they had been keeping a tally of the missions and were well aware what this one was.

As Steve went to climb aboard, Sarge murmured quietly, 'Have a smooth, trouble-free flight, sir.'

'We will,' he replied with a smile. He eased into the pilot's seat and they went through the checks, all business as usual.

From then on there wasn't time to think of anything but the task ahead. They all tapped the stars in their top pockets several times on boarding, calling on luck to be on their side this night. The flak over the target was fierce, but they managed to stay out of the searchlight beams, and on the way back they had a brush with a fighter, but came through unscathed.

When they landed and climbed out, the ground crew were all there with smiles on their faces. They stood beside the Lancaster and observed her with affection.

'We made it.' Ricky was serious for a change.

'And on my birthday,' Luke told them. 'February the twentieth, and I'm feeling lucky to be able to celebrate my twenty-first.'

'Hey, that's terrific!' Andy slapped him on the back. 'We'll have a right knees-up tonight.'

'We certainly will.' Steve drew the ground crew into the group. 'I hope you'll all join us in the pub.'

'We'll be there,' Sarge replied, 'and it'll be our pleasure to buy you all a drink. You've been a first-class crew and have only trashed one plane.'

That produced hoots of laughter as Sandy and his crew joined them.

'Party time tonight!' Ricky informed them. 'Everyone's invited to the pub. I'll find the girls and let them know.'

Steve caught hold of his arm. 'Debriefing first, then you can go fetch the girls.'

'Of course. Come on, then, let's get it over with.'

The commander congratulated them, and Steve asked, 'What happens now, sir?'

'Don't worry, you'll be kept busy, but now you've all earned a period of rest and relaxation.'

'Will we be asked to fly more missions?' Sandy asked.

'It's likely, yes, but for the moment enjoy yourselves.'

'We will, sir. It's Luke's birthday today and we're going to have one hell of a party tonight at the local pub. Everyone is invited to join us, if you have the time to come along.'

'I'll try to look in and have a drink.'

'You'll be welcome, sir, and the wing commander as well.'

'Right, I'll tell him. Now off you go and have breakfast and some rest.'

Nancy was sitting up in bed, hands curled into fists. She had heard the planes returning and longed to go outside but knew she couldn't do that. Jean could, though, so she was waiting anxiously for her return.

It seemed an age before her friend came back and sat on the edge of the bed. 'They're all back, with no injuries.'

Nancy let out a sigh of relief. 'Thank heavens for that. Have you seen them?'

'Only from a distance. They were heading for debriefing and they've been there some time.'

'I don't like the sound of that. I hope they're not being given a second tour of missions.'

'They're a good crew so that's always a possibility.'

Nancy looked at Jean and shook her head. 'And you know Steve won't be happy unless he's flying.'

'You're right, of course, but let's not dwell on that. Let's take each day as it comes and be happy they're back safely.' Jean shook her friend's shoulder. 'Get up and let's go to breakfast. I'm starving.'

Luke's birthday party was a riotous affair as everyone let off steam and drank too much, knowing they wouldn't be flying the next day. The commander and Robert joined them for a while and bought a round of drinks for everyone before leaving. The rest stayed until the landlord chucked them out at closing time.

The next morning, Steve was up before any of the others,

and knew from the condition they had been in last night that they wouldn't surface for hours yet. He always drank in moderation, so he was probably the only one without a hangover this morning.

He put his flying jacket on to shield against the biting wind and went in search of the commander. He was in his office and Steve knocked on the open door, and then stepped inside. 'Good morning, sir. Would it be okay if I left the base for the day?'

'Morning, Allard. You don't have any duties for a few days and are free to leave the base. Just you, is it?'

'Yes, sir. The others are still sleeping off too much to drink.'

The commander chuckled. 'What do you plan on doing today?'

'Just see more of the countryside.'

'You come from Alberta, I understand. Are you missing the wide-open spaces, or do you live in a city?'

'No, our home has plenty of space around it. I don't like being hemmed in.'

'So you want to go exploring today?'

'Yes, sir, with your permission.'

'You have it. Enjoy your day.'

Steve saluted and left the base, heading for the station.

He only had to wait half an hour for a train and found a seat in a carriage by a window. He relaxed and enjoyed the scenery as they went along. His thoughts turned to the crash. He would never cease to be grateful that he hadn't killed or badly injured his crew or anyone on the ground and he had managed to get the plane within fifty miles of Scampton.

He got off the train and then caught a bus to take him

close to the farm. The last mile he walked, and recognised the farmhouse the moment he saw it. There was smoke coming out of the chimney. He had been so low it was a wonder the house hadn't fallen down from the vibration.

His attention focussed on the field and he strode past the house, anxious to see if the clear-up had been thorough. And it had. In front of him was a clear, ploughed field, ready for planting. Lost in the memory, he didn't hear anyone approaching until he felt a small hand slip into his. He looked down at the child and smiled.

'Men came and took it away,' she told him seriously. 'Did you want it back?'

'No, it was too broken to ever fly again.'

'Hmm.' She tipped her head right back to look up at the sky. 'What's it like up there?'

'Beautiful. The stars are very bright and the moon looks much larger.'

She pulled a face and held the rag dolly up for him to see. 'Mary wouldn't like to go so high.'

'I'll bet she would once she was up there.'

'Might, suppose.' A cheeky glint came into her eyes. 'She likes to be picked up, though.'

'Oh, well, we mustn't disappoint her then.'

Her arms came up, still holding the dolly by the hair, and when he scooped her up she wrapped her arms around his neck and giggled.

'She's got the measure of you, lad,' a voice said from behind him.

Steve turned to the farmer and they grinned at each other. 'How old did you say she is?'

'Three, going on thirty.'

'I'm a pest,' she whispered in his ear.

He moved his head so he could look in her face, an expression of mock puzzlement showing. 'Really? That's hard to believe.'

She nodded. 'I get under everyone's feet, and ask too many questions.'

'Didn't your mummy tell you to ask Steve something?' her father reminded her.

She thought for a moment and then nodded. 'Will you eat with us? We've got sausages and mash, with treacle pudding and custard for afters.'

'I would love to. They are my favourites.'

Her face lit up with a huge smile. 'Tell Mummy he's going to stay with us. He'll need lots to eat 'cos he's ever so big.'

'Let's all go and tell her. Lunch must be ready by now.'

'Oh, goody.'

'Where is your son, sir?' Steve asked as they walked to the farmhouse.

'Spending the day with a friend, and he'll be cross he missed you. He watched as the Lancaster was taken away, bombarding the airmen with questions. One of them gave him a piece from the cockpit and he carries it with him all the time, launching into the story at every opportunity. That field is now referred to as the Lancaster field by everyone in the district. We can joke about it because no one was killed.' He looked up at Steve. 'From the mess that plane was in, I guess it was a close call.'

Steve just gave a dismissive shrug. 'I was sorry to have caused such devastation to your field, and wanted to come and check that the clear-up had been thorough.'

'You didn't need to worry about that. They stripped away all evidence of the crash, and even borrowed my tractor to plough it ready for planting again.'

'Yes, I saw that. They did a good job.'

The kitchen was warm and full of the smell of cooking and he put Beth down to greet the farmer's wife. As soon as her feet touched the floor she ran to her mother, gabbling away in excitement.

'Slow down,' her mother admonished. 'We can't understand a word you're saying.' She smiled and raised her eyebrows at Steve. 'While she's awake she never stops. The only peace we get is when she's asleep. Anyway, it's lovely to see you again. Please sit down; I'm about to dish up. Where are the rest of your friends?'

'They were still asleep when I left, recovering from a celebration last night.'

'May we ask what you were celebrating?'

'The flight engineer's twenty-first birthday and the successful completion of thirty missions. It was quite a party.'

'I'll bet it was. Does that mean you have finished flying?' Mr Collins asked.

'Oh, no. I came here to fly and that's what I intend to do.' Steve smiled. 'When we arrived, the commander told us never to volunteer for anything, which was a joke because we had all volunteered as bomber crew. If I have to, I will ignore that advice. We all will.'

Mrs Collins grimaced. 'Let's hope this darned war will soon end.'

Beth, who had been listening intently, came and leant against Steve's knees. 'Uncle Walt said we will soon be going to beat the bloody hell out of that man.'

'How many times have I told you not to repeat what Uncle Walt says,' her mother scolded. 'He swears too much, and you mustn't imitate him.'

She smirked at Steve. 'Don't know what it means, anyway.'

'Don't tell fibs.' Her mother tapped her on the backside. 'Go and get the salt and pepper for the table.'

She scuttled off and disappeared into a large cupboard while Steve tried to control the urge to laugh out loud.

'That child,' her mother sighed. 'She remembers everything. Her memory is extraordinary.'

'In that case she should go far, Mrs Collins.'

'We do hope so,' both parents said with feeling.

They were all laughing when the child reappeared.

'What you laughing at?' she wanted to know.

'Nothing to do with you.'

She glared at her father. 'Everything to do with me. How do I learn if you don't tell me things?'

'You already know far too much for your age.' Her father picked her up and sat her at the table next to Steve. 'Let's eat. I'm hungry and I'm sure Steve is.'

There was reasonable silence as Beth concentrated on eating her sausages and mash without making too much mess. After they had finished lunch, she helped her mother put everything away and they sat in front of the fire talking.

With her chores finished, she sidled up to Steve and held up her arms, indicating that she wanted to be picked up. He swept her up and she was instantly asleep with her thumb stuck in her mouth.

'Time for her afternoon nap.' Mr Collins pulled his daughter's thumb out of her mouth, hoisted her up and headed for the stairs.

He was soon back. 'She's sparked out and will sleep for a couple of hours. You seem interested in the farm, Steve, so would you like to have a look round?'

'Yes, please. I'd like to see a working English farm.'

After putting on their coats they began the tour. It was

quite a large farm with cattle and arable land. The farmer explained the everyday working of the farm, and the challenge they had faced in trying to feed an island nation during wartime. Steve was fascinated and noted that every piece of land was producing something; not one inch of space was wasted. He inspected all the livestock, paying special attention to the herd of cows. 'They are fine animals and in excellent condition,' he remarked.

The farmer studied him with interest. 'You appear to know what you are talking about.'

'We have a ranch back home and I've worked it with my father since I could walk.'

'Ah, that's why you were so concerned about tearing up my field.'

He nodded. 'I was relieved to see it had been cleared and made ready for planting again.'

'They did a good job. Now, I've got one more thing I think you might be interested in.'

They went to another part of the farm and Collins stood by the wooden gate, put his fingers in his mouth and gave a piercing whistle.

Steve watched in delight as two enormous horses thundered towards them. The farmer dug in his pocket and produced two apples. He handed one to Steve and a huge head took it gently out of his hand, munching with pleasure.

'Do you work them?' he asked.

'Yes, I hitch them up to a plough now and again just to let them know they are doing something useful. They like to work.'

'They're beautiful. Would you mind if I had a closer look?'

'Not at all. Go ahead.'

There was a grin on his face as he vaulted over the gate into the field. They allowed him to run his hands over them and inspect the enormous hoofs without the slightest complaint. Giving them a final pat, he climbed back, his eyes shining with pleasure.

When they returned to the house, Beth was up and rushed over to him. 'Did you have a good sleep, Beth?'

'I wanted to stay awake, but I couldn't. Mummy said you've been looking at the farm. Did you like it?'

'Very much, especially the large shire horses.'

She giggled. 'I sat on their back and they didn't mind. Daddy had to hold me else I'd fall off.'

'Can you stay for tea?' Mrs Collins asked.

He glanced at his watch. 'I'd love to, but it's time I was on my way. Thank you so much; I've enjoyed my visit.' He shook hands with them and swept Beth up to kiss her on the cheek.

'You'll be welcome to visit any time you feel like it. It's been lovely to see you again.'

'Thank you. I will certainly try to come again.'

It was dinner time when he arrived back, so he went straight to the mess.

'Where the blazes have you been?' Luke wanted to know the moment he sat down. 'We've been looking for you everywhere.'

'I had permission to leave the base, so I went back to see if the farm had been put to rights.'

'Why didn't you tell us you were going, we would have come with you?'

Steve raised his eyebrows in amusement. 'You were all fast asleep and didn't look as if you were going to surface for hours, Ricky.'

His friend smirked. 'Right. How was the farm?'

'Good. They did a fine clean-up job. What have you all been doing?'

'As little as possible,' Andy told him.

'Make the most of it,' Luke warned, 'because they're not going to allow us to be idle for long.'

'Yeah, I've heard a rumour a batch of new recruits is arriving soon, and we could be their instructors.'

'That's possible, I suppose. I don't mind as long as we still get some flying time.'

'Be a bit scary to have a novice at the controls, Steve.'

'We'll just have to wait and see what happens.' Luke handed round a packet of cigarettes. 'Wonder if we can get leave? It'd be nice to go and see Uncle Harry again, and Sybil.'

Chapter Seventeen

The rumours were correct, and as an experienced crew they were given the task of "knocking the new arrivals into shape", as the commander put it. It was the end of March before they were given any leave, and that was only forty-eight hours. They made a quick visit to see Harry, and as before, had a great time at the Jolly Sailor. Luke was disappointed not to see Sybil, though.

The day after arriving back they were called to a meeting, and Steve looked round the crowded room. 'Everyone's here, so I wonder what's going on?'

The commander came in and they waited expectantly.

'As you already know, plans are being drawn up for an invasion this summer. In preparation for that, all raids have been suspended for the time being.'

A murmur of surprise ran round the room, and the commander called order. 'Don't worry, you will have a part to play, but I can't give you any details yet. I will keep you updated when I receive further news.' His eyes fixed on

Steve. 'You are dismissed, except Allard. You are to come with me.'

Steve followed him to the office and was intrigued when the door was shut behind them. This door was never closed.

'Sit down.' He unlocked a drawer and pulled out a folder. 'I've had an urgent request for a pilot with certain abilities, and on reading your notes you appear to meet those requirements. Pack your kit. You're leaving immediately.'

'Where am I going, sir?'

'Tangmere. It's an airfield near the south coast.'

That sent a bolt of excitement through him – one of the Battle of Britain airfields – there would be Spitfires there. 'Why am I being sent there, and is this a permanent posting?'

'You will be told why they want you when you get there.' He closed the folder and glanced up. 'I resisted sending you, Allard, but you're the only pilot with the skills they require. I've told them that you are to return here as soon as they have finished with you.'

'So the posting is temporary?'

'It most certainly is. We're going to need pilots of your experience later in the year.' He sat back. 'You are not to tell anyone where you're going, and that includes close friends.'

'Understood, sir.'

'There's a car ready and waiting to take you to your destination.' He stood up and came round the desk.

Steve was immediately on his feet and was surprised when the officer shook his hand.

'Good luck, and make sure you come back as soon as you can.'

'I will, sir.' He hurried to his quarters to find the entire crew waiting for him.

'What did he want you for?' Luke asked the moment he

walked in, and watched with concern when his friend didn't answer and began to pack his kit. 'Where are you going?'

'I can't tell you.' That brought on a barrage of questions, making him stop packing and hold up his hands for quiet. 'I am being posted somewhere else, it is only temporary, and I don't know how long I will be away, but I will definitely be back.'

'Do you know what you'll be doing?' Ricky had a deep frown on his face.

'No, and I'll only be told when I get there, evidently.'

'Oh hell.' Andy shook his head. 'I don't like the sound of that. Steve, you be bloody careful. Anything this secret usually turns out to be dangerous.'

Steve swung his bag over his shoulder and smiled reassuringly. 'Don't look so worried. I expect I'll be back in no time at all. Behave yourselves.'

They all followed him out and the frowns deepened when they saw him get in a car and drive away.

On the long drive to Tangmere Steve puzzled over the mysterious posting. He had not been given any information except they needed a pilot with his skills, so it would certainly involve flying. But flying what? Not bombers, that was for sure, so it must be something smaller. He sat up sharply at that thought. Was his experience with small planes what they wanted? They had Spitfires at Tangmere – perhaps he'd get a chance to fly one of those.

It was dark by the time they arrived at the airfield and he was ushered straight to the commander's office. There were two men waiting for him – one RAF and one army. After being announced, he saluted and waited while the officers scrutinised him for a moment.

Appearing satisfied with what he saw, the commander stepped forward and shook his hand. 'Thank you for coming so quickly, Allard. My name is Grieves and this is Colonel Harrison. Leave your kit here and come with us.'

They walked in silence towards a hangar. What an earth was an army colonel doing here?

The hangar contained a Spitfire, Hurricane and one other plane. Grieves stopped in front of this plane and without looking at Steve asked, 'Can you fly that?'

'Yes, sir. I had the chance to fly a Lysander in Canada during my training.'

'We noted from your record that you hold a private pilot's licence and flew regularly before joining up.' The colonel had piercing grey eyes and they were now turned on Steve, assessing him carefully. 'So you are used to flying small planes by dead reckoning?'

'Yes, sir, I navigate at home by calculating airspeed, distance and direction.'

'You also have knowledge of Morse code, so how proficient are you at that?'

'I haven't used it for some time, sir, but I would still be able to manage it, if necessary.' *What the hell was this all about?* he wondered.

The two officers nodded to each other, and the commander smiled for the first time. 'Excellent. You will dine with us tonight.'

'Thank you, sir. Can I ask why you've sent for me?'

'All in good time.' The commander glanced at his watch. 'Let us eat, and then someone will show you to your quarters. You will need sleep because there's a busy day ahead of you tomorrow. Come on, you must be hungry.'

This was turning out to be very strange indeed, and Steve

was bursting with questions, but from their attitude he knew he wasn't going to get any information just yet, so he had to curb his curiosity. He gave the Lysander another careful look over, noting the extra fuel tanks underneath and a ladder in place by the rear seats. That was a fixture, by the look of it. This one had clearly been modified for a special task.

Once in the mess, the two officers were more relaxed and chatted away, but without giving a hint of what they were about to ask him to do.

'I hear you landed your Lancaster in a farmer's field,' the colonel said with a smile on his face.

'Oh, I didn't land it, sir. The poor thing was badly damaged and when a field came into view she dropped into it.'

This jokey explanation amused them, and he didn't miss the slight nod they gave each other. He felt as if he'd passed some test.

After an excellent meal he was ordered to present himself to them at seven the next morning. They were to breakfast together, and then everything would be explained.

He was given a room on his own, and although his mind was buzzing he slept soundly, as he always did. Tomorrow would take care of itself.

After breakfast they went straight to the office, and Steve waited while an airman was told they were not to be disturbed for anything.

The door was firmly closed, and the commander leant forward slightly. 'Right, let us get down to business. We had to send out an urgent request for a pilot with certain qualifications and experience. You were the only one who came anywhere near to meeting our requirements. You have experience flying small aircraft, are used to navigating by dead reckoning, and have a working knowledge of Morse code. You also have the necessary night flying hours.'

He gave the officers a studied look, wondering where this was going.

The colonel continued. 'What we are going to ask you to do is dangerous, and we would usually send our most experienced pilot in to carry out this mission, but at the moment he is too sick to fly. This is urgent, so we had to find someone quickly. Before I go into detail, I must ask you one question, and you must give me an honest answer. Is that understood?'

'Yes, sir.'

'Could you fly the Lysander into France at night, land in a field and then get out again in around five minutes? The only lights on the ground will be from torches.'

Some question! Steve drew in a silent breath before answering, then said with absolute confidence, 'Yes, sir.'

The commander showed him a folded map. 'Your only means of navigation will be a map like this, which you will have in one hand while you fly with the other.'

'How will I read the map in the dark?'

'You will be able to check the route with the aid of a small light, called a "wander light."'

'I gather the mission is either to drop off agents or to pick some up.'

'Pick up two.' The colonel lit up a cigarette and drew in deeply. 'They have information that is badly needed, and their situation is becoming perilous. We must get them out safely.'

'When?'

'Tomorrow night.'

Steve couldn't hide his surprise. 'That is short notice, sir.'

'We know, but an operation like this can only be carried out during a full moon. I will give you all the training possible in the time we have.' The army officer gave a slight smile. 'We know we're asking a lot of you, but we think you can do this. How do you feel?'

Excitement raced through him, but Steve kept his voice and demeanour calm. 'I'd like to give it a go, sir.'

Relief showed on the officers' faces, and the commander said, 'Right, first things first. Take the Lysander up, do a circuit of the field, come in and touch down, turn the plane round and then take off again. That should give you a feel of how she handles.'

Both men were on their feet and heading for the door, eager to see how skilful this young pilot really was.

The plane was ready and waiting for them, so Steve walked round it, taking in every detail. It was larger than the small planes he flew at home – he'd only ever had a go at this make once, and that was some time ago.

'All right, she's all yours,' the commander said after he had finished his inspection. 'See what you can do with a quick landing and take-off.'

He nodded, and then climbed into the aircraft. He knew he could do as they asked, and he was eager to give it a go. Once in the air there was a smile on his face, and once he was comfortable with the performance of the plane, he lined up for the next manoeuvre, which he accomplished smoothly. He was enjoying himself and would have liked to stay up longer, but he had his orders, so landed and taxied to the parking spot.

'Any problems?' the commander asked when he joined them again.

'None, sir, she handles well.'

'That was a smooth take-off and landing. Now all you have to do is the same thing in the dark, on a strange field and in enemy territory.'

'It'll be a challenge, Colonel, but not impossible.'

'We believe in you, son,' said the commander. 'You will be spending today with Colonel Harrison, and I will see you at dinner tonight.'

For the rest of that day and the next Steve learnt as much as he could about the Special Duty runs – what to do and what not to do. He brushed up on his Morse code and by the time the colonel had finished with him he felt he had every scrap of information to carry out the mission.

The army officer sat back and studied his pupil intently. 'I have prepared you as much as I can in the time available, but I will add one more thing. It is vital you get the agents out, but if you don't get the correct Morse code from the ground you are to abort and return at once. On no account are you to land if there is the slightest doubt. Is that understood?'

'Yes, sir.'

'Are you happy with the way the map is prepared?'

'Yes, sir, it is very clear.'

'Good.' The colonel took a deep breath. 'We have already sent a message to let them know you are coming tonight. Bring them safely back, and you will be doing a lot for the proposed invasion. These agents have intelligence we need.'

'I understand, sir. If they are there, I'll get them back.'

'Now, I suggest you get some rest. It's going to be a long night.'

Back in his quarters Steve stretched out on the bed, his mind going over and over what he had been told. He took deep breaths to relax. There was no need to keep running over it – the information was there when needed.

Within ten minutes he was fast asleep.

Chapter Eighteen

He was up and already in his flying gear when the orderly assigned to him knocked on the door.

'Is there anything special you would like to eat, sir?'

'Do I have a choice?'

'Within reason, sir. Some pilots don't want anything more than tea and a sandwich, others need something more substantial.'

'No good asking for a large steak, I suppose?'

The orderly smiled. 'I'm afraid not, sir.'

'In that case, how about a bacon sandwich and a cup of coffee? Is that possible?'

'For you it is. I'll get it straight away.'

While he was waiting Steve studied the map, making sure the directions were clear in his mind. It was a while since he had navigated like this and he was going to have to call upon all of his experience and knowledge to carry out this mission successfully. Getting those agents out was vital, so he was well aware that failure was not an option.

The airman was soon back with the food, and Steve picked up the cup, smelt it and took a sip. His eyes lit up with pleasure. 'Real coffee.'

'Yes, sir, we do have some, but it is reserved for special duty pilots.'

'Wow, what a treat. Do you know this is the first decent cup of coffee I've had since I left Canada.'

After finishing the very large sandwich and draining the cup, he glanced at his watch and stood up. 'Time to go.'

As he walked towards the Lysander his expression was tranquil.

The two officers were there to see him on his way, and when he reached them, he smiled. 'Nice bright moon shining tonight.'

They nodded, and the colonel asked, 'Any last-minute questions?'

'No, sir, you have schooled me well.'

Without wasting any more time, Steve climbed into the plane, ran through the checks and strapped himself in. He made sure the folded map was showing the section he needed, took several deep breaths to calm his nerves, and then taxied for take-off.

The moment he was in the air he relaxed. It was imperative he remained calm and focussed. This was going to be one hell of a challenge, but he was determined to complete the mission successfully. Flying three hundred miles at low level over enemy territory was going to be quite an experience, though.

The officers watched until the Lysander was out of sight, then they turned and walked towards the bar.

'There isn't anything we can do now but wait, and I need

a drink,' the commander said. 'I like that boy and I pray we haven't sent him on an impossible mission. I hate sending a pilot inexperienced in this kind of work. We are asking a hell of a lot from him. What do you think his chances are of even finding the right field?'

'I'm reasonably confident. He's got a good head on his shoulders.' The colonel smiled at the man walking beside him.

'True.' He sighed deeply. 'I know the man in charge at Scampton, and if that boy doesn't come back there will be hell to pay.'

'I'll take the blame, but you know we didn't have a choice. I only hope those agents haven't been caught before we can get to them. We should have got them out before this, and the delay could cost them their lives.'

'I know, and it's going to be a long night. Make mine a double,' he said as they entered the officers' bar.

Flying as low as he dared, Steve checked the map time and time again. The flight so far had been uneventful, but by his reckoning the field should be around here. Where the hell was it? He scanned the ground looking for the signal, but couldn't see anything. Certain he was in the right area he went round again, but knew he couldn't do this for too long or he would attract unwelcome attention. 'Come on,' he muttered, 'I'm not going back without you, so get those damned lights on!'

Then he saw a flashing light directly ahead of him, and when he approached he concentrated on the dots and dashes. It was right, but he let it flash once more just to be absolutely certain. Happy that he was receiving the correct signal, he gave a sigh of relief and headed in, touched down and turned the plane ready for a quick take-off.

Two figures were running towards him before he had even come to a stop. The moment it was safe to do so, they climbed the ladder attached to the side, and as soon as they were in Steve took off again. He had been on the ground for no more than five minutes.

It wasn't until they were well over the sea that he relaxed. That had gone well and he was elated he had the two important agents on board. All he had to do now was find Tangmere.

As he crossed the coast of England, he smiled to himself. Being over enemy territory was something he had done many times, but this was the first time he'd had to sneak in unarmed and without Ricky plotting the course for him. And to be honest, he had enjoyed the challenge.

His smile broadened when the airfield came into sight, and when he landed the two officers were waiting. He taxied to the parking spot and stopped, releasing his harness and jumping down. His passengers were already out and talking with the colonel. When he walked over, they thanked him for a smooth pickup, and shook his hand.

'Well done.' The commander, along with everyone else, had a look of relief on his face. 'I expect you could do with a stiff drink.'

'I could, and something to eat. I'm starving.'

'We'll see you are fed and watered. You did a good job tonight, and we are all grateful.'

He inclined his head. 'I'm pleased it turned out well.'

'Let's go to the officers' mess. There is food and drink waiting there for us.'

Steve walked with the two agents, discussing the difficulties and dangers of this kind of operation. During a lull in the conversation, he heard the colonel asking, 'How long can we keep him?'

'That would have to be negotiated. How long do you want him for?'

'Permanent.'

'Not a chance,' the commander told him. 'He's here on the understanding that it's a temporary posting, but I'll see if I can wangle more time if you need it.'

'Thanks.'

Ah, because he had carried out the mission successfully, the colonel was scheming to keep him. Well, as much as he liked using all of his skills, he was a Lancaster pilot, and he would make that clear when the subject came up. He wouldn't refuse to do another run if needed, though.

A full English breakfast was served to them, and the moment they had finished, the colonel whisked the agents away to do whatever it was they were here to do.

Steve stifled a yawn, suddenly tired, and the commander noticed. 'You need sleep. I'll buy you that drink tonight. Until then, rest and relax.'

'Will I be returning to my squadron now?' he asked, wanting to get the subject settled.

'We will need you for a while yet. The colonel is very impressed with you, and would like to keep you, but it was made clear to me that your assignment here was to be short. Before I start making myself very unpopular with your base commander, I would like to know how you feel about the possibility of doing another run.'

He took his time by lighting a cigarette before answering. 'I am quite prepared to do another run, but my place is at Scampton. After all, this kind of operation won't be necessary once the invasion is under way, and if what we have been

172

told is true, it isn't that far away now. I will want to be back before the end of April when all bomber crews will have to be standing by as the order comes.'

'I understand, and accept your willingness to help us out again, and I have no doubt that it will be needed. There will be quite a lot of coming and going over the next couple of weeks as every scrap of information is vital to ensure the success of the invasion. I promise we will release you in time for whatever you have to do.' He stood up. 'Now you must sleep.'

'After a mission I like to take a walk, so will anyone mind if I wander around the airfield?'

'Not at all. We'll see you for dinner tonight.'

He made straight for the Spitfires.

'Beautiful, isn't she, sir?'

He smiled at the airman who had come up to stand beside him. 'Can I sit in her?'

'Help yourself, sir. You'll find her very different from the Lysander.'

'And the Lancaster,' he said, eagerly climbing up to the cockpit and easing himself into the seat.

The airman had followed him, and now leant in to help fasten the harness. 'That will help you get the feel of her, sir. The pilots say the plane feels a part of them once in the air.'

'I expect it does.' He sat there imagining what it would be like to soar into the air in this superb plane. Before he left Tangmere he was going to fly one, he promised himself.

He reluctantly climbed out, thanked the airman, and began his customary walk. After half an hour he went to his quarters to get some sleep.

At dinner there was no sign of the colonel or the agents,

and he was told that they were now in London, but the colonel would be back soon. He guessed that would mean another mission, but until then he could leave the base as long as they knew where he was going. This gave him the opportunity to explore the surrounding countryside and enjoy long walks along the coast.

He hung around waiting for ideal weather conditions and then made one more trip to drop off agents and pick another one up. As much as he'd relished these runs, he was becoming anxious to return to Scampton, and was missing his friends and comrades. This was solitary work and he was very much on his own at this base.

After making his concern clear to the commander, it was the very same day that the colonel approached him.

'I am told you are anxious to return to your squadron.' He gave a wry smile. 'I would have liked to keep you longer, but I do understand you are needed elsewhere.' He shook Steve's hand. 'I am most grateful for your help. You have done a first-class job for us and helped us out of a difficult situation. Thank you very much.'

'I am pleased I was able to help, sir.'

When the colonel left him, Steve went straight to the commander's office, determined not to leave until he had flown a Spitfire. This might be the only opportunity he would get. 'The colonel has finished with me,' he said the moment he walked in through the door, 'so can I ask when I will be able to return to Scampton?'

'He told me he was, reluctantly, going to release you, and you also have my thanks for your excellent help. We'd have been hard-pushed to get those agents where they needed to be without you.'

'I enjoyed the challenge, and I would like to ask a favour, sir.'

'Name it.'

'I want to fly a Spitfire.'

The officer smiled. 'That doesn't surprise me. Why don't you fly back to your base in one of them, and I will ask one of the ferry pilots to collect it for us?'

Steve couldn't hide his delight at such an offer. 'I'd like that very much, sir.'

'Good, I'll let them know you are flying back. The plane will be ready for you at 9 o'clock tomorrow morning.'

'Thank you, sir.' He left the office elated at the prospect of taking off in one of those beautiful planes.

He was on the airfield before the time he was due to leave and another pilot was there to give him a few tips on handling the plane.

The commander came over to see him off. 'I've had a message from Scampton, and, before you land, they want you to show them what the Spitfire can do. You'll have the feel of her by the time you reach there, so have fun, but don't damage her.'

'There won't be a scratch on her, I promise.'

He chuckled. 'That remains to be seen. I know you young pilots when you get your hands on something new. Good luck in everything you will be doing over the next few months. It has been a pleasure to meet you.'

'The same here, sir. It has been an interesting assignment.' With excitement coursing through him, Steve took his leave and climbed into the plane, and the moment he was strapped in the usual calm settled on him and he was ready to fly.

'Robert.' The commander led the wing commander out to the airfield. 'Allard is on his way back in a Spitfire, and I've given him permission to give us a display before landing. He has checked in and is only about ten minutes away.'

'The lucky devil.'

They stood in silence, straining to hear the first unmistakable sound of the Merlin engine. Others had gathered as well, wondering what the officers were doing scanning the sky at this time of day.

'Here he comes.' Robert shaded his eyes.

The Spitfire came in fast and low, roaring over the airfield, making people come running from all directions to see what was happening. They were used to the sound of the bombers, but this was different and they all wanted to see what it was.

'A Spitfire!' Luke shouted to his friends. 'Come and have a look.'

After another low-level swoop across the field the plane climbed, rolled and dived, making everyone shout in delight.

'My God!' Ricky exclaimed. 'Look at him go.'

After giving a spectacular show for ten minutes, the plane swept into a victory roll and then came in to land.

Sandy was jumping around with excitement. 'I've got to meet that pilot. Who is he?'

The wing commander grinned. 'You'll see in a minute.'

When the plane landed and cut its engine the ground crew rushed over to help the pilot out and take care of the plane.

The onlookers watched, stunned, as the tall figure of their friend walked towards them.

Ricky swore under his breath, even though he was smiling. 'We might have known it was him.'

'Damn me,' Sandy muttered. 'How did he get his hands on a Spitfire?'

Steve stopped in front of the officers and saluted smartly. 'Reporting back, sir, and thank you for allowing me to let rip.'

'You are not trying to tell me you didn't have a sly practice on the way here, are you?'

'Ah well, I had to find out what she could do,' he replied, managing to keep a straight face.

'Don't try that with the Lancaster or you will turn your crew grey with fright.'

'Wouldn't dream of it, sir.'

The commander chuckled softly under his breath. 'Welcome back, Allard. Come and see me in an hour. I want to hear all about your exploits at Tangmere.'

'Yes, sir.'

He glanced around at everyone. 'I know you're all itching to get a good look at that plane. You can examine it and even sit in her if you want to, but don't any of you dare start her up. A ferry pilot will be coming tomorrow to pick it up.'

Robert looked disappointed. 'Does that include me?'

'Especially you, because the moment I turn my back you'll have her up in the air. Come on, we've got work to do.'

Robert held his hands up, and then walked back to the office.

His friends were delighted to see him and inundated him with questions.

'Where have you been? What have you been doing? We were worried you weren't coming back. What are you doing flying a Spitfire? Have you been with a fighter squadron?'

He stopped them. 'I have been on special duties, and the Spitfire was a reward for a job successfully done. That's all I'm allowed to say.'

'But you're back with us now?' Luke asked anxiously.

'I am, so what have you all been doing while I've been away?' He strode towards their quarters, and the others followed him, still hoping for more information.

'They've been keeping us busy, but things are moving, Steve. Raids will be stepped up because of the invasion. We'll soon be flying again, and they told us we would be given another pilot if you weren't back in time.'

'There was no chance of that,' he assured them. 'We're going to see this through together.'

The girls smiled at each other and watched the group of airmen walking away. Steve was completely surrounded, and it looked as if everyone was talking at the same time.

'They're so relieved to have him back. Ricky was worried that wherever Steve was would keep him.'

'I don't know what is more worrying – not knowing where he is and what he's doing, or watching them take off in the Lancaster, knowing the danger they will be in.'

'I'd rather have him here. His crew trust his flying skills.'

Nancy laughed. 'And we've just had a demonstration of that skill.'

'The commander ordered him to do that for everyone's entertainment.'

'How did he know he could fly like that?' Nancy asked.

'He knows Steve's full history from before and after he joined up.'

'What on earth was he – a stunt pilot?'

'That is information only the man in charge is privy to, but I doubt it. Remember, he's been flying from a young age and can probably handle anything he sits in.'

'I guess you're right, and I suspect someone has been taking advantage of that ability.' Nancy frowned.

'Secret and dangerous, no doubt.'

'We can be sure of that.' Jean glanced at her watch. 'I must get back to work now the entertainment is over. We'll catch up with the boys tonight. It would have been impossible to get near Steve with that crowd around him, but at least he's back and safe.'

'That's a lot to be grateful for. See you tonight, Jean.'

The girls went their separate ways, back to their duties.

Chapter Nineteen

The next morning they were sent for, and when they walked in they saw that all crews who had completed their missions were there.

'Uh-oh,' Luke murmured under his breath. 'Anyone want to bet what this is about?'

'Please be seated, gentlemen.'

They waited, all sure they knew what was coming.

The officer didn't waste any time. 'As you are all aware, an invasion is going to be launched soon and Bomber Command has a job to do in the run-up to this. When you all arrived here, I advised you never to volunteer for anything.' He paused and looked around at the faces all watching him intently. 'I take that back and now ask you to volunteer for further missions. Anyone prepared to do this, please stand.'

Every airman stood as one man, and the commander nodded. 'Thank you, gentlemen.'

'Do you have a date for the invasion, sir?' Sandy asked.

'I can't disclose that at the moment, but it is now the

beginning of May, the weather is improving, so it will be soon. However, everything will depend on conditions in the Channel. You will be fully briefed as the orders come through.'

Each crew walked out together as they contemplated what was ahead of them again. This was going to be a momentous undertaking and they were excited to play a part in it.

'Hey, Sarge,' Ricky called.

He came over to them, clearly eager to know what the meeting had been about.

'We're in business again.'

'I thought that might be the case. I'll get the boys together and we'll look after you again.'

'Thanks, we'd appreciate that,' Steve told him. 'We haven't any details yet, but the hint was we will be flying again quite soon. They are just awaiting orders.'

'Right. We'll start giving the Lancaster a thorough going over.'

They watched him hurry away, already shouting orders.

'That's settled, then. I'm happy with the same men we had last time.' Luke rubbed his hands together and grinned at them. 'Okay, what are we going to do tonight? Do we have a boys' only night out or are we asking the girls to join us?'

There was silence for a moment, then Steve said, 'I think we had better keep it to just our crews.'

Sandy agreed, but then looked at Ricky. 'Is that all right with you?'

'Yeah, as much as I would like Jean and Nancy to come with us, we can really let rip with just us boys.'

'Exactly,' Luke replied. 'I don't think we'll be suitable company for the girls tonight.'

That caused a few chuckles as they anticipated the evening ahead.

Two days later they were flying again, and there was an air of anticipation as the invasion of France was close.

Nancy watched Steve walking across the airfield, as he always did. Her thoughts turned to her brother and knew that, regardless of the risks, he would have volunteered to keep flying at this crucial time. The majority of them were little more than boys, but in her eyes the courage they showed made them men – special men. She was prejudiced, of course. She was well aware that the same kind of courage was present in all the services, but because of her family connection, and now the Canadians, she was close to this group of men. Too close for comfort most of the time, but it was unavoidable. The hardest part of this was struggling to keep a friendly relationship with Steve. They both wanted so much more, but she couldn't allow that to happen.

She saw him walking towards her.

'Morning, Nancy.'

'Good morning, Steve.'

'Are you on duty?'

'Not until two o'clock.'

'In that case, will you walk with me?'

This surprised her; he always walked alone. 'If you would like me to?'

'I would.'

They walked side by side out of the base and along a country lane. He didn't speak and she remained silent, knowing he didn't want to listen to mindless chatter. There were dark circles under his eyes, and it was clear they were all beginning to suffer with battle fatigue.

They had been walking for about fifteen minutes when he took hold of her hand, still saying nothing. After a few more minutes he looked down at her and smiled. 'It's a beautiful morning, isn't it?'

'Yes, lovely.' Now he had broken the silence she felt able to speak, but not about the missions, of course. 'What will you do when the war is over, Steve?'

'Go home. What about you?'

'I really don't know. It isn't going to be easy adjusting to civilian life again. You're a good pilot and could have an excellent career in the air force.'

He shook his head. 'Tempting, but not possible. I'm needed at home. Dad has been managing on his own, but it takes two of us to run the place.'

'Is it a big farm, then?'

'Big enough.'

'You'll miss flying.'

'I'll still be flying, but something much, much smaller than a Lancaster. I will miss that beautiful plane, though.'

'Is that all you'll miss?'

'Oh, no. I've come to love this place and the people we have met. It'll be hard to leave.'

'Yes, once the war is finally over there will be hard decisions to be made by many people.'

'True, but no obstacle is insurmountable, my father always says.' He turned them round and they started back. 'Thank you for walking with me,' he said, and pausing he bent down and kissed her on the lips.

It was no more than a butterfly brush, but it was the first outward sign of affection he had shown her. Knowing this was dangerous ground, she stepped back and said teasingly, 'My, you're in a strange mood. Get some sleep, you're tired.'

'We all are.' When they entered the gate, he gave her hand an understanding squeeze and walked towards his quarters.

As he strode away, Jean joined her. 'Did you actually accompany him on his walk?'

'He asked me to, and he's in a strange mood. He kissed me ever so gently, but I'm hoping it was more of a thank you for keeping him company. He didn't want to be alone today, and that worried me.'

Jean gave her friend a studied look. 'If you don't mind me saying, that gorgeous man loves you, and you feel the same about him. Why don't you just admit it?'

'I daren't, for both our sakes.'

Giving a shake of her head, Jean sighed, but dropped the subject. 'I've been told they had a very rough night, so he probably needed to release tension, and having you with him helped.'

She smiled at her friend. 'I worry too much about all of them.'

'Can't help ourselves, can we? I've just seen Ricky and he looks drained. But by tonight they will be laughing and joking again.' Jean tapped Nancy playfully on the back. 'The first night they have off we should challenge them to another darts match.'

'That's a good idea, and we could let them win this time.'

Jean looked horrified. 'Not likely. Don't let your sympathy for them cloud your judgement, Nancy.'

'True. Forget I said that. It was just a weak moment.'

'Well, don't do it again. Anyway, what did you talk about on your walk?'

'We were discussing what we would do when the war is over. I know you and Ricky are fond of each other, so it's going to be very hard to see him leave for home.'

Jean pursed her lips. 'More than fond of him, I'm crazy in love with him, and he feels the same about me. I know those boys won't make a permanent commitment until this conflict is over, but if he wants us to marry, I'll follow him to Canada.'

'That's a huge step to take. What about your family, won't they be upset?'

'I expect they will, but I'm the eldest of three. My brother and sister will still be at home, so I'm sure they'll understand. I have to make my own life, and all they will want for me is to be happy.'

'I hope it works out for both of you.'

'I hope so too, but the time to make such decisions is still a way off.' Jean broke into a wide grin. 'Do you know what Ricky told me the other day?'

'No, what?'

'While Steve was away, Luke travelled to where Sybil is stationed so they could spend a little time together. He appears to be quite attracted to her, Ricky said, and writing every day. I wonder if he's told Steve?'

'I really don't know, but I'm sure he would be happy for them.'

Jean chanced bringing up the subject of Steve again. 'What are you going to do about Steve when the time comes?'

'There isn't anything to do. We are just good friends and I expect we will keep in touch by letter when he goes home.'

'I don't believe that and neither do you. Be honest.'

'Alright, I'll admit that my feelings for him are more than that, but there is no future. He'll return to Canada, and I couldn't possibly go with him. You know why, Jean.'

Her friend nodded sadly. 'Is it any good pointing out that you have the right to choose your own future?'

'None at all.'

'I thought not. Ah well, all we can do is wait and see how things work out. Fate can take many unexpected turns, and things have a habit of working out for the best. Now, I must get back to work.'

'Always the optimist.'

'Is there any other way? Bye, see you for dinner.'

'Writing to your father?' Steve asked, sitting in a chair and stretching out his legs.

Luke glanced up. 'Already done that. This one is for Sybil, so shall I send her your love?'

'Please, and tell her I will write soon.'

'Okay. You've been a long time.'

'It's a lovely day so I went for a longer walk than usual.'

At that moment Ricky and Sandy arrived.

'Good, you're still up.' Sandy sat on Luke's bed. 'We're too keyed up to sleep yet, so we thought a game of darts might relax us.'

'Worth a try.' Luke put his letters in a drawer and stood up. 'What about you, Steve?'

'Why not.' He hauled himself out of the chair. 'I could do with a cup of tea and a bun as well.'

The four of them ambled over to the NAAFI and spent an hour seeing who could make the highest score. Ricky actually hit one hundred and eighty, which was a complete fluke, though he insisted it was skill.

Making their way back to their quarters they were all relaxed and laughing, ready to sleep and prepare themselves for another mission.

In the few minutes before drifting off to sleep, Steve's mind turned to his walk with Nancy. It was going to be very hard to leave her, but he knew he was going to have to. However, he was determined the parting wouldn't be permanent. He would find a way for them to be together. There was still time before decisions had to be made. The invasion was due to be launched soon. It wasn't going to be a quick victory, though, but victory it had to be, and they would all be playing their part in its success.

Chapter Twenty

It had been one hell of a bombing run, but they had come out of it without damage. They couldn't relax, though, until they were in sight of England.

'Fighters!' the rear gunner yelled as he opened fire, 'lots of them!'

There were thuds as the plane was hit many times and someone swore – then there was silence as the communications went down. The attack was brief but deadly as one Lancaster went down and others were damaged.

They began to veer off course and Luke called, 'Hold her steady, Steve.'

When there was no response, he studied his friend. He was still flying the plane but with obvious difficulty. Luke swivelled round to Ricky in the navigator's seat behind the pilot and saw he was slumped down and unconscious with blood running down his face. As much as he wanted to help him, they needed a pilot to get them home, and there was definitely something wrong with Steve.

'You're off course!' he shouted. 'The engines aren't damaged, she'll still fly. Come on, Steve, you can do it.'

Just then another Lancaster took up position in front of them. 'Steve, follow that plane. It will guide us back.'

He didn't know if Steve was hearing him and he watched carefully, then breathed out in a gasp of relief when he saw their course adjusted to follow the other plane. He was unable to find out how the rest of the crew were because their system had been knocked out. His job was to try and keep Steve conscious.

He kept talking, shouting instructions and encouragement, and although Steve never replied in any way, they remained on the other Lancaster's tail all the way back.

The guiding plane peeled off when they were approaching the airfield. Now all Luke could do was try to make Steve understand they now had to land – and pray. He could see his friend was in a bad way and fighting with all his might to remain in control of the plane. He touched the pocket with the lucky symbols in it.

'The airfield is in sight, Steve. Get us down. You can do it!' They began to lose height for the landing, but they were coming in much too fast. 'You're going to overshoot!' he shouted at the top of his voice.

The engines roared and they climbed.

The second approach the speed was better, and Luke knew they had to make it this time because, from the look of Steve, there wasn't going to be a third try.

They hit the ground with such force that the wheels buckled and the plane began to career all over the place.

'Brake! Brake!'

The moment they came to a stop, Luke released his harness and grabbed hold of Steve, who was now slumped in his seat.

It looked as if he had died the moment they hit the ground. 'Somebody get the door open. I need help up here.'

He heard the door crash open and Andy appeared. 'Get Ricky out and someone help me with Steve.'

One of the medics shouted for them to come out. 'Leave this to us, sirs.'

There were willing hands helping them out and once the way was clear the medics climbed into the plane.

'Where are the others?' Luke tried to run back to the plane and check, but he was told firmly to stay where he was as he would only hamper the rescuers. There was a look of horror on his face as he studied his blood-soaked hands and jacket. Andy was in the same state from trying to help their injured friends. 'There can't be only two of us unhurt, surely?'

'The wireless operator is dead, and I don't know about the gunners, but I suspect they didn't stand a chance.'

Ricky was brought out first and put in an ambulance, then Steve, who was also rushed away to hospital. A medic came over to them. 'Your pilot and navigator are alive, but the pilot is in a bad way. The wireless operator and one gunner are dead and the other so badly injured it is doubtful if he will survive.

Luke bowed his head in grief. He looked helplessly at Steve's blood covering his hands and clothes. 'Dear God, he's hit bad.'

'You helped. I could hear you shouting at him all the time. You kept him functioning enough to get us back.' Andy choked back a sob.

'Come with us, sirs.' A medic led them towards an ambulance.

Before they got in, Sandy rushed over. 'I'll come to the

hospital as soon as I've finished debriefing. Are Steve and Ricky still alive?' he asked urgently.

Luke just shook his head. 'We don't know yet. Ricky was unconscious all the way, but Steve got us down before he collapsed.'

'I saw you get hit and needed help so I flew in front, hoping you would be able to follow me.'

'That was you?'

Sandy nodded.

'That was just what we needed. It gave Steve something to focus on.'

'Glad it helped.' He squeezed Luke's arm. What about the rest of your crew?'

'Two dead for sure,' Andy told him.

Sandy swore before saying, 'I'll see you at the hospital.'

Luke and Andy climbed into the waiting ambulance and were sped off to the hospital.

This was one morning when Nancy and Jean were on early duties and had witnessed the drama unfolding.

'Oh, dear Lord, they brought out bodies. Only two of that crew were standing. Who were they, Nancy, did you see?'

Her face was ashen when she lowered her binoculars. 'That was Luke and Andy.'

'I want to know if the others are alive.' Jean lifted her tear-stained face and took off after someone. 'Sandy!' She caught him as he reached the building. 'How bad is it?'

There was a hint of moisture in his eyes and he just shook his head, unable to tell her.

Nancy rushed up to her. 'What did he say?'

'Nothing.'

'What do you mean – nothing?'

'It must be very bad if he wasn't able to talk about it.' Jean fought back a sob.

This was too much for Nancy and she snapped. 'I was wrong! So wrong,' she cried in despair. 'I convinced myself that if I kept our relationship friendly it wouldn't be so painful when this day arrived. I never told him how much I loved him, and now I'll never have the chance to tell him.'

Jean straightened up and wiped away her own tears. 'All we can do now is wait for news,' she told her gently, fighting to keep her own emotions in check. 'One of those carried out was obviously Steve, but nobody else could have landed the plane, so he must have been alive when they came down . . .'

Jean's voice had calmed Nancy's troubled thoughts. 'Luke and Andy are alive, and they are going to need our help. I'm off duty this afternoon, so if you are free, we can go then.'

'I'll get time off.'

'I'd better contact the hospital first to find out when we can visit, though.'

'I'll do that. Wait here.' Jean ran to her office.

She was soon back and clearly distressed. 'The sister I spoke to said we will not be allowed to visit as those that survived are too ill to receive visitors.'

The word 'survived' went through Nancy like a knife, and she had to force the next question out. 'How many are dead, and who?'

'She wouldn't tell me. You know they're not allowed to give out information unless it's to close family.'

Nancy pointed across the field to Steve's ground crew, standing by the Lancaster, and took off at once. 'I'll see if Sarge knows anything.'

When she reached them and saw their grim expressions she felt like turning round and running away, but they had to know. 'Sarge, can you tell me . . .' Her words tailed off when she saw the damage the enemy fighter had done. It was right along the fuselage, but the worst was where the pilot and navigator sat. She didn't dare look at the vulnerable gunner positions. Taking a deep breath, she steadied herself for the bad news she had no doubt was coming. 'You were here when they got the crew off, so do you know who survived?'

'Oh, my God!' Jean joined them, her face as white as a sheet.

'Sarge?' Nancy urged.

'All I can tell you is that only two of the crew were standing – Luke and Andy.'

'But Steve must have landed the plane, surely? No one else could have done it,' Nancy said hopefully.

'He did, but it looked as if once the plane was down, he died.'

'And the rest?' Jean's voice was trembling.

'We don't know. The medics were there straight away and wouldn't let us help get everyone out. There didn't appear to be any danger of fire, so they could be careful with the casualties. I'm sorry, girls, but from what we have seen inside and outside of the plane I wouldn't hold out much hope for any of them.

The distressed girls nodded and held each other for support as they staggered away in shock.

Luke and Andy were checked over and cleaned up when they reached the hospital. When told they could return to base and rest for a couple of days, they both protested vehemently; they weren't leaving until they knew how their friends were.

Ricky, Steve and Eddie were all in surgery, so, armed with cups of sweet tea, they waited.

Ricky was brought out first and they pulled up chairs to sit by his bed. Most of the damage was to his right leg, but he had been hit on the side of the head by something.

The sister gave them a stern look. 'You really shouldn't be here. We will take good care of your friends. Go back to your quarters and get some rest.'

'We're staying,' they declared together.

Another hour passed and then a doctor came up to them. 'I'm sorry to have to tell you that your gunner died on the operating table. There was nothing we could do to save him.'

'What about our pilot?'

'He's still in surgery.' His expression was grim as he walked away. He'd seen too much of this carnage over the years of war.

Luke laid his hand gently on Ricky's arm and studied him. His head was bandaged and there was a cage over his legs to take off any pressure from the bedclothes, but his breathing was deep and steady. A good sign.

They lost track of time as they waited for news about Steve, but suddenly Andy was on his feet watching a bed being wheeled in. 'It's Steve! He's still alive.'

Sister caught them as they made a rush over to see their friend. 'Sit down! You can see him when the doctors have finished, and he's settled comfortably.'

A curtain was pulled across and they couldn't see what was going on, but after an anxious wait it was drawn back.

'How is he?' Luke asked, as they drew up chairs and sat beside the bed.

'He has survived the surgery, but the next few hours will be critical.'

At that moment Robert Jackman strode in, and after checking on the patients he turned to Luke and Andy. 'The commander is waiting for you to attend a debriefing.'

Luke gazed at him in astonishment. 'You're joking, right?'

'Sorry, but you know it has to be done.'

Andy hauled himself out of a chair. 'Come on, Luke, let's get this over with, then we can come back.'

Robert had come by car and they were soon driving through the gates of the airfield.

'Sit down,' the commander ordered. His expression was grim as he studied the two exhausted men in front of him. 'Tell me exactly what happened.'

Painful as it was, Luke related the fighter attack. Andy also explained it from his position, and when finished they were both drained.

The officer had been making notes and threw his pen down. 'You've acted bravely, and the courage needed to get back here is of the highest. I shall be putting you all through for a commendation. Now, get something to eat and then sleep.'

'We'll do that later, sir. We must get back to the hospital,' Andy explained.

'That wasn't a request, it was an order. You are not to leave the base until after dinner tonight. I am in touch with the hospital, and if there are any changes in their conditions you will be informed at once. The pair of you can hardly stand up.' Then he said quietly. 'I know how you feel – I've seen it many times before, but Allard got you down. Don't dishonour his supreme effort by collapsing. If he pulls through it will give him some comfort to know that at least two of you are fit and well.'

Put like that, they couldn't argue. They were not going to

be any use to Steve and Ricky if they didn't do as they were ordered.

'I don't know if I can eat,' Andy remarked as they walked into the mess.

'Nor me, but we had better try.'

They sat at their usual table and lit up cigarettes while they waited for the belated breakfast.

Back in their rooms they agreed to meet for dinner.

Luke only removed his shoes before falling onto his pillows, turning his back on Steve's empty bed. He couldn't look at it. His nerves were in tatters and all he could do was escape into the oblivion of sleep for a while.

The sergeant leant on the stores counter and beckoned Nancy over. 'I've just seen Wing Commander Jackman and he told me that Ricky and Steve are alive and out of surgery but—' He held up a hand when he saw her face flood with relief. 'Ricky is not in too much danger, though they are concerned about his head wound, but Steve is critical, and the next few hours will tell if he is going to survive.'

A knot formed in her throat, but she managed to speak. 'What about the others?'

'Eddie died at the hospital and the other two were killed in the air. Only Luke and Andy have come out of that attack unhurt. Sorry it's such bad news, but I knew you would be anxious to know. Will you tell Jean?'

'I'll see her now, and thank you for letting me know. We wanted to go straight to the hospital, but visitors are not allowed yet.'

'I was told the same thing. Damn it. They were fine lads.'

'Colin,' she called as soon as Sarge left. 'I have an errand to run and will be about half an hour.'

He waved acknowledgement and she hurried out. She wasn't looking forward to giving her friend the news, but at least Ricky and Steve were still alive, and that was something to cling on to.

Chapter Twenty-One

'Any change?' Luke asked the moment they walked back into the ward.

'No, their condition is still the same.' She smiled at them. 'You two look more rested.'

Yes, we were ordered to eat and sleep,' Andy explained.

'That was just what you needed. You may stay for as long as you like.'

'Thank you, Sister.'

There was a chair by each bed, and they settled down, determined to stay all night if necessary. Neither felt like talking, so they remained silent, each lost in their own thoughts.

After about an hour a nurse brought them a cup of tea, and Sandy arrived just in time to cadge one as well. He borrowed another chair and the three of them waited, keeping a silent vigil on their friends. They were just dozing off when something brought them wide awake. A stream of expletives coming from one bed had them shooting to their feet, leaning over Ricky. His eyes were still closed, but his language was inventive.

'That's it, mate,' Andy told him. 'You bloody well let rip.'

'Sister!' Luke called. 'I think he's coming round.'

After checking him over she gave the hint of a smile. 'My goodness, he is cross.'

'That's a polite way of putting it. His language is only this bad when somebody shoots at him.'

'I'll send for the doctor.'

When she left, Luke touched his arm. 'Ricky, can you hear me?'

One eye opened, then the other and he looked around, rather confused. Slowly the memory returned, and he turned his head towards the other bed, grabbing Luke's arm in surprise. 'What the hell is Steve doing here?'

'He's badly hurt,' Andy told him.

'Was it a rough landing, then?'

'It was, but he was injured in the fighter attack.'

'Who landed us, then?'

'Steve did, but he'd lost a lot of blood and collapsed once we were down.'

Ricky laid his head back and screwed his eyes shut. 'How bad is he?'

'It's touch and go,' Andy replied.

He was going to ask more questions, but fortunately the doctor arrived and made them move away. It appeared that Ricky was going to be all right, but they waited anxiously for the doctor's verdict.

They were by Steve's bed and Andy reached out and gripped his arm. 'Come on, mate, keep fighting.

The doctor finished his check on Ricky and stood beside them, studying the still figure of Steve. 'Your friend in the other bed will make a full recovery. It was the head wound we were concerned about, but there doesn't appear to be any lasting damage. A few days' rest and he will be up and about again – on crutches, of course.'

'That's a relief, but what about Steve, Doctor?' they wanted to know.

'He was hit several times, but fortunately no vital organs were damaged. One was close to his heart and another couple of inches and he would have died instantly.'

'Along with all of us.'

The doctor nodded to Andy. 'I understand he continued to fly.'

Luke shook his head in disbelief. 'I don't know how. I shouted all the time to keep him with us. What are his chances?'

'Hard to say at this point, but he is physically strong and that is in his favour. However, the fact that he hasn't come round is worrying. Keep talking to him. Let him know you are here. All we can do now is wait.'

'Doctor?' Ricky called. 'Can I get out of bed?'

'No, you can't. You have concussion and must rest.' He gave his patient a stern look. 'So behave yourself, young man, and do as you are told.'

'That's asking the impossible.' Luke smothered a laugh, relieved to see his friend looking and acting more like himself.

'So I gather.' The doctor smirked. 'I understand he has rather a way with words.'

'Only when someone has tried to kill him,' Sandy explained, straight-faced.

'Ah well, at least it shows us that all his faculties are in good working order.' He walked away, his mouth twitching in amusement.

Ricky was leaning across his bed to get a better look at Steve. 'What did the doctor say? I didn't catch all of it.'

'They're concerned that Steve hasn't come round yet.'

'Oh, hell.' He was close to tears. 'Where are the others?'

That was the question they found hard to respond to as it was almost impossible to grasp they were no longer with them.

Seeing the trouble Luke was having in answering that, Sandy said gently, 'They're dead, Ricky.'

The shock rocked him back in the bed. 'What, all of them?'

'Yes.'

For once he was lost for words and tears began to run down his face; Andy handed him a clean handkerchief. His mouth set in a grim line as he looked across at Steve. 'We are not going to lose him as well! Steve, wake up,' he bellowed.

The sister came hurrying over. 'Stop that noise, or I will have you moved to a room by yourself.'

'Sorry, Sister, but he's got to wake up. I'm only trying to get through to him.'

'He will do that when he is ready, and shouting at him will not help.'

'Thank you. I've been shouted at enough.' A hoarse voice whispered.

All eyes turned towards Steve, not sure if the quiet words had come from there.

'He spoke. I know he did.' Ricky was struggling to get out of bed when Andy hauled him back.

Sister immediately checked to see if it had been Steve who had spoken. 'Nurse, call the doctor again.'

'Steve,' Luke said softly, 'can you hear me?'

The eyelids quivered and slowly opened, showing bright blue eyes clouded with pain.

'Welcome back. Doctor will be here in a minute. Are you in pain?'

He nodded slightly. 'Thirsty.'

'Nurse, a cup of strong sweet tea, at once,' she ordered, already holding a glass of water to his lips.

There was a rustling and muttering from the other bed and Sister gave Ricky a stern glance. 'Stop trying to get out of bed.'

'Can't move my bloody leg,' he muttered irritably.

'If you try, you will undo all the work the doctors have done, so you must remain quiet and rest it.'

'I want to talk to Steve.'

'Not at the moment. I understand how you all feel, but you must not bother him. He will talk to you when he is ready.'

A nurse arrived with the tea and held the cup to Steve's lips so he could drink. By the time the cup was drained the doctor had arrived and curtains were drawn around the bed.

They sat by Ricky and waited.

'I want to see Jean,' Ricky told them plaintively.

'I'm not sure that's a good idea. If Jean is allowed to visit, then Nancy will come with her, and do you want her to see Steve like this?'

'You underestimate her,' Andy pointed out. 'Both those girls have seen every kind of tragedy during this war, and they are tougher than you think.'

'Hm. I suppose you're right. Would you like me to arrange for them to visit, Ricky?'

'Oh, please.' He grasped Luke's arm. 'And tell Jean I'm okay and in one piece, will you?'

'I will, now rest.'

He nodded and laid his head back. 'I'll sleep when I know how Steve is.'

Eventually the curtains were pulled back and the doctor came to speak to them. 'We have given him something for the pain and he will sleep for some time. The next few hours will be critical, but now he has regained consciousness the signs are promising that he is recovering.'

Audible sighs of relief came from the friends.

'Why don't you leave now and get some needed rest? There isn't anything you can do here, so come back tomorrow and we will, hopefully, have good news for you.'

Glancing from one bed to the other told them that both patients were fast asleep, so they nodded and walked out of the ward, feeling easier now the news was better.

'Before we go, I'll ask Sister if the girls can come and visit.'

'Good idea,' Andy agreed. 'Tell her that it will help with their recovery.'

Sister listened to Luke's plea. 'Very well, tell them they can come tomorrow evening, but must not stay for more than half an hour. They both need rest and quiet.' She studied the boys in front of her and gave a hint of a smile. 'I know you think you have come through this unscathed, but there could be a delayed reaction to what has happened. If you have trouble sleeping, or feel unwell at any time, you are to come here at once. Will you do that?'

'Of course, but I'm sure that won't be necessary, I slept like a log for a few hours. And you did as well, didn't you, Andy?'

'No problems at all, but thank you for your concern. We will bring the girls with us tomorrow.'

When they walked in the NAAFI to get a drink, Nancy and Jean rushed up to them, desperate for news.

Luke explained and told them they could visit for a short time the next day.

'Oh, thanks for arranging that,' Jean told him with relief. 'We need to see them. Not knowing how they are is awful.'

'Ricky is talkative and almost his usual self but,' Andy glanced at Nancy, 'don't expect Steve to say much, if anything. They are keeping him asleep most of the time.'

'I understand. I'll just try and let him know we are there.'

'That will help, I'm sure.' Luke stifled a yawn. 'We've just come for a quick drink and then we must rest. Now the news is more hopeful I suddenly feel exhausted.'

They stayed only long enough for one drink, and then went back to their quarters.

After dinner the next day the five of them went to the hospital, and when they walked in the ward Ricky saw them immediately and waved, clearly thrilled to see all of them, and especially the girls.

He grasped Jean's hand tightly when she reached him.

'How are you feeling?' she asked after kissing him on the cheek, careful not to touch the bandaged part of his head.

'Bruised and battered, but better for seeing you.'

Turning her head, she glanced over at the other bed. Nancy was sitting in the chair, holding Steve's hand with her head bowed, praying, she was sure.

'How is Steve?' she asked Ricky quietly.

'Mostly asleep, but they told me he's doing well. All we can do is wait and hope. Tell me what you've been doing, and is there any more news about the invasion?'

'We're not allowed to stay long, and I can't tell you much. Mostly we've been worrying about all of you, and I haven't heard anything new about the invasion.'

'Once they see what a tonic you are to us, they will let you stay longer next time.'

They continued talking quietly.

'Steve,' Nancy said softly. 'I don't know if you can hear me, but I love you – we all love you and are praying for you. I want you to know that.'

'Thank you, sweetheart.'

Startled she looked up and saw his eyes were open. A smile lit up her face. 'Hello there.'

He smiled and curled his long fingers around her hand. 'I'm glad you are here. Tell Sarge I'm sorry I wrecked another one of his babies.'

Luke came forward, relieved to hear his friend joking. 'I've already done that, and he said not to worry, he'll get you another one.'

Steve had been looking at Nancy, but now he turned his head to see the other bed, then he fixed his eyes on Luke, making his heart rate increase. He knew what was coming.

'Where are the rest of the lads?'

They had been hoping to delay telling him about the others, fearing he was too ill to cope with the distressing news, but there was no avoiding it now. The steady gaze told him that, and knowing his friend, he wouldn't be put off with half an answer. So, he didn't hold back and stated plainly what had happened.

A look of anguish crossed Steve's face and he closed his eyes tightly.

'You got them back to their families, Steve, and saved the rest of us,' Andy told him firmly. 'That was one hell of a feat, and we will always be grateful to you for that. We are proud of what you did, and you should be as well.'

'I wanted to get you all down alive. The fact that I didn't is hard to take.'

'It wasn't your fault,' Ricky called across to him. 'It was over the moment those fighters riddled us with bullets. We needed you to get us back, and you did. In our eyes you're a hero. They should give you a bloody medal for what you did.'

'You say the daftest things sometimes, Ricky. Any pilot would have done the same, and it was my life I was fighting for as well. Anyway, how did you manage to survive?'

'Not a clue. Something hit me on the head, and that's the last I knew until I woke up here.'

'Ah, no damage done then.'

Ricky chuckled. 'That's more like it. You gave us a damned fright. We thought we were going to lose you as well.'

'Not a chance.' He turned his attention back to Luke, although he was clearly fighting to stay awake at this point. 'What about the funerals? We should be there.'

'I'll find out, but you won't be able to attend. I can go with Andy – Ricky, if he is mobile – and Sandy.'

'Leave it with us and we will contact the families. If they would like us there, then we will go,' Sandy told him. 'You two just concentrate on getting fit again. There's an invasion in the making.'

'Tell them to postpone it until we are flying again,' Ricky said jokingly.

Sister arrived, checked her watch and put on her stern look. 'You must all leave now. You are tiring my patients.'

'Just a little longer, please,' Ricky begged.

'Your friends can come again tomorrow, but now they must leave. The doctors are about to do their rounds.'

Before they left, Luke spoke to the sister. 'We had to give Steve the bad news about the rest of the crew. He seems to have coped with it quite well, but it hit him hard.'

'I understand, and thank you for letting me know. I will tell the doctor, and we will keep an eye on him. He is a strong, determined young man, so there is hope it won't delay his recovery.'

Sandy, Luke, Andy and the wing commander attended all the funerals, and as Steve was unable to be there, he had written to each family, praising their sons for their bravery and for being loved and respected members of the crew.

Although grieving, the families appreciated the show of respect and affection from the men they had been close to. It was distressing for all of them, but they came away feeling they had done right by their comrades.

Chapter Twenty-Two

During the next two weeks both patients made good progress, and armed with a pair of crutches, Ricky was released.

Early one morning when Steve was walking up and down the ward, he stopped to look out of the window. For early June the weather had been awful, but it looked a little better now, and he was longing to get out in the fresh air again. He was going to have to limit the distance he walked for a while, but he needed to build up his strength as quickly as possible. He hated feeling this weak.

Suddenly the ward doors burst open and his friends rushed in. They were so excited Ricky had even forgotten about using his crutches as support and was waving them in the air.

'What's happened?' he asked when he saw their smiling faces.

'It's on!' Sandy declared. 'The invasion is under way. There has been a delay because of bad weather in the Channel, but it has cleared enough for the fleet to sail.'

'That's great news.' Steve glanced around, searching for Sister, knowing she wouldn't be far away. She wasn't. 'Sister, would you please tell the doctor I want out of here today.'

'You will need to go to a convalescent home when you leave here.'

'That isn't necessary. I am perfectly fit and I must get back to base. We are all going to be needed.'

She knew it was useless to argue with this determined young man, so she gave way. 'I will see what I can do.'

'I know you can persuade him,' he told her, giving his most appealing smile.

'The nurses are going to miss you.'

Luke chuckled as she went on her errand. 'Been flirting with the nurses, have you?'

'The thought never entered my head,' he replied smoothly, sitting down on the edge of the bed. 'So, come on, tell me all the news.'

They were making so much noise talking, laughing and giving everyone the good news, including hospital staff, that they had to be told to quieten down.

When Nancy and Jean also arrived, Sister returned and sailed over to them. 'I know this is a momentous day, but it isn't visiting time and you really must leave.'

'But we've only just arrived,' Jean protested.

'I know you are all excited, but you must come back this evening.'

Ricky had a calculated glint in his eyes. 'We wouldn't have to disrupt you any more if you let Steve come with us. We'll take good care of him.'

'He can't go anywhere until the doctor says he can. Now, be on your way – all of you.'

Propping his crutches against the bed, Ricky grinned at

her. 'You can have those back now. Look, I can walk all right without them.'

He did a little dance with Jean. 'See.'

She gave a resigned smile. 'I'd be wasting my time if I told you to take it easy, wouldn't I?'

'We've got to get back to flying because the war isn't over yet.'

'I know that only too well, and as much as we like all of you, we don't want to see any of you back here again.'

'Not a chance, Sister,' Luke told her confidently, 'just so long as we can have our pilot back. We need him.'

'You know it isn't up to me to release him, but I have had a word with the doctor. He is considering it, and that is all I can do.'

'Thank you,' they all said at once, including Steve.

'Now you really must go.'

'We'll have a drink lined up for you tonight, Steve,' Andy winked at him as they were ushered out of the ward, and peace reigned once more.

Sister smiled at Steve. 'They think a lot of you.'

'We are a tight bunch who rely on each other completely when we are in the air. That kind of situation produces firm friendships.'

'I'm sure it does. Get back into bed and the doctor will be with you shortly.'

Ten minutes later he came into the ward. 'I understand you want to leave us.'

'Yes, sir. I feel quite well again. I'm grateful for everything you have done for me, but I need to get back.'

He studied the chart for a moment, and then glanced up. 'I'll release you on the understanding that you do not fly again before the beginning of next month.'

'But—' Steve began to protest and was stopped with a stern look.

'Those are my conditions, and your commanding officer will be given written notification of that. It is either that, or we send you to a convalescent home for three weeks.'

'I'll do as you say,' he replied, knowing it was useless to argue.

'Good, I'll see you each week and then decide when you are fit enough to fly one of those monsters again. I know this inactivity is hard for you, but you will be back in the air soon if you do as I tell you. I can't take any chances as you are a pilot, and you understand that, don't you? I must be sure that not only you, but the men up there with you are as safe as possible.'

'I do, and the last thing I would want is to be a danger to anyone else.'

'It's my duty to save men like you. I patch you up and then send you out to get shot at again. Remember to duck next time.'

Steve laughed, delighted at the thought of going back to base and his friends. 'When can I go?'

'As soon as the release paperwork is ready. You will feel weak and it is going to take some time for you to regain your full strength, so don't get impatient and overdo things. I'll see you in a week, and if I believe you have been pushing yourself too hard, I'll have you straight back in here. Is that clear?'

'Perfectly. I like to walk, so would that be all right?'

'Yes, but start slowly and build the distance up gradually. If you begin to feel unwell you must find somewhere to sit down for a while.'

'What about horse riding? I am sure that would help my recovery.'

'Is that something you are used to doing?'

Steve nodded. 'I have been riding ever since I could walk.'

The doctor pursed his lips in thought. 'Well, if you are an experienced rider, then it should be all right, but don't attempt it for at least another week. There are some stables nearby, so go and have a word with them.' He wrote the address down and handed it to him.

'One more question. Am I going to regain the fitness and strength I had before?'

'I don't see any reason why not, as long as you are sensible and follow instructions. When you were brought in, we feared you wouldn't live. However, when we heard that you had continued flying that plane even though badly injured, we understood that you had exhausted every bit of your strength on doing that. Now I have a question. How do you feel about flying again after what happened?'

'Can't wait.'

'Do you know, every pilot I've asked that has given me the same answer?' He sighed and shook his head. 'I'll see about your release, and then you can leave in a couple of hours.'

Eager to be on his way he began searching the bedside locker. 'Where's my uniform, Sister?' he called.

'It was beyond repair so it was burnt.'

Alarm crossed his face. 'But what about the things in the pockets?'

She held out a packet. 'We saved those, of course.'

He took it from her and emptied it out on the bed, smiling with relief when he saw the small leather wallet containing photographs of his family, and the star tokens.

'They were rather messy, but we cleaned them up for you.'

'Thank you, Sister; I wouldn't like to have lost those things. Now, how am I going to leave here without my uniform?'

'We have already sent a request that your clothes be brought here immediately.'

In less than an hour, Luke returned and dumped a bag on Steve's bed. 'That's your spare uniform, so let's get you out of here. The lads are all waiting to buy you a drink.'

'I'm supposed to take it easy.'

His friend grinned. 'That's easy; you can sit down while you drink.'

Steve raised his eyebrows at someone standing behind Luke, making him turn quickly. 'Hello, Sister, I've brought Steve's clothes.'

'And an invitation to what sounds suspiciously like a party.'

'Oh no, it's just a friendly drink to welcome our pilot back.'

'You make sure it is,' she warned. 'Only one drink, young man.'

'He never drinks much, so don't worry, Sister, we'll take good care of him.'

Looking completely unconvinced, she gave them both another stern look and walked away.

'They wanted to send me to a convalescent home,' Steve said as he dressed.

'What a terrible thought.' Luke helped him fasten the buttons on the jacket. 'Quick, let's get you out of here before they change their minds.'

Straightening to his full height, Steve put on his hat and they made their way out of the hospital. He had expected to catch a bus, but there was a car waiting outside, and he smiled when he saw the driver.

Sarge opened the door with a flourish. 'Good to see you. Your transport awaits, sir.'

'Thanks, and it's good to see you as well. I didn't expect this, though.'

'We've got to look after you.' Sarge got in and drove away from the hospital.

'Have you got me another Lancaster?' he asked.

'It's ready and waiting, and is a real beauty – one of the latest.'

'Great, I'll have a look at it tomorrow.'

'Steve, they are not going to let you fly just yet,' Luke pointed out.

'I know, and I wouldn't attempt it until I have my strength back, but I can look and have a sit in her. Just to see how she feels.'

Both men agreed that would be permissible.

They drew right up outside the NAAFI and Steve frowned. 'I'll have to check in first.'

'You can do that later.' Luke got out and opened the door, watching carefully as his friend eased himself carefully out of the car and stood up. 'All right?'

'Fine.'

With Luke and Sarge either side of him they walked in, and a cheer rang out as everyone rushed up to welcome him back.

Much to his surprise the base commander was there as well as Wing Commander Jackman. They came up and shook his hand, clearly pleased to see him. He found the outpouring of affection touching and completely unexpected. He glanced over the top of the men crowding round him and saw Nancy standing back and smiling. He motioned with his head to beckon her over. It wasn't easy getting through the crush, but she managed it just as Sandy made him sit down. He held on to the next chair for Nancy. The tables were pulled together, so they could all sit round.

The commander brought the first round of drinks, and when he put a small beer in front of Steve, he said, 'Don't let these men keep you late. Come and see me tomorrow afternoon, and take it easy.'

'I will, sir, and thank you for the welcome back beer.'

'Right, quiet everyone,' Andy called as soon as the commander left. 'To show how pleased we are to have our friend back amongst us, we have arranged a little treat for him.'

Ricky appeared and placed a plate in front of him with great ceremony.

'What's this?'

'A fried-egg sandwich. We've got to build you up.'

'A real egg?'

Ricky grinned and nodded. 'Two, in fact, so eat up before it gets cold.'

He did and enjoyed every mouthful. 'That was great, thanks a lot.'

'We tried to get you a steak,' Sandy explained, 'but it wasn't possible.'

'I enjoyed that just as much. We often have a fried-egg sandwich for breakfast at home.'

They sat around talking and after an hour Steve began to feel very tired. Although he was surrounded by so many friends, he was conscious of the three missing from the group. It must have shown on his face because Luke stood up and extended a hand to help him out of the chair. 'That's enough for tonight, Steve.'

He nodded and touched Nancy's shoulder. 'Walk me back to my quarters.'

She stood beside him and he smiled at everyone. 'Thanks for the welcome. It's great to be back.'

When they were outside, he tucked her hand through his arm, and they walked slowly, enjoying the warm evening. He didn't want to talk, and she was sensitive enough to know that.

On reaching the building he stopped and gazed up at the stars, then gathered her into his arms. When she didn't protest, he stayed like that for a few moments, then kissed the top of her head and stepped back. 'Goodnight, Nancy. Sleep well.' Without another word he walked into his quarters.

She saw Luke coming towards her, so she waited.

'Is he all right?' he asked immediately.

'I think so.'

He studied her face carefully. 'Why the worried expression? What's wrong?'

She shrugged. 'He's different. Not easy to explain, but it's as if his emotions are closer to the surface. Something inside him has changed. Does that make sense?'

'It does, and we've all changed, Nancy. We lost three of our friends, and that's hard to take. None of us are going to come out of this the same. Steve nearly died.'

'You're right, of course.' She smiled up at him. 'You all take care of each other, and if there is anything you need you can come to me and Jean.'

'Thanks, but you needn't worry about us. Once we are all fit, we will be back up there again. Nothing will stop us flying.'

'I know, and that's what worries me. I'm praying for a quick end to the war now.'

Luke shook his head. 'Don't bank on it. We may be moving into France, but there is a hell of a long way to go, and the bombing missions will start again soon. We will be a part of it as soon as Steve and Ricky are fit enough.'

'You bet we will.' Ricky joined them with his arm around Jean.

'It won't be for a while yet,' Jean pointed out. 'They're not going to allow Steve to fly again until the doctors pass him as fit enough, unless you plan on going with another pilot.'

Both men looked horrified, and Luke said, 'I for one will not leave the ground unless Steve is at the controls.'

'Nor me.' Ricky kissed Jean on the nose, smiled at Nancy, and then took hold of Luke's arm. 'Come on, pal, let's make sure Steve is okay.'

'Night girls.'

They entered the room quietly and nodded in satisfaction when they saw their friend was sound asleep.

'Everything all right?' whispered Sandy as he looked in the door.

'He's fast asleep.'

'Good. Luke, you call me if you need anything.' Then he left with Ricky, closing the door quietly behind them.

Steve slept right through until lunchtime, and then reported to the commander. He was told he could come and go as he pleased, and to see the medics at the first sign of any discomfort.

It was a pleasant day, so he left the base and walked. He had only been out for half an hour, and much to his frustration he had to stop and rest twice. He had never felt so weak in his life, but his focus was on getting back in the air again. It was abundantly clear it was going to take time, and as much as he wanted to speed up the process, it would be foolish to push himself too much and cause damage that could put his recovery back. He mustn't do anything to jeopardise his chances of a full recovery.

He walked a little further to a small tea shop, ordered a pot of tea, and spent a pleasant time talking to some locals. Feeling refreshed, he began to make his way back, stopping by a field to watch sheep grazing, who took no notice of the tall man leaning on the five-barred gate. Two rabbits shot out of bushes close by, stopped and looked at him, then turned and disappeared again, bringing a smile to his face.

There was one more thing he wanted to do, and then he would rest until it was time for dinner. Back on the base he went in search of Sarge, finding him in one of the hangars. 'Where's my new Lancaster?' he asked.

'Out on the field. Come with me.' The sergeant moderated his stride to match Steve's slow pace. 'There she is; the latest model.'

He walked round stroking his hands over the beautiful plane and nodded. 'You're right, she is magnificent. I want to have a look inside.'

'Er . . . are you fit enough to do that?'

'I'll be careful.' He climbed in and went straight for the pilot's seat.

Sarge was right behind him and sat in the flight engineer's position. 'You'll notice quite a few improvements.'

Steve grinned as he ran his hands over the controls. 'How many new ones have arrived?'

'Four.'

'Good, keep one for me.' A look of determination glowed in his eyes. 'I'll be fit for duty in four weeks.'

'That's very specific,' Sarge remarked. 'You've set yourself a tough target.'

He nodded. 'I know, but setting a time limit is something to work towards.'

After climbing out he gave the plane an affectionate pat,

and then went to have a rest. He was pleased with what he had accomplished that day. They were small steps forward, but he was on his way.

Chapter Twenty-Three

Steve went for a walk every morning, going a little further each day. Rain or shine he was out. The little tea room was at the halfway mark of his walk, and he always stopped there on his way back for a pot of tea.

'You are becoming quite a regular, young man,' the woman who served him said.

'Yes, ma'am. I take this route because I like to have a break, and you make excellent tea.'

She smiled at the compliment. 'The Yanks always want coffee, but you seem to enjoy tea.'

'I'm Canadian and my mother is English.'

'Really, well that accounts for it, then. Would you like some toast as well? You look as if you need building up.'

'Yes, I'm recovering from a stay in hospital.'

She had more sense than to ask what he was recovering from. 'That's good. You're from the base down the road, aren't you?'

He nodded.

'We hear the planes taking off at night and they fairly shake the house. They are huge great things and it's a wonder they are able to leave the ground.' She was looking at the wings on his chest, clearly wanting to ask more questions, but knew she wouldn't get any answers if she did. 'I'll get you that toast.'

Fortified with tea and four slices of toast, he left with a smile on his face. He was seeing the doctor tomorrow morning and was going to ask him if it would be all right for him to ride now. He had made progress in only a short time, so it was time to visit the stables in anticipation of that verdict. His heart soared at the thought of being on a horse again, and he was certain it would be the best way to regain his strength and fitness.

When he walked into the yard, curious eyes fixed on him – and they weren't all human. He breathed in the familiar smells reminding him so much of home, and stopped to enjoy the moment.

'Can I help you, young man?'

Steve smiled at the man he guessed was the owner. 'I would like to hire one of your horses to ride every day. An hour at first, but then for longer.'

'For a week or two weeks?'

'Until I am fully fit again. The doctor at the hospital suggested I come and see you.'

'Ah, been ill, have you?'

'Injured.'

The man held out his hand. 'I'm Charles Grayson, and I own these stables.'

'Steve Allard.'

'Nice to meet you, Steve. Are you an experienced rider, or will you need instruction?'

'I have been riding all my life.'

'Splendid.' He looked Steve up and down, assessing his height and weight. 'We will have to find you a strong animal. Come with me, and see which one you fancy.'

They walked along the stalls until Steve stopped and stroked the nose of a chestnut stallion. 'What about this one? He's a fine sturdy animal.'

'That's Ginger and he can be a bit difficult to handle.'

Steve was in the stall now and examining the horse who took exception to it and gave him a shove. 'Like your own way, do you? Well, let's get this clear from the start – I'm in charge and you do as I say.'

Charles laughed softly and called a stable lad over. 'Saddle up Ginger.'

'Yes, sir.'

They waited outside and Charles said, 'Walk him round the field so I can see if you can handle him.'

The horse was brought out and Steve paused for a moment, wondering if he would be able to mount all right. His movements were still restricted and it was a tall animal.

Charles noticed the hesitation. 'Bring the mounting block.'

The lad hurried away, and Steve grimaced at the thought of resorting to such a thing.

'There's no shame in it, and I'm sure you will soon be leaping into the saddle. Just take your time.'

Once in the saddle he urged the stallion into the field. He knew he shouldn't be doing this until the doctor gave him permission, but hell, it felt so good to be riding again. As long as he didn't set off at a mad gallop it should be okay.

First he walked the horse until it began to obey him, then they trotted and he made the animal weave and turn as he did at home. Aware he mustn't overdo it, he dismounted and led Ginger back to his owner.

'You sit well and know how to control a horse. Ginger will be ready for you. When do you want to start?'

'Tomorrow afternoon at three o'clock, if that is all right with you?'

'That will be fine. Look forward to seeing you then.'

The doctor was pleased with Steve's progress and gave him permission to ride, but he didn't get away without a firm talking to.

'Charles is a friend of mine and guessed I had advised you to see his stables, so he paid me a visit last night. I told you to wait until you saw me again before getting on a horse.'

'I wasn't on it for more than ten minutes,' he protested.

'So I understand.' He sat back again. 'Charles told me you appear to be a fine horseman, and you ride like a cowboy. Even though that was the first time on that animal you had complete control of him.'

'That was the way I was taught, and I'm sure the exercise will speed my recovery. So, do I have your permission?'

'Considering you have booked for this afternoon, I've got to trust you to be sensible, but I'm sure you will. You don't come across as the foolhardy type.'

'I'm not, and you can be certain I won't do anything to impede my full recovery.'

The doctor stood up and extended his hand. 'Don't start rounding up cattle, will you?'

'I'll try to curb the temptation.' He left, elated. With walking and now riding every day he should soon get back in shape.

He set a strict routine for the next three weeks. Walking in the morning, eating, riding in the afternoon, and sleeping, which left no time for socialising. If he went for a drink, he never stayed for more than an hour, and he hadn't touched a cigarette since he had been injured. His whole attention was on fitness. During this time there were frustrations and small triumphs, one of these being when he no longer needed the mounting block and could swing himself into the saddle with ease.

The prediction had been that he would be grounded for at least eight weeks, but he was damned well not going to be. He was due another check-up and he was determined to get signed off then. This dedicated regime of activity had done its job and he was back to normal.

There was a large empty field right next to the stables and he guided Ginger in there. 'Come on, boy; let's see what you can do.'

They thundered along and he shouted out in pure joy, oblivious to the people watching.

There was a broad smile on his face as he returned to the stables, and leaping off he handed Ginger over to the lad. 'He'll need a good rub down.'

'Yes, sir.' The boy gazed at him in something close to adoration. 'Gosh, you really can ride, sir. Just like the cowboys in the pictures.'

Charles came over to him. 'That was an impressive piece of horsemanship. I'd say you're fully fit now.'

'I'm hoping for a clean bill of health tomorrow, and if so, I won't be able to come very often in future.'

'You come along any time you are free.'

'Thanks, the riding has been a tremendous help.'

The walk back turned into a trot and then he was running, revelling in the feeling of strength in his legs and body again. There had been a niggling doubt that he would ever reach this stage again, but he had come through. The thought of spending time with Nancy again filled him with pleasure. She had quietly supported him over the last few weeks, never intruding, but letting him know she was there if he needed her. He was still a bit hazy about what she had said to him at the hospital, but he thought she had told him she loved him, and that had helped him fight to regain his full fitness again.

Nancy and Jean watched Steve jog through the gates, head high and the smooth elegant movement back.

'Just look at that,' Jean remarked. 'Fully fit and moving like a panther, the way he used to.'

Sarge came over and joined them. 'The speed of his recovery is remarkable.'

'His entire attention has been on getting fit enough to fly again,' Nancy said. 'He's been leaving the base every morning, and again in the afternoon, only appearing for an hour in the evening. He hasn't talked about what he's been doing, and I don't think even his friends know. So goodness knows what he's been up to. We have hardly seen him.'

'He's a determined person,' Jean pointed out to her friend. 'Now Ricky has been declared fit for action again, I suspect that spurred him on. They all want to get back in the air together again.'

Sarge nodded. 'He often comes and sits in a Lancaster, and you ought to see his face when he settles in the pilot's seat. That boy has got to fly, and nothing is going to stop him.'

'He's so like my brother in that way. I don't understand why they want to fly into danger. I was close to Dan, and when I asked what was so wonderful about guiding a huge lump of metal into the air, he would laugh and promise to take me up one day so I could experience it for myself. He never got the chance, of course.'

'Pilots like your brother and Steve are a special breed, and that includes all the pilots engaged in this conflict. This war must be won to preserve our way of life, and they are fighting like mad to help in the struggle to keep our freedom.'

'And die trying, Sarge.'

He gave Nancy a sympathetic glance. 'I'm sorry to say that is so, and I'm surprised to see you girls have become so close to them.'

Jean's smile was wry. 'We did try not to, but the heart wants what it wants, and before we knew what was happening, they had wormed their way into our lives.'

'That can happen. Ah, looks as if he's heading for the planes. I had better keep an eye on him or he will be starting up the engines and going for a ride around the field.' Sarge hurried off, chuckling as he went.

Steve was standing by a Lancaster, and he turned to smile at Sarge as he arrived. 'I'm going to take her up soon.'

'Not until you get a chitty from the doctor saying you can.'

'I'll have that tomorrow.'

'You sound very sure of that.'

'I am.'

'The doctor might have other ideas.'

'Then I'll change his mind.' He glanced at his watch. 'Time to eat; I'm starving.'

Watching him hurry away, Sarge shook his head in amusement. No ifs or buts, he was going to fly soon, and that was certain. The doctor was about to meet an unmoveable force.

Steve's friends were already in the mess and he joined them. 'Get ready to fly again soon. Only a training run at first, of course.'

Ricky nearly choked on a mouthful of tea. 'Who are we flying with?'

'Me.'

All eyes turned on him in astonishment.

'Have you been signed off as fit already?' Luke asked.

'Not yet, but I'm seeing the doctor tomorrow. He'll see I've completely recovered now.'

'Steve, we know you have been working hard, but don't you think this is hoping for too much. They did say it would be around eight weeks before you could fly again,' Luke reminded him.

'They were wrong. I'm in good shape now and won't take no for an answer.'

'Er . . .' Andy cleared his throat. 'Does the commander know about this?'

'I'll tell him when I get back from the hospital. He knows it is absolutely essential that we get back in the air, and once I'm signed off, he will want us prepared for what is to come.'

Ricky grinned in anticipation. 'Well, if anyone can get us on active service again, it's you.'

'That's what we all want.' Luke raised his glass of water. 'I say we drink to that. We are getting fed up with being grounded. Good luck tomorrow, Steve. We are with you.'

They all wholeheartedly agreed with that.

'Nancy said you had changed,' Luke told him. 'And do you know, she was right.'

'I expect I have, but haven't we all?'

He wasn't due at the hospital until eleven o'clock, so he went for his usual walk, and arrived in good time for his appointment.

The examination took longer than usual, and he wondered what on earth they were looking for. When he was eventually told to get dressed again, he watched the doctor poring over his notes, and a little concern crept in. He had been so sure he would be given a clean bill of health, so what was the problem?

Unable to stand the silence any longer, he said, 'I am back to full health, sir.'

'I can't deny that.' The doctor studied the tall boy in front of him radiating health and vigour, and shook his head. 'You have made a remarkably fast and complete recovery, but you are a strong young man, and I suspect that has been your saviour.'

He let out a silent breath of relief and nodded. 'So, will you sign me as fit for duty again?'

'I would like to delay that for at least another week.'

'Why? You didn't find anything wrong with me, did you?'

'Not a thing.'

'Then sign the papers, please. There is still a war to be won, and we want to get back to helping with that.'

'I don't have any legitimate reason for not releasing you, but you must promise me that if you experience any problems, no matter how small, you are to come and see me at once.'

'I promise to do that.'

He nodded, picked up his pen and signed the release papers in front of him. 'I'll send this to your base commander.'

'I'll take it with me, if that is all right.'

The paper was handed over and the doctor shook his hand. 'It's been a pleasure to see you recover so quickly, and against our expectations. To be honest, at first we thought your flying career was over.'

'Not a chance,' he declared with certainty. 'It's due to your excellent care that I have recovered so well, and I thank you for that.'

'You take care now. We are in the last stages of this war, so you keep safe.'

'I will.' He strode out with a huge smile on his face, clutching the document he had worked so hard for.

The first thing he did when he was back at the base was to hand in the document, and then he head for the mess. He saw Sarge nearby and gave him the thumbs-up sign, receiving the same back.

'How did you get on?' Ricky asked the moment he joined them and sat down.

'I'm fit for duty.'

Everyone was delighted with the news, and Steve settled down to enjoy lunch.

They had just finished lunch when they were told the commander wanted to see Steve, Luke, Sandy, Ricky and Andy.

'What, all of us?' Luke asked the messenger.

'Yes, and at once, please, sirs.'

Sandy grinned as they stood up. 'What have we been up to?'

'Nothing we shouldn't have – I think,' Andy replied. 'It's a bit puzzling he wants to see all of us, though.'

The office door was open as usual, so Luke tapped on it and they walked in, standing in a smart line in front of the desk.

The commander glanced up and the corners of his mouth twitched. 'Relax, gentlemen, I have good news for you. First, I must congratulate you, Allard, on your speedy recovery.'

'Thank you, sir.'

'I have the pleasant duty to inform you that all of you have been given awards. The Air Force Cross to Allard's crew – sadly three of them will be posthumous awards, but we hope the families will see how proud of them we are.' He then turned his attention to Sandy. 'For your bravery in guiding the stricken plane back although under attack, you are also to be given the Air Force Cross. Allard, for bringing that plane and your crew back although gravely injured yourself, you have been awarded the Distinguished Flying Cross, and promoted to squadron leader. Congratulations, gentlemen. That was a feat of extreme courage by all of you, and you deserve to have the achievement recognised.'

Steve was speechless. He hadn't expected this, and by the stunned expressions on his friends' faces, neither had they.

'There will be a ceremony tomorrow afternoon when the medals will be officially presented.'

'Thank you, sir,' they said in unison.

'Now to business. I have found you two gunners and a wireless operator to complete your crew. They are good men but inexperienced, so you will take them on training runs, and that will give you a chance to get to know each other. We have the luxury of a little time before missions begin again and I want us to make the most of it.'

There was a knock on the door and three young men were ushered in. They were only a year or two younger than the Canadians, but there the comparisons ended. Steve couldn't help wondering if they had looked like that when they had just arrived, untouched by battle experience.

The commander was on his feet and came to stand by Steve. 'Squadron Leader, these men have been assigned to complete your crew, and I suggest you all go to the NAAFI and get to know each other. You start your training runs tomorrow, early morning. You are dismissed.'

Steve smiled at the boys who hadn't taken their eyes off him. 'Let's go and get a drink – tea, of course.'

The moment they were outside the grins appeared, and Sandy left them to get acquainted with their new crew members. Because of the lads with them, they didn't mention anything about the awards, or Steve's promotion. The teasing would come later.

The NAAFI wasn't too busy, so they pulled two tables together and all sat round. The youngest of the boys seemed fascinated by Steve.

'It's an honour to join your crew, sir,' he said.

Ricky laughed and slapped him on the back. 'You might change your mind about that after he dumps you in a field full of cabbages.'

'Ah, but it was a nice field.' Luke joined in the fun.

'We heard about that, sir,' another one said.

'There you are, Steve, you are notorious.'

'Hey, that's a good word, Andy. He is so notorious he gets us a medal.'

Steve listened to the banter, his eyes glinting with amusement, pleased to see it was putting the new boys at ease. They knew darned well they were replacing men who had been killed, so this wasn't going to be easy for them. As soon as he saw them relaxing, he stepped in. 'First of all, we welcome you to our group.'

'Thank you, sir. We are pleased to join you.'

He nodded acknowledgement. 'When we are together relaxing like this, we only use first names. I am Steve and this is Luke, flight engineer, Ricky, navigator and Andy, bomb aimer. All we want now are your Christian names and your position in the crew.'

'I'm Geoff, wireless operator.'

'Jake, mid gunner.'

'Terry, rear gunner.'

'Good, be ready for a training flight in the morning, and don't be afraid to ask questions if you are doubtful about anything at all. Also, I am always around if you want someone to talk to.'

'Thank you . . . Steve,' Geoff said hesitantly.

He smiled. 'It seems strange, but you will soon get used to us.'

The three new members were nodding and smiling now. Cigarettes were handed round while they settled down to get to know each other.

After an hour they went back to their quarters and Luke closed the door before asking, 'What do you think of them?'

'They seem eager boys, but we won't know how good they are until we get them in the air.' He put his hat back on. 'I'm going for a walk.'

'Okay, but don't go far because we've got a big day tomorrow, Squadron Leader. I wonder if the girls know about this.'

'Ricky didn't come back with us, so I expect he is searching for Jean. It won't take long for the news to fly around now.'

Chapter Twenty-Four

The next morning the Lancasters were roaring into life as they prepared for a training flight. The new boys had been briefed and settled into their positions, trying to hide their nervousness, knowing they had to prove themselves worthy of flying as part of the Allard crew. There was also the added concern that they were replacing three of their friends who had been killed. It was only natural they felt the pressure, and Steve was very aware of this fact.

Steve and Luke went through their checks, then smiled at each other as they got into position for take-off.

As the plane gathered speed, Steve's excitement grew. This was where he loved to be, and the horror of the last mission could not dim his pleasure.

The flight went well, and after landing he made a point of praising the new boys, bringing smiles of relief to their faces. The next test would be to see how they performed under fire, but Steve felt confident they would do well.

After debriefing they sat around discussing the flight,

and at lunchtime went to the mess together. The youngsters couldn't stop smiling with pride.

The medal ceremony was to be held at three o'clock and best uniforms were pressed, buttons and shoes polished until you could almost see your face in them.

The commander took the salute and Steve was surprised to see Commander Grieves and Colonel Harrison there with him.

The achievements were read out as each had the awards pinned to their tunics. The three who had not survived were also honoured and the medals handed to Wing Commander Jackman, who would see the families received them personally. It was a heart-wrenching moment, but right they were honoured that way. They had paid the ultimate price, and no more could be asked of anyone.

After the parade, food and drink had been laid on and Colonel Harrison came over to Steve. 'I have people I would like you to meet.'

He was puzzled when they went to another room and saw four officers in there, one of whom was a general.

'Sirs, this is Squadron Leader Steven Allard. He is the pilot who successfully helped us out of a desperate situation.'

Steve saluted the army officers, intrigued.

The general returned the salute and smiled. 'It is a pleasure to meet you, Squadron Leader. Colonel Harrison has spoken highly of the way you carried out those missions for us. You made a vital contribution to future plans, and it is our pleasure to present you with the Distinguished Conduct Medal. Congratulations and our grateful thanks.' He stepped forward and pinned the medal next to the other one Steve had just received.

Steve saluted. This had come as a complete surprise and he was having a job to believe it was really happening. Those runs he had made must have been of the utmost importance. He had known they were urgent, of course, but to receive an award for his small part was unbelievable.

After staying for a while and talking to them, Steve made his way back to his friends, who stared in surprise at the new award, gathering round to examine it.

Luke gave him a speculative look. 'Distinguished Conduct Medal. Why would the army give you that?'

'It was for something I did for them at Tangmere, and I am as surprised as you.'

'Well, it must have been for something very special to not only give you that medal, but to let you fly a Spitfire. You can't tell us what it was for, can you?' Sandy asked.

'No, sorry.' He gave a smirk. 'They are a secretive bunch.'

Luke slapped him on the back and grabbed a drink for him, then raised his own glass. 'How on earth did four boys from Canada come to have medals pinned on their chests? All we did was fight to stay alive.'

'Damned if I know.' Sandy shook his head. 'All I did was guide you back.'

'With fighters shooting at us,' Luke pointed out. 'You could have got out of their way, but you didn't.'

'I knew it was you, and I wasn't going to leave my friends when they were in trouble. I told my crew what I wanted to do, and they all agreed we stay with you.'

'And for that we will always be grateful. I was barely functioning.' Steve pointed to the award on his friend's chest. 'You deserve that medal, and I'm so glad your part in saving us has been recognised.'

'Well, if you put it that way.' Sandy grinned at his friends. 'Wait until the folks back home hear we have been given medals.'

'I'm not going to tell them because it will probably make them worry all the more,' Steve said.

'You are right about that,' Andy agreed. 'It's best not to tell them too much, especially as you have been involved in some dodgy stuff.'

Steve took a swig of his drink and said nothing.

'Yeah, that about sums it up.' Ever hopeful, Ricky asked again. 'Can't you give us even a tiny bit of what you did for those guys?'

'Ask me in ten years' time.'

'He's going to leave us in suspense.' Ricky sighed and looked across the room. 'Where are the girls? They ought to be here as well.'

'I expect they are working. We'll see them tonight and have a party of our own.'

That brought the smile back to Ricky's face, and he beckoned to the new aircrew boys. 'Come and join us. You are part of the gang now and we're going to have one hell of a party tonight.'

Later that evening, and still in high spirits, they called on the girls and went to the local pub, which was already crowded with airmen from the base. With the first drink they raised their glasses to the three who had died – colleagues and friends who would never be forgotten. After that sombre moment of remembrance, the celebration began, and there was much to be grateful for. The award they had received, of course, but the fact that they were still alive.

As the evening progressed it became hot, smoky and boisterous, so Steve draped his arm around Nancy's shoulder and led her outside. He took a deep breath and smiled at her. 'That's better.'

'They will soon come looking for you. I think they are almost afraid to let you out of their sight now.'

He leant against the pub wall and drew her close. 'We are like brothers now, and I missed them when I went to another base. I was mostly on my own at Tangmere, but I did have time to explore the surrounding area. You have a beautiful country, so green and lush and I would like to see a lot more of it, but with the troops moving through France, the end should certainly come in early 1945. That doesn't leave much time for gadding about when we don't get a lot of free days.'

'You will be going home as soon as the war ends, then?'

Nodding, he said, 'I have to.'

'Before you leave, could you find the time to visit my parents? They would love to see you again.'

'Of course. I wouldn't dream of leaving without seeing all the people who have been so kind to us.'

'When you are home again, will you still be able to see Luke, Ricky and Sandy?'

'Certainly, we all come from various parts of Alberta, and I can always fly to meet them. We won't lose touch, and I hope we won't lose touch with you and Jean.'

'Not a chance. We shall be friends for life.'

'You know, I'm banking on us being more than friends to each other, Nancy. I can't bear the thought of being away from you, and want us to be together always.'

'I feel the same, but you know it isn't possible. You can't stay here, and I can't leave my parents. All we can do is enjoy whatever time we have together. When I thought you were dead I was distraught that I had never told you I loved you. I do, but that doesn't change anything, Steve. No matter how we feel about each other, when this war ends we are going to have to part. I wish with all my heart that things were different, but they aren't and we have to accept that.'

He shook his head. 'There has to be a way and I won't rest until I find it. I am not giving up hope, my darling. I can't.'

Just then, the pub door opened and Luke peered out.

'Hey, you two, come back and join in the party. The drinks are lined up for you.'

'Ah, that's the end of our peaceful moment together, and by the look of Luke I am going to have to put him to bed tonight.' He kissed her gently before stepping away. 'We'll talk again soon.'

Jake, Terry and Geoff were having a wonderful time, and clearly delighted to be included as part of this likeable group.

Sandy had his arm resting on Geoff's shoulder. 'How are you getting on with this crazy bunch?'

'We were nervous at first, but Steve has been encouraging and has complimented us on our performance, which was a huge relief, I can tell you.'

Terry joined them. 'To be honest, we were scared when they told us who we would be joining.'

'Why?'

'We heard a lot of stories about Steve and his crew, and we weren't sure we could live up to expectations.'

'Nonsense. They are grateful to have a full crew once more so they can fly again.'

There was a burst of laughter coming from Luke, Ricky and Jake. Sandy grinned at the two boys. 'See? There's nothing to worry about. You are part of the team now.'

'Er . . .' Geoff hesitated. 'The girls, Nancy and Jean, do they belong to anyone?'

'As Canadians far from home we have adopted them as family, but Ricky and Jean are an item, and the same goes for Nancy and Steve, I guess, so you'll have to find your own girls,' Sandy told them.

'Ah, that certainly rules them out.' Terry grinned. 'We wouldn't dare upset our pilot and navigator.'

'Sandy!' Steve called over to him. 'Try and stay reasonably sober, will you, because I think some of our friends are going to need help later on.'

'Okay.'

'Steve doesn't drink much, does he,' Geoff commented, studying the tall man.

'He never has, and he's drinking less after being in hospital.' Luke appeared beside them, swaying slightly, but still coherent. 'We help him out when he's got too many lined up.'

'From the look of you, I would say you have been helping him quite a bit tonight,' Sandy laughed.

Ricky peered over Luke's shoulder. 'There isn't anything we wouldn't do for our friend. He's one of the best, as you will find out when we are in action again.'

Someone started pounding on the piano and Ricky dragged them all over for a sing-song.

By the end of the evening everyone was still standing – just – and the two pilots managed to get them safely back to base.

Luke sat on the edge of the bed struggling to untie his shoes, so Steve knelt down to do it for him. When he looked up, he was shocked to see tears running down Luke's face. 'Hey, what's the matter?'

'It's so bloody good to have you back, Steve. When I saw you slumped in your seat with blood everywhere, I was sure we had lost you.'

'You daft thing,' he teased. 'You've had too much to drink, and you need to sleep it off.'

'I know.' He wiped a hand over his face. 'We had a good time tonight, didn't we?'

'It was great, and it helped the new boys feel they belonged.'

'Yeah, that's important.'

'Very.' Steve made sure Luke was comfortably settled in bed, and then climbed in his own. 'Night, sleep well.' But his friend was already snoring.

For the next few weeks they listened to the news, following the progress of the invading forces and flying missions to try and disrupt enemy supply lines. By October, it was clear the war wasn't going to end that year. With winter approaching that had been expected, but the end was in sight.

When they had a break, Steve took Nancy out on their own, Ricky spent much of his time with Jean, and Luke saw Sybil when he could get off base for a couple of days. They all knew their time in this country was coming to an end, and they weren't sure what was going to happen with the girls they had fallen in love with. Would they be willing to leave everything they knew and come to Canada, or were they going to have to walk away? It appeared that Jean was prepared to go with Ricky, but it was uncertain whether Sybil and Nancy would be willing to leave family and home.

After returning from his early morning walk one day, Steve found Luke looking rather dejected.

Steve shrugged out of his flying jacket. 'What's troubling you, Luke?'

His friend grimaced. 'A few more months and it will all be over.'

'Is that something to look miserable about?'

'No, it's a blessing, but what the hell are we going to do about our girls? Ricky's alright; Jean is happy to go with him

240

because she has a large family, so it's easier for her. Our two, however, are the only children their parents have.' He gave Steve a troubled look. 'How can we ask them to leave their folks and come to Canada?'

'It's complicated.' Steve sat on the other chair. 'But if we are sure they are the girls we want to spend the rest of our lives with, then we have to do all we can to keep them with us.'

'You're right, of course – but, as you say, it's complicated.'

Steve stood up and stretched. 'I know with time getting short this problem is gnawing away at us, but there is no point worrying about it just now. My mother always told us not to cross our bridges until we get to them. So, there isn't a damned thing we can do about it now, and no amount of fretting will bring a solution before its time. At the moment we still have a job to do, so let's concentrate on that.'

Without them even noticing, winter set in and Christmas was only days away.

'Hey.' Sandy peered in the door. 'I've just heard a rumour that we are standing down until after the New Year.'

'Where did you hear that?' Steve wanted to know.

'Sarge told me.'

Luke's face lit up. 'It must be true, then, because he knows everything. Wonder what the chances are of getting fourteen days' leave?'

'Let's find out.' Steve was already on his way out when he bumped into Ricky.

'Is it true?'

'We are on our way to check.'

They hurried into the operations building and went straight up to the duty officer. After explaining what they had heard he confirmed that operations were being suspended for two weeks.

'What about leave?' Sandy wanted to know.

'It will only be a limited number. The base has to be kept operational – Christmas or not.'

Ricky turned to Steve and implored, 'Go and put in a good word for us. We deserve a break, don't we?'

'I'll see what I can do.'

While they waited for him to work a miracle for them, Geoff, Terry and Jake arrived, along with a lot of the other crews. The rumour was flying around the base at great speed, and they all wanted to know if leave was possible.

'Steve's gone to find out,' Luke explained.

Steve was soon back and smiling. 'I saw the wing commander and he has all the details. My crew and Sandy's are to have ten days' leave, starting 23rd December.'

A cheer rang out and some of the others hurried off to find out if they were going to be lucky as well.

That evening, they all sat round a large table and decided what they were going to do with this unexpected stroke of good fortune. All the English boys were naturally going home, Ricky was invited to spend the holiday with Jean's folks, Luke was to stay with Harry and Sybil as he already knew she would be on leave at that time, and that left the two pilots.

'We could go to Harry as well,' Sandy suggested.

'Luke wants to spend time with Sybil, so we'll only be in the way,' Steve teased, standing up and pulling over another chair for Nancy, who had just arrived.

'Sorry I'm late. I've heard the good news, so what are you all planning to do?'

Steve explained. 'What about you? Are you on leave as well?'

'I am, so why don't you and Sandy come home with me? Mum and Dad would love you to spend Christmas with us.'

'That's very kind, but are you sure they won't mind?'

'I'm positive, Sandy.'

'Thank you. We would both love to come,' Steve said.

'Good, that's everyone settled.' Ricky was buoyant with excitement. 'We'll have to go on a food-scrounging expedition again.'

'Steve, you must both come and see Harry and Sybil while you are in London. They will be disappointed if you don't,' Luke pointed out.

'We'll come so we can all see the new year in together. What about your folks, Nancy, would they like to join us as well?'

'I'm sure they would love to.'

'We may possibly be into the last year of the war. It has been going on for so long it's hard to believe it could actually be coming to an end.'

That comment from Andy caused a moment of quiet as they contemplated what that was going to mean for all of them. For the Canadians, the prospect of spending the Christmas after this one in their own homes was bittersweet.

They had been very successful in scrounging food, and were in high spirits as they crammed their bags full.

The London train was crowded, as usual, but they managed to find Nancy and Jean seats in a carriage, while the rest of them got as comfortable as possible in the corridor. Jean and Ricky got off first, then Luke, and after a change of train Steve and Sandy were able to sit with Nancy in a carriage.

The moment they reached the Dalton home, the front door flew open and they were greeted enthusiastically. Inside was warm and bright and they had clearly done their best to make it look festive. The lounge was decorated with home-made paper chains and the small tree in the corner was decorated with brightly coloured ribbons. A log fire was burning in the grate.

'We are delighted you could all make it here for the holiday.' Tom shook their hands. 'Sit down, lads, and tell me what you have been up to.'

'Now, Dad, you know you mustn't ask questions like that.'

'Sorry, I couldn't help it. They have medal ribbons on their tunics, and you don't get them for nothing.'

'All the more reason for you not to ask,' she scolded lightly.

Steve shot her a grateful glance. She obviously hadn't told her parents what had happened, and that was a good thing because it could bring back distressing memories of the son they had lost.

She gave a slight nod, indicating he was right.

The conversation then turned to general subjects, and after relaxing with tea and biscuits they unpacked their bags.

'My goodness,' Sally exclaimed. 'You have been to see your friendly farmer again. We will eat well this Christmas.'

'I've got a contribution as well.' Nancy pulled a large white basin out of her kitbag. 'A proper Christmas pudding made especially for the top brass.'

'How did you manage to get that?'

'I spun a good story about how my parents were going to see the Canadians had a proper British Christmas.' She grinned at her mother. 'The chef gave me that the next day, suitably disguised, of course.'

Tom kissed his daughter's cheek. 'How did we ever come to have such a smart girl?'

'Just lucky, I guess.'

Steve watched the display of family affection and his heart dipped, knowing he was going to try and take their much-loved daughter away from them. There was a real chance that Nancy would refuse, of course, and he was well aware of that. He was in no doubt he wanted her for his wife, and she had shown, in many ways, that she cared deeply for him. Whichever way this went, hearts would be broken unless he could find a solution.

Chapter Twenty-Five

The holiday was relaxing and full of laughter. Tom and Sally made such a fuss of them they almost felt as if they were family. Being so far from their own folks at this time of year was hard, and they were both grateful to be made so welcome.

Dan was often mentioned, and Steve could see that having two pilots to share the festive holiday with them was helping, in a small way, to fill the void his loss had made.

A couple of days before New Year's Eve, they both went to visit Harry and found his small house filled with friends and neighbours. One glance was all that was needed to tell them that Sybil and Luke were crazy about each other.

'I hope you are going to come and see in the new year with us?' Harry asked.

With a glass of beer in one hand and a sausage roll in the other – at least he thought it was a sausage roll – Steve nodded. 'That's why we are here. We thought it was a night when we should all be together, so would it be all right if we brought Nancy and her folks with us? I know Ricky would love to have a night at the pub with everyone, so assuming you are in agreement, Nancy has gone to let him know we are meeting here. I hope that is all right?'

'Wonderful! Bring everyone and we can go to the Jolly Sailor and have a damned good party.' He raised his glass. 'We've really got something extra to celebrate this year, because there's no doubt next year will see the end of this bloody war.'

'There's still a way to go,' Steve cautioned.

'I know, lad, but there's no stopping now. That blasted man is already beaten and all he's got to do is accept that fact.'

There were murmurs of agreement, which called for another round of drinks for everyone.

When they arrived back at the Dalton house, Nancy hadn't yet returned from Jean's and the lounge was empty. Steve could hear voices in the kitchen, and hoping it was Tom and Sally on their own, he said to Sandy, 'Don't come into the kitchen for a while. I need to have a talk with Tom and Sally.'

'Okay – I know what's that's about, so good luck.'

He walked into the kitchen and was relieved to see them on their own. He pulled out a chair and sat at the large table with them.

'Hello, Steve, I thought I heard you come in. Do you want a cup of tea?'

'Please, Sally. Harry said he would be delighted if you would come and celebrate New Year's Eve with us. They are planning a huge party, so it will be lively, believe me.'

Tom chuckled. 'We'll look forward to that.'

Steve drew in a deep silent breath. 'I would like to

discuss something with you while we are alone, if you don't mind.'

They were both immediately serious, and Sally nodded. 'We are pretty sure we know what it is.'

'I feel it is only right you should know I intend to ask Nancy to marry me, and if she should accept it would mean her coming to live in Canada. I know this is hard for you and all I can do is assure you that I love her very much and can give her a good life.' Although they were doing their best to control their emotions, he could see they were devastated at the thought of losing their daughter as well. 'I know it is asking a lot, but I would like your blessing.'

Tom was the first to answer. 'We have been aware for some time this might happen. We like you, Steve, and would be happy to see our daughter married to such a fine man, but she is all we have and Canada is so far away.'

'Couldn't you stay in England?' Sally asked hopefully. 'You're a good pilot and the RAF would love to keep you, I'm sure.'

'I'm sorry, but I have to go home,' he told them gently. 'Nancy has already told me it is not possible for us to be together, but we love each other, and I can't give up hope that there is a solution to this problem. All I can do is promise you that I will not put any pressure on her. Whatever she decides, I will accept.'

Tom nodded. 'We can't ask for more than that. Our daughter's happiness is our main concern, and if this is what she wants, then we will have to let her go.'

Sally drew in a ragged breath. 'You both have the right to be happy, and if that means you be together, then you have our blessing.'

'I agree. Does Nancy know what you intend?' Tom asked.

'Not yet. I wanted to talk to you first because I knew this would not be easy for you to accept. However, with the end of the war in sight, it is now time to plan for the future – a future I want to spend with Nancy, if she will have me.'

'There is no doubt she thinks a lot of you. We have seen it in her eyes when she talks about you.'

'I fear she will refuse me because it would mean leaving you, but it is only right you know what I am going to do.'

'That was thoughtful of you.' Sally poured them all another cup of tea.

'I hope I haven't spoilt this time of year for you. Harry is looking forward to meeting you.'

'Not at all, lad,' Tom smiled then. 'You have been frank and straightforward with us, and at least we now know the situation, so we thank you for that. Our daughter deserves the best, and if she will have you, then we will have to accept that and be happy she is with a good man.'

'Thank you for taking it so well.' He stood up feeling relieved as he left the kitchen. They would not oppose the marriage even though it would tear them apart. Before closing the door, he saw Sally grasp her husband's hand and bow her head. He hated upsetting them like this, but far better they knew what he was hoping for, than having this thrust upon them. He'd had to be open with them because he doubted Nancy would even consider leaving her parents, regardless of how they felt about each other, and he might need Tom and Sally on his side.

Sandy looked up when he walked into the lounge. 'That took a while. How did it go?'

'Better than expected, considering I have just thrown their life into turmoil.'

'You've got a tricky situation to deal with, Steve, and I really do hope you can, somehow, marry Nancy. And while we are on that subject, will you be my best man when we get home?'

'I'd love to.' Smiling with pleasure, he shook his friend's hand.

'I'd like the whole crowd there, so do you think Luke and Ricky would act as ushers? It's going to be a big wedding.'

'I'm sure they would.' Steve eased himself into a chair and sighed deeply. 'That brush with death certainly brings life into focus. Each day is a treasure. Does that sound daft?'

'Not at all. You've never talked about it and I haven't liked to ask, but how did you fly that plane when you were so badly injured?'

'You and Luke helped tremendously. I was fighting to stay conscious, but there was only one thing in my mind, and that was to get the plane down safely or I was going to kill everyone on board.'

Sandy nodded. 'When they got you out of the plane, we thought you were dead.'

'It obviously wasn't my time, thank goodness.' He tipped his head to one side and listened to the front door closing. 'Ah, Nancy's back.'

She bounded into the front room with a wide smile on her face. 'Jean and Ricky are coming to the party.'

'Ricky wouldn't be able to turn down a visit to the Jolly Sailor,' Steve laughed, remembering his friend's antics when they had been there before.

'They are going to meet us there. Jean's family love Ricky and he's keeping them well entertained. Where are Mum and Dad?'

'In the kitchen.'

The two pilots watched her leave the room, and Sandy said, 'She's lovely when she's happy like that.'

'I've noticed,' Steve told him. 'But I think she's beautiful whatever mood she's in.'

'Of course you do.'

'Everyone's coming to the party.' Nancy felt the teapot and finding it hot, poured a cup, smiling at her parents. 'It's going to be a wild time with all four Canadians there.'

'I can't imagine Steve being wild. He's very controlled.'

'He is the quietest of the group, I agree, but he still enjoys himself and joins in the fun.'

'Are you in love with him?' her father asked bluntly.

She drained her cup before answering. 'We get on well together, but friendship is all there can be between us. When the war is over, he will return to Canada and we will never see each other again.'

'You haven't answered my question. Are you in love with him? We need to know.'

She looked directly at her parents. 'If you want a straight answer, then yes, I am.'

'And you are just going to let him walk away?' her mother asked.

Nancy nodded. 'That's the way it has to be. Just another casualty of this blasted war, I'm afraid.'

'You are going to sacrifice yours and Steve's happiness because we lost Dan?'

'Yes, Dad. Don't look so serious. He will be here for a while yet and we will enjoy each other's company while we can. All I want now is for him and his friends to be happy. They've had a tough time.'

'How tough?'

'Very, Dad. If it wasn't for the strength and courage of Steve, his crew would all be dead now. Sandy risked his own safety to guide them back.'

'Will you tell us about it?'

'If the boys haven't mentioned it, then it wouldn't be right for me to go into details.' When she looked at them, the pain in her eyes was clear to see. 'We nearly lost him; that's all I can say.'

'And I will tell you something, Nancy. You have your future ahead of you, and you mustn't jeopardise your happiness for us.'

'I will do what I feel is right, Mum. Now what are we going to wear for the party?'

Sally turned to her husband and sighed. 'She's just as stubborn as Dan. How did we manage to have such determined children?'

'Just lucky, I guess, as she has often reminded us.'

They all laughed then, and the serious subject was pushed into the background for the moment.

On New Year's Eve, they arrived at Harry's to find the house full to bursting, and the moment the pub opened they all trooped over. Ricky and Jean's arrival completed the party.

Tom and Sally got on well with Harry the moment they were introduced, and he spent some time in deep conversation with them. Steve could guess what they were discussing – their girls. Ricky pushed his way through the crowd and handed him a pint of beer. 'Having a good time at Jean's?' he asked.

'Terrific. They are a great bunch and happy for us, so we are going to get married as soon as this lot is over.'

'Congratulations. Are you going to marry her here or at home?'

'It will have to be here because that will make it easier for her to get the necessary permission to come to Canada. My family will be disappointed, of course, but we can have another little service for them later.'

'Good idea. They will be able to celebrate your marriage then.'

'Sandy told me you are going to be his best man, and he's roped me and Luke in to help out at the church. It will be fun for us all to be together again.'

'That's right.' Sandy joined them with Luke as well. 'The four of us have been together from the start, and I hope we will never lose contact once we get back.'

'Not a chance.' Steve lifted his glass. 'Let's drink to our continued friendship.'

They clinked their glasses and remained together talking and laughing.

'Those boys are close,' Tom remarked, watching them with interest.

'Not surprising when you consider the dangers they share night after night.'

'Do you know why they are now wearing medal ribbons, Harry?' Tom asked casually.

'No, they won't talk about it, but they must have done something very special to earn them,' he said proudly.

The pub had shut its doors at closing time and put up a private party notice. When midnight struck on the clock they cheered and went round hugging and kissing everyone in sight, and it was two in the morning before they made their way back to Harry's. With no buses or trains running at that hour, they had to sleep as best they could in chairs or on the floor. Some went next door to Gladys's and did the same. They had all had far too much to drink to care anyway. The war was nearly over and they were happy.

They were still slightly hung over and lacking sleep the next morning, so when they arrived back at Nancy's house they made their way through several pots of strong tea. After that they all crawled into their beds for some sleep.

At the end of their leave they packed their kitbags. Nancy's parents insisted on coming to the station with them, and as the train arrived, Tom spoke softly to Steve. 'We want you to know we are happy about you and our daughter, and as hard as it will be to let her go, whatever decision you both come to, we will accept.'

'Thank you, I appreciate that, and I will keep in touch.'

Sally hugged him and kissed his cheek, which surprised him. He got on the train, touched by their selflessness, and he was happy he'd had the sense to talk to them. He was very aware he was going to be asking a lot of the family – perhaps too much, but the prospect of not having Nancy by his side was something he could not accept, so he was left with little choice.

They met up with Ricky and Luke at King's Cross station so they could travel together. On the journey back to base his thought turned to home, and his mind roamed over the land, taking in every detail he knew so well, hardly being able to believe that it might not be too long before he was back there again. Someone tapped him on the shoulder and brought him out of his reverie.

'Are you all right?' Luke asked. 'You look miles away.'

'I was thinking of home and the future.'

'Ah, yes, our time here is running out.'

Steve grimaced. 'What are you going to do about Sybil?'

'We've talked it over, and she is naturally doubtful about leaving her father, which I fully understand, and I have to return home.' Luke propped himself up against the carriage partition. 'I know you are in a similar situation, so have you any ideas how we can solve the problem?'

'Not one, I'm sorry, but if I come up with anything, I will let you know.'

Luke sighed. 'What do you think our chances are?'

Steve shook his head. 'It will be up to the girls and their families. Whatever they decide we will have to accept.'

Shortly after that they were able to find seats for the rest of the journey, and they spent the time going over the lively party at the Jolly Sailor. There was little point fretting about the future at this point. It would have to be faced at the right time.

Chapter Twenty-Six

The weeks sped by and they were kept busy trying to knock out rail bridges and submarine bunkers.

On 22nd March the Allies crossed the Rhine, and they all knew it could only be a matter of weeks before the end came. That day was almost there when they were called in for a briefing.

'The people of the Netherlands are starving,' they were told. 'We have reached an agreement with the occupying forces there to drop food. Operation Manna it is to be called. They have promised that you will not be attacked.' The officer glanced around the room. 'You will be flying in low and on no account – I repeat, on no account – are you to use your guns unless you are fired on first. Is that understood?'

There were nods of agreement.

'Your first drop will be tomorrow, 29th April, and you will be fully briefed in the morning.'

After being dismissed, they stood outside discussing the

unusual mission, and became aware of the activity going on around the airfield. Vehicles were arriving all the time and being unloaded, and Nancy was in the thick of it, Steve noted, with a sheaf of papers in her hand as everything was checked in.

'Do you think they will keep their promise and not fire on us?' Luke was clearly very doubtful about that.

'We can hope so. This is going to be a humanitarian mission for starving people, and it must be desperate to get agreement for us to do this.'

'I agree, and the Germans must know the war is just about over, so I think they will keep their promise.' Sandy smiled. 'Dropping food will be a novel experience, and I for one am looking forward to it.'

'Going in low, not allowed to use guns, and in daylight will also be a change,' Ricky told them. 'Should be fun.'

The next day the Lancasters roared into the sky, heavily laden with food, and as they approached the dropping zone they searched the sky looking for enemy fighters.

'Nothing up here but us,' Terry, the rear gunner announced.

'Confirmed,' the mid gunner, Jake, said.

'Right, in we go then.' Steve approached the drop zone with the rest of the squadron and they released the large packages, filling the sky with life-saving food.

'Look at that,' Luke exclaimed. 'There are people every-where waving at us.'

They arrived back, buoyant that they had been able to help in this way. They did this several times, enjoying the unique experience.

They listened to the news every day, waiting, as everyone was. Then one day, while they were talking to some of the other crews, they saw the girls running across the field towards them, waving their arms and shouting something they couldn't hear.

'It's over!' Jean launched herself at Ricky. 'Germany has surrendered!'

Steve caught hold of Nancy and swung her off her feet, and then both the girls were running around and hugging everyone in sight.

The four Canadians watched the joy and relief on the faces of the British. They had arrived towards the end, really, but this country had endured over five years of war. It was good to see them celebrating with such abandon.

Sarge came tearing up with his entire ground crew. 'We are going to have one hell of a party in town. We've commandeered a lorry, so will you all come with us?'

'That would be great,' they all said enthusiastically.

'Terrific!' Sarge beamed with pleasure at the prospect. 'We have been through a lot, and it's only right we should share this triumph together.'

'We wouldn't have it any other way,' Steve assured him. 'Will it be all right if the girls come with us as well?'

'Of course.' He winked at Steve.

Sandy was laughing as he came over to tell them they had all been summoned to a meeting. The commander gave them details about the unconditional surrender. 'I'm sure that 7th May will be a date we will always remember, and while we celebrate this victory, let us not forget the many hundreds of bomber crews who are not here to join in. But you have earned the right to rejoice, so thank you, gentlemen, and enjoy yourselves.'

'Thank you, sir,' they all said together, standing respectfully as he left the room.

They gathered in groups, discussing this momentous

occasion. It was hard to grasp that it was finally over. No more taking off and wondering if they would return, no more watching friends being dragged out of wrecked planes, injured or dead, and no more trying to ignore the empty seats in the mess. There was the other side of things, though, like the comradeship they had shared. That was special, and when they did set sail for home, it was going to be hard to leave everyone. But before that day came there was still work to be done. The war might be over and their role changed, but they were sure there were many ways they could help, as they had done for the starving people of the Netherlands.

Later that afternoon, they piled into several lorries and headed in to town, The streets were full of people all celebrating, and the airmen were greeted with affection and much back slapping. Food and barrels of beer appeared, and a wind-up gramophone had been brought out so they could have music.

Nancy was standing beside him and he noticed tears in her eyes, so he put his arm around her and drew her close to him, knowing this was a bitter-sweet moment for her, as it must be for everyone who had lost loved ones.

She swiped a hand over her face, swallowed, and then the smile was back.

It was a boisterous time and the moment it began to get dark everyone rushed into their houses, pulled down the blackout curtains and switched on the lights. The years of darkness were over, and this brought a huge cheer from the crowd.

'I bet there is an enormous party going on in London,' Ricky said, 'Harry and his friends will be in the thick of it.'

'And rightly so,' Steve remarked. 'I wish we had been able to spend this time with Harry and your parents, Nancy.'

'That would have been lovely.' She tugged his arm, laughing. 'Look, Luke and Sandy are being pursued by two local girls.'

'Save us!' Sandy demanded, rushing over to them. 'Just because we spoke to them, they won't leave our sides.'

'Tell them you are both married,' he suggested.

Ricky and Jean appeared just then. 'Ah, there you are. Sarge said they are going to tour around the district, and do you want to come?'

'Good idea,' everyone agreed, and headed quickly for the lorry, with Luke and Sandy breaking into a trot.

'What's wrong with them?' Jean wanted to know.

'Some local girls have set their sights on them,' Nancy explained.

'And they are running away?'

A look of devilment crossed Ricky's face. 'Where are these girls? They might like a ride in a lorry.'

Jean punched his arm. 'Don't you dare.'

They climbed in and waved to everyone as they drove away. They spent the rest of the time moving from place to place, stopping now and again to join in the fun. It was two in the morning when they arrived back at base, and after saying goodnight to everyone, the Canadians walked towards their quarters.

'Just look at that.' Steve stopped and pointed into the darkness where the outline of majestic Lancasters could be seen. Their fighting days were over, and it was as if they were resting peacefully, proud of a job well done.

'I'm going to miss flying one of those,' Sandy said.

'Me too,' Steve admitted. 'But we will be here for some time yet, so let's make the most of any flying we can get – without being shot at.'

'I wouldn't mind doing more runs like we did for the

Netherlands. It was fun seeing people wave at us instead of running for cover.' Ricky shoved his hands in his pockets, still gazing at the planes. 'It won't be easy going back to our old lives, will it?'

Everyone agreed, knowing that the things they had seen and done would remain with them for the rest of their lives.

'I expect there will still be plenty for us to do. Remember, it isn't all over yet,' Steve reminded them. 'Troops are still fighting Japan.'

'That's true, and goodness knows how long that is going to last.' Luke stifled a yawn. 'I need sleep.'

They tore themselves away from their beloved aircraft and headed in to get some rest.

The defeat of Japan came much sooner than anyone expected. On 14th August Japan surrendered and VJ day was celebrated on the 15th. The relief that the fighting was finally over everywhere was enormous.

A week later they were given seven days' leave. Steve, Luke and Sandy went to Harry's, Ricky to Jean's home and Nancy to her parents, where the two pilots would join her later. The English crew members all headed for their homes.

'Time to think about our futures now,' Luke remarked. 'I would like to be home for Christmas.'

'So would I,' Steve admitted. 'But we have a couple of problems to solve before we board a ship. Ricky and Jean have it all sorted. They told me they are going to marry here, and when she can join him in Canada, they will have another ceremony to celebrate the marriage so his family won't feel left out.'

Luke was nodding. 'That's a good idea. I'll suggest it to Sybil.'

'Will she leave her father?'

'That's something we have to work out. Harry has said she must think of her own future and not worry about him, but I'm not sure she will feel able to do that. What about you and Nancy?'

'Honestly, I don't think I stand a chance, but I have to try anyway because the thought of sailing away and never seeing her again is the last thing I want to do.' He smiled at Sandy. 'I expect your girl is getting excited now it's all over, and is expecting you back soon.'

'From the letters I've received it is clear the families have got the wedding arranged, and all that needs to be penned in is the date.'

They arrived at Harry's and he was delighted to see them. 'Well, boys, your job is done, and I'm damned happy you have survived. Come in and drink a toast to peace at last. Sybil is on her way home, and should be here anytime now.'

They were savouring a fine whisky Harry had managed to get hold of when Sybil arrived.

After greeting everyone, she smiled happily. 'I've put in for demob and I will be out in about four weeks.'

'That's good.' Harry kissed her on the cheek and then held her away from him so he could look into her face. 'I suppose we will have a wedding to arrange?'

Luke was immediately on his feet, hope showing in his eyes. 'With your permission, Harry.'

'You have it, lad. This is a time for you youngsters now, and I know this is what you want, so go ahead and be happy.' He winked at Steve. 'After all, this won't be the first time a girl from our family has married a Canadian, and that has worked out all right.'

Luke was shaking his hand vigorously and Sybil was nearly in tears. 'Are you sure, Dad?'

'Positive. Hey, no tears, sweetheart. This is what we've fought this bloody war for, so we can live our lives as we want.' He put his hand on Luke's shoulder. 'Are you quite sure you want this foreigner as a husband?'

'Positive,' she replied, repeating what her father had said.

'Then that's all that matters.'

'I've got to buy you a ring now!' Luke was practically dragging her out of the door. 'We won't be long,' he told everyone.

As soon as they left, Harry turned to Steve. 'Their romance has been quite a whirlwind affair, mostly conducted from a distance, and although I like the lad, I don't know much about him. Will he be a good husband to my Sybil, and is he able to provide a home and look after her properly?'

'You need have no fears about that, Harry. Luke is financially secure and will be able to give her a good life. He is also one of the kindest men I have ever met. He will treat her well and probably spoil her.'

'I can confirm that,' Sandy told him. 'Your daughter will be safe and happy with him.'

'That's all I wanted to know. They will be too far away for me to keep an eye on them, and if she should be unhappy, I wouldn't be there to help her.'

'He only lives a short plane trip from me, so I will see them often, and if there is any sign things are not working out then I will step in.'

'Ah, Steve, that is a relief.' He refilled the glasses. 'Now I can relax. One way or another, you boys have caused havoc since you arrived.'

The two pilots suppressed smiles, and said together, 'Never.'

'No good you denying it. You've worried everyone flying those huge planes, got shot at night after night and nearly killed more than once, I suspect.'

'Yes, there is that,' Sandy admitted. 'But it's all over now.'

'And thank heavens for that. Now all we have to do is try to pick up our normal lives, and that isn't going to be easy. I doubt things will ever be the same.'

'They never will be, for any of us.' Steve tipped back the last of his drink. 'The things we've seen and done have changed us.'

'I certainly agree with that. You came here as boys, but look at you now. Confident, war-hardened men with ribbons on your chests. That's quite a transformation. Did you ever tell your mum and dad how badly injured you had been?'

'No, and I'm not going to. And how did you know about that?'

'I really can't remember, but someone must have mentioned it to me,' he said with a look of complete innocence on his face. 'Now, in all the excitement I forgot to ask how long you are staying.'

'Just two days, and after that we are going to spend a couple of nights with Nancy's folks, then we'll come back here. If that is all right with you?'

'That's fine. They are a nice family.'

'They have made us feel like family, and we are grateful for their kindness,' Sandy explained.

It wasn't too long before Sybil and Luke returned, and she held out her hand, grinning with excitement. 'Look at my beautiful ring.'

The solitaire diamond ring was examined and admired by all.

'Good heavens, that must have cost a fortune.' Harry was frowning.

'I wanted Sybil to have a really nice ring and that one fitted her perfectly.'

'I told him it was too expensive, Dad, but he insisted, and I liked it so much.'

'Even so . . .'

'I can afford it, Harry. We have hardly spent a thing since we've been over here, have we, Steve?' His expression was asking for support.

'Quite true. Our payments have been building up and we are loaded,' he joked.

'Well, if you are sure.' The frown disappeared and he beamed at his daughter. 'This calls for a right old knees-up at the pub!'

Two days later the two pilots arrived at the Daltons, looking forward to a more restful couple of days. They were welcomed enthusiastically, as always.

'Where's Nancy?' Steve asked immediately.

'Gone to do a bit of shopping, but she won't be long. We've managed to rake together some clothing coupons and there are a few essentials she needs,' Sally explained. 'She's been in uniform for quite a while and hasn't much in the way of civilian clothes.'

'Is she putting in for demob already?' Sandy asked.

'Not just yet, but she won't stay on for too long, and I must admit it will be good to have her home again,' Tom told them.

'Do you know when you will be able to go home?' Sally asked, handing round cups of tea.

'Not at the moment, but it can't be soon enough for me.

My girl has been waiting patiently, and we will be married once I am home for good.'

'That's lovely, Sandy, you have something to look forward to.' Sally turned her attention to Steve. 'I expect your family are waiting eagerly for your return as well.'

He nodded. 'My father will be relieved. He's been running things on his own, and it really needs the two of us.'

At that moment Nancy arrived back and put her shopping bags down so she could pour herself a cup of tea.

'Did you get all you needed?' her mother asked.

'As much as I could with the coupons I had. They were soon used up, though.' She sat down and smiled at the boys. 'Did you have a good time at Harry's?'

Sandy then told her about Sybil and Luke's engagement and the celebration that followed in the evening, making everyone laugh.

Sally stood up and beckoned to her daughter. 'Give me a hand with dinner, and then the boys can relax and sleep as much as they like. It sounds as if they need it.'

Chapter Twenty-Seven

The next few weeks dragged by as they lounged around waiting for an opportunity to fly. They began to feel useless.

Sandy threw the newspaper he had been reading onto the table. 'They don't need us any more. We've done what we came here for and now it's time to go home.'

The four Canadians nodded agreement. Now the danger and stress had gone their days felt aimless, and separation from their families was being keenly felt.

'Can we ask to be sent home?' Ricky wanted to know.

Steve shrugged. 'I really don't know, and I am sure they will tell us when we can leave.'

Luke stood up and stretched. 'If we knew how much longer we are going to be here, then we could sort ourselves out. I want to marry Sybil before leaving, and as my wife she will be able to join me quicker.'

'Yeah, same here.' Ricky sat down. 'Go and find out for us, Steve.'

He hauled himself out of the chair, quite used to being

asked to discover what was going on. 'I'll see what I can do.'

They waited and waited.

'What's taking him so long?' Luke was studying his watch.

'Perhaps he's got fed up and gone for a walk.'

That remark from Sandy made the others smile.

'I wouldn't put it past him,' Luke chuckled. 'Anyway, why do we always ask him to do everything?'

Ricky shrugged. 'People listen to him.'

It was over an hour before Steve returned. 'We need to put in an official request for a transfer back to Canada.'

'It's taken you all this time to find that out?'

'No, Ricky, it took me five minutes, and as it is a nice day I went for a walk.'

'Told you,' Sandy said smugly. 'So how do we go about this transfer?'

Steve pulled some forms out of his pocket and handed them to each one. 'Fill that in.'

After scribbling something quickly, Ricky held it up. 'Done.'

Luke peered at the form. 'What have you said?'

'I want to go home. What else is there to say?'

'How about – "Dear Sir or Madam, I have served Bomber Command and survived thirty missions. Now the war is over can we please go home to Canada? Yours faithfully," then just sign it at the bottom.'

Everyone found that hilarious, and Steve pointed out that it was forty-three missions, not counting the food drops.

'Ah, you're right. "PS, sorry, it's forty-three missions."' They were roaring with laughter now, their lethargy forgotten.

'Hey, with everything that's been going on, our return

match with the girls has been forgotten,' Ricky reminded them. 'Let's challenge them to a match tonight.'

'That's a good idea. A few drinks and a bit of fun is just what we need. Find Jean and throw down the challenge,' Luke told him.

'Before you do that, how many of us will be playing? Andy has a girl in the village now, so he won't be available, nor will the rest of the crew who have wangled a forty-eight-hour pass.'

'It will just be the four of us, then, Steve.'

Sandy grinned. 'That should be interesting. We couldn't beat them with eight of us, so what chance do we stand with only four?'

'We've been practising and they won't find it so easy this time,' Ricky said with confidence. 'What are we going to demand as a forfeit from them?'

'There speaks the man who couldn't even hit the board,' Luke teased. 'I think we should decide what we are going to do when they beat us again.'

'Pessimist.' Ricky headed for the door, turned back and winked. 'I can hit the board now and don't intend to lose.'

Jean leant on the counter and beckoned Nancy over. 'The four boys have challenged us to a darts match tonight.'

Nancy's face lit up with devilment. 'How do they think they are going to beat us on their own?'

'Ricky is sure they can because they've been practising. See you in the NAAFI.'

As Jean left, Colin came over. 'Did I hear right? You're taking on the Canadians at darts again?'

She nodded, laughing softly.

'Oh, this we will want to see. I'll tell the boys.'

'Who are you going to support?'

'The winning side, of course.'

The girls were already warming up when they arrived for the match.

'Damn, they are good,' Ricky murmured as they watched the darts flying to the target.

Nancy grinned at them, turned back to the board, and threw three darts in quick succession, landing expertly on one hundred and eighty.

'Show off,' Sandy called. 'Come and sit down and I'll buy you a drink before we start.'

They sat round a table and Steve asked, 'What are we playing for?'

'Silk stockings,' Jean replied at once.

'That can be arranged – if you win.' He turned to his friends and gave a sly wink. They had already discussed this, but they were going to have a bit of fun with the girls. 'And what will be our prize when we win?'

Ignoring the girls' amused smiles at that remark, they stood up, walked a few paces away so they couldn't be heard and went into a huddle.

After much whispering and waving of hands they sat down again and, as usual, Steve was the spokesman. 'We are going to play as two teams, Sandy and Ricky, Luke and myself. It will be the best of three matches for each team, so if you beat any team your prize will come from them. However, if either of our teams should win, then you will need to grant them a wish.'

The girls looked at each other, highly suspicious at this strange set of rules. 'And what will the wish be?' Nancy asked.

'Whatever we decide.'

'Oh, come on,' Jean exclaimed. 'You can't expect us to accept that without knowing what you are going to ask for.'

'We wouldn't ask for anything improper,' Luke assured them. 'Perhaps just a small favour when we need something.'

One look from the girls told them quite clearly that they didn't believe that for one minute.

'Suppose we give you the right to refuse any wish you consider impossible or inappropriate.'

'We'd want that in writing,' Nancy declared.

'Hey, they don't trust us.' Ricky was trying hard not to laugh.

'You bet we don't.' Jean gave him a wallop on the shoulder. 'If we agree, when would this wish be claimed?'

'Any time – or never.'

'What are you up to, Steve? This is ridiculous.'

He appeared totally innocent when he said, 'We are not up to anything, Nancy. We didn't know what to claim as a prize, and this was the only thing we could think of.'

'Come on, girls, you've known us long enough to trust us, surely?' Luke picked up the darts and handed them to Sandy. 'Take a chance and think of all those silk stockings you might win.'

'What do you say?' Jean asked her friend. 'It doesn't matter, because they are not going to win.'

'You're right. Let's show them how experts play the game.'

Ricky was already on his feet. 'It's me and Sandy first.'

As soon as they walked towards the dartboard everyone in the room stood up and gathered round to watch the fun. There was much calling of encouragement, urging them on to beat the girls.

They played well – but not well enough, and the girls won by two games to one, although it had been much closer than anyone expected.

Luke said quietly to his partner, 'They are not unbeatable, and they don't know how good we have become.'

Steve walked over and cleaned the scoreboard ready for their match. After throwing a few practice darts, making a hash of it on purpose, the match was on.

The first game went to the girls, and they had smug expressions on their faces, absolutely certain this was going to be easy.

'Okay,' Steve murmured, 'time to up our game.' From then on nearly every dart hit the desired number, and they won so quickly their opponents were silent with shock. The decider wasn't quite so easy, but eventually Luke threw the winning dart.

The place erupted with cheers at finally seeing these demons of the game being beaten. Many of those watching had tried in the past and been thoroughly thrashed.

'You really have been practising, haven't you?' Nancy said as they all sat down again. 'Ah well, we will still get stockings from the losing team.'

'I'll send right away, but it might be a while before they arrive,' Sandy explained.

'That's all right.' Jean sipped her drink and eyed Luke and Steve. 'So, we both owe you a wish. Have you any idea when you might claim them?'

'We don't know yet, and are banking that privilege until needed.'

Ricky arrived with more drinks and patted Jean on the shoulder. 'Don't worry about them. I'll make sure they behave themselves.'

That caused comments of disbelief that had everyone laughing. The rest of the evening turned into a party, and the girls relaxed. The rare defeat soon forgotten.

Back in their quarters, Luke asked his friend, 'What are you thinking of asking for?'

'No idea. As I said, I am banking that in case I need it in the future. What about you?'

'I'll have a word with Sybil, but I thought it would be nice to have them as our bridesmaids.'

'They'd like that, I am sure. When are you planning to get married?'

'The application has already gone in and we hope it will be in four weeks. You will be my best man, of course.'

'I'd be delighted to be your best man. It is going to be a church wedding, I take it?'

'Yes, Sybil and Harry are seeing to all that, and the reception will be at the Jolly Sailor. They've got a private room upstairs we can use.'

'What about a cake? How will that be possible with the strict rationing?'

'Gladys is going to make that, and as for a wedding dress, Sybil has asked me if I can get hold of a parachute.'

Steve thought for a moment, and then stood up. 'Let's go and have a word with Sarge.'

'Good idea. If anyone knows how to get things, it's him.'

They left the room and nearly bumped into Ricky. 'Where are you two off to this time of night?'

'Sybil wants a parachute and we are going to find Sarge.'

'What does she want that for? Is she going to jump out of a plane?' he joked.

'No, you fool; she wants to make a wedding dress out of

it. What about Jean, does she want a white wedding?' Luke asked.

'She said no fuss, so we are going to have a simple ceremony and in uniform.'

'Right, see you in the morning.'

'I'm coming with you.'

'So am I.' Sandy appeared then and raised an eyebrow in query. 'Where are we going?'

Steve explained the purpose of their mission. 'We are beginning to look like the four musketeers. Where one goes, the others follow.'

'I thought that was three.' Sandy rested his hand on Steve's shoulder. 'We came here together, and we stay together, so we will all go for a parachute.'

It didn't take long to find Sarge. He was standing outside the airmen's quarters smoking a cigarette, and when they reached him, he ground it out. 'I can tell by the look on your faces that you are up to something. What can I do for you, gentlemen?'

'We need a parachute,' Luke said, 'and thought you would be the man to ask.'

'You've all got parachutes.'

'Luke's getting married soon and his girl wants one to make a wedding dress,' Sandy told him.

'So you want me to steal one for you?'

'No, no, I only want one that can no longer be used,' Luke told him hastily. 'Do you know if that is possible?'

'Anything is possible.' Sarge lit another cigarette and drew on it deeply. 'I know where they keep the decommissioned items, but it will take a bribe, of course.'

'Of course.' Steve chuckled. 'What do you need?'

'A small bottle of whisky will do the job.'

'We'll get that and one for yourself,' Luke offered.

Sarge winked. 'It's as good as done. You leave this with me.'

'Thanks, and as soon as you can.'

'I'll have it for you by tomorrow evening.'

Luke was delighted, and as they began to walk away, Steve stayed behind and leant against the wall next to Sarge. 'What do they do with parachutes that are damaged and can't be used again?'

'Some are sent away for the material to be used for something else. We have learnt not to waste anything in this war, and I am told they make nice underclothes for the girls.'

'They also save lives, and it will be good to see Sybil walking down the aisle in one.' He pushed away from the wall. 'Thanks, Sarge.'

'I'm always happy to help my crew in any way I can – and I'll drink to the happy couple with a fine whisky.'

Steve was laughing softly as he ran to catch the others up.

The next afternoon Sarge found them kicking a ball at a makeshift goal. He ran to the ball, kicked it into the air and then headed it straight in the goal.

'Good shot,' Luke called. 'I can see you've played this game before.'

'I used to be quite good, if I say so myself. I've been checking your Lancaster and there seems to be something wrong with your seat, sir,' he said formally in case anyone was listening. 'Would you have a look at it? There's something stuck underneath.' He gave a crafty wink and walked away.

'Ah, thanks, Sarge.' He gave him a thumbs-up sign. 'I'll check it right away.'

They all went and climbed into their Lancaster, and tucked

underneath the flight engineer's seat was the material from a parachute, neatly packaged.

They took it straight back to their quarters, and Steve asked, 'How are you going to get that to Sybil? We can't leave base for any length of time at the moment.'

'I'll write and ask if she can come and meet me at the pub. If we are flying, I will ask Sarge to go and give her the package.'

'That will cost you several rounds of drinks.'

'I know,' he smirked. 'I wonder what he does in civilian life?'

'Goodness knows, but he's a fine mechanic.'

Sandy appeared at the door. 'Just heard, there's a briefing tomorrow morning. Supply run for someone, I expect.'

'Who cares as long as we can fly.' Steve's smile was one of pure pleasure.

His friend came in and sat beside him. 'Why don't you stay in the RAF, Steve? You would make a damned fine instructor, and I'm sure they would jump at the chance to keep you.'

'It's tempting, but not possible. I have to go home.'

'I suppose there is no way round that.'

'There isn't, and, anyway, we've all put in our transfer requests to return to Canada. That's where I belong.'

'Where we all belong,' Luke added. 'We've done the job we came here for, and now it's time to go home.'

With deep sighs they all nodded agreement, and Steve knew he was soon going to have a serious talk with Nancy. His time was getting short.

Chapter Twenty-Eight

The group was thrown into the excitement of planning the two weddings. Sybil, now demobbed, arrived two days later and met them at the local pub.

With drinks in front of them, Luke turned to Nancy and Jean. 'You owe me a wish, and I'm going to claim it now. Sybil and I would like you both to be our bridesmaids.'

They didn't hesitate and agreed immediately, excited by the offer, and also rather relieved that one of their wishes had been fulfilled so easily.

'We must have you in pretty colours.' Sybil studied the two girls, Nancy dark and Jean fair. 'I'll do some trials on the silk and see what colours are best.'

'Will you have enough material for all the dresses?' Luke wanted to know.

'I'll make it do. We are all quite small so it should be enough. I'll let you know if I can't manage it.'

The boys looked at each other, and Sandy murmured, 'Better get more whisky in case we need Sarge again.'

The girls got into a huddle, disappeared for a while, and when they returned Sybil nodded. 'Good, that's everything settled. Steve is our best man and Nancy and Jean bridesmaids. A week later I will be your attendant, Jean, and Sandy the best man. Although I am out of the army now, I still have my uniform, so I can wear it at the ceremony.'

Sybil had to leave to catch a train back to London, so Luke walked her to the station and the rest of them returned to the base.

When Luke arrived a short time later, Steve was propped up in bed reading. 'Goodness knows how Sybil is going to make three dresses in the time available, and how will she know if they are going to fit the girls?'

'She's got it all worked out. Gladys next door is a seamstress and has offered to help her. She has Jean and Nancy's measurements.' Luke chuckled. 'Remember when they all disappeared to the toilets? Well, she had a tape measure with her and took their measurements. Also, the girls are going to make a quick visit for a try-on session. She is quite confident that everything will be ready in time.'

'Nothing to worry about then.'

Luke pursed his lips. 'I wish my folks could be here. I'm sad about depriving them of this special day. They said they understand, but it must be upsetting for them.'

'Ricky feels the same, so we must have some good photos to send them.'

'Yes, that's all been arranged as well.' He kicked off his shoes and sat back on the bed. 'You know you will have to give a speech, don't you?'

'Already prepared.'

'What are you going to say?'

'You'll find out on the day, and as father of the bride,

Harry will have a few words to say as well.'

They looked at each other and burst into laughter.

'That should liven things up.' Luke became serious again. 'Have you asked Nancy to marry you yet?'

He shook his head. 'Not in so many words, but she knows how I feel about her.'

'You'd better do it soon, because I've heard a rumour that our transfers could be coming through soon. You won't have time to marry her here.'

He tossed the book aside and sighed deeply. 'She has already made it clear that she couldn't leave her parents, and I can't stay here, so there doesn't seem to be a way for us to be together.'

'I'm sorry, Steve, that's tough for both of you. You're going to ask her, though, aren't you? She might change her mind. Any fool can see you care for each other very much, so don't give up all hope.'

'I won't.' He settled down to sleep, but his mind began to go over everything that had happened since they had arrived here.

At the completion of their training their posting had come through. They knew they were coming to a country that had been at war since September 1939, and although there were tales about the strict rationing and shortages of just about everything, they really didn't know what to expect. As a precaution, Steve had brought extra money with him, and on the ship found out that the others had done the same thing. Ricky and Luke were now using that cash for their weddings, and his was about to be useful.

He looked across and saw that his friend was also still awake. 'Luke, I believe it's customary to buy the bridesmaids a gift of jewellery. Is that my job or yours?'

'Oh, heavens, I forgot that. I think it's up to me, but I'm not sure.'

'Why don't we buy one each, and then neither of us will be shirking our duty.'

'Well, if you don't mind, that would be a help.'

'I don't mind a bit. We will be free tomorrow. so let's go into Lincoln and find a decent jeweller. There is something I want to buy as well.'

'Right. What a good idea it was to bring extra cash with us.'

With that arranged they settled down to get some sleep.

The next morning the others were still in bed, so they left as soon as they'd had breakfast.

The first jeweller they came across didn't meet their approval, so they kept walking, until they came to another one. 'Ah, this looks better.' Steve pushed open the door and they went in.

'What can I do for you, gentlemen?' The owner smiled broadly at them.

'Can we have a look round?' Luke asked.

'Of course, and please take your time.'

'What about something like this for the girls?' Steve pointed to a pearl pendant set in a starburst of gold.'

'That's perfect.' He called the owner over. 'Do you have two of these, they must be identical.'

'I'm sure I have.' He opened a drawer behind the counter and took out two boxes, which he placed in front of them.

'We'll take those,' Luke told him. 'Now I must buy a wedding present for Sybil. What about that double strand of pearls, Steve?'

'I'm sure she would love those. Are they genuine pearls, sir?'

'We do not sell fakes in this establishment, sir.'

'In that case I'll take those as well. Didn't you say you wanted to buy something, Steve?'

He nodded. 'Could you show me a selection of diamond rings, please?'

The man's eyes lit up and he unlocked another drawer behind the counter and pulled out a tray of rings. 'These are the finest quality diamonds, sir.'

He immediately picked out a trilogy of diamonds set in platinum. He was going to have to guess the size, but she had slim hands and this one looked about right.

'That's beautiful,' his friend told him.

'I'll need a platinum chain as well. Have you got one?'

The man nearly fell over himself in his haste to find the required item, and in no time at all he placed two on the counter for Steve to examine.

'I'll take that one,' he said, choosing the better-quality chain. Then he put the ring, chain and one pendant together. 'I'll pay for those, and the other two are my friend's.'

'Certainly, sir.'

While the gifts were being wrapped, Luke grinned at Steve. 'Nice shop. Nothing is priced, so I hope we have enough money for what we've bought. Didn't think to ask how much they were.'

'We have enough because we've hardly spent a thing since we've been here.'

The shop owner handed each of them a bill which they paid easily, and putting the small packages safely in their pockets they walked out, well pleased with what they had bought.

'I don't need to ask who the ring is for. I hope things work out for both of you.'

Steve shrugged. 'That remains to be seen.'

The next day Steve borrowed a car and took Nancy out for dinner at the hotel they had visited before. Without the need for blackout now the hotel was ablaze with lights.

'Just look at that.' Nancy slipped a hand through his arm. 'Isn't it wonderful to see everything lit up again?'

He squeezed her hand, enjoying her pleasure at such a small thing. But of course it meant a lot to her after the years of darkness.

They were shown to the dining room and given a table in an alcove where they could have a degree of privacy.

After the meal was finished, he took the box out of his pocket and pushed it across to her.

Without looking at him she opened it and bowed her head.

'I love you very much, Nancy, and don't want to spend the rest of my life without you. Will you marry me?'

She looked up then, her eyes moist with tears. 'Are you going to stay in this country?'

'I can't, I'm sorry, my love.'

A tear trickled down her cheek. 'Then you know I can't marry you. If Dan was alive it would be different, but my parents have lost one child, and I can't deprive them of the only one they have left. Please understand, Steve, if it wasn't for that I would accept with the greatest of joy.'

'I do understand.' He'd known this was going to happen, but the pain of it still hurt. 'We are both in a difficult situation, but please don't give up on us. Once I get home, I will try to work something out. I promise.'

'I can't see any way around it.'

He reached across and grasped her hand. 'Please take the ring.'

'It's beautiful, but I can't wear it with my uniform.'

'I've thought of that.' He removed the chain from its box

and threaded the ring through it, then stood up and fastened it round her neck. 'It will make me happy to know you are wearing it, and one day I'll put it on your finger with a wedding ring.'

'Oh, Steve, can we get out of here, please?' The tears were now running down her face.

He paid the bill and they went back to the car. She was very upset and he gathered her in his arms, kissing the tears from her face. 'It will be all right, sweetheart; we must believe there is a way for us to be together. In the meantime, don't go and fall in love with someone else, will you? Give me time to find a solution.'

'There isn't any chance of me falling for anyone else. I think I loved you from the first moment I saw you gazing at that Lancaster.'

The fact that she loved him gave him hope. She was going to wait for him, and although their situation seemed impossible, he was certain they belonged together and there had to be a way. 'Now, my lovely girl, we must put our problems behind us because we have two weddings to attend. They are happy unions and we must show how pleased we are for them.'

'I wouldn't do anything to mar their special days.' She touched the ring he had put around her neck, then slipped her arms around him and kissed him. 'Damn you, Steve Allard, I didn't stand a chance. I'm going to snatch every possible moment with you before you sail away.'

He smiled and held her tightly for a moment, trying to comfort both of them. Through all the danger, drama and turmoil the bond between them had grown and grown. Now, very soon, they were going to have to part, and it was going to be a tough thing to do.

Luke was still awake and looked up expectantly when he came in. 'How did it go?'

Steve sat on his bed and ran a hand over his face. 'Much as I expected. We are at an impasse. She doesn't feel she can leave her parents, and I can't stay here.'

'What about the ring, did you give it to her?'

'I asked her to keep it until I can put a wedding ring beside it. Hell, Luke, I'm making promises I have no idea how to keep, but she is so upset – we both are. She's wearing it on the chain around her neck, so at least she accepted it.'

'There's a solution to every problem, remember?'

'Oh yes, I remember.' He gave a mirthless laugh. 'Anyway, you and Ricky don't have to worry that our problems will throw an air of gloom over your weddings. We have decided to enjoy them and have a bloody good time.'

'Glad to hear it. The last thing we need is a miserable best man at our wedding,' he teased. 'Hey, do you know what I have suddenly realised?'

'No.'

'I'll be a member of your family when I marry Sybil, and I can call Harry Dad instead of uncle.'

'And I'll be a part of yours.' He laughed freely then. 'That's something to be happy about.'

'It will be all right,' Luke said, echoing the very words he had spoken to Nancy.

He nodded, but didn't feel very optimistic.

Chapter Twenty-Nine

The organ began to play and both men turned to look up the aisle. Luke gasped when he saw Sybil in a flowing white dress, but Steve's gaze was fixed on Nancy. The two brides-maids were wearing long, pale blue dresses and carrying small bouquets of white flowers. Both were wearing the pendants.

Ricky was in the seat right behind them and he leant forward, smiling with pleasure. 'You'd never believe they were wearing a parachute,' he said softly.

Luke held his hand out to Sybil when she reached him, and the service began.

As soon as they were pronounced man and wife everyone gathered outside for the photographs, and Steve made sure some pictures were taken of him and Nancy on their own.

Harry came over, looking very pleased about his daughter's choice of husband. 'Fine turnout, lad. Our family is growing, and with the prospect of little ones in the future.'

'You are going to miss her, though.'

'Of course I am, but she has her life to live, and all I want is for her to be happy.'

Steve was pleased for his friend and hoped his own plans would go as smoothly, but he knew his chances were not good.

The Jolly Sailor had a good spread in spite of shortages. The cake looked impressive from a distance, but when it was due to be cut, the fake cardboard covering was removed to reveal a plain sponge cake.

Harry had friends who were in a band and they played dance music for the guests. Steve bowed elegantly in front of Nancy and asked her to dance. 'You look beautiful,' he told her, holding her close.

'So do you,' she replied, making him laugh, and then she looked around. 'This wedding has gone very well, and they look so happy. My best friend is next, so there is much to be joyous about. Against all the odds the four of you have survived, and it could have been very different, Steve.'

'True.' He smiled down at her. 'But we are all glad we came. Luke and Ricky have found lovely wives, and I have met you. Whatever happens in the future, I will always cherish the time spent in your lovely country.'

'Even though you were being constantly shot at,' she teased.

'Yes, but I got to fly a fantastic Lancaster.'

'You pilots are besotted with those monsters, but I am proud of every one of you. These years will be with me forever.'

'Agreed, although I am sure we will all have nightmares from time to time.'

'Probably, but let's put that all aside for the moment. We have been given fourteen days' leave, so let's have fun.'

'I will as long as I can spend most of it with you. I know you will be helping Jean prepare for her wedding, but will you find the time to show me more of England? There is so much I haven't seen – from the ground.'

'Where do you want to go?'

He thought for a moment. 'The New Forest; I hear there are ponies roaming wild there, and also find a nice sandy beach we can walk on in bare feet.'

'I believe some of the beach barriers are coming down, so we should be able to do that. Oh, look, Sybil and Luke are leaving.'

They followed the crowd outside where a car was waiting to take the newly-weds to the station for a short honeymoon. They would return in time for Jean and Ricky's wedding.

The party broke up then and they all went in different directions. Nancy and her parents went home, Jean to hers and the boys stayed with Harry to keep him company.

Steve wasn't able to see much of Nancy over the next couple of days, but after the next wedding they would still have a few days and he intended to make the most of them.

When the day arrived, Ricky was jittery, and as best man Sandy was doing his best to calm him down. 'Just imagine you are in the Lancaster and under fire while you plot a course to the target.'

'What?' He stared at Sandy, puzzled.

'I am sure you are perfectly calm then, or Steve would have had you replaced.'

'He's right,' Steve told him. 'You are icy calm under fire so use that now.'

Ricky took a deep breath and grinned. 'Hey, it works. I feel better now.'

'Good, hold that thought.' Steve stepped back to leave Sandy and Ricky waiting for Jean's arrival.

This was a full-uniform affair, but the girls each carried a small white Bible with a satin ribbon hanging down and dotted with pink carnations.

Ricky had insisted the reception be held again at his favourite pub, the Jolly Sailor, who did yet another good job.

Luke and Sybil left after Ricky and Jean so they could spend a few more precious days together. Sandy had a yearning to visit the Lake District, and took this opportunity to go there. That left Steve and he accepted the offer to stay with Nancy's parents.

For the next few days they jumped on and off trains to visit different places. Steve got his wish to see the ponies, and they even found access to a south-coast beach where they could walk in bare feet, holding hands and silently enjoying the experience. Neither of them mentioned the future.

On the evening before they were due to return to base, Tom caught Steve on his own. 'That's a beautiful ring you have given our daughter. She won't talk about it, but we are sure you have asked her to marry you.'

'I have.'

'And?'

'She refused.'

Pain showed clearly on his face. 'Because of us?'

'Yes, she said it is impossible for her to go and live so far away from you.'

'We have become very fond of you, and nothing would please us more than to see you married to Nancy. We wish you could stay in this country.'

'No, I'm sorry, Tom, I have to return home.'

Tom shook his head sadly. 'This isn't right.'

'I agree. We love each other very much, but this is the way things are and we can't see a way around it.'

'We don't want either of you to be unhappy.'

'She knows that and so do I. Although our situation appears impossible, I have asked her to wear my ring, and that is all I can ask for at this time.'

'I'm so sorry, Steve, you are a good man and you deserve to have the woman you love and who loves you.'

'Life doesn't always work out the way we want.'

'No, it doesn't, and too many sacrifices have been made during this bloody war.'

Sally looked in then, putting an end to this painful conversation. 'Come on you two, stop gassing. Dinner is ready.'

Steve could see Tom was greatly concerned and he was sorry to have caused this fine family more heartache.

They returned to base the next day and he was pleased to see Sandy already there. 'How were the Lakes?' he asked.

'Beautiful, and I even managed to fit in a quick visit to York. Did you and Nancy go exploring?'

'We saw as much as possible in the time available, and we really enjoyed ourselves.'

Everyone came back that day and they soon settled into the military routine once again. Two days later their transfers came through – much sooner than expected, causing a variety of reactions. There was excitement they were going home, but Luke and Ricky were sad they had to leave their wives behind after such a short time together. They had no idea how long it would take for permission to come through for them to come to Canada. Steve knew it was going to be distressing to leave Nancy not knowing if they would ever see each other again, but that was the situation and he had to accept it. The only one of the group who didn't have a problem was Sandy.

They were sailing from Liverpool in four days' time, and they all agreed that the speed of their departure was probably a good thing, as it gave them less time to fret over what they were leaving behind.

It was a frantic rush to see everyone. Steve had wanted to go and see the farmer and little Beth, but there just wasn't enough time, so he wrote them a long letter giving his home address, and saying that he would be pleased to hear from them if they felt like writing.

They all made a mad dash to London and spent an evening at the pub with Harry and the regulars.

On their last night at the base, they threw a huge party for the ground crews who had looked after them so diligently. Steve also handed Sarge his address, asking him to write and let him know how he was getting on.

Sybil had arrived from London, although they had tried to convince the girls not to come and see them off because it would be too upsetting for all of them. They flatly refused, determined to wave their men off on their voyage home.

'Wow! Look at that,' Ricky exclaimed, when they arrived at the dock the next morning. 'This ship is going to be packed. I haven't seen this many Canadians since we left home.'

A sailor came up to them and said they should report in at the office and then board as quickly as possible.

The girls were there to see them off, and so were many more who had come to wave off the men they had become attached to.

Steve gathered Nancy in his arms, and held on tightly for a moment, saying only, 'I love you,' then he turned and strode away, for there was nothing else to say.

They were soon being ushered up the ramp and on to the ship where they pushed their way to the rail for a last look at the girls. There were tears in many eyes as the ship sounded its horn and began to pull away from the dock. Slowly they began to move out to sea with everyone still waving frantically.

As the shore faded in the distance, Luke sighed. 'I'm going to miss Sybil, the Lancaster, as well as everything else, and everyone we have met.'

'Me too, it's hard leaving so much behind,' Steve admitted. 'It has been quite an experience, and those Lancasters were a joy to fly.'

Sandy nodded. 'It was like hell at times, but I wouldn't have missed it for anything. And to be honest, after the first mission, I doubted we would ever see our homes again.'

Ricky turned to face the open sea. 'Somehow we made it, and at least we won't have submarines chasing us this time. Let's go and find out where we can bunk down. Space is going to be at a premium by the look of things.'

Conditions on the troopship were crowded and uncomfortable, but the food was plentiful, and they didn't give a damn because they were going home. The weather was calm and they spent most of their time on deck, where all sorts of activities were going on, mostly gambling, and all four of them avoided that. Some of the men were going to be broke by the end of the voyage.

When their country came into sight, they crowded the rail, eager to see the place they called home, and very aware they were lucky to be seeing it again.

'Wonder if anyone will be there to meet us?'

'It will depend on whether they have received our letters in time, Sandy, but I doubt it.' Even so Luke scanned the crowd hopefully.

'I know, but it would be lovely to have someone to welcome us back.'

'Well, look at that crowd, and there's even a band playing,' Ricky pointed out excitedly. 'We are getting a big welcome home even if our folks aren't here.'

The moment the ship was tied up they disembarked and searched the crowd in the hope there might be someone there they knew, but they couldn't see any of their families.

'Sirs.'

They spun round to find a young airman standing behind them. He saluted and studied them for a brief moment before informing them that he had come to take them to the Shearwater base. 'If you will come with me, sirs, I have a car waiting outside.'

When they arrived at the base, their documents were checked and they were given a meal of steaks, much to their delight. After that they were shown to quarters and slept soundly all night.

The next morning, they were welcomed back by the commanding officer, and told there was a transport plane leaving in two hours for Alberta. 'It will be landing at your old training base, so you can catch a ride and that will get you home much faster.'

They hurried off to collect their kit, delighted to have this chance to fly back instead of a long train journey.

When they boarded the plane, they strapped themselves into the pull-down seats and smiled at each other. They were nearly home.

The moment they were airborne, Steve rested his head back and was instantly asleep.

'I wish I could do that.' Luke had to shout above the noise of the engines.

The other two nodded and settled down to wait out the journey.

The moment they touched down Steve awoke and they were all eager to get a glimpse of the place they knew so well. After reporting in they were given a meal and even a large steak.

'Now I know we are home,' Ricky said, popping a piece in his mouth and rolling his eyes with pleasure.

When the meal was over, they began to explore their old training ground. Most of the people they had known had moved on to other places, but they did find one flying instructor who was still there. He was pleased to see two of the pilots he had trained and had clearly acquitted themselves well.

It was the next morning before they were summoned to present themselves to the officer in charge. There had obviously been a change here as well, because they didn't know this officer. He greeted them with a smile. 'Welcome home.'

'Thank you, sir.' They all saluted smartly.

'Your requests for demob are being processed, but with the volume to be dealt with it could take several weeks. However, as of now you are officially free to return to your homes. You will be informed when your release comes through. You have served the RCAF with distinction, so go home, rest and relax. You have earned that.'

Just then there was a tap on the door and an airman came in. 'An urgent message, sir. A private plane is requesting permission to land here. He is only fifteen minutes away.'

'Name of pilot?'

'Allard, sir. He said he is coming to enquire about his son and friends.'

'Permission granted.'

The airman ran out and the officer fixed his gaze on Steve. 'Flying comes in the family, it seems.'

'Yes, sir.'

'You had better get out there, then.'

No sooner were the words out of the officer's mouth when there was a stampede to get out to the airfield, just in time to see a small plane make a smooth landing. The moment the plane stopped and the engines were switched off, Steve was running towards it. The man who got out was an older version of his son, and they hugged in joy at the unexpected reunion.

His father held him away so he could study him carefully. 'My word, your mother is going to be shocked. There is no sign of the boy we waved off to war. You have changed.'

He shrugged. 'Couldn't help doing that.'

'I don't suppose you could. You've matured into a hand-some man.'

'Must run in the family,' he joked, running his hand along the wing of the plane. 'Lovely Cessna, did you hire it?'

'No, we bought it as a home-coming present for you, and I'm glad you like it. I couldn't get a Lancaster,' he said dryly.

They looked at each other, both having the same vision of the huge plane landing on their small airstrip, and burst into laughter.

'She might be small in comparison, but I love it, and there will be plenty of room for my friends. Thank you, Dad.'

There was a hint of emotion in Bill Allard's eyes, but like his son he was quite good at hiding his feelings. 'Ah, but it's good to have you back. There were times when we listened to the news reports we wondered if we would ever see you again.'

'You don't want to believe everything the news puts out,

especially in wartime. They always exaggerate,' he remarked casually. 'You have arrived at just the right time because we have been told we are free to leave now. Come and meet my friends.'

The introductions were made and Bill said, 'I can't believe I had the luck to come this day and find you all here. My intention was just to try and find out when you would be arriving. We only received Steve's letter today. He tells me you have all been given leave to return home. I believe you all come from Alberta, so we can give you a ride, if you like.'

All accepted the invitation eagerly.

'We'll have to draw up a flight plan so we can drop you all off as close to your homes as possible.'

'Ricky is the best navigator you could find, Dad, and he'll plot you a course.'

'Thanks. I've got all the maps you might need.'

Armed with the various locations, the flight plan was soon ready and filed for their departure.

'I'll just go and have a word with the man in charge, Steve, and see if we can take on extra fuel here. You lads go and collect your kit and I'll be right with you.'

The plane was being refuelled when they arrived back, and Bill was overseeing the operation. 'Nearly ready,' he said. 'Do you want to fly her, Steve?'

'Would you mind?'

'Of course not, she's yours.'

When the tanker pulled away, they climbed on board, Steve in the pilot's seat and his dad as co-pilot. They strapped themselves into the comfortable Cessna with smiles on their faces, looking forward to getting home again, and for a moment the sadness at leaving so much behind was pushed aside.

As they took off, Steve noticed his father had the route in his hand and it reminded him of the flight he had made in the Lysander. Only this time it was light, he wasn't over enemy territory, and his father was beside him giving him course directions.

It took most of the day to drop off their passengers as there were lengthy goodbyes and promises to stay in touch. It was hard to part from friends who had shared the danger, highs and lows of that extraordinary time. It was then the full import of what was ahead of him struck home. Fitting in to his old life again was going to be damned difficult.

Chapter Thirty

Their ranch was a mixture of farmlands and cattle, and Steve took in the scene and nodded with satisfaction. 'I see the harvest is in. Was it a good one?'

'Excellent, and we have plenty of winter feed.'

A few more minutes of flying and the ground below was full of cattle spread over a large area. 'You've increased the herd.'

'There has been a constant demand for meat, and I've managed to buy land from a rancher who was selling up.'

He turned and nodded to his father. 'You've been busy while I've been away.'

'Very. I'll fill you in with the changes when you've had a chance to settle in again.'

When the ranch came into sight, Steve smiled. It looked impressive from the sky, and even more so when you walked into it.

'Buzz them to let them know we have arrived,' Bill suggested, a glint of mischief in his eyes.

'Do they know I am with you?'

'Of course. The moment I knew you were free to come home I sent a message. Your base commander was most accommodating and promised to see it reached its destination quickly.'

Steve altered course and as they came in low over the house, he could see people running from all directions.

'There's your mother,' his father laughed. 'I bet she's already crying, and all the hands are rushing to welcome you home.'

They landed and taxied towards the large shed that housed the plane. When he switched off the engine, they could see cars roaring towards them, and his father asked, 'Are you ready for this?'

'I guess so.' By the time he had unstrapped himself, his father was already out and opening the door for his son, not able to hide his pride as he watched him jump down.

The car his mother, Rose, was driving screeched to a halt and she rushed over to her son, throwing her arms around him. She was laughing through her tears as he lifted her off the ground and swung her round. 'I have missed you so much, and so has everyone else.'

'I missed you too.' He put her down and kissed her wet cheek, then turned to the crowd waiting to greet him. He took time to speak to all of the hands, although all he wanted to do was collapse in a chair with a large brandy. It had been an emotional day.

Eventually he managed to get away, and the moment he walked into the peace of his home he tossed his hat onto the stand by the door, loosened his tie, and then went straight to the huge lounge. His favourite chair was still there by the fire, and he sat down, giving a deep sigh of pleasure.

'Cook is preparing a special meal for you, but because we didn't know you were coming home today, it will take a while,' his mother told him. 'Would you like something while we wait?'

'I could use a stiff drink.' He glanced at his father.

'Brandy?'

'Perfect.'

They all enjoyed a welcome home drink together, and then his mother went off to see about dinner. Steve closed his eyes and was instantly asleep.

The next thing he knew his father was shaking his arm, his eyes shot open and he leapt to his feet before realising where he was.

'Steady, son, I didn't mean to startle you. Dinner is ready.'

He ran a hand through his hair. For a moment he had been back at Scampton with the sound of Lancasters roaring in his head. He gave a wry smile. 'I didn't know where I was for a moment.'

'I understand. It will take you a while to adjust to being on the ranch again. You just take your time, son.'

'I will.' He followed his father into the dining room and stared at the amount of food waiting to be served. This feast would feed several families for a week in Britain. His mind turned to the Daltons who had welcomed them into their home, Harry who had taken them to the British Restaurant and Nancy . . . Those memories hit him with such force he had a mighty struggle to keep his composure. Everyone was so pleased he was home he mustn't appear distressed in any way and spoil their pleasure. 'My goodness, I haven't seen this much food for the last couple of years,' he managed to say with a smile on his face.

'Sit down, son, and enjoy.' His father held out the chair at the head of the table.

'That's your place, Dad.'

'You are now ready to take your rightful place on this ranch. From now on I will be playing a supporting role. All important decisions will be made by you.'

'Are you serious?' he exclaimed.

'Perfectly. Your mother and I have talked this over, and decided this is the right time for you to take overall charge.'

His mother squeezed his arm. 'Don't look so shocked. You knew this was going to happen one day.'

'Yes, but not quite so soon. You're still a young man, Dad, and I expected you to be in charge for a long time yet.'

'Oh, I have a good many years in me, and I will work side by side with you.' He gave his son an affectionate slap on the back. 'But the responsibility of keeping this ranch running smoothly and profitably will be up to you. We have complete confidence that you will be able to do that, and probably a lot better than me. I'll be honest, Steve, I have missed your sound advice while you have been away.'

He grinned at his father. 'I don't believe that for one minute.'

'It's true.' He gave his son a sly wink. 'And your mother thinks it is time I took things a little easier.'

'Not possible,' he told his mother. As he looked at his parents' smiling faces, he heard the sound of a door closing and the key being turned in the lock. At the back of his mind, he had seriously been considering returning to England after a while to marry Nancy if there was no other way. The love and generosity of his parents could mean he would never see the girl he loved again. He felt like moaning in despair, but of course he didn't. Instead, he sat in the chair offered and smiled, giving the appearance of being delighted and honoured with their decision. Which he was, of course, but the pain of knowing that faint hope of having Nancy with him had been stripped away was hard to take.

However, using every bit of self-control he had, the meal progressed with laughter and his parents' obvious joy at having their son back home again. When they asked him about his time at Scampton, he told them the amusing stories about his friends, but nothing about the missions, or the friends they lost. Those memories were locked away, never to be spoken of.

After the meal, he went and thanked Cook and her staff, then joined his parents in front of a huge log fire until he was able to excuse himself and go up to his old room for some much needed sleep. It had been quite a day, and everything seemed strange, making it difficult to sleep in the large bed. He had been accustomed to bunk beds and friends close by, but eventually he drifted off.

The next morning, he was up early and when he put on his old working clothes he noted that they were loose on him. He had never put on the weight he had lost when injured, but with the amount of food here he was sure that would soon be remedied. His boots and jacket were all right, though, so he finished dressing, picked up the star tokens and tucked them in his jacket pocket, giving it a reassuring tap. He then made his way silently out of the house. He had become used to his early morning walks, and set out at a brisk pace to enjoy the open space he found so soothing.

After breakfast, he and his father flew over the ranch to see the changes that had been made in his absence, also noting where the cattle had roamed over the large expanse of land.

'Winter is approaching fast, so we will need to arrange a

round-up before the snows arrive,' his father pointed out when they landed. 'You'll have to get back in the saddle again.'

'I did ride a little in England, but only for a couple of hours at a time, and that's a lot different from sitting on a horse all day. It won't take me long to get back into it,' he said confidently.

They reached the house and went straight to the study and spent the rest of the day on the business side of running such a huge spread.

Over the next couple of weeks he immersed himself in work, writing letters, eager for news from his friends and Nancy. Would she write or would she think it better to cut ties completely?

Finally, a stack of letters arrived at the same time and he sifted through them, looking for Nancy's handwriting. Recognising it at once, he tore it open. It was a chatty letter telling him she was visiting Harry regularly, and spending as much time as possible with Jean and Sybil before they left for Canada. She hadn't found a job yet and couldn't decide what she wanted to do. Tom and Sally had also included a short note wishing him well, and hoping he was settling down all right. The last words Nancy had written were – Missing you all.

Yes, my darling girl, he thought, *that just about sums it up. I am missing everyone as well, especially you.* There were also letters from Luke and Ricky, and another from Sandy, enclosing an invitation card to his wedding in four weeks' time, reminding him of his promise to be best man. There was one more letter in a hand he didn't recognise. He slit it open and a couple of photographs fell out, making him chuckle softly.

His parents, who were also reading their mail, looked up, and his mother asked what had amused him. He handed over the photos and they studied the picture of a little girl holding a cabbage.

'Sweet child. Who is she?' his father asked. 'And why have they sent you a picture of a roof?'

'That's a picture of the chimney I nearly knocked off the farmhouse when I came down.' He just told them he had been out of fuel and had landed in the farmer's field, and what his little daughter, Beth, had said to him, sending him off into peals of laughter at the memory. 'She isn't holding the rag doll this time, she's holding up a cabbage to remind me that I ruined her father's crop.'

'You make it sound as if it was a huge joke, Steve, but it must have been dangerous,' his mother said, looking slightly worried.

'No one was hurt, and the only damage done was to the field. And what happened after was funny.' Still smiling, he put the pictures in his wallet and changed the subject. 'Have you received anything interesting in your mail?'

'We've had a letter from Harry telling us what fun you all had at the Jolly Sailor pub.'

'Oh, we did, Mum, you should have seen Ricky trying to do the "Lambeth Walk". Sandy has also sent me an invitation to his wedding, and as I've promised to be his best man I'll being going there for a few days. We had better start that round-up before then, Dad.'

'You're right. I'll alert the men to be ready to ride out. When do you want to start?'

'Monday, and that gives us two days to prepare. I'll go and spread the news.' He stood up and strode out.

As the door closed behind him, Rose gave her husband an anxious glance. 'That is the most animated I've seen him since he came home. Is he all right, Bill?'

'It's going to take him time to adjust, my dear. We don't know what he went through, and he's obviously missing his friends. We must give him time and space to adjust.'

'I realise that, but there is more to it. He isn't happy, although he's doing his best to convince us he is, and what about that girl he mentioned so often in his letters to us? I haven't heard him speak of her once. I'm worried about him, darling. Something is wrong.'

'I agree he is struggling with something, but let us hope that a few days with his friends will do him good.'

She sighed. 'I wish he would talk to us. He just goes out walking alone.'

'He'll talk when he's ready, and until then we mustn't push him.'

On Monday morning they were up before light, and after a hearty breakfast went out to the stables, where the men were already gathering. Steve swung himself into the saddle and, riding beside his father, they set off.

For the next few days, they rode until he ached in every limb, and at night they sat around a huge fire talking and swapping stories. The men loved the round-up as much as the horses did.

They were approaching the winter home for the cattle when Steve saw a couple of steers break away from the herd, and peeled off to bring them back. He followed them for quite a way and something came into sight that made him stop short. His parents' old house. It was tucked slightly out of the way, and he hadn't given this place any thought for a long time. Dismounting, he walked up the path and peered in the window. It was empty and had been for some time.

'I thought you were after strays.'

He turned as his father came up beside him. 'I thought you were going to pull this down?'

'Never got around to it.' Bill gave a wry smile. 'You were born here and it contains many happy memories. Shame to let it rot like this, though, so we ought to demolish it.'

'Don't do that. With a bit of work it could still be a nice home for someone. It's on the boundary of our land, and about half an hour drive to our ranch house. Have you got the key?'

'Not on me.' His father gave him a speculative look. 'Are you thinking of moving into it?'

'No, not me, but it's still a sturdy place and we shouldn't let it go to ruin.' He remounted. 'I'll have a look at it when we get the herd safely settled.'

It didn't take the two of them long to round up the strays and drive the cattle to the place they would be safe for the coming winter. Some had been separated and would be sent to market, but the experienced hands would deal with that.

They walked in dirty, tired, but well pleased the job was done.

Rose raised her eyebrows when she saw them. 'There's plenty of hot water, so clean yourselves up and then you can eat.'

Steve stretched and grimaced. 'I need to soak away the aches in a hot bath.'

'Off you go. You both look as if you've been crawling around in the dirt, but as usual, I expect you enjoyed it.'

Bill laughed and went to kiss her, but she backed away. 'Not until you have cleaned up.'

'Come on, son, we had better do as she says, but you would have thought she'd be used to it after all these years.'

There were three bathrooms in the sprawling ranch house and one of them was just off Steve's bedroom. He sunk into the steaming bath with a sigh of relief, and stayed there until the water was almost cold. Wrapping a towel around his waist he returned to his room and began pulling out clean clothes.

There was a knock on his door and his father walked in immediately, giving Steve no time to put on a shirt.

The smile on his face vanished when he saw the scars on his son's body. The shock made him draw in a deep breath. 'What happened to you, son?'

'It's nothing, Dad.' He quickly began to dress.

'Steve.'

'I don't want to talk about it. There is no permanent damage done, so just leave it, please. Don't mention what you've seen to Mum, it will only worry her.'

'She's already worried, and so am I. We know it's hard for you to talk about the things you have seen and done, but you always used to talk openly to us. Don't shut us out, Steve. We love you and want you to be happy, but you are not, are you?'

'Of course I am. It's just taking me time to adjust to life on the ranch again.'

'All right, but remember – when you want to talk, we are here for you.'

'I know.' He finished dressing. 'Let's go and eat. I'm famished.'

They threw a party for the hands that evening to celebrate a successful round-up. It had gone on until the early hours of the morning, but Steve was still up early, and after breakfast went to the study in search of the keys to the old house.

'I thought you would still be asleep.'

'Good morning, Mother.' He kissed her cheek. 'I'm used to being up at dawn and can't seem to break the habit. Do you know where the keys are to your old house?'

'What do you want those for? The place must be a wreck by now.'

'It isn't that bad, and I want to have a look inside.'

She opened the desk drawer and took out a large bunch of keys. 'I think they are on here, but I really don't know which ones after all these years. I expect your father will know.'

'Know what?' Bill walked in.

'Steve wants the keys to our old house.'

He took the bunch from her, sorted through them, then removed two and handed them to his son. 'Give me time to eat and I'll come with you. I'd like to have a look at the old place again myself.'

'Okay, we'll take the truck and I'll meet you outside when you're ready.'

Rose watched her son stride out and frowned at her husband. 'Why is he interested in that place? Is he thinking of moving in there himself?'

'I asked him that and he said no. I've no idea what he wants. But I could almost hear his mind working when he saw it. I had better not keep him waiting.'

After a hurried breakfast, Bill left the house and saw Steve propped up against the truck, deep in thought. Something struck him then, and on reaching him said, 'I haven't seen you smoking since you arrived back.'

'I gave it up.' He got in the driver's seat, and the moment his father was in he set off.

'Why?'

'I didn't want to smoke any more.'

Bill was wise enough to know that was all he was going to get, so he dropped the subject. In the short time their son had been home they had learnt not to push him for answers.

The moment they reached the old house, Steve was out of the truck and opening the door. They wandered from room to room, making a note of the work needed to bring this place back to a habitable home again.

'This is not worth the bother. Steve, you can't do anything with it.'

'I agree it will need gutting out and everything inside replaced, but the structure is still sound.'

'It is a solid building, but what on earth are you thinking of doing with it? Do you want it for one of your friends?'

He shook his head, but said nothing.

'Steve, tell me what is on your mind and I might be able to help.'

'It might – and I emphasise might – solve a problem for me. Can I have it?'

'Everything on this ranch is yours.'

'But this was your home before you built the big ranch house.'

'And a very nice home it was, but we don't have any sentimental attachment to it. Do what you like with it, son, I can see it means a lot to you.'

'It does,' he said softly.

'In that case, tell me what you want, and I will see the work is done as quickly as possible.'

'Everything renewed and fully furnished.' He began to pace up and down. 'Also, the ground outside needs to be cleared to make a garden with a fence round it. Do you think Mum would help with the interior? She's got a good eye when it comes to design.'

'I'm sure she would love to. How soon do you want it finished?'

'It will need to be ready by the spring.'

'Okay, that gives us time to do a good job – weather permitting, of course. The snow can be brutal, as you well know.'

'I'll pay for this work out of my own pocket.' When he saw his father was going to protest, he turned to face him. 'I insist, because it might all be for nothing. It's a crazy idea, but I have to try something, and this at least might give me a chance.'

'It would help if we knew who you want this place for.'

Steve walked over to the window and stared out, and then he spun round, anguish showing in his eyes. 'I left a part of me behind in England, and I'm finding it hard to cope with that. I'm sorry I am causing you and Mum concern, but all I can ask is that you give me time, and I will sort myself out.'

Bill walked over and placed a hand on his son's shoulder. 'We understand, and we'll make this into a home no one will be able to resist.'

He gave his father a grateful smile and they walked together out to the truck.

Later that evening, when Steve had gone to bed, Rose grasped her husband's hand. 'What's going on, darling?'

'I don't know for sure, but I can make a guess.' He then told her about his conversation with Steve when they were at the house. 'He's had to leave a girl behind; I bet that's what he meant.'

Rose took a deep breath, sadness flooding her face. 'That is a part of it, I'm sure, but whatever happened over there he has locked away.'

'Yes, he has, but he's seen and done things we cannot

even begin to imagine. However, time will heal whatever is troubling him. He and his friends have returned unscathed, but how many other friends has he lost? He loves this place, and it will work its healing magic on him. Until that time, all we can do is give him our help, love and understanding.'

'We certainly will. You're right. I expect there are thousands of men who have been in the thick of battle and are struggling to adjust, poor souls.' She smiled and pulled Bill out of his chair. 'Let's get some sleep.'

Bill felt guilty he hadn't told her about the awful scars on Steve's body, but he'd promised not to and he couldn't break that promise to his son.

Chapter Thirty-One

Steve was carefully folding his uniform to take with him when his father looked in the open door.

'Nearly ready? The plane is checked over and fuelled.'

'Thanks, Dad.' He looked up, his eyes alight with anticipation at seeing his friends again. 'Mustn't have any creases because Sandy is having a posh wedding and wants us all in uniform.'

'Will the air force want you to go back before your demob comes through?'

'Officially we are still in the air force, but they have released us, so I expect the papers will come through the mail. They don't need us any longer.' He grinned. 'Shame, really, because I'd love to get my hands on a Lancaster one more time.'

'I expect you would, but you'll have to make do with the Cessna.'

He laughed out loud. 'I'd cause a sensation if I came roaring in with a Lancaster. The Cessna is much more suitable and she's a beauty. I'll be able to take the boys for a joyride.'

'The mail has arrived and there are two for you, Steve.' His mother came into the room and handed over the letters.

'Great.' He reached eagerly for them. When he read the first one he gave a whoop of delight. 'This is from Luke. Jean and Sybil have arrived, and it will be marvellous to see them again.'

'How lovely. You must ask them all to come and stay with us. We've had photos of Sybil, of course, but it would be so good to actually see her.'

'You'll like her, and I'll try to arrange a visit.'

'Who is the other letter from?' she asked.

He looked at it and tucked it in his pocket. 'I'll read that later. I'd better get going.'

His parents came with him to the plane, and before getting in he tapped his top pocket.

'Why do you do that? I noticed you all did the same thing when I picked you up at the base.'

'Oh, just habit. We were given lucky tokens to keep us safe by friends at the base.' He took them out of his pocket and showed them to his father.

Bill studied them and then handed them back, smiling. 'Well, they obviously worked.'

'Not for everyone,' he murmured softly under his breath, feeling the sadness as he remembered his lost friends. Then he climbed in the plane and went through the usual checks before taking off. He would carry those stars whenever he flew, but he doubted anyone else would understand just how much they meant to all of them.

The usual feeling of sheer pleasure was there as soon as the plane began to climb, and once on course he relaxed and tapped his top pocket again to confirm the lucky tokens were there. Sitting in there with them was Nancy's letter, which he would read when he had a quiet moment to himself.

He was really looking forward to seeing his friends again. They had spent an unforgettable time together, sharing the dangers and lighter moments when they could relax for a few hours. It was hardly surprising he'd missed the close comradeship of those times, and he wondered if they were having as much trouble as he was in making the transition from war to peace. They now had their girls with them, though, so perhaps it was a bit easier for them.

When he looked back on their time in England, he thought of the people he had left behind. They had been there for a relatively short time, but for the people who lived there the war had been long and the price very high.

He made a course adjustment and smiled to himself. He couldn't wait to see Sybil and Jean again, and perhaps Jean could tell him how Nancy was coping. Her letters were chatty without saying much about her feelings, and it was frustrating not being able to look into her expressive eyes and talk face to face with her. The last thing he wanted in the world was for Nancy to be unhappy.

It was a smooth flight, and he was soon making his descent to a private airfield. The moment he jumped down, Sandy was running towards him with a huge smile on his face. They hugged, delighted to be together again.

'Ah, but it's good to see you. Let's get the business settled and then we can talk on the way to the house.'

When Steve checked in and went to pay the landing fees he was told it had all been taken care of, including refuelling for the return journey. 'I can't let you pay for all of this,' he protested.

'Of course you can. You are here to be my best man and it's only right I pay all your expenses.'

'But you've got enough expense with a big wedding.'

'Think nothing of it.' Sandy urged him towards a waiting car. 'Come on, I've got a treat for you.'

'What, another one?'

He laughed and held the car door open for Steve. 'We are going to have one hell of a boys' night out.'

They didn't stop talking all the way until they turned into a long driveway lined with mature trees. When the house came into sight, he could see this was the home of a wealthy family. They had never talked much about their lives here, but all four were well educated and clearly not youngsters from deprived backgrounds. He had known that Luke and Ricky were part of family businesses, as he was, but they had never gone into details. With the dangerous situation they had been in, it had not been important then. They had been in the fight together and that was all that concerned them at that time. However, none of them boasted about their wealth because they had wanted people to like them for themselves, and not for what they owned.

The instant the car stopped the front door flew open and familiar people were running towards them. Laughing, Steve opened his arms wide to greet the excited friends.

Jean and Sybil launched themselves at him with such enthusiasm he was nearly knocked off his feet. 'It's good to see you too.' He looked up to find their husbands standing there grinning at him. Detaching himself from the girls, he went over and hugged them. He had been excited about seeing them again, but he wasn't prepared for the flood of emotion surging through him. It was a healing moment when everything he had been struggling with since his return began to melt away.

He reached for Jean again and asked quietly, 'How's Nancy?'

'Putting on a brave face, as always, but she isn't happy, Steve, and now we've come here, she's alone.' She gave him a sad look. 'I'm so sorry it hasn't worked out for both of you.'

'I understood her reasons for not coming.'

'You are a good man, Steve Allard.'

'Why thank you, ma'am,' he joked, making her laugh. Then he tucked her hand through his arm and they went into the house.

Sandy's parents shook his hand, expressing their pleasure at meeting him at last, and then Sandy introduced him to his future wife, Helen. She was as lovely as the photograph they had seen.

'I am happy you could come. Sandy has told me so much about you.'

Steve raised his eyebrows at Sandy on hearing that, then politely replied, 'I wouldn't have missed this for anything.'

'As best man I am relying on you to look after everyone tonight. After waiting so long for the wedding, it would be good if you were all sober tomorrow.'

'He's an expert at looking after us, Helen,' Ricky told her.

'So I understand.' She slipped her arm around Sandy and smiled up at him. 'Enjoy yourselves, but don't get into any trouble or you will end up in front of your father, and he won't be lenient.'

'That word isn't in my vocabulary,' the father said dryly.

'Your reputation bears that out, Judge,' she teased. 'Now I am going to spirit your girls away. We have a party of our own planned.'

'You make sure you behave yourselves as well,' Sandy warned.

Laughing, she kissed him and then left with Jean and Sybil.

After that the boys were left to catch up on all the news.

315

'Is your father really a judge?' Steve asked.

'Yes, he is highly thought of and has quite a bit of influence.'

'For which we are very grateful,' Luke remarked. 'He helped to speed things up so Jean and Sybil could be here in time for this wedding.'

Ricky nodded agreement. 'We could have been waiting for months, but Sandy's dad managed to move things forward quickly.'

'Are you going to follow in his footsteps?'

'No, Steve, that isn't for me. I have been offered a position as a university lecturer.'

'Really, what subject, history?'

'Archaeology and ancient history.' He sat forward eagerly. 'I intend to go back to England some time. That country is steeped in history and I was sorry I couldn't see much of it while we were there.'

'We knew you were interested in history, but you never told us about the archaeology,' Luke said.

'We were too busy to think of much but the next mission. Anyway, none of us talked much about what we did at home, and Steve certainly didn't tell us he owned half of Alberta.'

Steve tipped his head back and laughed. 'Not nearly half, only a small piece of it. And what about Luke and Ricky – their families have successful businesses. Tell me, what did your wives think when they found out?'

'Shocked,' Luke told him. 'I believe they thought they might be coming to live in a shack.'

'Yeah.' Ricky roared at the memory. 'Jean couldn't understand why we had kept it a secret. She said other men boasted about wealth they didn't have so they could impress the girls, but I explained that we wanted them to love us for ourselves.'

'And they do. So, how many are coming to the party tonight?' Steve asked, changing the subject.

'Just the four of us. I wanted us to share the evening together, just like we used to. I have told everyone else they will have to party without us. I've booked a table at a local hotel, so we can reminisce and wonder how the hell we came out of that alive.'

'Pure luck,' Steve remarked.

'I agree.' Sandy stood up. 'I'll show you to your rooms and you have an hour to get ready. Have you brought your uniforms?'

They all nodded.

'Excellent. Helen wants us all to wear them, and our medals.' Sandy pulled a face. 'I tried to talk her out of it, but both families like the idea. I hope you don't mind?'

They assured him they were happy to do so.

'Thanks.' He opened the doors to their rooms. 'I'll see you in an hour.'

Later, dressed in smart suits, the four of them set off for a night out. The food was excellent, and they relaxed to talk over their time in England, remembering the amusing parts and ignoring the dangerous missions they had flown.

It was after midnight when they finally got to bed, and Steve remained awake for a while, recalling the evening. It had been good to talk freely with friends who had understood the difficulty in picking up their old lives again. He hadn't felt able to do that at home, fearing his parents would start asking questions he didn't want to answer. It was comforting in a way to find out that his friends were having similar problems. It wasn't just him who had locked away some details and thrown away the key. Perhaps one day that would change, but not yet.

The next morning the house was alive with activity, and when they were all dressed in uniform as requested, Sandy's parents inspected them with approval.

The rings were safely in his pocket and Steve checked the time, then he ushered the bridegroom into the car. Ricky and Luke had left earlier to carry out their duties at the church. When they arrived, Steve smiled at the girls who were dressed in clothes of the latest fashion. Their husbands had made sure they were suitably dressed for the occasion, and it did his heart good to see them looking happy and confident at such a prestigious gathering.

Helen arrived looking stunning in a gown of white satin and lace, with a long train flowing gracefully behind her.

It was a lovely service and went without a hitch. The reception was held at the same hotel they had been to the night before. As best man, Steve gave a short speech in his easy relaxed way and toasted the happy couple. After that there was dancing, and the boys were causing so much of a stir that Jean and Sybil had to stay close to ward off the interested females. Steve had no such protection and politely danced with several girls, avoiding their mothers who were eyeing him with a speculative glint in their eyes. When Sandy and his bride left for their honeymoon the party began to break up.

'I'm surprised you haven't been kidnapped by one of the mothers,' Ricky told Steve, laughing. 'I always said you were too damned handsome.'

Luke and the girls came over then and he placed an arm around both of them. 'Let's get out of here. My parents want to meet you, so why don't we collect our things and you can spend a couple of days with us?'

'Hey, that's a good idea. What does everyone think?' Luke asked them.

Ricky nodded eagerly, but the girls seemed rather doubtful.

'How are we going to get there?' Sybil asked.

'I've got the plane at the local airfield, and I'm quite safe to fly with,' he joked. 'Just ask your husbands.'

'Safest hands in the business,' Ricky told them. 'Come on, girls, you'll enjoy it, and I'm itching to see this spread he lives on.'

'I'm going, and I'd also love to see where this brute lives. It will be fun, Sybil.'

'All right,' she agreed, but still didn't look very sure about the idea of flying.

'Sandy has lent me a car, so let's say goodbye to the families and be on our way.'

It took them nearly an hour to finally take their leave, and then they were speeding towards the airfield. Steve was to leave the car at the airfield, and it would be picked up by someone the next day.

After filing a flight plan and checking over the plane, he saw his passengers comfortably strapped in and climbed into the pilot's seat. Luke sat beside him out of habit, leaving Ricky to cope with two nervous girls, and from the noise coming from their seats he could tell his friend was thoroughly enjoying trying to calm them down.

The weather was good, so it was a smooth flight, and when they approached the house he flew low over it to let them know he was back. By the time he landed, his parents were there waiting for him as they always did.

Rose gave a cry of delight when she saw his passengers and instantly made for Sybil, recognising her from the many photos they had received from Harry. Then she turned to the others, arms outstretched. 'You must be Jean, and the two handsome men must be Luke and Ricky. We are so pleased you could find the time to visit us. How long can you stay?'

'Just a couple of days, if that is all right, Mrs Allard?' Luke asked.

'Of course, please stay as long as you like.'

Ricky smirked. 'We had to make a hasty retreat because Steve was being pursued by mothers eager to find a husband for their daughters.'

'I'm not surprised.' Bill was laughing as he studied the three in front of him, still smartly turned out in their uniforms. 'They must have been disappointed to discover two of you were already married. Whatever your reasons for a hasty exit we are delighted to have you here, and welcome to the Allard ranch.'

'Thank you, sir; we'll just get our bags from the plane.'

'No need for you to do that, Ricky, it will be taken care of. Come on, you must want to change and have something to eat.'

Bill had brought the truck, so they were able to cram in together for the short drive to the house, and he asked Ricky to tell him about all the new gadgets now being used in the bombers. They chatted happily about the subject that fascinated them both.

'Did you enjoy the flight?' Rose asked the girls.

'We were nervous about it,' Sybil admitted, 'but it wasn't as bad as we imagined.'

'I know. I was the same, and I admit that I still like my feet on the ground, but these two men of mine love aeroplanes.'

When the ranch house came into view, Jean gasped. 'Wow, Steve, and you told us you were just a farmer.'

They were even more stunned when they walked inside.

'Oh, my goodness,' Sybil whispered to him. 'Dad never told me you lived in anything like this.'

'It's hard to grasp what a place is like unless you have actually seen it, so I expect Harry just thought of it as an ordinary farm.'

'Well, it certainly isn't that.' She smiled up at him. 'I'm going to enjoy exploring and telling Dad just what this place is like.'

Although faced with unexpected guests, this didn't faze Rose, and organised as ever, she soon had the maids preparing rooms and Cook busy making a feast for their visitors.

They sat around in the evening talking, and Steve could see that his parents were thoroughly enjoying the company of his lively friends.

The next morning, Luke and Ricky found him in the stables. 'I didn't expect to see you up so early.'

'We haven't broken the habit yet.' Ricky patted a horse that was showing an interest in him. 'Do you still walk at dawn every day?'

'Of course. Where are the girls?'

'With your mother. We were wondering if you would fly us over your ranch so we can get a good look at it,' Luke suggested.

He studied the sky and nodded. 'Just the two of you?'

'Yes, we received a firm no when we asked if the girls would like to come with us.'

'Okay. We can go now, if you like.'

'Great, I'll navigate,' Ricky joked.

It didn't take long for Steve to inform his parents what they were going to do, check the plane was ready, and climb into the sky. He did a complete circuit of the property, and then flew over the interior, pointing out the different things it was being used for.

When they landed, Bill came over to them. 'Did you enjoy seeing the ranch?'

'Very much. We understand now why Steve learnt to fly at a young age. The only way to see it properly is from the air,' Luke said.

'Yes, we find a plane very useful,' Bill said as they made their way back to the house.

The girls had clearly enjoyed themselves exploring the huge ranch house with Rose, but promised after lunch to come outside and see the horses.

'Riding is another thing you have to be good at on a spread like this,' Steve explained. 'I'll get you both up on a horse this afternoon.'

'First he makes us get in a plane and now he wants to sit us on one of those animals.'

'You can't come to a ranch and not ride a horse, Jean,' he teased. 'We'll find you a docile animal.'

'Steve, there's an official-looking letter in the study for you,' Rose told him.

The three boys glanced at each other and stood up together. 'That might be demob papers. Let's go and have a look.'

Luke and Ricky followed Steve to the study and watched while he slit the envelope open.

'Do they want us to report back?' Luke asked while the letter was being read.

Steve shook his head and held out the paper for them to see. 'We are no longer in the air force. They don't want to see us again. I expect your letters will be waiting for you when you get home.'

'Thank goodness that is settled. I was afraid they would

find some reason to keep us on for a while longer.' Luke grinned. 'This calls for a celebration.'

'It certainly does.' Ricky was already heading for the door and calling out the good news to the girls.

Steve and Luke smiled at each other, remembering the many times they had been side by side in the Lancaster as flak burst all around them. They slapped each other on the back, saying nothing, as they both knew their thoughts were with that terrible time when Steve had been injured. Now, with their release from the air force, they could look forward to the future – a future they had been so close to not having.

They walked together into lunch, which turned out to be a lively affair, with his parents eager to make plans so they could celebrate that evening.

After lunch they all went out to the stables and the hands saddled the horses and then stood back to watch the fun. As usual, Ricky kept everyone well entertained.

By the end of two days, Steve's friends were able to trot round a field without falling off their horses and were very proud of themselves.

'I'm afraid we shall have to leave now,' Luke told them over breakfast the next day. 'We've had a wonderful time and thank you very much for putting up with us.'

'It's been a pleasure to have you here,' Bill told them. 'You must come again and bring Sandy and his wife with you next time.'

'I'm sure they would love to come.' Ricky turned to Steve. 'I didn't notice a field of cabbages when we flew over the ranch. If you have got one, then please don't fly anywhere near it.'

'It wouldn't be the same without little Beth there to tell

us off, anyway.' Steve took the photos the farmer had sent him out of his wallet and handed them round. This produced roars of laughter.

Rose glanced round at the youngsters. 'Steve has given us only a very sketchy account of this, so would anyone like to fill in the details for us?'

Steve nodded to Ricky. 'Okay, you tell the tale.' Then he sat back, a slight smile on his face as his friend launched into the story, knowing he would make it sound hilarious without mentioning the danger.

By the time he had finished, everyone was doubled over with laughter and Sybil grabbed Jean's arm. 'Were they safe to be let loose with a Lancaster?'

'Of course we were,' Ricky said before Jean could answer. 'The only problem was someone kept shooting at us.'

Jean raised her hands in protest. 'Please, don't anyone get him started on that subject.'

Ricky grinned and kissed his wife on the cheek. 'That's a story for another time.'

'I know what happened because I was there, remember?'

'So you were, and you still love me,' he said smugly.

Still chuckling, Steve stood up. 'Get your things and I'll fly you back now. It looks as if the weather might deteriorate later in the day.

The journey back was a little bumpy this time, but not enough to upset the girls. He landed at the same airfield, as it was the best stop for both couples. Then he refuelled and headed straight back.

He arrived back just in time, because when he jumped out of the plane the first snowflakes began to fall.

Winter was upon them.

Chapter Thirty-Two

During the dark, cold months Steve kept busy overseeing work on the house, and using their snowplough to keep access to vital places open. Most of the hands left during these months, but some stayed. In severe weather the animals had to be fed and cared for, as the farmland was dormant under a blanket of snow waiting for the thaw.

Since Sandy's wedding and spending that time with his friends he was more relaxed, and the constant stream of letters from everyone was something he looked forward to.

He smiled to himself when he lit the log fire in the house they were renovating. It was bitter outside and he wanted to keep the place warm now the work was finished.

The front door opened and his mother walked in. 'The mail has just arrived, and I thought I'd bring it to you and have another look to see if we need to get anything else for this house.'

'Thanks, Mum.' He took the letters from her and shuffled through them quickly.

'There is one from Nancy. I know her writing after all these months. The others are from Luke, Ricky, Sandy and Jean. Sybil sent one to us, which you can read later.'

He grinned at her. 'Have you read them as well?'

'Certainly not!' She kissed his cheek. 'I don't have to because you always let us see them, except for one, of course.'

The door opened again and Rose called, 'Wipe your feet, Bill. We don't want a mess on our nice new floor.'

He came in and raised his eyes to his son, then lifted up his foot to show he had taken his boots off. 'The gas tank is now connected, so we can make a pot of coffee. I've brought everything with me.'

'Lovely, the place is habitable again.' She smiled affectionately at her husband. 'We had some good years here, didn't we, darling?'

'Yes, we did, and it is good to see the old place in fine order again.' He gave his son a steady look. 'Are you going to tell us what you plan to do with it now?'

He nodded.

'Let me make the coffee, and then we can sit by the fire while you tell us about it.' Rose hurried to the kitchen, and soon returned with coffee and cookies. They settled in the comfortable chairs Rose had chosen and waited for their son to begin talking.

He began with the moment they had arrived at Scampton, and their growing friendship with Jean and Nancy, telling them all about their visits to Nancy's parents. Without mentioning anything about their missions or his time at Tangmere, he explained why Nancy felt she couldn't leave her parents. He then outlined his idea, and for a while they didn't comment.

'You think I'm crazy?'

'No, I think you are desperate, Steve,' his father replied. 'You will be asking a lot of them.'

'I know they probably won't accept my offer, but what else can I do? I've gone over and over this, trying to find a way we can be together. I couldn't stay in England, and Nancy won't leave her parents. This is the only way I can see for us to solve the problem.'

Rose poured more coffee for them. 'This is a difficult situation for both of you, but we'll do everything we can to help.'

'Of course we will,' his father added. 'The first step will be to get them out here, so when you write to them, we could put in a letter from us. Would that help?'

'I'm sure it would, because I suspect it won't be easy to persuade them to make the journey.'

'When do you plan to send the invitation?' Rose asked.

'As soon as the thaw sets in I'll make all the arrangements.'

It would be another three weeks before spring began to show it was on the way, and Steve drove into town to put his plan into action.

When he arrived back, his parents were waiting anxiously to hear the news.

'Did you manage to get everything you wanted?' his father asked.

'Yes, the package is on its way, and all we can do now is wait.'

The post came through the letter box and hit the floor with a thud. Sally picked it up and stared at the thick envelope addressed to them in Steve's handwriting. She found her husband in the kitchen. 'Look at this, it's from Steve and addressed to us, not Nancy.'

He took it from her, slit it open and tipped the contents onto the table.

'What has he sent us?' Sally was frowning at the unusual collection of things her husband had spread out.

He picked up an envelope with a picture of a ship on it, gasping in surprise when he saw what was inside. 'These are tickets for a ship going to Canada in six weeks.'

'Who for?' she asked, bemused.

'All three of us. There are also three letters as well, and one is a sealed envelope for Nancy.'

Sally had to sit down. 'Why on earth would he do that? I could understand if it was a ticket for Nancy, but three must have cost him a fortune, Tom. He must want to see Nancy very much.'

'And she needs to see him again. Our daughter pretends everything is all right, but she isn't happy.'

'I know. I've tried talking to her, but she won't discuss it. She's sacrificing her own happiness for us, and that doesn't sit well with me, Tom. There are two letters for us, so we had better see what they say.'

They read one each, and without saying anything swapped letters, then both stared at each other in astonishment. The one from Steve's parents was an invitation to stay with them for a holiday, stating that their son had told them of his time with them and they would like to repay them for being so kind. They hoped very much they would accept the invitation as they would love to thank them in person. Steve's letter gave details of what they would have to do to board the ship, saying he would be waiting for them when they docked.

'What are we going to do?'

Tom hesitated for only a moment before stating, 'Go. We must give Nancy and Steve this chance to be together, even if it's only for a short time.'

'But why invite us as well?'

'Because he knows Nancy wouldn't go without us.'

She nodded and studied the tickets again. 'That darling boy must have been saving up ever since he returned home so he could buy these.'

'That settles it, we have to go. If we refuse, then all this money will have been wasted, and that wouldn't be right. Where is Nancy?'

'She said she was going to look for another job.'

'She just can't settle, can she? Now, we must be enthusiastic and convince her we really want to go. Make it seem like a dream come true, then she won't be able to refuse.'

Sally leant forward and kissed her husband. 'We don't have to pretend; it is a dream come true, and I really do want to go to Canada.'

'So do I. It would be lovely to see Steve again.'

They were silent for a moment, remembering the son lost to them, then Sally said softly, 'If Dan was here, he would be urging us to go.'

'And he would be right. Something like this is what we all need.'

Nancy arrived back an hour later looking downcast.

'No luck with another job, sweetheart?' her father asked.

She grimaced and shook her head. 'All the men just out of the services are being given priority.'

'Ah, well, we've got the very thing to cheer you up.' He handed her the envelope from Steve. 'Go on, open it.'

They watched as she studied the content, read the two letters, and then exclaimed, 'This is crazy. We can't go.'

'Why not?' her parents asked at the same time.

'You won't want to travel all that way.'

'But we do.' Tom sat beside her. 'Look at all this, Nancy. Steve has gone to a lot of trouble and expense to arrange this for us.'

'And his parents want to meet us,' Sally pointed out. 'It's a trip we would be silly to turn down. Just think how exciting it will be to travel on a really big ship and see another country.'

'Your mother is right. We will never get another chance like this. Everything is paid for; he has included all the papers we need to enter Canada, and even sent a cheque to cover any other expenses we might have.' Then he played his ace card. 'Come on, Nancy, we can't go without you so please don't deny us this chance. We would love to see Steve again, and I am sure Jean would be so happy to see you as well.'

'Wouldn't it be wonderful to see all the boys again, as well as Sybil and Jean?' Sally added softly.

'Aren't you going to read Steve's letter?' her father prompted, seeing it was still unopened on the table.

She picked it up, opened it and read in silence, then a smile spread across her face. 'Oh, Steve, you devil.'

'What does he say? Why are you so amused?' Bill wanted to know.

Nancy then told them about the darts match and the outrageous prize. 'Luke claimed his wish by asking us to be bridesmaids at his wedding, which we were delighted to do. However, Steve has never mentioned it, and I thought he had just forgotten, but he's claiming it now. He's asking me – no, *telling* me to honour our agreement and grant his wish by coming out to Canada for a holiday.'

Both parents glanced at each other with a smile on their faces, and Tom said, 'That was rather reckless of you and Jean to agree to such a thing.'

'We honestly didn't believe they could beat us, and they did promise not to ask for anything inappropriate. We agreed if they would put that in writing.' She paused and shook her head. 'Come to think of it, the crafty devils never did.'

'So, we are going?'

'I really can't refuse, can I? A debt must be honoured.'

Tom and Sally dragged their daughter out of the chair and took turns in hugging her in delight.

'This is so exciting, isn't it, Tom? We must think about clothes; we can't arrive in Canada looking shabby.'

'How are we going to do that, Mum? We've used up all our clothing coupons.'

'We'll find a way. We are both handy with a needle and your dad's got one decent suit, so that will have to do.'

'I can't wear that all the time.'

'You won't have to. We will be staying on a farm, so dress will be casual, and there isn't rationing out there, so we can buy ourselves a few things.' Sally beamed at her daughter. 'We must look smart when we get off the ship because Steve will be waiting there for us.'

'You girls always look smart,' Tom declared as he stood up. 'I'll send a reply straight away to let them know we are coming, unless you want to do it, Nancy?'

'No, this was addressed to you and Mum, so go ahead. I'll also send separate letters to Steve and his parents, thanking them for their kind invitation to stay with them.'

That night Nancy couldn't sleep as her mind was in a whirl. She was frightened that seeing him again would reignite all the feelings she had for him, feelings she had been trying so hard to keep locked away – without much success, she had to admit. On the other hand, there was the excitement of knowing they would be together again, even if only for a short time. Would she be able to see Jean? She really hoped so. They had shared so much and she missed her friend terribly. She had waved goodbye, not only to the man she loved, but to Jean as well, certain she would never see either of them again, and tears welled up in her eyes as she admitted that she was dreadfully lonely. But she was being given the chance to spend a little time with them, and she was going to make the most of every second, because it was going to have to last her for the rest of her life.

It was a busy time of the year and the Allard men were working every daylight hour. A lot of the regular hands were now returning, all eager to get the vast fields of barley and wheat growing again. Once all that was underway the cattle could be moved to the grazing lands, where they would have all the space they needed.

Every evening when they returned to the ranch house dirty, tired and hungry, Steve would check the mail, waiting anxiously for a reply.

'Anything?' he asked his mother the moment he walked in the door.

'We've had a letter from Nancy and another from her parents. There is also one addressed to you.'

He took a deep breath. 'What did they say? Are they coming?'

She held the letter out to him. 'Open it and see for yourself.'

He took it, an anxious frown on his face, but didn't open it. 'For heaven's sake, Mother, tell me what they said.'

'They are coming.'

He quickly tore open Nancy's letter and after reading it he ran a hand through his hair, closing his eyes for a moment in relief. 'I really didn't hold out much hope they would accept the invitation.'

'Well, they have.' His father had been reading Tom's letter and the brief one from Nancy. 'And they sound excited about coming.'

Steve began to pace up and down. 'I'll have to let the others know.'

'I know how much this means to you, but would you mind not making the floor so dirty,' Rose scolded gently. 'Both of you go and get cleaned up, then we can eat and discuss what arrangements we need to make.'

Father and son made a hasty retreat, leaving a trail of dirt behind them. Half an hour later, scrubbed clean and in fresh clothes they reappeared.

'Right, now we can talk,' Rose told them. 'The first part of the plan is underway, but the next part will be the most difficult and could easily fail. Are you ready for that, son? Are you prepared to say goodbye to Nancy again and know that is the end?'

'Yes, I have thought this through very carefully and know my chances are very slim. I have sent them open tickets that can be used anytime within the next six months.'

'Her parents won't be able to stay that long,' Bill pointed out. 'It depends how much time her father can get off work. What does he do, by the way?'

'He's an accountant and has his own office, so I'm hoping he can take as much holiday as he likes. I don't want them to have to make a hasty decision, as that could be disastrous for everyone concerned.'

'That's very wise.' Bill looked thoughtful. 'He's an accountant, you say. We could do with one of those now ours has retired. It's a chore neither of us enjoys. So, assuming we can keep them here for a while, what are your plans?'

'I'll fly to the most convenient private airfield and hire a car to finish the journey to Vancouver. I'll meet them from the ship and bring them back here. I want at least a week with them, and that will give them time to settle in and get a feel of the place. Nancy will want to see Jean and the others, so, with your permission I will bring them all here for a few days.'

'That will be lovely,' Rose exclaimed. 'We will have a full house.'

'Very full,' Bill remarked. 'It will be a squeeze fitting that many in, even in this house.'

'You can use my room and I'll sleep in the bunkhouse while they are all here.'

'Will there be room in there?' Rose frowned. 'The men are nearly all back.'

'There's plenty of room at the moment, and if I sleep there, then the six rooms here should be enough.'

'Well, if you don't mind bunking down with the men it will solve the accommodation problem.'

'Of course I don't mind.' Steve laughed. 'After some of the places we slept in, the bunkhouse will be luxury. When we visited Harry we often slept on the floor or any chair we could find. Mind you, after a night at the Jolly Sailor with him and his friends, we didn't care where we slept.'

'He must miss Sybil,' Bill said. 'We should invite him to visit us sometime.'

'You can try, Dad, but I doubt he would come. He has a group of friends, and there is a woman next door, Gladys, he is very friendly with. Not sure if it's more than friendship, but she looks after him. Anyway, Luke will take Sybil back to London occasionally.'

'I expect you're right.' Bill stood up and went over to the drinks table. 'Want an after-dinner drink, Steve?'

'I'll have a small whisky, please, because I will be flying tomorrow, weather permitting, to invite the others to join us when Nancy and her parents arrive.'

It was a clear bright day and Steve was on his way early to visit everyone. It took him nearly all day and a date was finally agreed when they could all come to the ranch. Jean was overjoyed to know she would be seeing Nancy again. There was one more stop to be made before he flew back, and after a lot of searching he managed to find what he was looking for.

The light was fading when he arrived back, and carrying his precious parcel he walked into the house.

'Is it all arranged?' Rose asked the moment he came in.

'It took a bit of deciding to find a date they could all manage, but we eventually got there. They are coming ten days after Nancy and her parents arrive.'

'Lovely. What have you got there?'

He laid the parcel on the table and removed the wrapping.

'A dartboard? What do you want that for?'

'I'm going to put it in the bunkhouse, Dad, then while Nancy and Jean are here you and I are going to challenge them to a match.'

'I'm not sure I could even hit the board,' his father laughed.

'You've got time to get your eye in, and we will need to be good. I've used up the wish I won, and I might need another one.'

'What on earth are you talking about?' his mother wanted to know.

He then told them how expert the girls were, and the fun they had trying to beat them at the game.

'Ah, now we are beginning to hear about some of the things you boys got up to in England. I thought you went over there to fly Lancasters and help win the war,' his father said jokingly.

'We did that as well.' He picked up the board and boxes of darts he'd bought to go with it. 'I expect the hands will like using this, so I'll put it in the bunkhouse now. Then I'll get cleaned up. I'm starving.'

They watched their son rush out of the house and looked at each other.

'All we get from him are the amusing stories,' Rose sighed. 'Is he ever going to talk about the missions he flew and how he got those medals?'

'He is opening up a little at last and, hopefully, he will soon be able to say more. I expect we'll get it a little at a time.' Bill placed a hand on her shoulder. 'Don't worry about him, darling. He isn't the only one having trouble adjusting. There are thousands like him, I honestly believe most of his problems seem to be with the girl he loves and has had to leave behind.'

'I hope that Nancy coming here will help him.'

'Of course it will.' He smiled confidently at his wife, hiding his concern. He knew only too well that this plan was a last desperate effort by his son, and the visit would either help or make matters worse. Ever since Steve had been born, Bill had worked tirelessly to build this ranch up for him, and his son was well aware of that. Because Nancy was needed at home and Steve was needed at the ranch, they'd had to part. What a sad situation these two young people found themselves in. This visit was going to be a worrying time for all of them.

Chapter Thirty-Three

The ship's horn blasted as she approached the harbour, and there was a stampede to the rails with everyone eager for their first glimpse of Canada.

'Look at all those people,' Sally exclaimed. 'Steve said he would be there but how are we going to find him in that crowd?'

'He'll find us.' Tom leant on the rail, excitement on his face. 'I'm almost sorry the voyage is over because I've really enjoyed it. We had the best cabins and everything was laid on for us. That boy thought of everything.'

Sally nodded and continued to scan the crowd as the ship manoeuvred into the dock, then she grabbed Nancy's arm. 'Look, that's him, isn't it?'

Nancy focussed on where her mother was pointing, and after a moment she said, 'No, Mum, he's taller than that. He's over six foot, remember.'

A few girls who had married Canadians were on the ship, and two near them began to shout and jump up and down, waving frantically when they saw their husbands on the dock.

The moment the gangplank was in place the passengers began streaming off the ship.

Tom took hold of his wife and daughter's arms. 'It's time to set foot in another country for the first time in our lives. Let us enjoy every moment of this wonderful experience.'

They joined the line of people, and every step she took made Nancy's nerves increase, and she had to fight to stop herself shaking. Was she doing the right thing? Could she walk away from him a second time? The pain of that first parting was not something she wanted to experience again, but it was too late for doubts. She was here now, and to be truthful, she was yearning to see him again. All she could do was make the most of every minute.

Stepping on to firm ground again felt strange and she gripped her father's arm to steady herself. Then she felt a hand on her shoulder and turned round to find herself enveloped in familiar arms. She didn't have to look up at his face, she knew who it was, and the joy of being with him again overwhelmed her as she gave a quiet sob of relief.

'It's all right, sweetheart,' Steve murmured in her ear, holding her close until she had control of herself again. Then, with one arm still around her, he smiled at Tom and Sally. 'Welcome to Canada, and thank you very much for coming.'

'It's good to see you again, Steve.' Sally reached up and kissed his cheek. 'Thank you so much for inviting us.'

Tom shook his hand. 'We really enjoyed the voyage, and thanks for arranging everything so perfectly for us.'

'I'm glad it was all right.' He looked down at Nancy. 'You weren't sea seasick?'

'No, we were all fine, but some of the passengers were bad for a couple of days.'

Tom was gazing at the milling crowds. 'Where do we collect our luggage, Steve?'

'Come with me.' Tucking Nancy's hand through his arm he took them to a large building.

All they had to do was stand there while Steve dealt with everything, then they were allowed to collect their cases and be on their way.

While walking out of the building, Sally whispered to her husband, 'My word, he has such an air of authority about him, I had forgotten that.'

Steve led them to a car and put their cases in the trunk and then opened the doors for them to get in; Nancy in the front and her parents in the back.

'The first part of our journey is by car,' he told them as he drove away from the dock.

'How long is the journey, Steve?' Tom wanted to know as they drove out of the dock.

'We have quite a way to go, but should be home in time for dinner, so sit back, relax and tell me what you have all been doing since we left.'

After almost two hours, Steve turned on to a small airfield and got out. 'I won't be a moment.'

'Er . . . what are we doing here?' Sally wondered as she watched the tall figure disappear into a building.

'Well, he is a pilot, so I suppose he wants to find out something,' Tom replied.

Nancy said nothing, but she had a good idea what was going to happen.

He was soon back and opened the doors for them to get out, then he opened the trunk and two men picked up the cases and headed for a plane. 'Right, we can go now.' He took Nancy's hand and began to walk towards the plane, but turned when her parents weren't with him as well. 'Something wrong?' he asked, winking at Nancy, who was having difficulty controlling her amusement. Their stunned expressions were a picture.

'You want us to get in that?' Sally had turned quite pale.

'What's wrong with it?'

'It's an aeroplane,' she gasped.

'Yes, I would say that is right. She's a beauty and a lot more comfortable than a Lancaster.'

Tom hadn't said a word, or moved, and this was too much for Nancy, who dissolved into helpless laughter. He hadn't changed a bit. He was still the same man she had fallen in love with.

'Steve is safe to fly with,' she managed to tell them. 'His crew wouldn't go up with anyone else. They trusted him completely, and he's flown everything, including a Spitfire.'

'You don't seem concerned, have you been up in a plane before and never told us?' her father wanted to know.

'No, but I'm looking forward to seeing what those men loved about taking to the air. And Steve is right, it is a beautiful plane.'

He squeezed her hand, then turned his attention back to Tom and Sally. 'Come on, you'll enjoy it, and it will save you a long journey. She's a good, sturdy, little plane. My parents gave it to me as a homecoming present.'

'They gave you an aeroplane as a present?' Tom asked, hardly able to believe it. He took hold of his wife's hand. 'So far this has been a journey of new experiences, we might as well add one more to the list.'

When they reached the plane, the two men had finished stowing the luggage away.

'She's all ready for you, sir,' one of them informed him.

'Thank you. Will you see my passengers on board while I do my own checks?'

'Of course, sir.'

'Nancy, you sit in the front seat with me,' he called as they climbed in.

'No need for you to be worried,' the man said, as he helped the nervous passengers to fasten the seat belts. 'Squadron Leader Allard is a fine pilot and you'll be quite safe with him.'

Tom stared out of the window and watched Steve checking everything and talking to the men. 'Nancy, I'm confused. He sends us expensive tickets, gets an aeroplane as a present, and those men call him "sir". What the hell is going on?'

'I don't know any more than you, Dad. He said he was a farmer, and that's all I know about his life here.'

'Haven't Jean or Sybil said anything in their letters about him?'

'Not a word.'

Their speculation ended when Steve joined them and settled in the pilot's seat. The engine sprang into life and they took up position for take-off.

His whole attention was on what he was doing, and Nancy could just imagine him in the Lancaster. There was an air of calm efficiency about him that was reassuring. Was that what the men who had flown with him had seen?

They gathered speed, lifted off and climbed. Once levelled off and on course he glanced across at Nancy. 'All right?'

'Yes, it's wonderful.'

He reached across, took hold of her hand and kissed it. 'That's my girl.'

Smiling happily, she turned round. 'Are you and Mum all right?'

'Very comfortable,' Tom replied. 'Quite exhilarating, really.'

'That's what I like to hear, so settle back, ladies and gentleman. I'll tell you when we are nearing our destination.'

The drone of the engine had a soothing effect after an emotional few hours, and the passengers dozed off.

Steve could hardly believe he had Nancy with him again, but he knew it could turn out to be only for a short time. One thing he was sure of, though, was that he wouldn't be able to stand on that dock and wave goodbye to her, knowing it really would be for the last time. If that did happen, then they would have to get on with their lives without each other, but that was something he was not ready to accept at this time. Getting her and her parents here had been the first hurdle, and now the most important and difficult part was to come. Everyone's future happiness depended on that being a success.

He glanced across at her sleeping and smiled. For the moment he was content to have her with him. It was something he had never expected to happen.

Half an hour from home he reached across and shook her gently, and when she started awake, he said, 'We will be landing soon. Wake your parents.'

'Oh, I didn't mean to go to sleep,' she said with dismay, turning round in her seat. 'I've missed everything. Wake up, Mum and Dad, we are nearly there.'

Steve began to lose height, and when the ranch house came into view, he flew low over it. This time, though, he had asked his parents not to come and meet them, but wait at the house. He banked to make his approach and then came in to land.

A man with a spanner sticking out of his top pocket opened the plane door as soon as the engine was switched off. 'Had a good flight, sir?'

'Perfect thanks, Jim. Help my passengers out and put the luggage in the car, please.'

When this was done Steve got in the car and as they drove along, Nancy couldn't help smiling. 'That man reminds me of the ground crew who couldn't wait to get their hands on the Lancaster when you got back to see what damage you'd done to it.'

He chuckled softly, remembering Sarge and the boys. 'Yes, they looked after us well.'

'Steve, how long before we get to your farm?' Tom wanted to know.

'We're on it now.'

There was a confused silence for a moment. 'You've got a landing strip on your farm?'

'Yes.'

'But how big is it?'

'We've been flying over it for some time. We have something like three thousand acres; some of it for crops of wheat and barley, the rest for beef cattle.'

Tom began to laugh. 'And you told us you were a farmer.'

'I am, but not as you know it in England.'

'How on earth do you manage a place of this size?'

'We have good hands, some are permanent, some transient, and we all work hard.' The house came into sight and he hooted to alert his parents. Rose and Bill appeared, followed by a couple of servants to deal with the luggage.

Bill immediately stepped forward to help them out of the car and shake their hands. 'Welcome to the Allard ranch. We are delighted you could come.'

Steve could see they were quite overwhelmed with everything and he shot his mother an imploring glance.

She stepped forward, smiling brightly. 'It is lovely to meet you at last. Steve has told us how kind you were to four Canadian boys a long way from home. Now, I am sure you are gasping for a cup of tea.'

Even after all these years his mother still spoke with a very English accent and this seemed to settle the Daltons a little.

Rose led them inside and he stayed by his father's side, quite happy to let his mother take charge of welcoming them to their home. A table had been laid with fine bone china, tea and delicate cakes. A maid was waiting to serve them, and Nancy's parents had a look of astonishment on their faces, but their daughter seemed to be taking it all in her stride.

Bill murmured under his breath, 'You didn't tell them?'

Nancy was staring at Steve and his father as they stood side by side, and seeing it Rose laughed. 'I know, they do look like two peas in a pod.'

'They certainly do.' Nancy took a cup from the maid and sat down, looking more relaxed. 'Do you know your son never mentioned any of this? When asked what he did at home he would simply say he was a farmer and change the subject.'

'That's what Bill told me, and I expected to be living on a farm something like the ones at home, and I was staggered when he brought me out here.' She gave her husband an affectionate smile and then turned her attention back to Nancy. 'The Allard men never boast about their achievements, and I thought that a fine trait. They never talk about themselves much, but I love them both dearly.'

'We are pleased to hear that.' Looking highly amused, Bill settled in a chair.

Steve did the same and his parents asked about their journey, letting their guests talk so they could get to know them.

After a while, Rose stood up. 'I'll show you to your rooms so you can freshen up. Dinner will be in an hour.' She led them along a wide corridor, up an elegant staircase, and opened two doors next to each other. 'You will find everything there you need, but if there is anything else, then please do ask.'

Nancy stepped into a spacious room, decorated in pale apricot with a touch of gold on the bedspread. 'This is beautiful, Mrs Allard.'

'I thought you would like this one, and the name is Rose. Make yourself at home while I settle your parents in and show them where everything is.'

Steve and his father were still downstairs. 'What do you think, Dad?'

'First impressions are good. Tom and Sally seem like good sensible people, and Nancy is lovely.'

'I can hear a "but" in your voice.'

'Only a small one. They are city folk and appear to be unsettled by so much space around them. Would they be able to settle here?'

'Mother did, and she came from London.'

'Yes, thank heavens. It was a very short courtship, and I took one hell of a risk, but I was sure I had picked the right woman. I was right: she settled in quite quickly and loves the life. Would Nancy do the same?'

'I believe she has the strength of character to make such a radical change if she gets the chance to. Only time will tell.'

'Well, you have done the right thing by giving both of you the time to see if it would work for you. Your mother and I will do everything we can to see they enjoy themselves.'

Rose came back then. 'We'll leave them to settle in. They are still in shock, but they will soon get over that, as I did. When you come from the crowded streets of London, it's hard being faced with so much space.' She turned to her son. 'Nancy is lovely, but have you thought that finding you live and own such a huge place might make her want to run back home?'

'I've considered every eventuality,' he told her. 'I know the risks and will accept disappointment if I have to, but this has got to be settled one way or another for all our sakes. To be honest, I will be devastated if this doesn't work out, but as I've said before, I had to try.'

'You have done the right thing, and your father and I are behind you all the way.'

'Thanks, I can't ask for more.' Steve stood up. 'I'll clean up before dinner.'

He was at the top of the stairs when Sally caught him, looking worried. 'Steve, do you dress for dinner? Only we don't have any posh clothes. You know what it is like with rationing.'

'We wear casual clothes all the time, so just wear whatever you have. Don't be fooled by the size of this place; it is a working ranch, and everything comes big around here. Dad did rather let his enthusiasm get the better of him when he had this place built.' He gave her a reassuring smile. 'You wait until you see us after we've been rounding up cattle.'

That made her smile and the worry disappeared. 'I can't wait to see more of this beautiful place.'

'There's plenty to see. I'll fly you over it one day so you can see everything.'

'Thank you, Steve. This is so exciting. Is there a town nearby where we can buy suitable clothing to wear around the ranch? We'd like to do some shopping while we are here.'

'I'll ask Mother to take you to Edmonton tomorrow. You'll get everything you want there.'

'Lovely. Are you sure she wouldn't mind?'

'She would be pleased to take you. She loves going on a shopping spree.'

'I'll go and let Tom and Nancy know.'

He watched her disappear back into her room and continued on his way. After a quick bath and change of clothes, he found his mother coming out of the kitchen after talking to Cook. 'Mum, Sally is worried about their clothes, or rather the lack of them. Can you take them shopping tomorrow so they can get something suitable to wear here?'

'I would love to. There are a few things I want as well.'

'They will need pants, shirts, a jacket, boots – and don't forget hats.' He handed her a roll of notes. 'Try to pay for as much of it as you can with that, but don't upset them. They have their pride, but at least pay for the most expensive items as a gift from me.'

'I will, my dear. Ah, here are our guests.' She smiled as they came down the stairs with Bill who was talking to Tom about something that was making him laugh.

It was an interesting meal, and by the end it was as if they were old friends of his parents. It was an encouraging sign to see things going so well up to now.

Coffee and brandy were served in the comfort of the lounge. Steve longed to have Nancy to himself, but this evening was for their parents to get to know each other, and he accepted that. He would have plenty of time later to be with her.

The next morning Rose drove them away on their shopping trip, leaving Bill and Steve to their work.

'They will be gone for the rest of the day, so let's go out and check the herd.'

'Okay.' Steve put on his hat and walked with his father to the stables.

Two more of the regular hands had arrived, so the four of them rode out together. They spent most of the day checking the condition of the steers, and making a note of when they could send some to market. The Allard ranch was noted for its high-quality beef, so they only sent the finest animals.

It was late afternoon when they returned, and there was food laid out in the bunkhouse for everyone to help themselves.

'We had better get cleaned up before your mother gets back. We can deal with some paperwork while we are waiting for them. I've advertised for an accountant but haven't had any luck yet. When are you thinking of taking Sally and Tom to see the house?'

'In a few days. I'll have to be careful and pick the right moment when they are relaxed and enjoying themselves.'

'I'm damned sad about the situation you find yourself in, son. And I don't want to sound callous, but if this doesn't work out, then time will heal, and there will be someone else for you.'

'You taught me never to accept second best, Dad, and I'm not going to lose her without doing everything I possibly can to keep her. I've already begun the procedure for them all to live in Canada.'

'Have you? When did you do that?'

'The day I sent the tickets.'

'Good heavens, Steve, I never thought of you as a gambler.

You've thrown your dice in the air without knowing if they are going to fall in your favour.' He looked at his son in astonishment, which turned to respect and pride. Then he grinned and slapped Steve on the back. 'Hey, if you win, we might get our accountant as well.'

'Or we might not.'

'They don't stand a chance against the Allard men.'

The father and son smiles were identical, as they went indoors to make themselves presentable again.

They were waiting when Rose drove up to the house, and stepped forward to open the car doors.

'The shopping is in the boot,' Rose told them.

'Trunk, Mother,' Steve corrected.

'Don't waste your time; you know your mother refuses to speak our language.'

'It isn't your language, it's English, and you have just made changes without our permission,' she told her husband, a glint of mischief in her eyes.

That had everyone laughing, and she ushered her shopping companions into the house. 'Leave the shopping to the men. We need a strong cup of tea.'

As they disappeared, Bill winked at Steve. 'She's a clever woman. That little act distracted them so they didn't have time to confront you about paying for their purchases.'

'She's only delayed it. Look at this lot.' The parcels were piled up to the top. 'There isn't room for one more package.'

They loaded themselves up and walked into the lounge where the others were already sitting down with cups of tea in their hands. After dropping everything onto a large leather sofa, Bill tossed the car keys to a servant who left to put the car in its parking spot. They poured themselves tea and sat down.

'Did you get everything you wanted?' Steve asked innocently.

'Everything and much, much more.' Tom was shaking his head. 'The boots and jackets you bought us were far too expensive. You have already given us so much and we can't keep taking from you, it isn't right. I'll make a note of everything you and your mother have paid for and send you the money when we get back home.'

'And we will send it right back, Tom. I brought you here and you must have the proper clothes to be able to enjoy your time on the ranch.' He turned his attention to Nancy, who hadn't said a word. 'Are you going to refuse my gifts?'

'I wouldn't dream of it because I know I will be wasting my time, but I'll get my own back on you somehow.'

'Sounds interesting. What will it be – a darts match?'

'You haven't got a dartboard.'

'Yes, I have. It's in the bunkhouse.'

'Really?'

He nodded. 'Dad and I will play you and Mum. Go and put on your new ranch gear and we'll have a game before dinner.'

They were soon back and they all walked to the bunkhouse. There were a few hands there and they gathered round when they heard about the challenge.

It was a hilarious match, which Nancy and Rose won with ease, while the two men told themselves they had been perfect gentlemen and allowed the girls to win.

Chapter Thirty-Four

It was another week before Steve felt it right to take Tom and Sally to see the house. It was vital Nancy didn't know about this because it could sway whatever decision her parents made. They had to stay because they wanted to, and not for any other reason.

Rose had agreed to keep Nancy occupied, and they went off somewhere immediately after breakfast, leaving Steve alone with Tom and Sally. He stood up. 'Fancy coming for a drive to see more of the ranch?'

They readily agreed and were soon on their way. As they drove along, Steve explained the working of the ranch, the different seasons and how many men they employed. He wanted them to have a fuller picture of what it was like to live here. They reached the house and he pulled up outside. It was looking a picture now, with a fence around it and a garden ready for someone to do what they liked with.

'What a lovely place,' Sally remarked. 'Is it still on your property?'

'It is.' He opened the car door for them. 'Would you like to have a look inside?'

'Yes, please.'

He unlocked the front door and let them walk in, following close behind. 'Have a wander round while I make some tea, or would you prefer coffee?'

'Coffee for a change, please Steve.' Sally took hold of her husband's arm and urged him to explore this fascinating place with her.

While they were doing this Steve put a match to the log fire, which was already laid, then went to the kitchen to make a pot of coffee. By the time they came back it was ready. They settled in comfortable chairs and he asked, 'What do you think of it?'

'Very nice,' Tom replied. 'Spacious and comfortable.'

Sally was still looking around the room. 'It has a nice homely feel about it.'

'It was my parents' home until I was born, and then Dad had the large ranch house built. This has been empty for some time, which was a shame because it would make someone a lovely home.'

'It certainly would, but it is rather remote.'

'It's only around twenty minutes from our house.' Steve walked over to another door and opened it. 'This room houses a two-way wireless, so anyone living here could contact us at any time. A small town with quite a few shops is only an hour's drive from here, and a car comes with the house.'

'My goodness, in that case you won't have any trouble renting it, if that is your plan.'

'You like it then, Sally?'

'Oh yes, and I'm sure your parents were very happy here.'

'They were.' He paused briefly – now was the time. 'Would you like to live here?'

'Anyone would, don't you agree, Sally?' Tom said.

'I certainly do.'

'Then it is yours.'

They stared at him, not sure they had heard correctly. 'Pardon?'

'I said it is yours, if you want it, Tom.'

'We could never afford a place like—' He stopped and shook his head. 'Nancy. If we stay here, she will as well.'

'Yes, but I don't want you to think about that. You took four young Canadians into your home and made them feel welcome in a strange country. That meant more to us than you know. You suffered years of war, lost so much and I wanted to give you the chance of a new life – a life where you will be surrounded by family and friends. Of course, I want to marry Nancy, I won't deny that, but this is for you. That is all I want you to consider.'

Sally was near to tears, so Tom did the talking. 'You will have to give us time to think about this, Steve.'

'Of course, I don't expect a quick answer, and I would be worried if you did agree too quickly. Take your time, and promise me your decision will be based on one thing only, and that is what you and Sally want. The last thing in this world I want is for you to be unhappy, so think carefully. The house and everything that goes with it is yours if you want it. Oh, and if you are worried about finding work, Tom, then we are in desperate need of an accountant.'

Tears were rolling silently down Sally's face now, so Steve stood up. 'Don't tell Nancy about this, then if you decide against it you can all return to London, and no harm will have been done. I'll wait outside until you are ready to leave.'

He walked out, leant against the car and found himself reaching for a cigarette, regretting he had given up. He had done his best to make them see that it must be what they wanted, regardless of anyone else. He could do no more.

An hour later they were back at the house and Steve went looking for his father. He found him in the study with Nancy at the large desk, writing in a ledger.

They looked up when he walked in. 'Hiya, Steve. Nancy took pity on me. She's very good at sorting out paperwork.'

'I know she is, but she didn't come here to work.'

'I insisted,' she told him. 'You were nowhere to be found and I could see your father needed help.'

'I was going to do that tonight,' he told her defensively.

'No need, it's all done now.' She beamed at Bill. 'It didn't take us long, did it?'

'No time at all,' he replied, trying hard to hide his amusement.

'Well, if you are quite finished, why don't you go and get yourself into your cowgirl gear and I'll teach you to ride a horse.'

'Oh good, that's on my list of things to do while I'm here.'

'You've got a list?' Bill asked.

'Of course.' She gave the Allard men a cheeky grin. 'After I've learnt to ride you can teach me to drive, and fly a plane. How long did you say our tickets last?'

'Six months.'

'Hmm, that might be enough time for some of the things on my list.'

They watched her leave the room and began to laugh. 'I think she means it, Steve.'

'I'm sure she does.'

'How did your visit to the house go?'

'They were shocked, but didn't turn the idea down straight away. They are going to think about it, and I did my best to make them see it must be something they want, and not to accept because of Nancy and me. I hope they keep that in mind, because it wouldn't help us if they stayed for the wrong reason and were unhappy.'

'Yes, that is vital.'

They didn't have time to discuss it further because Nancy reappeared dressed in hard-wearing trousers, shirt, boots and carrying the hat.

Steve's heart did a flip when he saw her. She really looked as if she belonged there. He walked over, removed the hat from her hand and placed it on her head, then stood back. 'Now you look the part. What do you think, Dad?'

'Hmm.' He walked round her, then nodded. 'Almost perfect, just needs a bit of wear on the seat of the pants.'

'A few hours in the saddle will put that right.' He held out his hand to her. 'Come on, let's get you started.'

Bill was just filing away the last of the paperwork when Rose came in. 'Steve's looking happy. Do you know how he got on this morning?'

'We didn't have much time to talk, but they are thinking about it. I hope it works out because the more I see of Nancy the more convinced I am that she is the right one for him. She's a good sensible girl and would make him a lovely wife. I like her.'

'So do I.'

There was a tap on the door and Tom and Sally came in looking worried. 'Sorry to disturb you, but could we talk to you, please?'

'Of course. Come in and sit down. What can we do for you?'

Tom launched into their visit to the house and what Steve had told them.

'And what is worrying you about that?' Bill asked.

'He can't give us that lovely house and everything that goes with it,' Sally blurted out.

'Why not? It is his and he can do what he likes with it.'

They stared at Bill and Rose, lost for words.

'Tell us your concerns,' Rose prompted, 'and perhaps we can put your minds at rest. Coming to live in a place like this can be a bit of a shock, as I well know, but it didn't take me long to realise I didn't want to live anywhere else.'

Sally was clearly agitated. 'We must only stay if it's something we really want to do – Steve was very clear about that, so we mustn't make a mistake.'

'That is very important, because if you are unhappy then your daughter will be unhappy, and that will not make for a good marriage. It would be disastrous,' Bill pointed out plainly. 'We are already fond of Nancy, but if you have the slightest doubts about moving here then you must refuse, for everyone's sake. Steve understands that.'

Tom nodded. 'Yes, he is a fine boy. He raised the question of a job for me and said you needed an accountant.'

'Desperately. The man we had for years has retired. Your daughter pitched in to help me this morning. She's marvellous at organising things.'

Sally smiled. 'She takes after her father in that way. They kept her at Scampton because she was so good at her job, but I understand the commander didn't think she should be there because of our son. He was killed, you know, and she waited for him to return, but he never did. He was a Lancaster pilot, the same as Steve.'

'Yes, he told us. It must have been terrible for you.'

'We were hurting bad, but then Nancy brought the boys home, and that helped so much. Our two boys would have liked each other if they had met.'

'I'm sure they would,' Bill agreed, then turned his attention to Tom. 'If you do decide to stay, then the job as our accountant is yours, if you want it.'

'Thank you. We need to give this a lot of thought, you understand.'

'Consider it carefully, and remember what Steve said. You won't be doing either of them a favour if you base your decision on their needs. If you decide this is not the life for you, then enjoy your holiday and go home with happy memories of your stay here.'

'Yes, we understand that.' Tom smiled at his wife. 'We will give this serious consideration, won't we, my dear?'

'Take all the time you need. No one is going to pressure you into making a decision. The offer is there, and you must only do what you feel is right for you.'

'We will.' Tom stood up and helped his wife out of the chair just as a burst of laughter came from outside.

They went over to the window and saw Steve running round a field leading a horse with Nancy on it, and whatever she was saying had him in fits of laughter.

'He's teaching her to ride so she can help with the next round-up,' Rose told them jokingly. 'Let's go and watch the fun.'

Bill rested his hand on Tom's shoulder as they went outside. 'What about you two? Fancy learning to ride?'

'I'd love to have a go. What about you, my dear, do you want to become a cowgirl like Nancy?'

'I would love to,' she replied eagerly.

'Excellent. Go and get into your boots and I'll have the horses saddled and ready. You too, Rose; you can show us all how it's done.'

For the next hour all problems were put aside as they tried to ride a horse for the first time in their lives.

Over the next few days Steve took over teaching them how to ride, and his father was the driving instructor. Nancy and her parents were eager to learn new skills and were now obviously enjoying themselves.

Tom was soon driving on his own, and Steve knew he took Sally to the house several times, but they never mentioned it and he didn't ask. There were days when Steve and his father had to ride out to oversee the work of the ranch, but they had good hands and delegated as much as they could while they had guests. When they weren't around, Rose spent her time with them, and as she was a good rider and could drive, she took them to see places of interest. However, he had a lovely surprise for them, and was eager for that time to arrive.

Nancy heard the plane swoop over the house and ran outside in time to see the Cessna climbing into the clear blue sky.

Bill came out and stood beside her. 'Lovely sight, isn't it?'

She nodded. 'I watched him take off many nights, roaring up towards the stars, and I prayed – oh how I prayed for each and every one of them.'

'You must have seen many distressing things.'

'Working at the base was a mixture of laughter and tears. They each had their own ground crew who looked after them, and they would be waiting for their boys to return. Many times I saw them standing by an empty parking space

359

gazing up at the sky with tears in their eyes. It was hard on everyone, but the day Steve didn't come back was terrible. I was so afraid I had lost him, just like my brother.'

Bill turned her to face him. 'What do you mean – he didn't come back? What happened?'

'Didn't he tell you about the time he crashed into a farmer's field?'

'Oh, yes, he did mention that, but he said he landed, not crashed.'

'That's what he would say. We all thought we'd lost them, but during the day a lorry came through the gates and they were all there, unhurt. Evidently the plane had been badly damaged, but Steve had managed to coax it across the coast.' She smiled then. 'They made a huge joke of it, of course.'

'You said they were all unhurt, but I've seen scars on Steve's body. He won't tell me how he got them, but I have no doubt you know.'

'I do, but if he doesn't want to talk about it, then I can't tell you. All I can say is that you have a son to be proud of. Where has he gone?' she asked, changing the subject.

'He has an errand to run, but will be back in time for dinner. Want a driving lesson?'

'Yes, please.'

It was late afternoon while Nancy was being shown how to groom a horse by one of the stable hands when she heard the plane. She rushed outside to find everyone had suddenly appeared and were watching as the plane flew over the house, banking, turning and coming in again. As he came over this time, he waggled the plane from side to side.

'That boy of ours would make a good stunt pilot,' Bill remarked.

'That's nothing. You ought to see what he can do with a Spitfire. He gave us an exhibition that had everyone on the ground cheering.'

'He never told us he did that,' Rose said giving a sigh.

'He didn't tell you about the aerobatics he performed in that plane?'

'Not a word,' Bill replied. 'He was a bomber pilot, so why was he giving a flying demonstration in one of those?'

'No idea, but he certainly had fun with it. There are things he did that even we don't know about.' She laughed softly. 'You should have seen his face when he landed. He looked like a kid who had been let loose in a sweet shop.'

'Steve doesn't talk much, does he?' Bill sighed.

'I agree with that. When he said he was a farmer, I imagined a little farmhouse with fields of crops, similar to the ones at home. Then I came here, find everyone calls him sir, and he owns a spread the size of England.'

Rose and Bill laughed and she grinned. 'An exaggeration, I know, but you must admit it seems like that to us.'

A few minutes later two cars came tearing up and stopped right by them. When the passengers got out, Nancy and her parents gave cries of delight and rushed over to hug them all.

Nancy was running from one to the other, so excited, also hugging Helen who she had never met before. 'Oh, it's wonderful to see you. Are you staying? And don't you girls look terrific.'

'Hey, how about us, don't we look terrific as well?' the three men wanted to know.

'That goes without saying,' she teased, giving them an extra hug, then turned to Sandy's wife and towed her towards Tom and Sally. 'You must meet my parents.'

Steve was standing back, watching with a slight smile on his face, happy to see everyone together again.

After the introductions, Nancy rushed over to Steve and wrapped her arms around him. 'Thank you, thank you, my darling.'

'Come inside, we just have time for a celebratory drink before dinner.' Rose had to raise her voice to be heard above the excited chatter.

With drinks in their hands, Steve noted that Tom and Sally were just as thrilled to see all of them again. There was a lot of laughter as they discussed what each one had been doing since their return.

Out of the corner of his eye Steve caught something that made his heart beat a little faster. Tom and Sally were watching the youngsters, and then turned, a smile on their faces as they nodded to each other.

Bill came over and stood beside his son. 'It looks as if they might have come to a decision.'

'You could be right.'

Tom took hold of his wife's hand and made his way over to them. 'Steve, we would like to accept your kind offer of the house, and Bill, if the position is still available, I would like to apply to be your accountant.'

Bill shook their hands. 'It's yours.'

Steve drew in a ragged breath. He hadn't dared hope for this, he admitted, as he shook Tom's hand and kissed Sally on the cheek. 'You will be happy here, I'm sure.'

'I am so pleased you have decided to join us and make Canada your home,' Bill said. 'What made you decide to stay?'

Sally indicated the lively crowd in the room. 'We would be fools to turn down the chance to be a part of this. There isn't anything for us in London, and this is our family now.'

'Don't say anything to Nancy just yet, Steve,' Tom asked. 'We want to take her to the house and tell her there. How long are the boys and girls staying?'

'Three days.'

'We will tell her after that.'

'Okay, I'll wait.'

'Thanks for everything, Steve. You have been patient and understanding.'

'Hey,' Ricky called. 'What are you looking so serious about? Come and join the fun, Steve. The gang is all together again.'

Chapter Thirty-Five

After dinner they sat around talking about their time in England – only the amusing stories – and their plans for the future. Steve said very little, as usual, and sat there with an amused expression on his face, just happy to have all his friends there. Ricky was the best storyteller and had everyone laughing.

'You sound as if you had quite a time in England,' Rose remarked, then glanced accusingly at her son. 'Steve's letters told us very little.'

'We couldn't, Mum. They were all checked before being sent on. Anything considered useful to the enemy would have been cut out. Secrecy was very tight, and rightly so.'

'What was it like to fly on the bombing missions?' Bill asked. 'We've heard stories, of course, but you boys were there.'

They were all quiet for a moment, and then Sandy answered the question. 'It is impossible to describe it. We were the lucky ones who came through – many didn't.'

'Our luck was having tough skilful pilots,' Luke told them. 'We wouldn't be here now if it wasn't for Steve and Sandy.'

Ricky was nodding. 'Yes, but that last time I missed all the fun.'

'You were better off that way, believe me.' Luke shook his head as he remembered that flight. 'Goodness knows what your language would have been like that time.'

'Ah, yes, no one will ever forget the time you found a hole in the plane close to your position, Ricky, and when we landed you let the whole base know what you thought,' Steve reminded them in an effort to steer the conversation back to the funny side. He really didn't want his parents to know how close they had come to dying that day. It would upset them too much, and he couldn't talk about it – yet.

Everyone who had witnessed Ricky's tirade roared with laughter, and then the incident had to be explained.

After that, much to Steve's relief, the conversation turned to what they were going to do while they were at the ranch.

For the next three days there wasn't a dull moment as the friends revelled in each other's company. Nancy proudly showed them how she could ride a horse when she cantered around a field on her own. Then, of course, everyone had to have a go.

Rose and Bill watched their antics with relief when they saw their son laughing and happy. 'He's back.' Rose hugged her husband. 'We heard a little of what happened to them, but no details. Do you think Steve will ever tell us exactly what happened?

'Probably not. Nancy knows, but she wouldn't tell me either, so we must just respect that and be glad he is now happy once again. They all need to put the past behind them, and not talking about the bad times is just their way of dealing with it.'

'And by the look of them that is working for them.'

Nancy ran over to them, her face shining with pleasure. 'Come with us, we are going for a ride.'

'They can hardly sit a horse,' Bill said.

'They are willing to try and it should be fun. We won't go far, though.'

'Okay, we had better go with them, Rose, and catch anyone who falls off.'

By that evening all the inexperienced riders were stiff and needed a strong drink to ease their soreness, then it turned into a party.

As they prepared to leave the next morning, Nancy was tearful when she had to say goodbye to the girl she had shared so much with during their time at Scampton.

When they were in the air, Steve told them about Tom and Sally's decision, and they were going to tell Nancy while he was flying them back to their homes.

'If you weren't flying this plane, I would hug you, Steve Allard.' Jean was thrilled to hear such good news.

After dropping off his passengers he refuelled and headed straight back.

Tom found his daughter grooming the mare she had become fond of during her riding lessons. 'I can drive now as long as I stay on the property,' he told her proudly. 'Leave that and come with us. We want to show you something.'

'All right.' She handed the brush to one of the stable hands and followed her father to the car. Her mother was already there and sitting in the back. 'Are you allowed to borrow this car?'

'Bill said I can use it any time I want. Hop in.'

As they drove along she asked, 'What are you going to show me?'

'You'll see. It isn't far,' her mother replied.

Nancy watched how her father was confidently handling the car and had to admit he was quite good for a beginner. She relaxed and enjoyed the scenery.

They stopped outside a ranch house, and her mother hopped out of the car with keys in her hand. 'What do you think of it?'

'It's lovely. Is this what you wanted to show me?'

'Yes, come and have a look inside. It's really beautiful.'

Nancy didn't understand why her mother was so excited, but she obediently followed her into the house.

'Tom, you show Nancy round while I make us a pot of tea.'

'Er . . . are we allowed in here, Mum?'

'Of course, dear.'

Her father took her from room to room, and was particularly enthusiastic when he showed her the wireless room. 'You can keep in touch with the big house on that.'

'That's handy.' She was puzzled. Her parents seemed to know everything about this place, and her mother was even in the kitchen making tea!

'Tea's ready.' Her mother came in carrying a tray with not only tea on it but cookies as well.

They made themselves comfortable and Nancy wondered what on earth was going on. She hadn't seen her parents this excited for a very long time.

'Bill and Steve have completely renovated this house, and Rose chose the furnishings. It was their home before they built the large one,' her father explained.

'Really? Are they going to rent it out or something?'

'No, they have given it to someone.'

'Who?'

'Us.'

Nancy looked from one parent to the other. 'What did you say, Dad?'

'They have given the house to us, along with a car, and I am to work for them as their accountant.' Tom reached out and took hold of his daughter's hand. 'We are going to live here, darling. Don't look so stunned. We have thought this over very carefully and have come to realise that there is nothing for us in London now. We would be fools to turn down the chance of a new life.'

Her mind was in a whirl. Steve had said all along that he would try and find a solution to their problem – but persuading her parents to live here wasn't right. As much as she wanted to marry Steve, she couldn't let her parents sacrifice their happiness for hers. 'You mustn't do this for us. Steve should never have asked you to.'

'We are doing this for us,' her father declared. 'Steve emphasised that the only people to be considered while making this decision was your mother and I. He pointed out that neither of you could be happy if living here was something we really didn't want to do.'

'Bill told us the same thing when we talked about it with him.' Sally smiled at her daughter. 'Please believe us, darling, we are doing this because we want to, and for no other reason. Even if you decided not to marry Steve, we would still want to make our life here now.'

'But you two do want to be together, don't you? Neither of you are happy being apart. You are made for each other, any fool can see that.'

'Of course we do, there is no question about that, but

368

it would be disastrous for all of us if you make the wrong decision.' Nancy sat back and folded her arms. 'Convince me you really want to live here.'

For the next hour they talked, giving every detail of what this would mean to them, and then she made them go over everything again. She had to be absolutely sure they meant what they were telling her.

Finally, her mother smiled. 'So you see, darling, when Jean, Sybil, Helen and the boys arrived, we realised they were our family now, and this is where we want to be, this is where we belong – all of us. We will have to return to London to sell the house, and then we will be right back. You will be able to stay.'

'We can't just do that. We need permission to settle here, and goodness knows how long that will take.'

'It's already being dealt with,' said a familiar voice from the doorway.

She shot out of her chair to find Steve standing there. With a cry of joy she leapt at him, nearly knocking him off balance. 'This is why you invited us here, wasn't it? What would you have done if Mum and Dad had refused?'

'Then you would have gone back to London, and no more would have been said about it. This was the only way we could be together, but it had to be your parents' choice.'

'That's right.' Tom was smiling broadly. 'Steve made us the offer, but put no pressure on us. There is a better life for us here, Nancy – a better life for all of us.'

Steve still had his arms around Nancy and held her slightly away from him so he could look into her face. 'So, do I have to propose again?'

'The first proposal will do nicely,' she told him, not bothering to hold back tears of joy.

Sally could hardly contain her excitement. 'Let's get back and tell Bill and Rose the good news.'

That evening was spent going over everything they needed to do so they could all live in Canada.

Bill walked over to the drinks table and took two bottles out of the cupboard below. 'We must have a celebratory drink after all that talking.'

The glasses were filled with champagne, handed round, and then lifted to drink a toast to wish them all a happy life in their new country. Bill refilled the glasses. 'Now we must drink to Steve and Nancy. They faced an impossible situation, but handled it with courage, thinking of others before themselves. We wish them happiness and a bright future together. They deserve it. Nancy, we are absolutely delighted to be able to call you our daughter.'

'And now we have a wedding to arrange.' Rose turned to Sally. 'We will need to invite Harry, all the boys and their wives . . .' She was already writing down names as fast as she could. 'Then we must go into town and choose smart outfits for ourselves, and if we are quick the wedding can be held before you go back to London and settle your affairs there.'

'Hold it,' Bill told them. 'Our youngsters haven't had time to decide when they will get married, and I must point out that it's their wedding, not yours.'

Steve was listening to all of this with that familiar half-smile on his face, but saying nothing.

'It's the mother's prerogative to interfere in wedding plans, Bill, so how long have we got?'

'Six weeks,' Steve declared, glancing at Nancy for confirmation, which she gave.

'My goodness, we are going to have to move fast. Have

you any idea what kind of wedding you would like, Nancy?' Rose asked.

'I haven't had time to give it much thought, but a white wedding, of course, and Jean, Sybil and Helen must be my maids of honour. Apart from that, I really don't mind.'

'Write to them straight away, my dear, then Steve can bring them here to shop for dresses. Who is going to be your best man, Steve?'

'Luke,' he said without hesitation.

'You will have to live here at first,' Bill said. 'We can give you rooms to yourself until you build a house of your own. Any ideas where you would like it to be, Steve?'

'I have a place in mind about two miles from here. I'll show it to Nancy tomorrow.'

'Good, good, decide what you want and then we can get on that right away.'

Rose was still scribbling notes and then looked up. 'We must give Ricky and Sandy something to do, so they can help to look after the guests.'

Tom had nearly finished his second glass of bubbly and said with a glint of amusement in his eyes, 'Do you think that's safe?'

'You and Bill can keep them in order.'

The two men grinned at each other and Bill chuckled. 'I doubt that's possible when they all get together. Did they cause havoc at Scampton, Nancy?'

'I wouldn't call it that, but they did like to have a good time when they were free, just like all the crews. Your son was always well behaved, though, and looked after them on the ground and in the air.'

'They were all well behaved,' Sally told them. 'When they stayed with us, they were perfect gentlemen.'

Steve gave Sally an affectionate smile. 'We were often exhausted and came to you for a rest. A few days in your peaceful home and we were back to normal.'

'I don't know about a rest. I found you in the garden one day digging over the vegetable patch, remember. You said you found it relaxing, but to me it was just hard work.'

'Well, you'll have a bigger patch this time, and I'll come and dig that over for you if you like.'

'We are not growing vegetables this time, Tom. I want shrubs and flowers,' Sally told him.

'Ah, yes, flowers.' Rose was scribbling on her pad again, turning her thoughts back to the wedding. 'We'll have to decide on those, as well. With all the people we have to invite this will be a big affair. How do you both feel about that?'

Steve placed an arm around Nancy. 'Is that all right with you?'

'I'm happy to let our mothers do the arranging. The only thing that matters to me is that we will be married.'

'Me too.' He pulled her out of the chair and steered her towards the door, calling over his shoulder, 'Do what you want, mothers.'

They walked a little way from the house, happy to be on their own at last, and after a long embrace, Steve looked down at her. 'Are you still wearing the ring around your neck?'

'Yes, I've never taken it off.' She then removed it from the chain and handed it to him.

He slipped it on her finger. 'We are now officially engaged. I promised that one day I would put a wedding ring next to it, but at that time I couldn't see how that would ever be possible.'

'Neither did I, but you will now be able to keep that

promise. I tried so hard not to fall in love with you, but I just couldn't help myself.'

'We were in a very difficult situation while flying missions, and although I had fallen in love with you, I held off because you had lost your brother and would be wary about forming a loving relationship with someone who could suddenly disappear from your life.'

'But thank heavens you came through.'

It was a clear night and, wrapped in each other's arms, they stared up at the sky. 'On a night like this we would have been heaving Lancasters off the ground and into the sky to join all the others.'

'Yes, and leaving the rest of us to worry the hours away until we heard the sound of the planes returning, and wondering how many weren't going to come back. Do you miss flying those monsters?'

'Yes, they will always have a special place in my heart, as will the friends we lost. It was a time that will never be forgotten.'

'It is a part of who we are now.' She sighed and tipped her head right back. 'The stars are very bright here.'

'They are even brighter when you are up there with them. As a crew we were under those stars together. But right now, this is the only place I want to be, and that is looking up at them with you, knowing that against all the odds we are going to spend the rest of our lives together.'

Epilogue

6 Years Later

When Steve walked in with his friends and their families there was a yell of delight from his three-year-old son, William Daniel. He grabbed hold of Luke's son, Stevie, who was about the same age, gathered up Ricky's two daughters and dragged them over to see his new toy – a model of a Lancaster.

The three men stood watching the mayhem with smiles on their faces. 'Shame Sandy couldn't come,' Luke said, 'but Helen is eight months pregnant and it wouldn't have been wise for her to make the journey, especially as they are expecting twins.'

'Twins!' Steve exclaimed. 'He didn't tell me that in his letters.'

Ricky grinned. 'Yeah, they are hoping for two boys or one of each, as they've already got a daughter.'

'I'm going to have to get a bigger plane.'

Nancy came over and handed her husband their sixteen-month-old daughter, Sara Jean. 'Look after your daughter while I see if everything is ready for the buffet lunch.'

The little girl smiled as she settled in her father's arms, after giving him a smacking kiss on the cheek, then she leant towards Luke and Ricky. 'Kiss.'

Steve held her out so she could do this, then she settled down again. Suddenly something caught Steve's attention and he caught hold of her hand before she could put it in her mouth. 'No, sweetheart, you can't have those. You mustn't take things out of your dad's pocket.' He prised the star tokens out of her fingers and put them in his trouser pocket.

'Do you still carry those with you?' Luke asked.

'Every time I fly, and they are precious to me, not only because of who gave them to us, but because they hold many memories.'

The two men nodded and also tapped their pockets, indicating they had them with them as well.

'Of course, Steve, you have one more memory we don't know anything about,' Ricky reminded him. 'Surely you can tell us what you did at Tangmere now?'

'I flew a Lysander into France and picked up agents.'

The friends stared at him in amazement, and Ricky swore under his breath. 'How many runs did you do?'

'Two.' He then went on to tell them about the flights.

By the time he finished, Luke was shaking his head. 'It was just as well we didn't know, or we would have been frantic with worry.'

Sara Jean was getting restless and began hitting his shoulder to gain his attention and repeating 'Bes' over and over again. He began looking round the room and found the item on a chair behind him. She beamed when he gave it to her.

'Hey, a rag doll,' Ricky exclaimed. 'Where did you get that, Steve?'

'From a market stall one day when we were out shopping. I named it Beth.'

'Do you still hear from that farmer?' Luke wanted to know.

'We receive a card and a letter every Christmas.'

Bill came over and held out his arms. 'Come to your grandpa, my darling girl.'

She reached out eagerly, and Steve handed her over. 'Kiss,' she said, wrapping her arms around Bill's neck and giving him a kiss.

Steve sighed. 'Some day I am going to have to persuade her not to kiss all the men in sight.'

'We're hoping for a girl next time,' Luke told him, smiling broadly as he watched the little girl kissing Tom as well.

'Have you had any luck getting Harry to come out here and live?' he asked Luke.

'No, he won't leave London and all his friends, but we've made it clear there is a place waiting here for him if he changes his mind at any time.'

The three men fell silent then and gazed around the room. Their wives were busy seeing to the huge layout of food, and the grandparents, Bill, Rose, Sally and Tom were joining in a boisterous game with the children. Tom and Sally had never regretted their decision to make Canada their home, and the addition of grandchildren had helped the loss of their son. His loss would always be a sadness, of course, but they had learnt to live with that and enjoy what they now had.

'If we hadn't survived, then none of this would have happened,' Luke pointed out. 'These children would never have been born, and I am grateful for the happy years we have been given.'

The other two nodded agreement, each one of them remembering their time together under the stars, knowing they had been among the lucky ones.

BERYL MATTHEWS was born in London but now lives in a small village in Hampshire. As a young girl her ambition was to become a professional singer, but the need to earn a wage drove her into an office, where she worked her way up from tea girl to credit controller. After retiring she joined a Writers' Circle in the hope of fulfilling her dream of becoming a published author. With her first book published at the age of seventy-one, she has since written over twenty novels.